Paradise Salvage

Paradise Salvage

John Fusco

Scribner

First published in Great Britain by Scribner, 2001
An imprint of Simon & Schuster UK Ltd
A Viacom Company

'Highway Star' Words and Music by Jon Lord, Ritchie Blackmore, Ian Gillan,
Roger Glover and Ian Paice © 1972, Reproduced by permission of B. Feldman
& Co Ltd trading as HEC Music, London WC2H OEA

'Lady Marmalade' Words and Music by Bob Crewe and Kenny Nolan © 1974,
Stone Diamond Music Corp/Tannyboy Music Co/Kenny Nolan Publishing/Jobete
Music Co Inc, USA.
Reproduced by permission of Jobete Music Co Inc/
EMI Music, London, WC 2H OQ7

Scribner and Design are trademarks of Macmillan Library Reference USA, Inc.,
used under license by Simon & Schuster, the publisher of this work.

1 3 5 7 9 10 8 6 4 2

Simon & Schuster UK Ltd
Africa House
64–78 Kingsway
London WC2B 6AH

Simon & Schuster Australia
Sydney

A CIP catalogue record for this book is available
from the British Library

Hardback ISBN 0–7432–0861–7
Trade Paperback ISBN 0–7432–0862–5

Typeset by Palimpsest Book Production Limited,
Polmont, Stirlingshire
Printed and bound by Omnia Books Limited, Glasgow

*For the three Giovannis,
my grandfather, my father, and my son*

In the Neapolitan dialect of my tribe, *storia* means the history, the true story. But it can also mean a myth, a fiction. I could not have bottled the two in the ritual jar without the following people:

The entire *Famiglia* Fusco and my beloved Glasgow Mary Isabel. Richela from America Street, Francesco Gallippi and family, my gear-head advisor Jim Silver, Richie 'il capo di tutti capi' Fusco, Uncle Domenic, Johnny 'Cowboy' Shea, Sando Bologna, Tony the Barber, the Pontelandolfo Community of Waterbury, Connecticut, and all the *Goombaraggio*, my many godfathers and godmothers.

And my friend Robert De Niro. Sorry Bob, but to us factory kids you were, and remain, the King. Yes, I'm talking to *you*. And I want to say just one thing: thank you.

Several writers, film-makers, book-makers and magicians: Howard Frank Mosher, Ray Bradbury, Robert McCammon, Lorenzo Carcaterra, Stephanie Cabot and Marcy Posner at William Morris, Ian Chapman, Martin Fletcher and the S&S gang. And Casey Silver, who believes in the movie.

Mille Grazie!

Prologue

As a New England boy, I believed in the prophecies of the *Old Farmer's Almanac*. Since I was five I had longed to see a woodchuck rise to see his shadow, or 'geese on the wing, come home for Spring'.

But in Saukiwog Mills, Connecticut, where I grew up, the first sign of the vernal equinox was the Italians setting fire to their front lawns.

Sometime between late February and the Ides of March, the West End would go up in a controlled bonfire as our fathers and uncles and grandfathers lit the dry brown grass with torches to renew the soil; as the lawns burned, they worked the flames with potato hoes like they were cultivating rows of fire. Black clouds would billow and we hyphenated-American kids would race our bicycles through the smoky gantlet, honking our rubber horns, pretending we were in *The Great Escape*. When the Irish in the Longview section saw the dark clouds drifting, they threw open their shutters and brought their screens up from the basement, assured that winter was over; the Lithuanians just down the Overlook section shut their windows and cursed the raining ash; the Yankees in the Mill Plain section rolled their eyes at our pagan rites even as they came to our neighborhood to buy imported cheese; while the blacks and Cape Verdeans in the North End expressed gratitude that at least somebody was burning the devil out of town; in the South End, the Dominicans and Puerto Ricans had their own liturgy going – old men came out on their porches to smoke Munimakers and play dominoes while the old women let out the clotheslines and hung sheets like the official flags of a great festival. But no matter the enclave one dwelled in, or the country his forbears sailed from, we were all glad for spring.

Although the rich kids in Greenwich and Westport called our immigrant city 'the Armpit of New England', there was a time when we were known as the Cradle of the Industrial Revolution and more recently as the Brass Center of the World, though they had all but stopped rolling brass by the time I turned twelve, the birthday which occurred on the first day of spring in 1979. Forty lawns were lit before my twelve candles, and the woodchuck came up to see his shadow – smoked out of his hole by my grandfather who shot him and marinated him in red wine and basil in the garage while my friends sang Happy Birthday.

My name is Annunziato Paradiso; Nunzio for short.

Although I lied and told my fifth-grade teacher that my grandfather was a fourth-generation American who played semi-pro baseball with Ty Cobb, he really came over from Southern Italy in 1919 to roll brass with the Irish. He had never *seen* a baseball, but he brought with him a leather satchel filled with the salvages of the Old Country – what he called his *storia*: his fables and cantos and nightmares and memories; basil seeds from the old land; a fig sapling in balled burlap, and of course, a slab of cheese and some *soprasatta*.

Storia, like many words in the Southern Italian tongue, has two meanings at once. It means 'a story', but it also translates as 'the history'. How fact and folktale could be bottled in the same jar was a mystery to me, but the longer such a jar sits, the more the two seem to ferment into something very close to true. The Paradiso family history was one composted from folklore and fact and ancient recipes in an unwritten tongue. There were dark secrets, too, in Grandpa's satchel. The Old Country often followed our ancestors to the New, and there comes a time when the second or third generation has to stick a hand into the gaping maw of *La Bocca della Verità*, the Mouth of the Truth.

It was my time.

But I wasn't ready for any Italian rite of passage. I had earmarked my twelfth summer as the last, unfettered and wondrous season of my American life. My mother whispered that it would be the last absolute one before things changed for ever.

And so I seized the last days of May with a gusto: me and Eddie Cocobianco ran roughshod and wonder-bent in Nikes through our neighborhood that the Irish called 'The Little Boot', high on the smell of anisette and my grandmother baking a thirty-two layered cake (a layer for each year of Christ's life) that she called the *torta di Pasqualina*.

Although we could see the brick obelisks and smokestacks of Saukiwog from our highest point, The Little Boot was a green and groomed neighborhood with an Italian market called Coangelo's, and if you walked past it on Sunday morning, you would find your steps slowed by the aromas of fresh Italian pastries baking and the first spices of the day being kneaded into sausage, and if you walked in, you would hear Italian women speaking in the melodic tongue of their regions, and music from Naples on the radio. There was nothing, nothing in Coangelo's Market that would make you think you were in America on a Sunday morning. The best *panini* were made with a passion for food on the first floor of the two-family home of the Croccos on Mary Street, and if it was a hot day, Mrs Crocco might give you a tart Italian ice cream for your walk home which would last you all the way up the stucco and vine alley behind Cafe Benevento, the espresso bar where the old Italian men gathered for their daily card games of *tresette* and *briscola* and to complain in their native tongue about us kids who didn't know much Italian, and recall the old days when the North End was all *paesani*, but was now all black, or, as guys like my Uncle Baptiste would say: *zootzooni* or *mulanyom*.

Boys and men got their ears lowered at Tony's Barbershop, women permed and colored at Yolanda Perugini's litttle pastel house with multicolored rose garden and shrine to the Blessed Mother. Within weeks of the Great Spring Fires, the grass would burst back Uganda green and dandelions rioted; the old women, plump and small in sleeveless floral prints of summer, went out with steak knives and bent at the hip to cut them for salad. The old men unearthed their fig trees, the ones that they brought over as saplings on the ship and buried in the yard every winter so they'd survive the frost.

Every house had a garden: our tiered vegetable plots were the stuff of Guinness Record Books. No one could raise miracles from the soil like the old-timers I lived amongst. I had once, in an earlier less-endangered summer, gotten hopelessly lost in Mama Orsini's magnificent rainforest of green. Somewhere in a tangle of vines and giant growths I swore I had seen a small South Asian tiger. But it turned out to be a Bengal striped blouse my dad had found in our family wrecking yard and gifted to our neighbor the previous winter. When I screamed for help and stumbled in a blind panic through tomato vines, the corporeal Mrs O. stood up in her tiger muumuu and pointed me east: 'Go'a right at the beans, go'a left at the radish, follow the anisette alla the way down to the corn but, Nunzio: no step on the squash, *capisce?*'

Fifteen minutes later I stumbled out into the light, eating a fresh cucumber, intoxicated by the wet smell of greens. '*Buono figlio,*' she sang out to me as I ran home. *You're a good boy.*

But things were changing in 1979.

The last of the mills were closing down. The price of gasoline was going up.

And my voice. That was changing, too.

As sure as the Shah was in exile and John Wayne buried with his boots on, the summer of 1979 was destined to be the last true summer of my boyhood. Somewhere inside I think I knew that there is a colossal difference between summer when you're twelve and summer when you're thirteen. Eddie Coco was twelve and still slept with his Jerry Mahoney ventriloquist dummy; Rick Massi was thirteen, had acne, was on drugs, and beheaded his grandfather's vintage Charlie McCarthy doll with a coping saw. I knew for sure when Father Vario told me that near summer's end I would – if I could meet the test – make my Confirmation and be anointed a Christian and a soldier. And I knew it for certain when my father found a black composition tablet gunwaled with tales I had written, the one my mother had hid under the sofa: a wild fantasia that I titled *The Amazing Summer Adventures of Nunzio*.

Dad led me next door to meet with Grandpa down in his stone basement where the old man sat amongst wine-making equipment and a hanging *prosciutto*. As he and my father spoke in the secret tongue of the home village, I began to realize they were discussing my place in the world. As Dad spoke and Grandpa slowly nodded, his eyes on me, I felt my summer sliding into the abyss. I did not know what *La Via Vecchia* meant, but my gut translated it as no wiffle ball in Eddie's backyard; no makeshift raft to ride the Mattatuck River; no rainy Saturday mornings of vintage *Creature Feature*; no more writing stories.

Dad did it when he was twelve, and so did my brother Danny Boy. *La Via Vecchia* – it was the old way, the only way lest I become a dyed-in-the-wool *Americano*.

The gospel said, *Know Thy Work and Do It*.

My father said: 'Let go of your *minglilone*, kid, and get your boots on.'

And so, on the 1st of June, it was decided that I would work my summer side-by-side with my father and brother at Paradise Salvage, our family wrecking yard. I didn't know it then, but *The Amazing Summer Adventures of Nunzio* were just beginning.

The Mouth of the Truth was opening, and I was going in.

I need to take you with me. If I'm ever going to close that trunk again – and lock it – I need to make you see this memory.

This is my *storia*.

Most of it is fact, some is ancient folktale.

All of it is true.

ONE

Renaissance City

Pandora's Pontiac – America Street – *La Strega* –
Brass Balls – Dead Man's Derby – *Mal'occhio* –
Super 8 – Napoleon at St Helena –
Another Man's Treasure

CHAPTER ONE

Pandora's Pontiac

'Junk? *Junk*? Never call it junk. *Salvage* – that's the word. Comes from salvation.'

Big Dan's hands are enormous, the color of Chinese pork. Aslant on the wheel of the tow truck, they vibrate with a diesel pulse.

'Like when them guys go diving after shipwrecks,' he says. 'They call it salvage. And that's what we're doing, Nunzio. Like Jacques Cousteau. Only we ain't Frenchmen.'

'Diving for shipwrecks?'

'Bringing up treasure.'

Big Dan downrakes hard into second gear and I hasp my legs, protect the nuts. I am wedged in the frontseat between Big Dan, my father, and Little Dan who is not so little. He is nineteen, whiskey-dead. My big brother. With every retch from third to low his head knocks the passenger glass, his eyes aperture like a guppy dropped into ice water. Until he gets his bearing, sees where he is, where he's going – then he closes his eyes. We know him as Danny Boy, but my father knows him as the *mamaluke*. Or the *gigolo*. I'm not sure about *gigolo* but I know what *mamaluke* means. Means Mama's boy; but can also mean moron.

'Now, the *mamaluke* over here,' Big Dan says, coasting the wrecker down Genoa Street, 'he takes it all for granite. Your mother says fix him up a car, I fix him up a car. But what's he do? He goes to the Swizzle Stick or Gigi's or JuJu's or whatever they call it, and he looks for women. Not young women – old women. He finds himself a divorced *goomare*, and she takes him home and gives him a six-pack. I'll tell you what your brother is: he's a welfare woman's *gigolo*.'

I know what *goomare* means. Means godmother. But it can also mean mistress. The Italian kind of mistress. The kind who sneaks you out her back door with half a hard-on and an aluminum pan of lasagna. That's how Big Dan says it.

But my father's eulogy cannot tarnish the truth about my brother: he was – as even Mayor Longo proclaimed with a key to the city – the greatest defensive back and punt returner in the history of Kirby High School. He was, always would be, the 'Junkyard Dog', a nickname awarded him as much for his kamikaze head-knocking as for the local fame of our family wrecking yard.

I don't see myself ever growing as raw-boned handsome as Danny Boy. He has it: the prominent Paradiso nose like Big Dan's. Mom calls it Romanesque; I think of it more as the strong beak of a raven. Has the eyes, too: large, dark, almond-shaped – like Valentino's, our mother says. Mine are cue-chalk blue. Aye, for the dram of Celtic blood, says Mom. Even so, people can always tell me and Danny are brothers. Maybe the dark brows that always look knotted, that make us appear to be brooding or roiled with gas and cramp.

'The Big Clock,' Big Dan says now, as the city's landmark comes into view. 'Our famous Big Clock.'

The clock-tower, an imposing brick structure 250 feet high, is an exact replica of a clock-tower in Southern Italy and, Big Dan always reminds us, a tribute to the early immigrants. 'You never heard that, did you, Nunzio?' Dad says, smiling, and now he affects a voice not his own. '"What a city, a Big Clock city, with that famous Big Clock."'

When I shake my head, stumped, Big Dan is pleased. 'Willie Loman,' he says. ' It's from a play by Willie Loman.'

A sound comes from Danny Boy, barely audible. Maybe gas and cramp. 'What was that over there?' Dad says. 'The cadaver wake up?'

'Willie Loman,' my brother says with a heavy tongue, 'is the salesman in the fucking play, not the playwright.'

'I see,' Dad says, driving south. 'And who told you that? A topless professor down the Thirsty Turtle?'

'Oh, Christ,' Danny Boy moans as if fully awake, painfully aware that he is in the Paradiso family tow truck on a muggy summer morning, out searching for a junk car.

'What are you a scholar now?' Dad says. 'Who wrote the play then? Who wrote it?'

'Miller.' My brother's lips are so close to the window it would fog if it was cold. 'Arthur Miller.'

My father and brother are powder and wick; any stray spark can set the charge. I feel blood warm my ears and something at work in the gut. My legs are in tight, my hands clutching the three brown lunch bags Mom packed for us with our names on them in red magic marker: Big Dan, Danny Boy and Nunzi (with a tiny heart dotting the i). I am small, but smaller still when pressed between my father and brother as they shuttlecock their words over my head.

'That's how much you fucking know, Casanova.'

'And he wasn't talking about our clock, he was talking about the Waterbury clock.'

Big Dan looks as if the judges have scored a round against him. I think of different ways to cleave the silence, to switch the train onto a new rail. Baseball, no. Could trigger a football association, open more scabs. Big Dan is going to blow. Danny Boy is tightening against my shoulder. I can smell beer, aftershave, gasoline, all of it combustible, about to go and so I yell: 'Look! Look there!'

A bright banner hanging between lamp-posts. Bold letters spell AMERICA'S RENAISSANCE CITY.

'What's that, Dad? What's that all about?'

Well, Big Dan explains as we clamber into the Puerto Rican South End, we aren't going to dress up as historical ass-holes and assemble on the Green; and no, there will be no feathered masks, no pewter steins of beer, the Italians will not be jousting against the Irish, nor will we get to see Monica Lafontaine's outsized breasts stuffed into a corset. 'The Renaissance City' is Saukiwog Mills' new slogan, coined by our mayor Frankie. Mayor Frankie is cleaning up the city, Dad says. The old housing projects are being restored, the parks fixed, dingy architecture scrubbed; the unemployed are being schooled at new trades and the druggies are being flushed out like rats from rice sacks.

'And they're gonna fix the Big Clock, too,' he says. 'The famous Big Clock.'

'Why?' Danny Boy stirs again. 'What's wrong with the clock?'

'*What's wrong with the clock?*'

'What's wrong with the clock.'

'The north face. It's been quarter past ten for seven years.'

'That's why I keep coming home so late,' Danny Boy says, nudging me.

'Yeah?' Dad spits out his window. 'What the *goomare* give you for your services last night? Food stamps?'

'Renaissance City,' I say, as we drive past sordid tenements and boarded brick buildings.

Big Dan grows solemn, just drives.

'I'm glad they're fixing up the city, Dad.' I say this while looking for evidence of such an ambitious claim, find none.

'That's right. We're a part of it, too, this Renaissance.'

'We are?'

'You bet your life. Junk? No, not junk, Nunzio. *Salvage.* We clean up the streets. We pick up the eyesores, all these old wrecks, scrap metal, and we use everything. Every part of it. We're like the Indians were with the buffalo.'

Dad is shrewd, knows I am nuts about Indians. And I like buffalo. But it is still too early in the morning to make the connection between the Paradisos, Jacques Cousteau and the Sioux, or scrap metal and bison and salvation, or even the Renaissance and Saukiwog Mills. I am still trying to figure out just what a renaissance city is; I envision guys in armor with lances, not Mayor Longo refurbishing the clock and increasing the tax base like Dad explains while looking at Danny Boy as if awaiting some contention. But there is no riposte: my brother is dead to the daylight as we fast approach a hilltop that I recognize.

'Okay, boys, stay alert,' Dad says, driving through rusted gates into a roily gray haze, the heat fog of summer. If Ahab wore a baseball cap that said *Dr Pepper*, Big Dan could pass for an obsessed whaler. 'One man's junk, another man's treasure,' he says. 'Let's bring her home, boys.'

This is how I remember sunrise on 11 June, 1979.

My father and brother, powder and wick.

And a '73 Pontiac Bonneville I would soon wish we had never found.

WELCOME TO HOLY HILL, USA

To us second- and third-generation Catholics growing up in a dry-rot mill town, it was our Agawam Park, our Disney World. Built high on Maple Hill in the early 1950s, the improbable Biblical shrine was the passion of an Irish judge and evangelist known as the Deacon Michael Flynn. The emigrant from County Kerry, Ireland, claimed to have received a message from God to construct the site. The result was impressive: a 32-foot neon peace cross glowing on the hill and leading travelers toward Saukiwog Mills like a blue beacon on shore. It hovered over the rubble and rust and the new interstate, a Day-Glo crucifix big enough to make itinerant vampires jump off the next exit and never look back at Saukiwog (which many people would tell you was wise).

It was still dawn so the peace cross was electric blue when we approached and the wind rapped and rustled the Day-Glo plastic on its metal frame. Dad fished out a little scrap of paper from his shirt pocket. He read the pencil scratch, confirming our mission.

'A '73 Pontiac Bonneville, boys. Where is she? Where's our buffalo?'

In the fog on the hill I could see a concrete slab and the carved passage:

WHY SEEK YOU THE LIVING AMONG THE DEAD?

'There it is!' I said, pointing out the old blue Bonneville abandoned near the fence. It had some rust on the rocker panels, no tags. Bald tires. And in the rear windscreen, a rubber troll with iridescent hair peering glass-eyed over the trunk.

Dad studied his new acquisition for a moment or two, his eyes breaking down the zinc, the chrome, the ferrous metals, the rims and the condition of the windshield – front and rear – and the value of the rubber troll. I was more intrigued by the bumper stickers:

THE AYATOLLAH IS AN ASSAHOLA.

A second read: KEEP ON TRUCKIN'.

Danny Boy was out of the wrecker; opening the driver's door of the old junker and spinning the steering wheel hard to starboard.

He unbuckled his belt, hissed it through the loops in his jeans, doing a kind of cat's cradle with it, and running it through the wheel and back out the vent window where he tied it to secure the wheels for towing.

While Dad circled the car, inspecting, I walked past a small cement structure that once served as the Holy Hill concession stand and gift store. I could see figures in the mist: used statues long-ago purchased by Deacon Flynn from various churches, which meant they were of varied sizes and designs. Blessed Mary was twice the height of Moses, and The Three Wise Men were from three different statuaries. A plaster marker said they had journeyed from the Orient; they looked more like they had been stolen from Barnum's Museum in Bridgeport.

Walking through hundreds of tiny temples and tombs constructed from factory scrap and upturned soup pots and chicken wire, I came upon a Christian being tortured for his faith: a store mannequin laid out over an electric fireplace log that had short-circuited years before. All within a few acres one could venture through Bethlehem, Egypt and ascend into Moab where my grandmother once, on a long-ago Easter, left a *torta di Pasqualina* at the feet of the Blessed Mother.

In Egypt, there was an isolated display that told the story of Lot's wife who disobeyed and was turned into a salt pillar. Behind the sign stood a lopsided white concrete block representing salt. I pitied Lot's wife. Not as much for being trapped in a big lump of cement as for being left up here on Maple Hill where there were no maples, and never had been any.

Everywhere lay heavy concrete slabs with equally heavy-handed Biblical imagery: *Eye hath not seen nor ear heard, neither have entered into the heart of man.* And there beneath the passage was an ineptly-carved picture of an eye, an ear and a heart.

Some had said that Deacon Flynn never heard the voice of God as much as he'd heard the voices of slow madness from drinking Sterno during the Depression. But this was the place, the Mecca that at one time had as many as 15,000 people a day visiting from around the country. Now there were no pilgrims, no signs of life – just an abandoned Pontiac and the distant sounds of dawn traffic far down on the interstate.

Grown over with mullein and fire weed, Holy Hill USA was not how I remembered it. Mary's arms were busted off at the elbows and someone had spray-painted a pair of lewd nipples on Her; John the Baptist still had his head but no left leg, and he had been broken off his stand; a winged devil creeping up on an innocent angel had been knocked on his back and now stared with cement eyes at the sky, his demonic face sanded smooth by twenty-five winters; and the entombed Jesus, a plaster child mannequin, was missing an arm and half His head. The catacombs that me and Danny once loved to descend into were now roped off as a hazardous area.

What was once a place of solace and pilgrimage and childhood wonder, now made me uneasy. The heat fog seemed to lay heavier around me and for a moment I was lost in Moab.

'Nunzi,' Dad called and I bolted toward the wrecker lights, bounding over miniature temples and mangers, toward the safety of my father's tan uniform. 'Hook her up.'

I took pride in being the hook rat. I was small and suited to the task. Dropping to my belly I would ferret under the chassis – dragging two large and rusted hooks – and rack them on the undercarriage.

'They on good?' Dad always asked, no matter how many times I performed and perfected it. He was, it seemed, always fearful of losing the car on the highway and getting a ticket from the Motor Vehicle Department, an agency he felt was his nemesis.

'They on good?'

'Yeah.'

'Hah?'

'Yes, they're on good.'

'Then check them again, make sure.'

While I was under the Bonneville in gasoline and gravel an odd thing occurred. Perhaps I was spooked by the defaced Jesus, by the mists of Moab, by the whole sickening desecration of the urban shrine, but I thought I heard a voice say something that sounded like, 'Dio.'

I went still, one hand on a hook, and I listened.

'Dio,' the voice said again, more distant.

I knew the word. Nonni, my grandmother, used it like a liniment: Dio or Dio mi', the Italian for My God. And so for a fleeting second I thought of a catechism story of St Francis of Assisi and the voice he heard from above telling him to go repair the ruins of crumbling churches. But why would God send a voice to me, Nunzio Paradiso from the Italian neighborhood, lying in oil beneath a '73 Pontiac? Surely not to go repair crumbling churches. I was not yet a confirmed Christian, and I could barely assemble the Lincoln Log set Big Dan once found in a Renault.

But there was a more disturbing thought down there under the car with me.

The Legend of Deacon Flynn.

According to my mother, the judge who turned to preaching began to deteriorate at a pace with his beloved shrine, and in the late 1960s had disappeared from Saukiwog Mills. Some said he had grown disillusioned and went back to Ireland. But others had another version, one that kids like the Doyle brothers repeated ditty-style in school:

> *Gather, Kerries and Kerry kin,*
> *This is the story of Deacon Flynn.*
> *They say the ghost of Deacon roams*
> *For he sealed himself in the catacombs.*

Our mother said it was just a tale, the story of Deacon Flynn going down into the ersatz catacombs of his beloved shrine and sealing himself inside the plaster walls, block by cinder block, a Christian torturing himself for his faith. I sure didn't want to hear the voices *he* heard, so I slid out from under the Pontiac and almost knocked my father off-balance.

'Hey-hey!' Dad squirmed. 'Easy there, kid.'

'Let's get outta here,' I said.

Danny Boy, himself looking off at the pitiful ruins of Egypt, took a last deep inhale on a Kool, dropped it in the gravel and heeled it out with his work boot. He started off a few steps into the shadows, toying with his zipper.

'What you doing, Danny?' I said.

'Gotta take a leak.'

'In Jerusalem?'

My brother stood there, hand at his fly. He looked up at the peace cross as if noticing it for the first time, then returned to the tow truck without relieving himself. For the next half-hour's drive,

Danny Boy, like the mannequin on the hill, would be a Catholic tortured for his faith.

Somewhere on the stretch of Route 8, parallel to the leaden green Mattatuck River, Big Dan was proffering wisdom again as we towed the junk car away; something about how people drive a car until it expires and they just leave it where it croaked. People did it with washing machines, he said. Record players, pets and other people, too.

'One day a guy looks at his wife and he realizes he's going on old memories. Because the fact of the matter is she's got too many miles on her. She's not the young Dodge he brought home to his mother in 1953. The front-end's out of line, shocks are gone, and her rocker panels are saggin'. So he junks her. Just like that. Junks her, goes shopping for a new ride, a used one, but a little younger model, less mileage. New color. Red, say. And what happens to the old Dodge?'

There was a pithy silence and then Danny Boy said, 'I snag her at the Swizzle Stick, for a price.'

He was awake and rapt now, Danny, his hangover having burned off like the dawn fog and he looked past me with a wink. 'One man's junk, another man's treasure,' he quoted, stirring the shit fire.

'The food-stamp *gigolo*!' Dad yelled with sarcastic glee, kept his head turned to look out the rear windshield. 'They on good, Nunz? The hooks, they set right?'

We crossed the old trestle and drove through the area that was once the hub of the brass industry but was now being called the Rust Bowl: mill after fallen mill, sitting fallow or already demolished. Piles of dusty brick, steel rods and gutted backsettlements.

'Who would do something like that, Dad, to Jesus and Moses? They broke the Blessed Mother's arms off.'

Dad needed no time to ponder. 'That's how people are, Nunzio. They're like those lamprey eels that suck onto a big walleye and keep sucking till the fish is dead, and then they move onto another one. You're going to find out, kid, that in this world, people use up people like they use up cars, then they leave the carcass for lesser animals.'

Then Big Dan sucked his teeth, said, 'Hey, but you can't think like that. You got to have faith in people.'

His disclaimer did not soothe me. This lamprey eel philosophy, if it was true, made me fear what lay beyond my twelfth summer, and so I did what I always did whenever fear or uncertainty became too much for my body weight: I repeated the name of Saint Rocco four times, looking down then back up between each incantation. A strange ritual, I confess, but it was my own way to render evil harmless, to put myself at ease. It was a superstition going back to when I was four or five and I first began laying my socks in the shape of a crucifix at the foot of my bed, or leaving a broom in the corner to keep away *La Strega*, the Italian witch who had come over from the Old Country on a tramp steamer. The ultimate talisman, taught to me by my grandmother – and reserved only for close encounters with *Il Diavolo* – was to grip my testicles and count backward from seven in Italian. I was never able to locate this one in my old, hand-me-down copy of Italo Calvino's *Italian Folktales*, but it existed in my Nonni's household as sure as pickled eggplant.

'What are you doing?' Dad said, suddenly concerned. 'You're not doing that tic again.'

'Leave him alone,' Danny Boy said. 'He's superstitious about shit.'

'He's got a nervous tic,' Dad shouted back. 'They're going to put him in Southbury, he does that in public. They'll throw rocks at him, they'll give him shock treatments.'

'Leave him alone,' my brother said, firm in his role of protector.

Dad let go a breath like clean-jerking the weight of the universe; he often felt like he never got a fair shake. 'I got one son with a nervous tic, and one with a bargain-rate dick,' he complained, and he seemed amused by his own little haiku.

'Maybe Mayor Longo will fix Holy Hill, too,' I said hopefully.

'Maybe,' Dad said. 'But they'll only ruin it again.'

The north face of the Big Clock read quarter past ten, but on the east face, it was ten minutes to eight and somewhere back in the small park that separated The Little Boot and Lithuania Town, my friends were mourning my loss on a baseball diamond and Monica Lafontaine, sweet thirteen – a descendant of the extinct

French-Canadian section – was walking barefoot and bored down
America Street, trolling for adventure.

PARADISE SALVAGE – USED PARTS – SCRAP METAL REDEMPTION

That's what the big sign said as you drove through the chain-link
gate and into our family junkyard: ten acres of old cars spread
across a plateau and down into networks of ravines and scrap
rows. A bargain-hunter's treasure trove, a dinosaur park of old
machines: 1950s Chevys and Buicks with their snarling front grills
and lewd bullet-shaped projectiles; battered muscle cars like the Le
Mans and the ponies like the 'Cuda and old Mustangs; Aerospace
fantasies from the 1960s and rococo roadsters from the 1970s; old
school buses and vans and totaled Mac trucks packed chockablock
against the fence; there was a VW Bug section that looked like a
multicolored insect pod, and an exclusive Japanese section; there
was even a Woody hearse, black and ominous and bearing the
legend *Saturday's Children*, the name of the rock outfit that restored
it before they drove into steel guardrails and decapitated a girl sitting
on the drummer's lap. That one was down in the little valley Dad
called The Boneyard, a taboo area of fatal wrecks.

Big Dan had found an 8×10 photo of Saturday's Children in
the Woody and pinned it up on the office corkboard among his
collection of polaroids that he took from the junked cars; a black
family huddled around a birthday cake, some Puerto Rican guy
posing with a sea bass, a graduation photo of some redheaded
girl and postcards from people he never knew in places he'd never
been. The strange thing was, there were no photos of our family
on the corkboard wall. Just strangers who had died in wrecks or
had retired their cars in his junkyard.

There was other salvage: the city's last steam engine, retired in
1949, rusted now and used to house secondhand generators. But the
feature that set our salvage yard apart from others was the vegetable
garden oasis in the middle, lovingly tended by my grandfather, and
boasting the biggest, reddest, heftiest beefsteak tomatoes in the
city. If our salvage yard was unusual, our routine was steady and
disciplined. When Big Dan had stripped a vehicle's carcass of every
valuable resource – right down to its door locks – it went to the

open lands out beyond the garage where it was picked clean one more time before the sacrifice on the mantel of The Crusher, the wide-mouthed beast. If the junkyard was a kingdom, as Big Dan had often proclaimed it, then The Crusher was King. Almost something of a family pet, the gargantuan baling machine had gaping jaws of rust and steel, and the heartless, soulless gluttony of a great white shark; like the natives offering a chaste girl to a mythical beast, we made daily offerings of old Pintos and Impalas and wrecked GTOs, mollifying the smoking monster. Invariably, it shut down on Toyotas and Hondas, stalling with compressed scrap wedged in its jaws.

'The Crusher don't like Japanese food,' Big Dan would say as he sprayed starting fluid inside the baler's pipes. As ferocious as our junkyard dog was, when he heard that hydraulic press start up, he slunk panther-pawed into the back of the Wonderbread truck he was chained to, and coiled himself in the shade.

My friends who had visited the junkyard before, held a mythic view of The Crusher. They always scrunched their noses and grinned at the bold and humorous legend my father had spray-painted across the machine's yellow body:

I can't Believe I ate the Whole Thing

While my brother would manage the tire bunker, Dad and I would go through the new arrivals in our customary way: Big Dan laying down across the frontseat and searching the glove box, bagging a pair of sunglasses or an old paperback, the odd ball cap, Kleenex boxes with some viable tissue left. I would squirrel about in the backseat, shimming my small hands under the upholstery. For all the grim boredom of being sentenced to hard labor, I found great joy in this part of the job. It was a treasure hunt and one never knew what booty would be salvaged, what dirty secrets we would find under the seats – like the nubby pink French Tickler we once found under the seat of a red Rambler that belonged to an alderman's ex-wife.

Inevitably, Dad would get in back with me, take his old jack blade and cut a neat incision along the bottom of the front seat. Coins would sometimes rain like a slot machine, and I'd flip my hat under Dad's blade catching the lost nickels and pennies, the odd button and a few ossified French fries.

'Hey, look at this, Nunzio,' Dad whistled through his teeth one afternoon during my first week at the yard. He'd found something in the frontseat and he held it up like it was the Golden Fleece. 'Hah? What do you say, kid – look at that.' The bounty was an old High School letter jacket, God-awful pumpkin orange with a big black W.

'Aw, Dad, I don't know.'

'Try it on. It's a nice one.'

Big Dan, like Crazy Horse, let nothing go to waste. If I rejected the jacket he would, after a brief address about children freezing in Greenland, hang it in the office like a trophy.

Now, on this muggy Thursday, as we lowered the blue Bonneville, Danny Boy went shuffling off to the tire bunker; thunder was grumbling and the sky was a dark sponge that wanted to let go but only managed to wring off large and scattered raindrops. I pushed up the sleeves on the letter jacket – which Dad had encouraged me to wear with pride daily – and prepared to ransack the new acquisition. I had my eye on the troll.

But Dad told me to go feed the dog and he, too, walked off toward the garage.

'What about the Pontiac, Dad?'

'Scrap,' he said. 'She's on deck.'

In our salvage yard argot, this meant the car would not be stored and used as a parts trove. Once its tires were removed and its engine yanked, it would be fed to The Crusher. I started to the office to open a can of Alpo but there was something about this car, this old blue beater with rat-holed rocker panels that you could crumble with a kick. I was thinking of the coin collection Dad had once found in an old sedan and carried home with all the ceremony of presenting the Lost Chalice. Now, I watched him go around the back of the garage as thunder cracked like a bullwhip somewhere down near the fence. I left the Pontiac and set off in his footsteps.

But that pink-haired troll beckoned.

I wanted it for my room, for the archaeological collection I kept in a Puma Clyde shoebox. And so I went for it. Working fast and with all the anticipation of Christmas morning, I hurried into the backseat, tucked away the troll then crawled into the front. I peeled back the floor mats and found a pack of matches with an ad for truck driving school on the back. I slid my hand in the crevice of the frontseat and combed the distance, coming away with sixteen cents in mixed change, some kind of brass token and a small hat pin. On closer inspection I could see that the pin was a tarnished fake gold, a tiny globe-shape with some numbers on it and the logo *1973 – Chicago*. The pin was broken off but I took it anyway. I tucked the coins, token, pin and matches away in the pocket of my letter jacket, squirreled over the frontseat and cased the glove box. It was empty but for a tiny red cellophane package. Hopeful, I removed it, but found it empty. I would have left it behind but for the picture of a Chinese dragon on it and some foreign words. Some kind of Asian cigarettes I surmised, and so I nabbed it and crawled out, richer than I was when I crawled in. This was the singular benefit to working the summer in the family salvage yard: I got to be an archaeologist.

Out back, I could hear The Crusher starting up like a monster waking with a diesel protest.

But the treasure chest was yet to be opened.

If junked cars were our buffalo then the trunk was the raw heart; if an old Pontiac was a shipwreck, it was the trunk that held the treasures, the mystic cargo space that had provided me through the years with a catcher's mitt, a set of golf clubs, a box of *Police Gazettes* from the 1940s, a pair of bowling shoes and a box of canned rations from the Korean War.

I withdrew the keys from the ignition and went around to the trunk of the Pontiac, brimming with anticipation. The first key didn't fit, the second popped the latches, and I hefted the trunk lid open with a promising ancient creak. There was something large in there and I felt my heart lift with excitement, remembering the set of golf clubs we found the week prior. Whether I saw it or smelled it first, I do not know, but my breakfast came surging upward.

In the trunk was a man.

A man in a dirty white dress shirt and blue slacks.

A dead man.

His face was a moleskin hue and one leg was tucked under him in an unnatural bend. It couldn't be a real man. But it was. Something, some unseen and malignant force pushed down hard on me and kept my boots from lifting. It was the smell. That's what held me to the bumper.

The man was old and he wore horn-rimmed glasses. One of the lenses had been smashed and the shards were what seemed to pin the glasses to his face. Behind the cracked lens was a red splotch, no eye. There was another mark near his temple, crusted with a brownish putty.

I was looking at a dead body.

'A body is in the frigging trunk!' I wanted to scream, but there was no wind to set my voice to sail. Thunder bullwhipped so close I felt it in my back. Again, I tried to holler, but couldn't. The trunk lid must have been pressing the body to the carpeted tire space because as it released, the dead man's left arm seemed to thaw from repose.

His head lolled slightly, his tongue purple, exposed, like a rotting plum. He looked straight into the rain with the eye that had not been punctured and he let out a gaseous sound, like a deep and resonant fart finding its way up and out his lungs. It was the sound, the voice I had heard while I was under the car in the Biblical ruins on Maple Hill earlier that morning. The man had been alive then, in the dark constraints of the trunk, alive, listening to somebody clank hooks just under him.

'Dio.' It came from the deep well of the man's lungs and a thin bubble formed in the red froth at his nostrils and lips. The undamaged eye fixed on me, and then, as if in violent reflex, his left hand unfurled and smashed me in the throat. It was the hand of an old man, a leather raptor talon that squeezed, twisting my T-shirt at the neck, pulling me toward him like he wanted to whisper something to me, or maybe he was trying to pull me into the trunk space with him. My spirit was running for the garage, but my body was going into the trunk of the Pontiac with a ghoul.

'A ghoul is in the frigging trunk!'

And then he released me.

Just like that.

His arm retracted, his head went still. His eyes filmed over and stared into the rain, like a bluefish I once saw decomposing on the beach at Milford. In his other hand was something that looked like the strung beads my Cousin Lena had hanging on her bedroom door. Love beads, she called them – the dead man had love beads twisted around his knuckles. I took no chances on another resurrection: I grabbed the trunk lid and slammed it closed, heard it latch. I ran for the garage but went the wrong way, banging into hoods and bumpers and an old mail truck, I vaulted the hood of a wrecked Renault wagon, came down again yelling. Thunder sledge-hammered at something overhead and a silent flash of lightning reflected in a thousand car windows, no matter how cracked.

'DAD!' I screamed, grabbing hold of the bumper of an old Hudson Terraplane and launching myself for the garage. The junkyard German Shepherd lunged at me in a mad lather, but the chain held him short. I was running through a flood of terrible thoughts:

Who is this man? Is he some bum who was staggering around the shrine looking for a warm place to sleep? What was that smell like the Porta-john at the Danbury Fair? Is that what death smells like? What happened to his eye? Where is my dad? Where is my – DAD!

He wasn't in the garage.

The little cubby hole office was unlit and quiet. And then I heard the sounds of machines warming up in back: the whoomph-whoomph-ROAR of the Caterpillar fork machine and the punishing chainsaw moan of The Crusher. I could smell diesel fuel, stale gas, and still, the fetid odor from what had touched me. I couldn't tell where Dad was on his Caterpillar but the quickest route out was through the front door again. I would have to look at the Pontiac once again as I ran, and some remote part of me expected to hear the ghoul banging from inside the trunk. I felt part victim-on-the-run, part criminal for locking the trunk on a man.

That's when I realized the car was gone.

Vanished. Just rain puckers in the small dark fuel stain where it had been moments ago. I could hear now, behind the garage, the jack hammering of the air wrench shooting off lugs. If Danny Boy was removing the tires from the car, I had to stop him. I came around the corner and there was Big Dan high on the Caterpillar, working the wheel and levers and driving the two huge forks through the driver's door of the Pontiac, piercing metal.

'Dad, stop!' I yelled, but I might as well have been calling into a typhoon: the diesel machinery was ear-damaging. Danny Boy stood by The Crusher, the air wrench still in his big work gauntlets, his eyes shielded by foggy safety goggles. In his early morning haze, he watched Big Dan place the car onto the gangway of The Crusher as it did its mechanical inhale, drawing the old Bonneville in, crushing metal like tin foil. The car buckled, lurched, and slipped deeper into the giant machine's double-rowed molars. The man in the trunk, dead or still alive, was being taken into a seven-ton baler. The world was skidding on black ice, and for all my yelling and flapping my cap in the air, I couldn't stop it.

'Dad! No!'

He looked at me, just a glance, and he must have thought my gyrations were another nervous tic because he looked away, resuming his routine and helping force-feed the Pontiac into the hydraulic press.

'WOH! There's somebody in there! Woh! Shit!' I fell and got up a half-dozen times, ran to the Caterpillar and threw myself at the steel ladder on its frame, scaled up to the driver's seat where Dad was concentrating on the flattening process.

'Dad!' I yelled right into his ear, and now he could see something was awry. He shut down the big Caterpillar, pushed the brim of his Dr Pepper hat up an inch.

'What is it?'

'There's a frigging guy in the car!'

'There's a what in the what?'

'There's a guy in the car!'

Dad glanced toward the garage. 'Okay, give him a cup of coffee, tell him I'll be over there in a minute.'

'No, Dad! There's a guy in the Pontiac!'

'What Pontiac?'

'*That* Pontiac!'

Dad blinked at me in the rain then turned his gaze on The Crusher. The old car was already ingested, only its rear bumper remaining in sight, and then that too folded in and became enmeshed with the trunk, the roof – one flat square extruding out The Crusher's spillway. It eased out in its new contour, ten feet over the ground, and then dropped next to other flattened hulks of assorted makes and eras. Big Dan did his shrill whistle and signaled for Danny Boy to shut the baler down.

After a few heaves and seizures, The Crusher made a diesel hacking sound, let out some hydraulic air, then went still. And then it did the repugnant thing it always did when its engine was cooled: it belched out a foul wash of red fluid and diesel silt. My eyes fixed on the legend Dad had painted across The Crusher's girth long ago:

I can't Believe I ate the Whole Thing.

What had once been amusing to me now seemed the stuff of a violent dream. Everything had fallen into the strange, ear-ringing silence that follows unbearable noise. Dad stared at me, his brow furrowed.

'Say this again? Slow it down, Nunzio.'

'I opened the trunk . . .'

'Okay.'

'And I saw a guy.'

'What do you mean, you saw a guy?'

'He had a white shirt and blue slacks and black penny loafers, he was alive for a minute because he grabbed me and then, do you remember that bluefish on Milford Beach on Nonni's birthday about three years ago?'

'You smoking something?'

'No!'

Dad was prepossessed with this thought now. He had made up his mind, swift and certain as was his way. 'You sniffing starter fluid or something?'

'Dad, please.' I resorted to the sacrosanct. 'May Grandpa MacLeish turn over in his grave!'

'Between you and your mother, that poor bastard is turning like a pin-wheel.'

'Dad, *please*. I know what I saw.'

Thunder was far off now, a buffalo rumble on the edge of town. Aware of the situation now, Danny Boy trudged over, his plastic pilot goggles beaded with light rain and motor oil.

'Hey, Dad,' he said. 'Maybe it was Jimmy Hoffa.'

'Don't even joke like that,' Big Dan said. 'You're going to get this kid looking at everything three times again and holding his nuts.'

'Four,' Danny corrected him, starting off for the tire room. As much as Danny Boy loved and protected me, I could see he didn't believe me.

'Danny,' I called to him, but he was already gone.

'Come up here,' my father said, and he made a little room for me on the tattered black upholstery. Together we sat up high, looking over the sea of junked cars. My eyes were locked on that one blue metal block of 1973 Pontiac Bonneville, and I felt ill.

'Nunzi. You're a good boy. You got a little too much of the Scotch in you, but we're working that out of your system. You're doing good. See, what the problem is . . .'

'There's a dead guy in that car, that's the problem.'

'Will you stop for one second?'

He looked long and hard into my eyes. 'The problem is, your mother says you got a good imagination. You write stories about dinosaur bones in the woods, Indian carvings and Blue Beard's gold in the Mattatuck River, and your mother, she says' – here, Dad affected my mother's Scots brogue and high fluted timbre – '"he's got a wonderful imagination, he's a dreamer, going to be a writer". You know Horton Judd? The bum who walks the railroad tracks? He's got a wonderful imagination, too. He's a dreamer. Sonuvabitch dug up the back lawn of the library looking for oil. He's got a wonderful imagination, too. And now the *mamaluke* lives in a cardboard box under the trestle. You know what you saw in that trunk?'

'Horton Judd?'

'Dead puppies.'

I looked at Dad, my mind ajar now and no less sickened. It all seemed a strange dream; maybe I had inhaled gasoline fumes.

'Didn't I tell you to leave it alone?' Dad said.

'Yes.'

'Didn't I tell you it was scrap?'

'Yes.'

'Thirty-five years in the salvage business, I've got this.' Big Dan touched his ample nose. 'I smelled it. Once I opened a trunk and found a side of rancid beef. Another time, baby diapers. Some guy must've had six kids and was stuffing diapers for six years in the trunk of that little Chevy Nova. I opened the trunk – I almost passed out. When I tell you a car is scrap, you leave it alone. I've got this.' Again, he tapped his finger against his nose.

'Okay, but—'

'You saw a dead dog.'

'No, Dad—'

'Are you going to argue with your father? What's with you guys?'

'I'm sorry, Dad. But—'

He cupped his hand on my shoulder and smiled. 'That's a nice jacket. You know what kids in the North End would give for a jacket like that?'

I dropped from the ladder and took a few dazed steps toward the crushed vehicle. I was looking for an arm twisting out, a shoe, something to prove my case.

'Feed the dog, sweetheart,' Dad called after me as I swerved toward the vista of hubcaps and radiators. 'Eyes on the ground,' he reminded me. 'There's gold down there.'

Another decree: in the salvage business one always walked with eyes on the ground lest you pass right over a chunk of Number 2 cast iron or a buffalo head nickel. But a few half-buried pennies in the grease were nothing against the scope of my trauma. I walked away with my eyes ahead and my heart pulsing so heavy I could feel it bruise against my ribs.

I knew what I saw.

Danny Boy was in the cinder-block tire bunker, deep in the ritual that began his day. On the cement wall he had air-nailed pages from magazines, newspapers, and other publications that paid tribute to his patron saint. There was even a big black-and-white image of the figure, showing him bleeding from the eyes like a stigmata. Above the image was the name RAGING BULL.

And in the center of the shrine, a large Mac truck mirror was mounted so that Danny Boy could look into his own soul as he reflected and appealed to his guardian angel.

'Wait a minute,' he said into the Mac truck mirror, narrowing his eyes and making his bottom lip strain into a grimace even as he grinned. 'Are you talkin' to me?'

Danny Boy visited this junkyard sanctum several times a day to commune with St Robert. The conversion began at the farthest edge of the junkyard, on the high ridge overlooking the Mattatuck Drive-in where Danny Boy would occasionally go to drink beer. The movie *Taxi Driver* had been running for two weeks, and for eleven nights he sat on the hood of a stray Mercury on the edge and watched like some spiritual seeker looking for a message in the Aurora Borealis.

He took me up there one night to 'see Bobby'.

I drank a Yoo-Hoo, he drank a Miller, and he made me watch, the two of us seated side-by-side on the hood of the old Montego. 'Loneliness has followed me my whole life,' he would say, in perfect synch with the colossal De Niro's lips. At the end of the picture, he would climb back down the ridge with a certain peace about him. Far as I can tell, that's when it started; the only ritual that seemed to fill the void after his football dreams were taken away.

Now, Danny Boy – who gave himself that little twist on his name in tribute to Johnny Boy from *Mean Streets*, not from the Irish song *Oh, Danny Boy* as our mother believed – was working on his face like it was pliable clay. He sensed me standing there in my wet letter jacket and he angled a cheekbone at me, crooked his head. Like when a dog tries to make sense of humans.

'There's nobody else here,' he said, entrenched in the mannerisms of the actor. *'There's nobody else here.'*

'We just crushed somebody,' I said.

He studied me for a moment and his face slowly resumed its natural shape.

– Nunz, man.

– I saw him. He was still alive. Like that duck Grandpa killed that time, kept jumping up. He grabbed me.

– He grabbed you?

– I don't know.

– You just says he grabbed you.

– I don't know if he grabbed me. He moved, like. He twitched, like.

Twitched like.

– I don't want to say he grabbed me because maybe he was just like, reaching.

– Reaching. Or twitching?

– I don't want to accuse him of grabbing. Remember what happened with that Portuguese girl and Father Vario when she said he grabbed her.

– Nunz. Hello? If you're saying a guy just went through The Crusher in the trunk of a fucking Pontiac, he can't get into any more trouble than he's already in.

– He grabbed me. He tried to, but I shut the trunk and—'

'Dante,' my brother said.

It was what my grandfather called me because of my penchant for writing stories when I was supposed to be out helping in the garden.

'Is this one of your stories, Dante?'

'May Grandpa Mac turn over in his grave if I didn't see what I saw.'

My brother weighed this with more gravity than our dad. He gingerly touched a raw pimple at his hairline. 'Nunzio, come on, man.' He laughed. 'This is Saukiwog Mills, not New Jersey. Maybe . . . you're watching too much *Godfather*.'

'Me?' I said, looking at his shrine where De Niro loomed as young Don Corleone, training a sawed-off shotgun on old Fanucci.

Danny stared at me, then he wiped something from my chin with a maroon gas rag. 'Okay. I'm your big brother, right? Listen to me—'

– Okay.

– I saw a body in a car once.

– You did?

– Last winter.

– My God, Danny.

– In a '68 Skylark. A woman. A baldheaded woman in the cargo space.

– Holy shit.

– She had no face.

– No face?

– None. She was a mannequin – from Sears. That's what you saw. A mannequin somebody was throwing out. Or a rubber sex doll.

– No, this guy wasn't a rubber sex doll. And he had holes in his head – two holes – one of them right through the lens of his glasses.

– What are you saying over here?

– I'm saying if he was a rubber sex doll he would have deflated. And I've never seen a guy like that at Sears.

– *What are you saying over here?*

– Same thing I said over *there*. We crushed somebody.

'I don't know anybody named Iris,' Danny said. In his odd commitment to his newfound religion, this meant he didn't know what to say, how to unscramble a predicament.

I don't know anybody named Iris.

Most of the world didn't have a clue what he was saying when he did that, but I did, and sometimes I used it myself, and sometimes he and I shortened it just to 'Iris', which was to say 'Hell if I know.'

It was unnatural behavior, I was aware of this. But Mom said it was just a phase like when he took up Kung Fu after his football career ended and he went shoeless, even in the junkyard, walking softly over crushed glass and asking for water in a vague and disembodied voice. 'Grasshopper,' my father would say to him then. 'Put your fucking shoes on and go get some fourteen-inch snow tires.'

'Hey,' a voice clipped, startling the two of us. Jimmy the Puerto Rican stood squat and bowlegged in Bermuda shorts and a faux Polo shirt, knee-high athletic socks and black shoes. A flavored toothpick bobbed in his tight lips, his eyes tiny wedges of disdain. 'I need two tire, man,' he said. 'For my Cha-velle, man,' he said. 'I need good tire. Nice tire. Good tread, man. Don't be giving me no bald shit tire, I want two good fucking tire, man. Don'ju fuck with me, man.'

As Jimmy the Puerto Rican laid out his order, he tugged at his Bermudas like there was a live mouse in there. Danny Boy stared at the customer for a long moment then looked at me with a smile and testy nod. It was that odd down-turned smile – that almost impossible mix of comedy and tragedy on the same face – and he turned it on Jimmy the Puerto Rican who seemed bemused by the collapse of my brother's facial muscles. 'You talkin' to me?' Danny said.

'No, I'm talkin' to my balls, man,' he said, menace in his tiny eyes, sweat beading on him like rainwater on Turtle Wax.

Danny Boy flipped me a dime, the tread inspection tool, and said, 'Find two nice G-14's for Jimmy the Puerto Rican.'

Jimmy lifted his chin and gave me an autocratic eye. He seemed to take pleasure in my young servitude. When I didn't hustle right away, he stomped a loafer toward me like one spooks a cat. 'Pssst!' he hissed. And I hustled outside.

That's where I saw them.

Four Hispanic men standing outside Jimmy the Puerto Rican's Chevelle, silent. Still. One of them, wearing a teal-blue bowling shirt, rested an elbow on the roof of the Chevelle and stared up at the stack of crushed cars. So did the others, all of them, just gazing up there as if trying to pick out something in the rubble. The guy in teal turned suddenly, looked down the alley of used tires. Looked right at me. I ducked into rubber and scrambled through the tall rows of Goodyears and Uniroyals. When I surfaced to look again, they were gone.

All my young life, summer had been mine to catch and release, like an endless vein of sunfish. Now it was out of my grip; I had hooked something deep in the gills under muddy water and it was pulling me with it, wherever it was going.

Danny Boy's only wisdom was to salvage his favorite line from *The Deer Hunter*: 'This is *this*.'

CHAPTER TWO

America Street

And that was that.

We drove home for the night, into the oasis of grape vines and gardens and ceramic porch saints that was my neighborhood. It was still light out and the streets and yards yet alive with black-haired girls and olive-skinned boys, the people of my ilk, the *ragazzini*, playing themselves into the sweet fever of summer. Gooma Lucia, short and bent in her sleeveless flowers, was crossing her yard with a basket of laundry. She yelled in Italian at some boys who spoked her garden rows on two-wheelers. But when we drove past in the tow truck, she threw her cursing into a helium-shrill and joyous, 'Heeeeyyyy, Donato! *Come va?*' waving with her chin as Dad waved and swung us up around the buff-brick Our Lady of Mount Carmel Church.

They were mostly people from the *Mezzogiorno*, the lower half of Italy: *Pontelandolfesi* like my grandparents (there were more Pontes in Saukiwog than there were in Pontelandolfo, Italy); *Cercimaggiores; Avelenese.* But there was a stronghold of *Calabrese* around Our Lady, and some Northern Italians had taken up residence near St Lucy's. Our idea of an intermarriage scandal was when a Ponte married a Sicilian.

Our home was a two-story Cape at 11 St Mary Street. Muted green. My mother called it Lincoln Green, but said it held shades of pistachio at dusk. My brother's ex-girlfriend Cheryl Vaughn, who grew up in the wealthier enclave of Saukiwog, called the color of our house avocado and said it upset her stomach. I saw it more as the color of a plastic Malox bottle, so in an odd way, it kind of soothed my insides. Our cedar hedges were trimmed in a neat, flat row and our planters were made from old tires that Dad cut a design on and whitewashed; our lawn ornaments were harvested from the family wrecking yard: a vintage pink flamingo, a stone birdbath, and a plaster Blessed Mother holding vigil over the *zucchini*. Next door, at number 13, was my grandparents' older home, part yellow plaster, part brick, and dwarfed by an almost supernatural garden.

My grandmother was Italian but she was a dead ringer for Chief Dan George. This satisfied my questions about why they always used Italians to play Indians on TV; give Nonni a head-dress and she could pass for an Ojibwa even as she favored black scarves and flesh-toned stockings rolled at the ankle. Always peeking through her flowered curtains when she heard us come home, Nonni knew all in The Little Boot.

When we walked Indian-file into the breezeway, my mother was there, apron on and big wooden sauce spoon in her hand. She smiled her gay Celtic grin as she assessed our greasy states and gathered up our work-clothes in a basket. Born on the banks of Loch Lomond and brought over at my age by her mill-worker father, my mother was a Scotswoman living happily among Italians. Like me, she knew how to count in Dad's Neapolitan dialect, and she had command over curse words. She was far from a cursing woman but once I heard her get cross with Dad and tell him *vafangoolo*, which in her thick burr sounded like a soft calypso on a pan pipe.

'How's my working men? Hungry horses make clean mangers.' Mom looked me over for any wounds, physical or otherwise, as I entered the kitchen and went right for the sink and a drinking glass. Mom did not like the idea of me sacrificing the last free summer of my life, and she had fought like a clanswoman for my rights, only to surrender before matters turned worse. Now she 'hoped well to have well', 'listened for the music of hope in grief', and her favorite, 'tine heart, tine all, Nunzio'.

She gently removed my Mao cap and pushed my hair from my eyes. 'So what wonders did ye find today, love, that you'll put in your box of treasures?'

I looked past my mother to make sure the two Dans were still at the sink, arguing over how hot the water should be to clean effectively. I wasn't sure how to broach what had occurred. I feared the wrath of Big Dan if he heard me recounting what he thought was a nervous tic or mere child's play. So I stood there, thin in my underwear and opened a fist to show my mother the hat pin, the token and the sixteen cents. Then the other fist: the troll, the matchbook and the small red cigarette pack with the yellow dragon on its cover. Mom smiled, clucked her tongue in approval and put my cap back on my head, backward to be playful.

'Tell her,' my father said, entering the kitchen. 'Tell your mother what you saw in the trunk.'

'A body, Mom.'

It sounded so odd that my own face went warm and I was grateful for the mask of grease.

'Oh, dear Columba,' Mom said and she brought a hand to her mouth. 'What kind of body was it? A secret agent maybe?'

Mom meant no condescension, she just thought I was playing the game she and I had enjoyed since I was 'a wee bairn', a game in which I would describe my abduction by a German submarine in the Saukiwog River to explain why I was late for supper. She would go along with me until a fantastic narrative was spun by the two of us, like two mad weavers from the book of Grimm. This was the very stuff Dad was hoping to rescue me from lest I became an irretrievable *mamaluke*.

'Did you check under the body?' Mom asked. 'Perchance there was a briefcase of money. Millions of dollars, hidden in the trunk.'

'There was no million dollars,' I said flatly. 'There was sixteen cents, and a dead man. I'm not fooling. I saw a body in the trunk of a Pontiac, but it went through The Crusher before I could tell Daddy. He doesn't believe me. The guy is up there right now.'

Danny Boy passed by with a slight bounce in his step. 'What a day, Mom. We sold six pair of tires and Nunzio met Jimmy Hoffa.' He dipped a finger in the stove pan and sampled the stew as he headed toward his bedroom.

My mother stared at me for a spell, knitting her reddish brow. She was still smiling, but when I swore on Grandpa MacLeish's soul turning, her smile dimmed and her eyes lost their playful shimmer. Dad stood in the hall in clean Bermuda shorts, drying his hands with a towel.

'Will you leave Grandpa MacLeish alone? The poor bastard's spinning like a Kansas windmill!'

'Oh, Dan,' Mom clucked her tongue. My father sat at the kitchen table and turned his attention to the *Saukiwog Mills Republican* while Mom stirred the pan of mince, one eye looking down at me. I never swore on her father's soul unless I was telling sacrosanct truth, and at this moment, in the kitchen, Grandpa Hamish MacLeish was looking down at us from the wall, a black-and-white figure in kilt and bagpipes and Woolworth's stockings. I never knew him – he died before I was born – but by all accounts he was a mystic, a member of the Foreign Legion, a banjolin player and a straw-weight boxer. To me, he was in a league with Johnny Appleseed, and his death in a chemical fire at the rubber shop long before I was born, a dark wound in my mother's history.

She said nothing for a time as she served the stew. But she was watching me as if looking for signs of fever. 'Maybe he's too young to be working up there,' she said to Dad as he read the front page. 'The sun is dreadful. Is he wearing a hat?'

'Don't body-block for him, Nancy,' Dad said. 'He's a big boy, he's doing good. You oughta see him strip tires.' And then, Big Dan offered his theory about the mystery cargo. 'Last Fourth of July at the beach, do you remember? A big piece of driftwood was washed up. Nunzio came running over, screaming that it was a mako shark. He sees things, Nunzio.'

'Aye, well, art improves nature as they say.'

'Not when you see dead puppies in a trunk and say you saw a dead man.'

'Why couldn't somebody just leave the poor things on a door-step?' she said. 'Locking them in the trunk of a car, *och*!' She looked at me as I stared into my stew. 'He's not lifting too much, is he? He can get a hernia.'

I knew my mother was not disregarding my story. There were just some things that were best worked out between us with silent looks or porch whispers. And there was something else: my mother did not believe in the evil of men. She tined heart and tined all, in all people and events, and she was outspoken on this tenet. So in her optimistic way, she soon let the dark waters run south and out of her mind. 'There's going to be a big shindig on the Green, Sunday,' she announced. 'They have refurbished *The Soldier's Horse* and they're going to unveil it.'

'That right?' Dad said.

The Soldier's Horse was a fountain monument erected, before the flood of immigrants, in honor of a local hero from the Revolution named Asa Bean. Although it was known as *The Soldier's Horse* it was, in reality, a mule that saved the life of old Asa. Big Dan referred to it as *The Soldier's Ass*, and no one could challenge his accuracy.

'So they sand-blasted *The Soldier's Ass*. That's good,' Dad said now, sitting down at the head of the table, turning the pages of the *Saukiwog American*. I tried not to be too obvious in scanning the headlines, but when Dad creased the newspaper at the local section, I saw a word that made me choke on my own air.

MURDER, it said, in the lower left column. MURDER UNSOLVED IN SAUKIWOG.

I must've made an awful sound, but I wasn't aware.

Dad looked up, startled. 'What the hell's the matter with you? You choking? Nancy, he's choking.'

'A murder,' I said. 'In the city.'

'Och, dear,' Mom burred.

Dad looked down at the paper, found the headline. 'See what I mean about Dante? It's not a real murder. It's about a play. A mystery play.'

'In Saukiwog?' Danny Boy asked. 'At The Playhouse?'

'*Ten Little Indians*,' Mom said.

'Who cares,' Dad answered.

'Agatha,' Mom cooed. 'That should be a chiller. Agatha Christie. That's the one they made the movie from. *And Then There Were None* – that was it.'

'Auditions are open to the public,' Danny Boy read at an angle before Dad had the practical sense to round his stew bowl over the article.

'What's this to you?'

'Open auditions.'

'What's this mean – open auditions?'

'It means I'm going to go down to The Playhouse and audition.'

My father stared at him. For a long time, he stared at him.

'Wonderful,' Mom said, smiling, and then trying to remember the cast in the old movie version.

'What do you wanna do that for?' Big Dan said.

'Forget it, Dad. Let's just – there, there you go, read about Mayor Longo scrubbing *The Soldier's Horse.*'

'This is kind of *mangia* stuff, ain't it? I mean plays.'

'Is De Niro a *mangia?*'

This was the Neapolitan slang for gay. *Mangia bracciola.*

Big Dan glared at his oldest son with what seemed a mix of irritation and profound sadness. He went back to eating his stew an inch from a photo of Mayor Longo. 'You're going to embarrass me,' he said, his cheek full.

'They try to say that Tyrone Power was a *mangia*, too,' Mom brogued.

'I've already embarrassed you, Dad,' Danny Boy said. 'I'm thinking this could be like the encore. In front of the whole city, the show-stopper.'

'Danny,' Mom warned the both of them, one name for the two.

Outside, the ice cream truck was belling somewhere over on St Francis Street. I considered grabbing some change from my box of collections and heading the truck off at Genoa and Lucia. A toasted almond might take the curse off the day. Make things right again.

That's when my father lurched slightly. His fork fell into his empty bowl and he fixed his eyes on the far wall as if trying to identify some sudden and sharp pain.

'Dan?' Mom said. 'Dan, what is it?'

'Oh, Jesus,' my father said. His fingers raked at the newspaper, balling the sports section, and his legs stiffened. His free hand slapped his big chest and clawed.

'Dan!' Mom screamed out, pushing past me as I sat frozen.

My father fell from his chair and struck the linoleum elbows first. He made a choking sound and then went still. Mom and I were on him, the both of us screaming over each other. *Get up, Dad, get up, Dan, oh my God – call 911. Now, Nunzio, NOW!!*

I made my move toward the phone, but something held me in place – a powerful grip on my ankle. Dad had me. 'No, Nunzio,' he said. When I looked at him, he was trying to suppress a smile, his lips twitching.

'Shame on you,' my mother hissed, pulling away. 'Shame.'

Danny Boy remained in his chair, observing the whole charade with a passive eye. He shook his head, resumed supper. He had seen this before. We all had, in fact, but Big Dan had become a master of the fake heart attack, planning the episodes far enough apart so as to catch us offguard.

'Now *there's* acting,' he said to Danny Boy as he got up from the floor.

'Yeah, brilliant.' My brother left the table, tossing his napkin.

'Why, Mom?' I asked her when Dad went out back to weed the garden.

'You have to understand your father,' she said with great patience. 'You might think he's a hard man, but the fact is, he loves hard. He loves too hard. All of us. And he wants to make sure we love him, too. A man who passes away rarely gets to see the effect it would have on his loved ones. Your father enjoys seeing what his passing would mean to us.'

'911 gets him every time,' I said, and Mom smiled.

'Try to understand that it's all about love, laddie.'

After my father rose from the dead and went next door to his mother's for espresso and *biscotti*, I went to my bedroom, shut the door and tried to conjure magic. I turned on the lava lamp that Big Dan had found in an old Volkswagen Bus and sat over my Puma Clyde shoe box full of salvages. I dropped in the brass token, the gold pin, the red cigarette pack with dragon emblem, the troll, and the sixteen cents. I hefted the box to appraise its weight.

Sitting in the strobe flicker, I let my mind reel back to the terrible morning in the warm rain. Big Dan had me questioning myself now: when he'd brought up the story about the mako shark in the surf at Hammonasset Beach, I was astounded to learn that it was actually driftwood. No one had come down to see the shark with me that overcast afternoon; they'd looked up from under their sun umbrellas and said, 'Driftwood.' But I had seen its steely eyes, its rigid dorsal fin and raw bruises on its underbelly where I surmised dolphins had ganged up on it.

It was a shark, not driftwood.

Or, was I improving on nature as Mom said? Had I done the same this morning?

One thing I knew: the man I saw in the trunk was no improvement on nature.

Out in the kitchen, I heard the phone ring and my mother saying, 'Aye, Maria, och, Maria,' so I knew she was on the phone with our neighbor Mrs Cocobianco and some neighborhood minutes were brewing. Even though Southern Italians never trusted outsiders, my mother was viewed as part of the Italian neighborhood and they often phoned her, the levelheaded Nancy, to weigh the gravity of things, to maybe offer up one of her optimistic proverbs like 'the mill won't grind with waters past' or 'Tyrone Power was not a *mangia.*'

But she wasn't giving anyone proverbs now. She was making a mournful little sound in her lowland burr, out there in the kitchen: 'Och, no, dear. Och, *no. Och* no, *dearie.*'

Now I could hear her discussing the old man, Mr Cocobianco, Eddie's grandfather. He had to be a hundred years old and I feared he had finally died. But that was not the case. The small disaster was a recurrent one: he had wandered away from the Cushman Rest Home once again.

'He's done this before,' Dad reminded her when she came out to the garden, her arms folded across her chest and her face pinched with worry. I followed her out on the back porch to hear the village news. Dad was right: it was always in the summer, the old Italian man trying to find the beach. His youngest child, Franco, had drowned in the ocean in Milford when Papa Coco was only twenty-eight, a caster at United Brass. Mom said that sometimes in the summers, Papa Coco would wake from his sleep and walk out of the Rest Home, calling Franco and trying to get to the beach. Once they found him wading in the polluted Mattatuck River, just looking into the shallows and sweeping his right hand through it – the one that left two fingers and a thumb under a metal roller at the factory in the 1950s.

Thoughts collided like pool balls and banked. A missing man in the city? Senile and wandering? Deeply religious, had he gone to the city's Biblical shrine to fall on his knees before Mother Mary or Lot's wife? Then leaving, disoriented, perhaps cold, had he crawled into the open trunk of the old car at the fence, thinking it his bunk, settling in for a sleep.

'He'll be back,' Dad said casually, bent over, yanking weeds from around the *zucchini*. 'They'll find him down Benevento's watching soccer on Italian TV.'

Mom looked to the porch. 'You should go and comfort poor Eddie,' she advised me. 'The poor dear with his poor feet.' She was referring to the corrective shoes Eddie Coco had to wear, which gave him an odd wobble when he walked. If I had a best friend, it was Eddie Cocobianco. If there was a kid in the world that I could share my dead man story with, it was Eddie. But now I found myself in a squeeze. What if we had crushed Eddie Coco's missing grandfather?

'Go on, love,' Mom said. 'Go and comfort the wee boy.'

'He's gone for good this time. I know it, Nunzio.'

Eddie Cocobianco was sitting in his bedroom, forcing his face into the wind of an electric fan in the window. 'He's so old. He probably walked right in front of a train or something.' I wished Eddie would turn away from the fan because the rotating blades chopped his voice into a weak vibrato and made him sound like some kind of lost ghost from across the divide. 'H-e-e-s-gone-f-o-r-good-d-d-d.'

I knew Eddie since kindergarten, and from the first time I saw him, I thought his skin color odd. He was green. Green as a pea soup, and in his pigeon-toed trundle he reminded me of a frog.

'Olive,' my mother insisted. 'A good healthy olive.' Maybe I was color-blind but he was green to me then and he was a shade of chartreuse now, hanging his long face in the breeze of the fan. But whatever Eddie's color, I loved him.

I couldn't bring myself to tell him that his grandfather might be in the trunk of a crushed Pontiac at my dad's junkyard and that I'd slammed the trunk on the old man as he grabbed out, desperate for his medication perhaps. I just stared at Eddie and he seemed to appreciate the awful dread on my face.

'I hate Rest Homes,' he said, his eyes welling. 'Grampy worked his butt off in the mill, took care of everybody. Now they got no use for him. They put him in The Home with a bunch of sad, thrown-away people. Sure, he's going to try to escape. Wouldn't you? Won't *we*, me and you, Nunz, when we're old? Escape. Like Butch and Sundance.'

The image of an elderly Butch and Sundance loping across the Green in blue pajamas was more disconcerting than inspiring, but still I commiserated; Eddie was right. The Home was like a junkyard for people with nothing to salvage but old stories, and Old Man Cocobianco had volumes. But they had all disintegrated like brown parchment with only one page remaining: Franco and the sea.

I can no find, he had confided to me once, in the loud voice of a man who had worked too long near pounding mandibles, and Eddie's mother scolded him like he was a child. '*Basta!* Frankie is in the Heaven! *Finito!* He's gone!' I remembered the old man folding his hands that looked like warped knots of cottonwood, seven fingers altogether, and bringing them to his lips, whispering Italian into his fingers. '*O, Dio, o povero mio.*'

I felt like a criminal, sitting in front of my troubled friend and I had to get out of there. I got up and gave Eddie a tentative hug – heavy on the backslaps to make sure we weren't queers – then left him alone with his Dallas Cowboys banners and his glow-in-the-dark Led Zeppelin poster.

'Hey, Nunz,' he moped as I headed out. 'Sucks the moose that you have to work this summer.'

'Yeah. Sucks the moose.'

'I miss you, man.'

'I miss you, too. Ed. Man.'

'But it must be cool with all those old cars. Smashing them up and stuff. Can I go with you some time? Look through some of the old cars with—'

'NO!' I lashed out, one of my arms knocking over his collection of tiny plastic American Presidents. 'I mean, no, Ed. It's hard work, man.'

'Yeah,' Eddie accepted. The fan segmented his response into a 'yeh-eh-eh-eh'. I picked up President Polk and the corporeal Taft, my hands trembling as I tried to fit them back on their Styrofoam stand. I noticed that President Taft had some grease on his cravat and I hoped that Eddie didn't know my birthday present to him in 1977 came from a 1969 Impala.

'If you see Grampy out walking or anything . . .' he said with a hint of hope, his voice quivering in the fan like it was a thousand miles away.

'I will, Eddie.'

I started out, but Eddie stopped me. 'Hey, Nunz. Wait,' he whispered. He made sure his door was locked then he dropped to his knees and probed under his bed. He pulled out a Nike sneaker box covered with muslin. With a reverence, he rose with it, smiling like he held the Holy Grail.

'Look here,' he said, pulling back the muslin. Inside the box were four caterpillars on green leaves.

'Cool, Ed.'

'I was hoping you'd be with me when it's time.'

For the past three summers Eddie and I had shared the ceremony that was, to us, a miracle before our eyes. We would gather up leaves and bring them to the box. Some years it was in his room, others mine; together we'd watch them molt and grow and molt again and pupate, and at the end of summer either I would call out my window or he would call out his: 'Here they go!'

Breathless, shoulder to shoulder, we would watch butterflies emerge from the chrysalis and unfurl their wings. Carrying the box delicately, we would take it out to the back lawn and remove the muslin. Up they would go, black-and-orange angels doing air surveillance over The Little Boot which was a haven with all its flower gardens and fig trees. My Nonni, who at the beginning of summer would step on a caterpillar with one of her big black shoes and proclaim it 'the devil's worm', now beheld it with a peaceful blush to her face. *'Bella, bella, farfalla,'* she would say. 'Beautiful butterfly.' Then she'd add, 'Thanks'a God.'

'Make sure you bring new leaves to them every day,' I reminded him, starting backward out the door. 'And make sure your sister's cat's not around when you let them out of the trunk.'

'Out of the what?'

'Out of the box.'

'You said trunk.'

I was out of there, jogging down the Cocos' hall past the kitchen where Eddie's mother and father and uncles and aunts argued in Italian about the Rest Home and the old man. In the front hall, a framed photo of a young Papa Coco looked out at me from where he posed with the United Brass Bowling Team beside a rolling machine in the factory. He looked as proud as if he'd been posing in front of a prize marlin. I hit the front walk and ran for home where I would sit in my room and sort out my archaeological collection of salvages.

There was an old *Police Gazette* that I wanted to read, one about the body of a woman that turned up in a cornfield in the 1950s and was never identified. I read half of it, but it spooked me, so I took my shoe box to bed and spent the last hours of the terrible day, trying to link a troll, a brass token, a hat pin and sixteen cents to a missing old man from the Rest Home.

Nunzi-ooooh.

He called for me like he always did, like a monk summoning a stray goat in some mountain hollow, and it usually meant he wanted to put me to labor. Watching the old Italian, in his salvaged sombrero, pulling springs and fuse boxes from the scrap heaps, one could see he was a man who needed to understand how broken things worked and having done so, find a way to make them work better and in a more practical manner. 'What go arounda, she come back arounda,' he would say, shoving a wheelbarrow full of parts toward the secrecy of the place he called his *laboratorio*, the place where he transformed junk into salvage, and salvage into genius.

I spotted his sombrero and wove through the maze of used parts until I found him hunched over one of his new inventions. 'Hey, Grandpa. Hot one today.'

All of Saukiwog was near parboiling, but the hottest place in the city was our family wrecking yard. Acres of glass and metal magnified the sun, and gas fumes did slow hoola-hoops, making the place look like some apocalyptic vision of the future, a post-nuclear parking lot on the edge of a dead city. Behind the old train engine was a taboo area that Danny Boy called Area 51. My grandfather forbade us entrance to this section which was where he worked on his inventions, secreted inside a tarpaper shed. Nailed to the east wall of this shed were two salvaged metal signs: one advertised a BURMA SHAVE and the other was a rusted 1950s relic that said: FALLOUT SHELTER.

Once Danny Boy wandered in close and caught sight of twisted sheet metal and a large bent disc and he convinced me that our grandfather – under the auspices of the Motor Vehicle Department and the United States Government – was storing the wreckage of a UFO that had crashed in the woods of Litchfield.

'Stand'a here, boy,' Grandpa instructed me now. He wanted me to distribute my weight on a flat sheet of roofing tin which had been welded as a base onto some odd-looking contraption made from the salvages of an Evinrude boat motor, a Renault generator with fan belt and the steel claw of a potato rake.

'What is it, Grandpa?' I asked, endlessly intrigued by his inventions. During my first week at the yard he had invented an electric pasta spoon that twirled spaghetti when the handle was squeezed. The only problem was it did not ground correctly and anyone who tried to twirl their spaghetti got high voltage and screamed. Gooma Rosa, upon receiving a jolt, had thrown the spoon away after a moderate tussle with Grandpa. This new machine he called 'the weed chop'. Looking at him, a wise old man, I would have loved to *sfogarmi* – confess to him about what I had discovered five days earlier. But I knew how he'd react; I knew he would smile and call me 'Dante' – not in a mean way but with grandfatherly amusement – and then he would explain what he viewed as the truth by telling an Old Country fable about the Fox and the Wolf or some such instructive tale.

'Okay, *allora*,' he said, 'here we go.' He lifted his foot onto a kick-start and pumped downward. The machine made an encouraging clack-clack but didn't catch. Grandpa tried twice more then wiped his brow with a rag. 'Sonamabitch,' he wheezed.

He tightened the kick-start with a ratchet, then had me spray ether into the duel carb on the backside. The old man jumped on it again. This time it started with the deafening grind of a chainsaw, and pinkish smoke hung in the garden. The tin base vibrated wildly under my boots and in the sudden panic of the moment I remembered Eddie Coco saying that Monica gave 'hum jobs' and I wondered if this was a similar effect; everything under my belt was humming.

Grandpa maintained a tranquil look as he ushered me aside and tilted the boat motor downward. He slid the contraption into the junkyard's prodigious albeit wild garden. I could see now that the tin base had old roller-skates welded to its underside and a single ski from a snowmobile for harrowing a smooth row. He guided the invention between tiers of young beans, his stubby torso aquiver like a plastic man on an electric football board.

Grandpa was getting a hum job, too.

His sombrero seizured and his bottom teeth clamped on his lip while he worked the loud machine through the garden. He did not see the carnage his device left behind: the steel claw, driven into a cyclonic spin by the motorized fan belt not only chopped weeds, it whacked the bean plants into diced herbs and dug an ugly furrow a foot deep, uprooting tomato plants. Soil flew and a potential blue-ribbon *zucchini* that Dad had ogled the day before was now lacerated by the steel claw, sucked into the machine, and a fine yellow detritus sprayed out the other end through what I assumed was the housing from an Oldsmobile transmission.

I stood with the can of ether in my hand, watching nervously as the machine jack hammered out of my grandfather's control.

And then a shrill sound cut the air.

Dad appeared, doing his two-pinkied whistle. Grandpa heard it – even over the Evinrude – but he didn't look up. He knew it was Dad, and so he began cursing him in Italian as he swung the weed-chopper around and wrestled with it along the next row.

'What the hell are you doing?!' Dad screamed from knee-high pole beans. I couldn't hear Grandpa's retort but his lips moved as fast and mean as Primo Canero biting at his food. Dad set his hands on top of his head in a cringe – pushing his hat down close to his eyes – as his father's invention trammeled another squash and turned it into a frothy Orange Julius. A wedge of gut and seed struck Dad square in the chest. '*Vafangoolo*,' he called out, flicking it away as he ducked some more fleshy strings.

'He's nuts!' Dad yelled to me. 'He'll electrocute you like that fucking twirling spoon.'

'Shut up!' Grandpa yelled loudly, wrestling with the boat motor. The housing was clotted with vines and weeds and tomato plants and dry soil and finally, to my relief, it stalled.

Hard.

But it put up a determined after-kick before it was brought to bear.

There was a welcome silence as Dad stood there, hands still flat on his crown. Grandpa could see, in his periphery, the damage his new machine had caused but he had too much pride to acknowledge this. He dropped stiffly to one knee and began wiping motor oil off spark plugs as if this was the small glitch in the design. I felt obligated to fill the silence. 'It's a weed-chopper, Dad.'

'No shit,' Big Dan said. 'Stay away from fucking Edison. You're going to get hurt.'

As Grandpa cursed Dad and his machine in the Italian tongue, Dad started away, eyes on the ground. 'I need you up front, Nunzio.'

As I left the old inventor in the newly-furrowed garden, I tried not to look up at the crushed Pontiac sixty feet atop ferrous scrap, but it was nearly impossible. It towered over the yard and no matter where I happened to be, it watched me, the way eyes in an old painting follow the observer from wall to wall.

What I could glimpse of the rear end was no more than a flat alloy of blue and rust. The red plastic of the left tail-light had been crushed out and now a flat socket remained. It was from inside the dark hole of this socket that I thought I could feel the man's eye staring down like Quasimodo in the bell tower.

I tried to forget it, tried to concentrate on sorting Nash hubcaps from Buicks, but the darkness within the tail-light socket followed my movements. On one such crossing, I looked up at the car four times.

And then a fifth.

Sitting on the remains of the vehicle was a crow, large and glossy black, cocking its head and pecking like an efficient scavenger over a road kill. It gazed down at me and cawed in a sound like an angry Commanche.

Another crow lighted on the Bonneville.

And another, cawing, shriller than the first two.

They came out of the west, a half-dozen more – maybe they were ravens, they were that large. Thirteen I counted, converging, gathering on the metal mountain, deafening in their jabber. A bold flock. No, not a flock. Crows did not form a flock. I could not recall if the information had come from one of my tattered *Peterson Field Guides* or from my mother's wealth of crossword curios, but the word came.

A Murder.

When geese darkened the sky it was called a Gaggle. Quails made up a Bevy, finches flocked in a Charm.

Crows gathered in a Murder.

Primo Canero, the junkyard dog, barked at us from the shade of his tether as we helped a redheaded kid from Testa Refuse load scrap radiators.

I harbored a healthy fear of Primo Canero. Glances from the skinny redhead told me he did, too. The black Shepherd was kept by a rusted skidder chain to a 1957 Wonderbread truck out in the middle of the sea of old cars but I had once seen him pull the carcass of that bread truck a half-inch off the cement blocks it rested on, his chest heaving like an enraged wolverine and brownish lather discharging from his leathery snout. There was only one way to feed Primo Canero: spoon out his meal – usually some leftovers like sausage and *calamari*, stuffed shells or some bread – onto a hubcap and skim the makeshift bowl to him from a safe distance. Often, he ate his own stools. Water: he lapped what the rain left in the rusted wheel-well of a nearby Chevette. Dad got too close once – he liked to spar with the black dog and keep him mean – and he now had ribbons of blue scar tissue on his legs and hands to show for it.

He barked at us now as we heaved scrap radiators into the bed of a dump truck that looked ready for the graveyard itself. Dad stood by with a heavy man in a bright acrylic shirt and green polyester slacks. He wore white shoes like Pat Boone and seemed concerned at times that he might get grease on his pink socks. Salvatore Testa had a shock of silver hair and yellow tinted wire-rim glasses that Dad called 'mod'. In the peculiar manner of fat men, he was forever unbuckling his slacks and tucking his shirt in, even when it needed no correcting.

'Twenty-six, twenty-seven,' Dad counted off as each radiator crashed into the bed. Sally Sheet Metal – Dad had a nickname for everyone – seemed less concerned with an accurate count and more interested in my brother.

'I remember that interception he made against Wilby. He jumped right in front of that tall Polack – ba-boom – clean pick, right down the fucking sideline. The whole place was going "Junkyard Dog!

Junkyard Dog!" *Madonna*. Run? The kid could run like a fucking Corvette.'

'Thirty-one, thirty-two, thirty-three.' Dad kept his eyes on the scrap as we hefted it.

'I told my wife right there,' Sally went on, '"That kid's going to UConn. You're going to see him in the papers." Then that big *zootzoon* cheap-shots him. On a fair catch. Bada-boom! Fucking nigger hits him high. Dislocates the whatever it was. All over, just like that. Hey . . . whatta ya gonna do? That's how life is. Hey.'

He said *hey* a lot, fat Sally Sheet Metal – especially when he was imparting his wisdom.

'It only gets worse, kid. Hey, I promise you. Watch.'

'Thirty-nine.' Dad didn't miss one. Danny Boy cast an opaque eye on Sally Sheet Metal. The scrapmetal merchant unbuckled his green slacks and struggled with his shirt-tails.

'It wasn't your fault, Paradiso,' he assured Danny. 'You took a cheap shot. These fucking *zootzies* they got big hard eggplants for heads.' He knocked on his own head in illustration. 'Fucking cave men. Their tails only fell off about sixty years ago.'

If this was supposed to be a salve on my brother's wounds it was as ineffective as it was offensive. Danny Boy tried to ignore the fat man but he pitched each radiator with a little more muscle behind it, and he spit once, dangerously close to the man's white shoes.

The scrawny redheaded kid grinned with bad teeth every time his boss used a crude word about coloreds.

'Sixty-seven,' was Dad's final tally. Sally did a take.

'Sixty-seven? What, are you pulling a short con on me, Paradiso?'

'Sixty-seven, they're all there.'

Sally winked at me as he reached behind himself and slapped for his wallet. He drew a billfold and pulled some cash.

'Who's the kid with the blue eyes?'

'My kid.'

'Your kid?'

'Nunzio. He's working this summer.'

'*Nunzio? This* is Nunzio?'

'Yeah.'

'Good-looking kid,' he observed. 'He talk Italian?'

'No. Nunzi's the American in the family.'

Fat Sally tightened his belt and brought his green slacks to bear high upon his ample stomach. 'Come here, *guaglione*.'

I didn't speak the dialect of my tribe, but I knew *guaglione* – pronounced *wahl-yo* meant 'boy'. Respectfully, I approached the large scrap man. He hid one of his hands behind his back and stared down at me through his tinted specs. I knew what was coming next and I held my breath. I had seen my father's cousins, Zi Bap and Zi Toine, duel in the garage doorway; Grandpa had taught me the rules as a child, and me and Danny Boy often settled disputes with it instead of tossing a coin. It was the Southern Italian fingers game – *morra*.

I slid my right hand behind my back. Sally Testa drew.

I drew just as fast.

'*Quatro!*' he yelled.

'Seven!' I shrilled over him.

He had three meaty fingers held out. I had four small ones. Seven total. My win.

'Kid's good,' he said, looking at my father as Dad put his cash away and made sure the dump truck tailgate was secured. Sally hid his hand again, and I followed suit. The redheaded kid sat on some scrap tires and stuck a cigarette right into a hole in his teeth. He squinted, puzzled by the ritual.

'*Cinque!*' Sally cast two fingers.

'Seven!' I yelled again and my voice sounded high and girlish as I pronged all five fingers like flicking sand, winning yet another round.

'Well, I'll be a sonuvabitch,' Sally said under a labored breath. 'For a little Italian, this kid's got the luck of the fucking Irish.'

'I'm half Scotch,' I announced. Sally Sheet Metal looked down at me and his face crinkled into an infectious grin, his glasses sliding up a notch on his nose.

'The Scotch was never lucky. Cheap bastards but never lucky.'

He began to laugh and repeated his joke so my father could hear it and when he laughed, I noticed that Sally had sagging breasts like a hermaphrodite I had seen in my book about *Very Special People*. Then suddenly, he pitched. I felt my breath shorten. He lunged forward, ducking low, his yellowed glasses sliding down the bridge of his nose; with a ballerina dexterity belying his size, he spun and unfurled his fingers:

'*CINQUE!*'

'*QUATRO!*' I predicted.

He had two fingers out.

So did I.

Quatro. Danny Boy laughed. 'Yo, Nunzi! Way to go.'

Sally straightened himself and pulled his billfold again. I reached for the dollar and Sally jerked it back. He folded the bill in half, crimping George Washington's head down over his neck. As he displayed it to me he said, 'The father of this country never told a lie, did you know that?'

'Yes, sir,' I answered.

'You know what that makes him?'

I admitted my ignorance.

'A lying pecker head.' And with this, Fat Sally presented the dollar bill with the flourish of a magician. It was an impressive albeit irreverent illusion: the first President transformed into a large phallus not unlike the way Danny Boy used to turn the Land O'Lakes Indian woman's knees into prize-winning mammaries. Sally seemed to savor my studious reaction.

'Nobody goes their whole life without telling a lie. Not George Washington, not the Pope – nobody.' He studied my quiet reaction. 'Bet they never taught you that in school.'

The redheaded kid hissed a laugh and Sally smiled, surrendering the buck. He seemed to size me up as he mussed my hair with his large hand. Then he moved away gingerly on his white shoes, doing a little *salterello* to dodge an oil puddle. He spun and pointed at my dad. 'We'll see you, *paesan'*.'

'Yeah, we'll see you, *Salvador*.'

We all stood admiring Sally Sheet Metal's vehicle: a luxury muscle car with a big power plant, shining like a candied apple in the sun. Sally looked over his shoulder at his redheaded skeleton help. 'Let's go, Dummy,' he ordered, and the scrawny kid lit his cigarette then climbed up into the battered dump truck that would follow the red Monte Carlo.

Sally's weight made the new car strain on its springs – it seemed to groan like a camel being packed for a long trip. He pushed in an 8-track and as he drove off through the junkyard gates, I could hear strains of Tom Jones' 'What's New Pussycat'.

Sally Testa dropped her into low, punched gas and gravel spun
as he drove away, Dummy following him in the big, rattletrap truck
somewhere under a mountain of scrap radiators.

'Everything on this island is odd,' Danny Boy said, rehearsing on
his way back to his rubber sanctum.

'What's that?' Big Dan said.

'He's rehearsing,' I informed my father, afraid he might mis-
interpret my brother.

'Rehearsal's over, kid,' Dad called out to him. 'This is life.'

Nunzi-ooooooo.

Grandpa was calling to me from down in the garden. He was
disassembling his weed-chopper and needed me to bring him a
nine-sixteenth wrench.

And someone else was summoning.

High over Paradise Salvage, watching my every move through
the empty socket of the missing tail-light.

CHAPTER THREE

La Strega

'Nunzio, get on your skateboard and go to America for me.'

I could see her in the garden, the old woman, dressed all in black as she had been, according to my mother, since 22 November, 1963. When the news of Kennedy's death had reached her, she reportedly threw herself on the front porch and clutched her rosary beads.

'He was like a son to me!' she had heaved from her belly, pumping her fat fist at the sky, until Grandpa threw a pot of cold water on her. My mother had said she was just looking for an excuse to wear all black like the widow Gooma Chiara who drew great community sympathy and free bread from Coangelo's with her black veil and shawl.

On her kitchen windowsill, she kept a little plastic monk my father had found in a wrecked stationwagon. She was always dusting under the little relic she called San Anthony, or gently repositioning him to face the sun. The irony there was that Nonni didn't realize it was a novelty friar and if one pushed down on his bald pate a plastic appendage would spring up from beneath his vestments. Whenever I saw her dusting Little Tony, I held my breath.

My grandmother was a kind of medicine woman. In Italian 'hoods like ours – as in the ancient villages we came from – one referred to a woman like this as a witch – a *strega*. Not like the Bad Witch of the West or the Good Witch of the East, but more like a traditional country healer from the South of Italy. If my grandmother was one of these rare and endangered witches, it was despite herself, for she was a reluctant healer, afraid of her own powers and the mysterious energies that made them manifest.

Yet, when forced to, she could do the oil and water treatments, the Italian incantations, she knew how to lift an infant and sweep him through the air in the sign of the cross to cure colic, and once or twice a year some relative or neighbor came to seek her treatment if they suspected someone had given them the evil eye, a malady that was often disguised as a compliment, which is why in my neighborhood, if you complimented someone you should always say God Bless you. *What a nice dress. God bless you.*

'Nunzio, he has the good teeth,' I remember her saying once when I was about six. Then she blessed herself, shivered and said, 'Godda bless him. Godda bless his teeth.'

Get on your skateboard and go to L'America.

Nonni referred to everything east of Highland Avenue as *L'America*. She never went there alone. She did all her shopping at Coangelo's Market and had her hair colored in the home of young Yolanda. But Casa Savings and Loan was two blocks removed from the easternmost boundary of The Boot, so when she and Grandpa needed a deposit made, she gave me her little blue bank book and a sealed envelope, and sent me to America.

On this warm night I was in my room finecombing my archaeological collections from the junkyard, trying to piece together clues to the man in the trunk: the Chicago hat pin with the mysterious number, the brass token, the few pennies. The silly troll.

Nonni was on her front porch, watching me through my screen window as she often did. I wanted to tell her the bank was closed, but she was a shrewd woman; it was Friday and the bank would remain open until 6:15. So with the envelope, which couldn't have held more than thirty dollars, I mounted my silver skateboard with urethane wheels and high-tech trucks that Grandpa designed at the junkyard, and I made the pilgrimage.

'*Buono figlio*, Annunziato,' Nonni said as I pushed off and skitched up Mary Street. 'Good boy, Nunzio. God bless you, God bless the children.' And she crossed herself twice.

Truth be known, I liked going to the *banca* and making deposits for my grandmother. Firstly, the place was carpeted and air-conditioned like a Polar igloo. And the bank president, Mr Domenic Carmella, if he was in, always waved me into his little office and gave me a new nickel for my own bank book and his signature butterscotch candy wrapped in brittle paper. Once, he even gave me a crisp two-dollar bill and made me the envy of the school yard. *Carmella* meant butterscotch in Italian, and *Domenic* meant Sunday, so we kids from The Little Boot – in honor of his name and golden candy habit – christened him Mr Butterscotch Sunday.

When I reached Casa Bank on this day however, Mr Sunday was busy in his office. I could see the friendly little man on the phone, shuffling papers while I stood at the teller's counter making a deposit in my grandfather's name. Grandpa had bought stock when Casa Bank started up, and the old man always told me to walk with my head high to the counter. Mrs Lewicki, the tall stork of a teller who was always blinking her contact lenses wet, looked down at my filthy hands. 'Looks like you're getting into mischief, Master Paradiso,' she said.

'No. I'm working with my father.'

'Oh? Good boy,' she said. 'My son Tommy's at camp.' She smelled faintly of baby powder and her hands were so clean I felt impelled to hide my dirty ones from her. Maybe I was defensive, but it seemed to me that she was searching for a jealous reaction from me, knowing that her son was fishing at some camp.

And then someone shouted, 'How's Nunzio?'

Mr Butterscotch Sunday was heading to the men's room when he recognized me from the back, or in one of the many mirrors, because he stopped to make a certain identification. He was always smiling and knocking a butterscotch around with his tongue in his molars, his eyes sheeny behind his big glasses like the sweetness from the candy was touching a ticklish spot in some secret place inside where adult calluses had not yet hardened.

'Nunzio's good,' I said. We always played that game: How's Nunzio? Nunzio's good. And then he probed into his jacket pocket and fished out a butterscotch for me.

'Where you been playing? In the old factories?' he said, looking me up and down from head to rust-dusted construction boots. 'Those places can be dangerous.'

'Working,' I said. 'At the yard.'

'There you go,' he said. 'That'll make a man out of you.'

Little did he know.

That dark thought triggered an idea as Mr Sunday started for the men's room again. 'Mr Carmella?'

He turned, eyes shimmering, candy rolling in his mouth like a walnut in a wooden cup.

'Could you look at a coin for me?'

He stepped forward, held out a hand and I dug deep into my pocket to find the brass token. 'What you find, Nunz? Something up the salvage yard? Place is a gold mine. People don't know that, but it is. Talk about precious metals. Scrap metal's a gold mine. Let's see what you've got.'

When I gave him the token, he took it in his fingers which were even cleaner than Mrs Lewicki's, and manicured. He didn't bite his nails which was a sign, my mother told me, of a secure man. With the hands of a gemologist he glanced at one side of the object, turned it and held it to the light, smiling as he squinted. 'No, she's not a coin,' he said.

'She's not?'

'No way, José.'

'What is she?'

'Some kind of token.'

'Token?'

'It looks like the kind of slug we used to put in Lady Fortuna at Savin Rock Amusement Park when we were kids. You put the token in and she told your fortune.'

'Wow,' I said, seeing more worth in this slug than the bank president apparently did. 'You ever get your fortune done there?'

'Sure. When I was a kid,' he confided. 'I remember it said "you will have a romance with a tall, dark and handsome man". That's how accurate Lady Fortuna was. I gave the fortune to my sister and look what happens: she marries a short Polish brick mason.'

We both laughed and he crushed his butterscotch into sweet dust in his molars, looking pleased when Mrs Lewicki and two other tellers laughed at his joke from the counter.

They were putting up the Closed placards.

Mr Carmella handed the token back to me and made his overdue trip to the men's room. 'See you, Nunzio. Keep looking in that junkyard. There's gold in them thar hills.'

And he pushed through the door with a little painting of a man holding an umbrella. I pocketed the amusement park token, stuck the butterscotch in my mouth and headed back to my skateboard for the journey home in the falling dusk. Nonni was sitting on her front porch, her legs straddling a black kettle as she sliced red and green peppers into it. Her black dress was hitched over her knees and she wore fleshy stockings as far up her black-veined calves as they would stretch. She watched me intently as I did a slalom up the walk, and when I handed over her bank book, she opened it, gave it a studious, almost suspicious look, then she smiled at me.

'*Buono figlio*,' she said, and she resumed slicing peppers.

Summer was sloughing off June like old snakeskin and July was showing its head with humid cruelty and record temperatures near 96. I always slept on my back with my hands folded on my chest, but tonight I was squirreling in the damp sheets, turning and punching my pillow over onto the cooler side until there wasn't one.

The more I thought about the man in the trunk the more his face took on the characteristics of old Mr Cocobianco who was still missing. Did the blank token I found belong to the old millworker? I wondered if maybe in his senility he was trying to find his way to Savin Rock to take a chance on Lady Fortuna, maybe hoping she would say 'Never take your son swimming in the ocean,' and he'd have another chance to spare himself a life of pain.

I could not get the smell of the dead man out of my nostrils. Wherever his destination was, heaven or hell or some industrial port in Tokyo, he took my image with him: a kid in a godawful pumpkin orange letter jacket, slamming the trunk lid shut on him and all his history, for ever.

Now as I tried to sleep in the heat, I kept checking the red marks near my throat where the old man had grabbed me and tried to pull me into the trunk with him. 'Zits,' Danny Boy had diagnosed the week before. 'Don't squeeze them.'

As I lay there, I remembered the phone call that came to our house the night before we towed that car. When I had answered it, a man said there was a junk car that had to be towed, and he asked for my father. There was nothing special about his voice, but behind him, I could hear music, what sounded like soap opera music; I might have heard it on one of my mother's 'plays' after school, a kind of music that seemed boring then.

Maybe that music teased at my imagination now, but I heard something in the corner of my room and I hoped it was a squirrel nesting in the insulation. A false hope: Grandpa had invented his own type of rodent trap and it was highly effective. I would be more likely to find a squirrel in Nonni's sauce than in the house.

Still, the sound baited me.

In the darkness between my dresser and the heating baseboard, down behind the box of Nick Savage comics and a rolled-up kite, I heard faint breathing. I stilled my own breathing to listen. It was there, deep and guttural and moist and I felt my heart start pushing too hard; I tried to lift my head but could not. I tried to move my arms but they were asleep, buzzing numb. And now, the thing in the dark corner manifested into a dark shape and emerged from the corner. It made a slobbering sound along the floor, like a quahog sucking onto linoleum and pulling itself along. It was exactly as my grandmother had described it to me.

She had often spoken of the *Strega* and the word alone terrified me. She was a demon, a dreadful devil's daughter – a female monster who would overtake the sleeper and crawl upon his chest, sit there with an incomprehensible weight, then she would lower her vile mouth over the sleeper's and suck his breath out until he died, mysteriously, in his sleep.

Some of the older women in our family refused to even call it by name, lest they invoke it, so they referred instead to the night visitor as 'the Mist'. Years later, I would come upon a description of something called the Succubus in a book on European beliefs, and learn that the Italians were not the only culture who had encounters with this bad girl. Some believed she was spawned by Adam's first wife, Lilith, and she had a reputation for invading the sleep of celibate monks, hoping to steal their virginity and their semen while they slept. American experts on sleep disorders named the malady 'sleep paralysis with hypnagogic hallucinations'. But the *Strega* was no scientific sleep disorder to us in The Little Boot. It was a classified species in Nonni's *New World Field Guide to Old Country Horrors*, and it had come over from the Sania Mountains the way burdock or poison sumac was accidentally transmitted from some immigrant's boot heels.

The Mist had suffocated my Aunt Nicoletta when she was

fourteen. They had found her in the morning with her mouth and eyes open, her head turned completely around, and all life drawn from her. Now the *Strega* was moving toward me with a smell like musk.

Nonni had taught me the only defense: a broom must be kept in the corner and when the beast drew close, I was instructed to yell at her and order her to 'count the straws in the broom.' This would make the apparition retreat. I struggled to lift my head and for a moment I thought I saw a dark amorphous thing hovering over me. It had a female contour. An impressive female contour. The Succubus was upon me.

'THE BROOM!' I yelled. 'Count...the...straws...on...the... BROOM!'

Just then I heard a tremendous yelling from the hall. I had woken my father and he was up, grabbing for his .22. 'What is it?!' he yelled, waking Nonni in the window next door and she yelled 'O Dio!' and lights went on all around The Little Boot. That's what life in an Italian 'huddle' was like. Sneeze in your bathroom and you'd get a *saluti!* from someone's garden.

Mom calmed my father. 'It's Nunzio. He's having a nightmare.'

The lights from the Orsini's house lit half my room and the *Strega* drew back until I could not separate it from the shadows of my dresser.

'What'd my mother do to this kid?' Dad said, shutting the light.

Nonni meanwhile, was outside on her porch with Mama Orsini and Gooma Chiara and Mrs Pisani, all in their nightclothes, heads wrapped in bandannas, speaking in hushed Italian. The word was out and it would travel up Mary Street to Genoa by morning, along America Street by noon, and by the time we'd come home from work the next day, the old Italian women would be hanging up extra red peppers and sweeping all corners of their homes.

La Strega was in the neighborhood.

And she wanted Nunzio, the American and unconfirmed Christian.

Sunday dinner was sure to serve as a forum for my grandmother's security council regarding ancient evils. She watched me with suspicion all through salad, and she even tried to smell my hair at one point while I was reaching for the bread.

It was my mother's turn to make the sauce and this double-barreled the tension: once again she would be tested by the Italians. Our Sunday dinners were lavish eating ceremonies with fresh harvest from the gardens, unsparing *antipasti*, freshly baked bread, enormous pots of rich sauce and *maccherone*, *buffala mozzarella* and, of course, Zi Bap and Zi Toine's homemade red wine, pulpy and sweet and stored in the recycled bottles year after year; the capper was Nonni's *ciambelli* cookies.

After putting two tables together under one big and colorful cloth, we began eating at noon and did not leave the table till three or four, all but for Goomba Rocco, Big Dan's godfather, who usually fell asleep in his chair with his hands folded on his generous belly while Grandpa talked to him about his new inventions and Rocco snored.

Mom carried a fair-sized bowl of her sauce to the table, her face ruddy and jaw set firm, balancing it with the same care she took in crafting it. She set it down and I scanned faces, hopeful: Grandpa lifted his nose slightly to smell it as he chewed on some fresh bread, Nonni bent forward to inspect the thin surface of oil atop the sauce. Zia Concetta, one of my father's sisters, sat between me and Danny. A widow, she was still wearing black after four years and was always accompanied on these Sundays by her three daughters: Giustina, Maddelena and Pina Maria. All three were olive-skinned and favored big earrings, jangling bracelets, and silk summer tanks of bright red or fuschia. Their fingernails were bright red, too, and long. Castilian red, Mom told me; she always maintained that the Del Vecchio girls were striking. But what struck me the most was the contention they seemed to bring to any chat at the table; there was no subject they relinquished claim to and they often took each other to task. Giustina, Maddelena and Pina Maria; I forever thought of them when a teacher mentioned Columbus's three ships. I would never share that thought with Giustina however, as she resented her Italian name. Only her mother was allowed to call her Giustina. For us, it was Tina.

'I'm going to eat a lot today,' Goomba Rocco announced. 'Who knows? This might be my last Sunday at this table.'

'Oh, come on, Goomba,' Giustina said to old Rocco. 'Don't be so Italian.'

Rocco Caro had long been the source of much whispering between me and Danny when we were younger. His hands quaked so terribly when reaching for food that Zia Concetta often came to his aid but no one discussed it. My mother had told us that he had 'spelter bends' – a result, she said, of working for thirty years in the casting shop at Saukiwog Brass and inhaling zinc fumes. Whenever he reached out for the heavy plate of *pasta fazool* I averted my eyes, hard as it was.

As I observed the gathering now, I thought of a picture I had found in an old Hudson up the junkyard, one I kept with my *Police Gazettes*: a painting of Indians by the artist Charles Russell. The picture showed a group of Sioux standing on the cliff overlooking tepees, and the caption read: *Give me a camp where I savvy the people.*

What made me think of that picture during dinner was this: I did not savvy these people. Not in this camp. I wasn't entirely sure what savvy meant, but I knew I did not savvy Gooma Rosa as she lamented something in her foreign tongue and my Nonni lifted Lena's little boy, Vinnie, off his chair and moved his body through the air in the sign of the cross, and Dad said, 'Don't drop the kid in the sauce, Ma, it's hot,' and then, passing the bread he said, 'That's right, Gooma,' to Rosa. 'You got it, Gooma. *I figli in questi giorni.* The kids today, that's how they are. But see Nunzio? He's learning. Good worker.'

'*Il figlio fa scrito la storia?*'

'No, Gooma, he doesn't write stories any more. He's working, doing good.'

'*Buono,*' the old woman said. 'Read too much story, make you blind. Write the story, make you crazy.'

Gooma Rosa looked at me, read my eyes. There were only two pairs of blue eyes around the entire table: mine and Mom's. Cousin Giustina, who liked my eyes for their American hue, told us all one Sunday that the Ancient Romans held a dim view of blue eyes because they were a sign of the Celtic water deities and sea-coast enemies. Whatever deities they may have been, they were now swimming in Mom's eyes as she held her breath, watching Grandpa sip some red sauce off his spoon. He said nothing as he twirled his fork in the spaghetti, perhaps lamenting the failure of his electric pasta spoon. Nonni dabbed some bread in the sauce, smelled it, tasted it with caution, said nothing.

Danny Boy, already half done, came to our mother's rescue. 'Excellent, Mom,' he said.

Grandpa nodded as he ate; this was promising. Dad monitored his own mother's reaction like reading sign. 'Something's missing, I don't know what.'

Nonni shrugged, coy.

Zia Concetta said nothing. Goomba Rocco ate quietly as did Tina, Lena and Pina Maria. Then it came: Giustina held the sauce in her mouth, shut her eyes, dabbed a napkin at her lips and said – with some sauce still on her tongue, 'Oh, my God.'

My mother and I watched her, hopeful.

'Oh, my God,' she said again. 'Did you hear about Yolanda? She's getting a nose job.'

'She should,' said Pina. 'She's got a big guinea schnozz.'

Zia Concetta clucked her tongue. 'No say the guinea.'

'Yeah,' said Giustina, 'but if she shortens it, she's going to look like a Puerto Rican.'

Gooma Rosa wailed high-pitched at such an observation.

Nonni crossed herself, fingered her scarf and said, just above a hoarse whisper to Dad, and only Dad: 'Maybe the *zucchero*.'

'Yeah, Nancy. Did you put the pinch of sugar in?'

'Yes, I did,' Mom answered, with a touch of stubborn Scot.

'Maybe not enough,' Big Dan said.

'It's fine, Aunt Nancy,' Pina Maria said, somewhere in her gossip about Yolanda having a big crush on Danny.

'My mother puts a whole fistful of sugar right in there,' Big Dan said.

Nonni shrugged again. 'Maybe it's me, I no' know.'

I wanted to praise my mother but I could not get the sauce to my lips. The crushed tomatoes made me think of the dead man and the crimson splotch behind his shattered lens. I weighed the memory on my fork and my hand trembled like Goomba Rocco's. Mom eyed me, concerned. If I ate it, I might turn it loose. And if I threw up at Sunday dinner, it would reflect poorly on Mom's excellent sauce. This was my quandary, sitting there with the Paradiso tribe.

'*La Strega*, she come back,' Nonni promised me. 'Make'a sure you wear *il corno*.'

'The what?' I asked.

'*Il corno. Come si chiama?*'

'The horn,' Zia Concetta explained.

'He doesn't have one, Ma,' Dad informed her.

'Oh, don't start that *Strega* stuff,' Cousin Pina Maria protested, but I noticed her move her napkin in the sign of the cross shortly after. That was how they were, the *Nina*, the *Pinta* and the *Santa Maria*: they blushed often about their own heritage and condescended to the old Italians, but as soon as someone mentioned the *Strega*, they genuflected despite themselves. Lena even wore a small plastic red pepper pinned to her bra to ward off the Evil Eye. I know she did, because once when she was bending over the table to get the *mozzarella*, I snuck a look at her enormous bubbies. There it was: a small plastic pepper capped in gold, held to the right strap of her bra by a large saftey pin. And if one of the girls got a severe headache, they visited Nonni and asked to be treated for the *mal'occhio*, which they supposed was cast by an estranged boyfriend or 'that jealous bitch at work'.

'I think I oversalted the meatballs,' Mom said. 'Who was it who used to like the meatballs salty?'

'Salt is bad for the blood pressure,' said Giustina.

'No,' countered Pina. 'Now they're saying that's not true.'

'*Non e vero*,' said Goomba Rocco, twisting a forkful of spaghetti into his hungry maw.

'Sure it is,' Lena threw in. 'Who's *they*? I want to know who's *they*?'

'Anybody outside the family is they,' Dad said. 'Right, Gooma?'

'See, Uncle Dan, you're so Second Generation,' said Giustina.

'*O Dio*,' proclaimed Nonni at the mention of blood pressure and this prompted Zia Concetta and Gooma Rosa to trade discourse on their favorite subject: gallstones and doctors.

Give me a camp where I savvy the people, I said in silent prayer.

Mom, a true Scots terrier, held fast to her anecdote. 'Was it Zi Toine who liked the meatballs salty?' she burred.

'Zi Toine has no taste buds left,' Dad put in. 'He drinks a gallon of vinegar a day. His tongue is pickled.'

Pina Maria let out a raven-like laugh and Zia Concetta covered one of her sensitive ears and made a long shrill howl of protest. '*Uffa*! No so loud.'

'Oh, you know who it was?' Mom remembered now. 'You know who it was who liked my meatballs?'

No one allowed Mom the room to speak; Italian language all but drowned my mother out. I saw a look in her eye then, the Celtic Water Sprite maybe. Or maybe the look of someone who knew they had a weapon that could do untold damage with the roll of a brogue. And so she said it. One word, a name.

'Goomba Angelo,' she said.

The kitchen fell so silent I could hear the far-off sprinkler wetting tomatoes in the Garatonis' garden. 'Angelo,' Mom said again 'Dan's second cousin, *Angelo*.'

Nonni pulled her napkin to her face and yelled, '*Dio!*'

Zia Concetta made a long, mournful sound of disapproval while Giustina suddenly spoke Italian for the first time, and fluently. Grandpa began spewing clipped Neapolitan expletives about the aforementioned cousin.

'Nancy, come on,' Dad said. 'Don't say that name at this table. What's' a matter wich' you?'

'*God* is on the table,' Nonni explained. 'So no speak of the Devil.'

'The *food* is on the table,' Grandpa said, slapping a hand down. 'So *shot up'a* and eat. Everybody.'

'Yo, Mom didn't say the Anti-Christ,' Danny Boy said, 'she said Goomba Angelo.'

'*Dio, non parla del diavolo!*' three of the women screamed all together like a rookery of bluejays.

Mom meanwhile, was slowly chewing a salty meatball, her eyes fixed ahead. She could play her Italian in-laws like her father could play the pipes, using their superstitions, scandals and Catholic fatalism as reeds. A sea-coast enemy could not have scored a better coup.

'*Pregliammo per noi!*' Nonni said. 'Pray for us,' crossing herself as some squabble broke out between my father and Goomba Rocco and Cousin Lena's husband Joe scolded Little Vinnie for cutting his pasta with a fork. 'That's a sin,' he whispered. 'You don't cut the *maccherone*. You do that again, Uncle Dan'll take your bicycle up the junkyard.'

'*Si*, it's a sin you talk about *Il Mamone*,' Nonni said firmly. 'Why speak about the dead? Why?'

'Is he dead? Angie die?' Giustina inquired. Her Associate's Degree warded off any Old Country superstition, I concluded. Rocco, his spelter bends making him quake now, was engaged in a heated Italian dialogue with Big Dan about the relative my grandmother had called *Il Mamone*. I grew intrigued by the power the name alone yielded.

'What's *Mamone* mean?'

A silence fell over the spread for a moment.

'The monster,' Giustina whispered.

Grandpa put his fork down hard. 'When you work you work, when you talk you talk, when you eat you *eat*.'

'I don't know anybody named Iris,' Danny Boy said, wiping his mouth with his napkin. Everyone looked at him.

'Now who the hell is Iris?' Dad said.

'Another *goomare*, Danny?' Lena said, lifting a spirited eye. 'Don't let Yolanda find out, she'll put the *mal'occh'* on her.'

'Or she'll give her a butch next time she comes in for a perm,' Pina Maria said.

I had heard mention of the *Mamone* once or twice in my childhood but I did not know that he was one and the same with my Dad's second cousin Angelo, who I had also heard called Goomba Angelo, but never met. I wondered if it was the same guy Dad was referring to whenever he couldn't break a lug off a wheel and prayed the tire iron 'up Angelo's ass'.

Mamone, Dad explained to me, meant The Freak. Had we, I wondered, a pinhead in the family? A dog-faced boy? A Borneo Strong Man? Now *that* I might savvy.

But whatever his affliction, my Dad's second cousin's seemed a dark history that my family forbade vent at the dinncr table. Mom knew it, even as she closed out the conversation with a little Highland aphorism: 'A sairy wood it is that has not a withered bough in it.'

Then Big Dan said, 'Okay, no more talk over here about devils, about salt, about gallstones, and no more talk about crooked cops. Nancy? Get the anisette and some Stella D'oros. Okay, honey? Don't worry about the sauce, it was fine.'

I was rapt as a hawk now. 'What crooked cops, Dad?'

'I said that's enough.'

'You haven't touched your *maccheron*',' Gooma Rosa observed. All eyes were on me now. 'You're too skinny. You're a stick. You look like one of those *figli* from Africa.'

'*O Dio*,' Nonni responded fearfully, inspecting my ribcage and causing me to seek refuge behind the big gallon of olive oil. I ate best as I could and wondered why no one had ever told me that amongst junkmen and highway workers and toolmakers at the brass mills, we had a cop in our ranks.

After dinner, Grandpa sat in Dad's easy chair and sipped a grappa, telling Danny the fable about the Frog and the Scorpion. Cousin Giustina got into a debate with Big Dan about Jimmy Carter and the Shah, while the women talked in Italian about the Pope, cysts, gallstones, and who the best ear doctors were in the city's history.

Me, I watched a rerun of C.P.O. Sharkey.

That's when Nonni approached me. She handed me a small gold horn on a frail chain. '*Il corno*,' she whispered. 'The horn. Put on the neck, never take off. Or She come for you.'

And so at five o'clock when we loaded into Big Dan's Bel Aire to head to the unveiling of *The Soldier's Horse* on the Green, I had a golden amulet draped around the crew neck of my *Disco Sucks* T-shirt and I felt protected from all the evils of summer.

CHAPTER FOUR

Brass Balls

In the band shell on the city Green, Lou Napolitano Massi was singing the theme song from *Rocky*. A heavyset lounge singer in his forties, Louie Nap wore his blond-going-silver hair in a disco style pruned from a 1950s pompadour. He had a chest like a lowland gorilla, matted and silver and testing the seams of a white suit that looked like a cross between 1970s Elvis and a Mexican mariachi as he swiveled his hips like Tony Orlando and punched at the air, the microphone at his mercy. Behind him, the Crosby High School Marching Band, rusty on summer break, brassed round and triumphant notes.

I stood deep in the gathered throng with Danny Boy and my parents, trying to see over old Polish ladies' *babushkas* and young Portuguese women's poodle perms. There were a lot of old-timers from all our various ethnic enclaves, and clutches of young people here and there like the brooding guys wearing the Saukiwog tuxedo: a white sleeveless T-shirt and blue jeans. With their arms folded, they stood about, chewing gum slow and cynically. Most of the young women with the kinky perms or outdated shags wore halter shirts, high-waisted jeans and high-heels or tube tops and European clogs. Everyone, it seemed, smoked cigarettes.

One of Danny's ex-teammates, Dave Zuraitas, appeared at his side in a ball cap and T-shirt that said *Dunning-Bickford Munitions*. He and my brother had a conversation, lost under Louie Nap who was now taking the *Rocky* number to a truculent pinnacle and singing so loudly into the microphone that the power seemed to wane in the city; there was awful feedback as the speakers rattled and knocked, and then it ended with a spattering of applause.

'All right, Lou,' somebody yelled from the crowd.

'Let's hope he don't pick up his accordion,' Dad said to my mother. 'If he picks up the accordion, go start the car.'

But Lou Napolitano Massi did not pick up his accordion. He took some time collecting his breath and fingered a gold chain free of his matted white chest hairs. From where I stood I couldn't tell, but I wondered if perhaps Louie Nap wore the horn, too.

'The man I'm about to introduce to you used to deliver my newspaper,' he said in a gruff Brass City voice. 'Always on time, never late. Frank. Frankie, the Boy Scout. Sonuvagun, if I knew he was going to become Mayor, I would've bought some Pecan Sandies.'

Laughter came from the front of the crowd, but back where I stood everyone just looked warm. 'And back when he was an election day runner, runnin' in his Keds from the polls to the Republican headquarters – Christ, I would've given him a lift.'

That one garnered Louie Nap a solid laugh and he savored it, nodding and grinning and winking at some locals down in front.

'Ladies and germs, it's my pleasure to introduce you to Hizzoner: Mayor Longo.'

It was mostly the poodle-permed girls who whistled and cheered but everyone clapped respectfully as Mayor Longo threw a few playful punches at the fat Louie Nap. But when he took the center of the band shell, the Green fell silent. Someone whistled from the street near the old Eaton Hotel where young people sat on parked cars.

'Frank-eee!'

The bellow came from a short muscle-swollen guy in a shrunken tank top, baggy California pants and clean, unlaced work boots. Ray Bonacascio, better known amongst my brother and his friends as Ray Beans, leaned on the hood of a silver Camaro. 'Give 'em hell, Frank-eeee!'

Mayor Longo was only ten years older than guys like Ray Beans, Dave Zuraitas and my brother. He had been elected the year before – an upset, landslide victory over Edgar Dunn. The Republicans had been out of power for nearly twenty years and Frank Longo had given Saukiwog Mills a much-needed injection of young, aggressive leadership. Handsome in a dark Euro-American way, my mother thought he resembled a combination of Tyrone Power and Joe DiMaggio, which is why she said she voted for him.

My father was somewhat indifferent until the medical bills came for Danny Boy's MRI following his injury. The charges would have cleaned out my father's savings but Mayor Longo found my dad at Tony's Barbershop and told him that although he was met with city opposition, the town would find a way to cover the hospital bill. Dad left Tony's with his ears lower and his spirits on the wing, and from that day on, Frankie Longo was the 'best mayor this city ever had'.

The fact that he was Italian and Republican didn't hurt much either.

And so Dad was rapt as Mayor Longo looked out at us and a few hundred others. He singled out an old woman near the World War II monument and smiled at her.

'Mrs Conigliaro. How are you?'

The Italian elder laughed self-consciously and covered her long yellow teeth with her hand, but her daughters smiled openly at the handsome mayor; one of them popped some purple Bubble Yum and did a slow throw of her hair like Cher.

'I'm sure you've all been seeing signs around town. Banners and things that say "Renaissance City". I'd like to say that I came up with that slogan but I didn't. It was someone in congress up in Hartford. They were discussing what's happening to the city of brass, all the changes going on. The movement, the motion, the historical sections being restored. And they said, "Saukiwog Mills is going through a rebirth. A renaissance." And you know what? You're damn right it is.'

Some cheers rose from down in front and equally over near the parked cars. Ray Beans shoved a muscled arm into the Camaro and rapped the horn.

'My grandfather came over here from the little village of Pontelandolfo, Italy, in 1929. He came with a dream of making enough money to bring his wife and daughter over. "They have a beautiful fountain on the green," he told my grandmother in a letter. "The most beautiful horse you ever saw. *Un cavallo bello*. And it is said that if you drink from this fountain, you will never leave the city." Well, he never left the city. He went to work in the brass mills. He worked as a caster in a blast furnace and he saved every penny. Seven dollars a week for fifty hours a week, he made . . . these.'

Mayor Longo inserted his hands into the pockets of his suit and produced two small spheres of burnished metal. 'Weights for a scale,' he explained, tossing one of the golden balls in the air and snatching it back again. 'Rolled brass.'

The mayor went on: 'Some people say we've lost our hold on manufacturing, that we're going to go belly-up like Bridgeport, become another dead New England factory town, mill town, you know – an east coast cliché in red brick. Well, that's not going to happen, people. And I'm going to tell you why it ain't going to happen.'

''Cuz you're the man, Frankie!' Ray Beans drew some laughter, but then silence overtook the humid air. Mayor Longo took a few steps toward the edge of the shell and studied faces with his eyes, that even from a distance, looked young and vital.

'Because we are the descendants of the men and women like Mrs Conigliaro down there and Mr Renkunis and Mrs Doyle who worked for fifty-two years in the clock factory.'

On my toes, I located Mrs Doyle in the crowd: there she was, ruddy-faced and somewhat startled that she was being recognized for her labors. She lay a finger on her flowered blouse as if to say, 'Me?'

'And Mrs Conigliaro's late husband, Mike, who lost four fingers in the mill.'

A morbid twelve-year-old, I tried to see Mrs Conigliaro's face but could not.

'We are a melting pot,' Mayor Longo went on. 'We are black, we are Irish, Lithuanians and Poles; Scots and Germans, Portuguese and Italians; Puerto Ricans and French-Canadians and more. But we all have one common denominator. We all have one thing in common. Like our grandparents who came here, we have . . . *these.*'

Again he held up the two perfectly round brass weights. But now it seemed to take on a different meaning. Lou Napolitano Massi began to chuckle from near a tuba and it spread through the marching band, out to the young people sitting on parked cars

– Ray Beans whistled – and when I looked at my brother, he and Zuraitas were grinning.

There was some sort of sign language going on because the handsome young mayor was smiling at the crowd and there was a rumble of laughter.

'What do we have?' Mayor Longo asked Louie Nap and the band.

'Brass Balls,' the lounge singer shouted back.

'What do we have?' the mayor now asked the throng, shoving the microphone toward us.

'BRASS BALLS!'

'I can't hear you.'

'*BRASS BALLS*!'

'Say it again?'

'BRASS BALLS!'

My mother blushed and my father's lips twitched, and Danny Boy and Zuraitas cupped their hands around their mouths and joined the chant. The whole Green was yelling it and many of the old women exchanged disapproving looks, but many laughed; some didn't speak English well enough to understand and so they asked their children. Mrs Orsini, I was certain, thought the mayor was referring to the manufacturing of brass weights for scales because she was chanting in her helium-squeal: 'Make'a some brass ball! Make'a the brass ball!' She must have had fond memories of the days when brass was King, I reasoned.

I liked our mayor.

I began to recite the victory chant at the peak of my lungs, and it was exhilarating, having permission from His Honor to swear on the Green on a Sunday in front of my own mother.

And now with the town in a pep-rally heat, Mayor Longo began shouting over them. The way our mayor was punching at the sky, I imagined Louie Nap wouldn't last two rounds with him – especially with the brass weights Frankie had in his fists.

'We were once a city of promise and we will be a city of promise again!' he yelled. 'We will make gold again!' With more ardor than Father Vario on Good Friday, he worked himself into a spitfire and brimstone homily, the likes I had never seen before.

'My mother once said, God gives the milk but not the pail. No pain, no gain.' The young people liked this one. Ray Beans and his friends yelled something dumb and inaudible about bench pressing.

'No pain, no gain,' the mayor repeated, pointing their way. 'We, the people, might have to gamble, but I want the unemployment line to become an *assembly* line! Where there are lack of skills, let us train the *unskilled*! Let us increase the tax base and where there are buildings in decay let them find a new purpose! As our grandparents walked across this Common with American dreams, let us, too . . . dream again.'

I thought that for a moment, his eyes caught mine, and I wondered if he, like my father, saw a dreamer there. Maybe he was a dreamer, too.

'We can be a city of promise. Again,' he said. 'We will drink from the horse again. We will be a fine city, again.'

There was a lull.

And then the sward began roaring like an Aerosmith concert and Ray Beans started the big power plant on the Camaro, began revving muscle. Then as everyone sobered and waited for more fireworks, someone shouted from the crowd, 'Have you dragged the river?'

The Common fell silent. People tried to locate the voice, which sounded like it had been aged for seventy years in an oak cask. 'Have you dragged the river?'

As the throng parted and the man came into eye-line, I nearly collapsed against my brother.

'Oh, my God,' my mother whispered. Old man Cocobianco stood in a furrowed suit and bare feet, holding a green plastic garbage bag stuffed full with some unknown contents.

'Have we dragged the river?' the mayor asked, trying to spot the caller in the crowd. 'As part of our restoration effort we are cleaning all lakes and ponds and rivers. In fact, I guarantee, we'll be fishing again in the Mattatuck.'

'Bring back the salmon!' Dave Zuraitas shouted.

'Bingo,' Mayor Frankie said over the speakers. 'Salmon know how to find their way back to where they started, right? So do we. Leave the porchlight on, we're coming *home*.'

Some residents cheered and some residents laughed their doubts.

But most pointed to the old man, and I heard my friend Eddie make a whimpering sound behind me.

'It's Grampy!' He tugged at his mother and a troop of Cocobiancos pushed past residents toward their senile patriarch.

'I'll give to you: my blood!' he bellowed, hoarse and ancient.

'They found him,' Mom sighed, relieved.

'Yeah, he don't go far,' Dad shrugged.

As the mayor went on with his speech I joined Eddie at the small reunion in the middle of the gathering. Tears were shining on his olive cheeks as he hugged his grandfather.

The old man, ruddy-faced from missing his meds, seemed confused by the welcoming and as he wrestled with Eddie's mother, he lost his grip on the garbage bag and it hit the ground. I retrieved the bag for him, and as I did – I could not help myself – I looked in. It was brimming with seashells and fragments of driftwood. And an empty Pepsi can. The mayor said something now that drew all eyes back to the band shell.

'Before I go, I'd like to ask everyone to turn around and look at that *Soldier's Horse*.'

With an inquiring murmur, the crowd did a slow shift in the heat, inverted, and gave their attention to the far edge of the Common. Two public workers were standing high on the fountain, waiting for a cue. With a reverent circumspection, they folded away a canvas to reveal the sculpted donkey. It was scrubbed clean and refinished. What I always thought had been a black mule was fine brass. It was restored: a symbol of the city's renaissance.

'Bingo!' Mayor Longo shouted. 'There she is,' his voice echoed across the Green.

My father started telling me something about *The Soldier's Ass* but it was now buried under a respectable ovation and some catcalls from the VFWs young Lady Auxiliaries as the mayor left the stage with a youthful bounce. Around the town car waiting for him was a small but official-looking assembly of men in suits, all of them old enough to be Frank Longo's father, or even grandfather. I recognized old Mr Sforza amongst them. He was the deli manager from Coangelo's Market and the coach of the girls' basketball team at the new Kirby High. And I knew Mr Campobosso as the nice old man who owned the large hardware store downtown. Mr

Butterscotch Sunday was there to shake the mayor's hand, too. But I didn't know what they were doing, these men, dressed to the nines and carrying clipboards, and flanking the mayor like they were secret service agents. I asked Big Dan if our local banker and hardware chief were undercover Pinkerton men, and he told me they were. And then he laughed. But later, he told me a more boring truth.

Mr Sforza was an alderman; Mr Campobosso, a former GOP chairman who had been 'grooming' Frank Longo for City Hall since he was eighteen; Mr Sunday, a Young Republican who had campaigned hard for Longo, hosted a dozen dinners to raise money for him.

Now, watching the mayor get into his town car, smiling and shaking hands, I tried to imagine him in his Keds, running from the polls to the House.

'Look at the old bastards holding onto his coat-tails,' Dad said to my mother, working a toothpick in his teeth.

As the city crowd jostled toward the town car and my mother clucked her tongue at the statue's beauty, the Cocobiancos led Papa Coco to their family stationwagon at the curb. The old man covered his ears as the Crosby High School Marching Band broke into something nostalgic which they played off-key and maddeningly out-of-synch. Lou Napolitano Massi had his accordion strapped across his large chest and he was singing so loud the microphone fed-back like a rabbit being tortured. My father clapped his hands once, sharply.

'He's got the accordion, Nancy. Let's go.'

We were almost out of there when Danny Boy caught sight of something and his eyes went hard. And then distant. He was looking across the Green at his ex-girlfriend Cheryl Vaughn. With her blonde hair coiffed in a sensible bob, she walked slow and composed with her new boyfriend, a tall guy who she probably met at Yale. He walked slow and composed, too. Big Dan had been pleased when Danny Boy was going out with the girl who 'looks like Morgan Fairchild and her family's got more money than Morgan Bank'.

Two months after Danny's injury, when Cheryl broke up with him, Dad had encouraged Danny to hold onto her and this angered my brother. Now, as she made eye contact with him, there was a small silence. And then she told Danny Boy she was home from Yale for the summer. She also said she had just come back from an art trip to France where, she said, 'I spent two weeks in the Louvre.'

'How's Ivy League?' Danny said, trying not to look at the guy with her.

'Not as hard as I expected. Love New Haven. How about you? What are you up to?'

When Danny Boy said nothing, I looked up at him. He was staring at the curly-haired guy with Cheryl. 'I'm leaving, at the end of the summer.'

'Yeah? What's going on?'

'I'm going to study some acting.'

'Acting?' Cheryl's boyfriend said, chuckling.

'Danny saw *Taxi Driver*,' she said.

'Oh, yeah?' the boyfriend said, polite at first. Then he said, 'Rotsa ruck.'

Zuraitas was there now, his cap off. His hair was thinning, his scalp red from the sun, and I could tell Danny Boy was embarrassed by his presence. 'Hey, Paradise, man,' Zuraitas said. 'Can you give me a ride to the Brick fucking Wall?'

Cheryl and her boyfriend looked uneasily at Zuraitas, even though Cheryl was still smiling. 'We'll see you, Danny. Take care.'

'Take it easy.'

And they were gone.

When I asked Danny what a Louvre was, he said it's what the British people call the bathroom.

'She spent two weeks in the bathroom?' I asked, bewildered.

'Yeah, probably from the water over there in France,' Zuraitas reasoned.

As we passed the fountain, Danny started to stoop for a drink, but changed his mind. I was thirsty but refrained; I wasn't sure if I wanted a lifetime lease in the city of brass, especially with a murderer walking around. So I went thirsty.

'You fucking guineas,' Zuraitas said. 'Superstitious.' He took a drink, then soaked his cap and put it back on his head.

Mom found me at the fountain and said Dad was waiting for me in the car.

'I'll ride with Danny, okay?'

'All right, love.'

There was something I wanted to say to my brother that I could not say to my parents. If Papa Coco was not the dead man in the trunk of the Pontiac Bonneville . . . who was?

CHAPTER FIVE

Dead Man's Derby

Down in the lower seven acres of the junkyard, just beyond the place where the wrecked and rusted VWs were kept pastured, I harbored a secret. My friends, the free lads and lassies of summer, may have been home horsing around on skateboards and three-speed bicycles, but I had a toy that would have left them salivating, and I knew it.

On the backside of a big junked cement truck sat a 1952 Pontiac Chieftain Eight with a working high compression engine. It was black as an 8-ball, one of those big American cars – luxury over logic – with a front grill like a snarling shark and massive bullet-shaped headlights that Dad called 'Dagmars' presumably after a starlet with big bosoms. Chieftain was my black stallion, my club house and my demolition super car.

Whenever I forced open the driver's door and crawled in on tattered upholstery, I could smell the scent of a lost era, smells from the 1950s. There were still cigarette butts in the ashtray called Hotshots – a brand long ago extinct, and in the huge glove box a 1952 magazine called *Vue* that was chock-full of Dagmars. I had a boyish fascination with the centerfold, Bettie Page; *Page is all the rage* it said above her picture. She had black bangs and little leopard-spotted bikini bottoms and not much else.

When the time was right – when Grandpa was out in his shed tinkering and Dad was off towing a car and Danny Boy was watching the front – I would slip down to see The Chieftain and conjure up the wild furies.

I felt the need on this warm Monday and made my secret sojourn. Crawling in, I felt a little flash-flood of adrenaline. The Chieftain had a dual-range Hydra-matic tranny and its ignition was a rubber push-button. I got her going with a few pumps of the gas and backed out between old wrecks.

With a clear lane ahead of me, I let Chieftain sit and do a throaty idle for a moment as I adjusted my driver's cap and secured my position at the wheel. Then I floored it.

Crushed diamond glass spun out from under the bald tires as I thundered forward, gaining a respectable speed, slamming into an old Rambler with a great crash. My body lurched like a test crash dummy then back again. I pushed the R button and punched stale fuel. In reverse I could see my opponent, a '67 VW bus with a peace sign on the hood. I clobbered it and caved in the peace sign. I jabbed the D button and Chieftain growled forward, taking out a Bug from the same pod as the bus and smashing right through a pile of dead tires. We bumped down into a ravine, motor throttling like a big, mean racing machine. This was demolition derby in the junkyard; Nunzio Paradiso in Car Number 8, the black Chieftain, taking on all-comers of all makes and models.

I looked at myself in the big round side mirror. It wasn't often I got to see myself at the wheel of a car. There was grease on my face like war-paint, but squinting in the glare I thought I saw something out of place.

In the undulating heat haze I could see the dull shine of a junked vehicle moving slightly. I had conjured up collisions and sideswipes before, but this car, a red '59 Rambler wagon, was actually rolling forward. Not fast, but methodically. I must have upset the sardine arrangement of junkers, I postulated. Knocking away the bus probably freed the old Rambler from its twenty-year repose. I saw its left side, part sheared off, and now I recognized it.

The vehicle was one of the cars from The Boneyard: a car that Dad had said lost its brakes in the early 1960s and struck a cement train trestle, killing an entire family on their way to Hammonasset Beach.

I sat there, my heart bumping with every knock of The Chieftain's big engine and I wondered if it wasn't something to do with the Rambler's faulty brakes that had caused it to roll. But it wasn't just rolling now. It was idling. Its motor was alive and exhaust was making a thin fume and I thought I could hear, on the wind, the sound of children. Singing. Closer. The fine hairs on my arms stiffened.

In the passenger seat, a woman in a headscarf and cat's-eye sunglasses half-turned and handed something that looked like a large pickle into the backseat. She looked like a woman I had seen in a frigidaire ad in the 1950s sex magazine. She, too, was singing the song. At the wheel, a shirtless man with a butch crewcut and wayfarer sunglasses joined in with the singing, affecting a Lawrence Welk voice and making his wife giggle and poke him.

'Ninety-eight bottles of beer on the wall . . .'

I pushed the R button on Chieftain and punched gas. But as I reversed, the Rambler wagon picked up speed and came at me. I could see a little girl with reddish hair hanging her head out the back window, singing while her siblings jumped around unrestrained in the backseat, eating big kosher pickles. As the Rambler came at me, I was drawn to the little girl. I knew her from somewhere. The red hair, the upturned nose, gapped teeth.

Oh my God.

She was in one of the old photos up on Dad's cork board, striking a cabaret pose and hamming for her Mom's camera. The photo always made me uneasy. Now I knew why. It was a snapshot of a dead girl. And now she was coming at me, singing oblivious as her mother opened her large mouth and screamed, clutching at the dashboard.

I backed into another junker and bounced forward, chest into the wheel. It was a brown '73 Pinto, half-burned. Dad had recounted for me, on more than one occasion, how this model of Pinto had been recalled because of a gas-tank problem. But not before this particular acquisition was rear-ended and exploded like a cherry bomb, killing two teenaged girls on the Post Road. That's when I realized where I was.

The Boneyard.

The Rambler was coming down the ravine fast and I could see that the guy with the butch was pumping the brakes and screaming, 'Oh Christ, Debbie, I'm down to metal!'

'Ninety-four bottles of beer on the wall . . .'

I tried to yell – my voice was gone – as the Rambler hit my Chieftain head on. There was a terrible rocking and sliding and skidding sideways as I wrestled with the black wheel. The little redheaded girl was delirious with joy and laughter, behaving like a child on too much sugar. Or was it the ghost-child's reaction to a vast unknown, a little dead girl's tantrum of denial?

I floored the Chieftain, trying to climb back up the ravine, back to the living world, but another wreck left its stall, cut me off: a 1960 salmon-pink Chevrolet Biscayne with its nose pushed in. Working the twisted wheel was a tall black man in a wide brimmed hat and a macintosh raincoat, sipping from a bottle. His wipers were on.

'Hennessey an' me,' it sounded like he said as he rumbled by me and looked over glassy-eyed. 'Woman broke me but she don't take my Chevy and she don't take my Hennessey.' He took another long sip and smiled at me. And then the flaming Pinto broadsided him and he howled with laughter. 'I'm gown' the wrong way,' he laughed – the slow, mellow laugh of a cool daddy. The burning Pinto was determined to take him out and the two girls in the frontseat were screaming like they were on a rollercoaster going down; I was caught in the bumper cars of the Living Dead.

'Help me, Chieftain,' I said to the steering wheel and I pushed the Low Drive button. There was a rutted lane strewn with old drive shafts and scrap but it was my only way out of The Boneyard.

Or so I thought.

Up ahead, another death car entered the derby and sat idling at the end of the rutted lane out. In sunspots I could not see which car it was but I could hear music, audible at one moment then just a feeling on the air, like picking up a faraway place on a shortwave radio. A repetitive three-chord noise. A falsetto scream.

Nobody gonna take my car, I'm gonna race it to the ground . . . oh, it's a killing machine, it's got everything – like a driving power, big fat tires, everything – I NEED *it, I* WANT *it, I* LOVE *it . . .*

Coming out of the dust and wreckage was the killing machine: a Woody Hearse with the name *Saturday's Children* on its paneled side. The metal music was coming from the Bose speakers of the rock wagon and I recognized the song as 'Highway Star' by Deep Purple. What disturbed me was that I knew the old vehicle had an 8-track player with a tape permanently lodged in the deck; Danny Boy once tried for half an hour to get it out with a screwdriver while I begged him not to because Dad said there was a guy's anklebone still wedged under the brake pedal.

As the Woody came out of the clouds of dust and exhaust I could see an assembly squeezed in the frontseat, some guys were crammed in back, too, with amplifiers and guitar cases and heavy smoke. In the middle of the frontseat was a young girl with a shag haircut, sitting on a bearded guy's lap and snorting at a roach clip. What struck me was she was probably only fourteen with small breasts the size and shape of tennis balls. She seemed enamored of the guys who were all singing, screaming shrill that song:

Nobody gonna take my girl, I'm gonna keep her till the end . . . whoa, she's a killing machine, she's got everything – body controlling everything – I NEED her! I WANT her! I LOVE her! . . . On a highway . . . staaaar . . .

Metal against metal sent sparks up with the squeal of electric guitar feedback; I tried desperately to loop away from its path. When it struck me, Chieftain went into a fishtail; I heard the girl with the haircut scream and drum cymbals crash and somebody with a slow voice say, 'Hey, where's the fire, man?'

I collided with the pink Biscayne; I was so close I could see that the whites of the black man's eyes were jaundiced, his pupils hazy. He looked at me and laughed his slow hip laugh as he dropped the car into reverse. 'Southbound on the Northbound – that's a no-no, Daddio,' he said, then he took another purposeful swig from his cognac bottle and hissed. His car had stalled and he glanced at me as if to share his disgust. But then he did a strange double-take. He fixed his hazy eyes on me. 'Whatchyou doin' in here, boy? How'd you get in here?'

I was wedged between the black man's Biscayne and a dead Skylark. I stomped gas, but Chieftan's tires only spun.

'You too young,' the black man in the pink Biscayne said, and he said it in a voice that sounded like it hurt him somewhere, years in. 'Quit this game, son. *Now.*'

I stomped gas and raced for the lane out. But the Woody set chase, a long-haired guy with sunglasses looking out, dispassionately.

I WANT her, I NEED her, I LOVE her! Deep Purple screamed.

The girl screamed.

'*Forty-two bottles of beer on the wall . . .*'

Then I heard nothing. Just my brother Danny Boy, calling my

name. He was crying, and that's when I knew I must be dead. My ghost sat behind the wheel, staring at him.

'Nunzio!' he yelled into my face. 'Wake up! Wake up!'

'I *am* awake.'

'You were sleeping with the car running and the windows up, man. Jesus Christ! You could've killed yourself! You *ass*hole.'

As he dragged me from the car, I looked down into The Boneyard. It was just a lot of wrecked cars and forgotten tires. But Primo Canero was still barking at something down there, his hackles high and his eyes crazy.

Danny Boy drove the torch wagon slowly around the hem of the yard, me beside him.

He was convinced that I'd tried to commit suicide in the Chieftan, and I wasn't so sure he was wrong.

'You were doing something you didn't even know you were doing,' he explained.

Maybe I had. Like those lemmings that throw themselves off of cliffs despite themselves; I had a picture of the act in one of my old *National Geographics*, and I used to stare at it for hours. Maybe I had stared at it for too long.

– I don't want to talk about it.

– I think you better, man.

– I'm pretty sure now, almost ninety percent, that I didn't see anybody in that trunk. They found Eddie's grandpa, you know. I think maybe it was dead puppies I saw. My imagination.

– It idles a little high, like Daddy says, right?

– Right.

– Dante, right?

– Right.

– So let's say it's the imagination of a young superstitious dink.

– Okay.

– In your imagination you see like some ghoul with penny loafers and blue socks.

– White socks like.

– White socks like. Okay. And something wrapped around his fingers. Amber rosary beads you said.

– No, I said red. Red. Like those love beads Cousin Lena used to have.

– Then it must be your imagination.

Danny Boy stopped the car. He lifted a small ratchet box, opened it. Gingerly, he removed four or five, maybe six small beads of honey-colored plastic.

'Because these are amber.'

'Oh!' I yelled. Or 'Ow!' because it felt like the dead man was looking at me again. There was no doubt those were the beads – though now unstrung – and several were dark with a brownish crust that looked like ossified apple butter.

'Where, Danny?' My throat was arid. 'Where'd you find those?'

'There was a jackdaw kept going up to the crushed Pontiac, pecking around.' Jackdaw was what my brother called crows. 'It was taking some shit down and stashing it in the old school bus, in a nest. There was pieces of chrome and broken tail-light – they like shiny things, these jackdaw. And in the bottom of the nest were these beads.'

Danny Boy seemed to study me. 'I believe you,' he said in a hoarse whisper and he sounded grim. 'I had a funny feeling about that car. I smelled something too, but Dad told me not to open the trunk.'

Danny Boy was now looking straight up into the sunspots that clustered around the crushed Pontiac and although his vote of confidence provided relief, it also deepened my fears.

'What if there was just some beads wrapped around something in that trunk, and I thought I saw a hand? Remember that guy in Beacon Falls thought he saw Jesus's face on a catalytic converter?' I didn't believe the weight of my own voice as I treaded plausibility. 'Maybe it was like a mirage.'

'That's what I thought, too,' Danny said. 'And then I found . . . this.' He pulled some old keys from the box, the silver V from 'Bonneville', and then something tiny that he pinched gingerly in his fingers.

It was a spent bullet, the shaft smashed flat and grooved.

'We got us a magic bullet, Bro,' Danny said.

'What do you mean, a magic bullet? That's a real bullet.'

'Oh yeah, it's a real bullet, and these are real rosary beads. And there's a real body in that car, no bigger than a bread box now.'

My brother's voice began softly, but it quickly rose to alto heights and soon he was shouting at me.

'The only people who know where he is, is us . . . *and* whoever put him there. And somebody someplace has got to be looking for the guy, whoever the flying *frig he is.*'

'Do you think it could be Jimmy Hoffa like you said?'

– It could be fucking Elvis for all I know.

– What do we do, Danny? If Dad knows there was somebody in there . . .

'What do we do, Danny?' my brother mocked me. I wasn't offended, I could see it was just stress. He lifted his gas rag to his forehead and sopped up sweat and dirt and I could see that he needed this crisis like he needed one of Miss Page's ample Dagmars in the middle of his forehead; this could complicate his condition, I worried.

He gently pinched the spent bullet back into the ratchet box and snapped it shut. He looked off across the yard, out over the tarpaper fence, toward the Big Clock in the haze.

'I don't know anybody named Iris,' he said.

CHAPTER SIX

Mal'occhio

My father was The Strongest Man in the World.

It was in the books, he told me – though I never knew for sure just which books – but I had been comfortable with his title since I was four or five and there was never much occasion to doubt the claim which came with plenty of supporting evidence. He had defeated the Arm Wrestling Champion at the Connecticut Junkyard Association annual picnic, and years before I was born, he had allowed Zi Bap and Zi Toine to crush a cinder block on his chest with a sledge-hammer. Once, in an argument with my grandfather, I saw him drive his head through sheet rock, and on a long ago Thanksgiving morning the entire neighborhood witnessed him shot-put a half-cooked twenty-pound turkey forty yards, one-handed, into the neighbor's compost heap. A sin for which my grandmother never forgave him.

There were not too many customers at the yard who would argue long with my father. He had a reputation for having a short fuse and no ability to stop himself if you upset him. The word was out that he had once hefted a used transmission and thrown it through the windshield of a petulant customer's car. 'There you go,' he'd said. 'There's your four on the floor, now get the hell out.'

Yet, driving home in the wrecker, I could see something happening to him and it troubled me. His shock of black hair was moving away from his forehead like the slow retreat of a glacier in the Ice Age. His eyes, at midday, looked like they usually did only in the morning, bee-stung and small, and he ate more Tums than usual, a residual white powder forever at the corners of his lips.

My dad was growing old. Was it the stress of his junk license being up for renewal or was it something more?

'Movie acting,' he said, more to the street in front of him than to my brother, 'it's something that people like us can't do. I know you look at a picture on the TV set and you think you want to be one of those people in there, in the box, but – it just don't happen.'

'You think movie actors are little people *inside the TV set*?' Danny Boy asked, nonplussed.

'No, I didn't say that, but they might as well be, see. They're people who . . . they just come from different places. They're one in a million.'

'You ever think maybe I could be one of the one in a million?'

My father threw a bewildered look at him. 'You ever think maybe Zi Bap could be the President of the United States? You're not a movie actor.'

'Rosalind Russell was from this valley.'

'Rosalind Russell had a big pair of Dagmars. Do you have a big pair of Dagmars?'

'Jane Russell had the big Dagmars, not *Rosalind* Russell.'

'What are you, an expert now?'

'On Dagmars I am,' he smiled, knowing this would get Big Dan's goat.

'Yeah,' Dad snorted, looking off into the traffic.

Danny Boy looked down at his army boots and let out an audible moan.

'I got a headache,' he complained.

'Well, you stay up all night chasing *goomare*, you're gonna—'

'Knock it off!' Danny Boy fired, and the exertion made him drop his head back on the seat. 'I've had it for three days. I think somebody gave me the *mal'occhio*.'

A silence filled the cab as we headed for The Little Boot. The mere mention of the subject filled me with equal parts fear and fascination. The malice was a Neapolitan rendering of *mal'occhio* – the Evil Eye. It was, in most circumstances, rooted in envy. If someone cast you a jealous glance, the *mal'occhio* could set in. In other cultures, if someone spoke clandestinely about you, your ears might burn. In our culture, you grew ill with the *mal'occhio*.

'You better go see my mother,' Dad suggested and there was

an atmosphere of truce in the tow truck. 'Okay, Danny? Go see Nonni, kid.'

Danny Boy closed his eyes and worked a thumb against his temple. Since The Hit, he had frequent headaches but never for a three-day run. If Danny had been afflicted, it best be remedied, and our own grandmother was one of the few old women left in The Little Boot who knew the medicine.

In the silence, Dad tuned the AM radio and he stopped for a moment on a rock song. It was Alice Cooper singing 'School's Out' which reminded me, like salt in my open sores, of my lost summer. Dad listened to the rock star banshee. 'That's not music,' he decided. 'That woman's getting a two-by-four up her ass and they're recording it.'

I did not see much use in telling Dad that Alice Cooper was a man. I was more concerned about other things.

My father may have been The Strongest Man in the World, but there was one individual he had never defeated at arm-wrestling.

His mother.

Assunta Fante Paradiso was five feet ten and boasted forearms like the wrestler Bruno Samartino. Growing up in the mountain village of Pontelandolfo, Nonni had hauled fifty pound bags of chicken feed and baskets of oranges. Like her witchcraft, Nonna's own strength spooked her.

At one of our large family weddings, my father, slightly besotted with wine, herded all the men, all the cousins and uncles and *goombas* and lined them up at his mother's table for arm-wrestling. She dispatched them easily, and even took Zi Bap and Zi Toinc at the same time with each arm in opposite directions. They tensed and trembled like they had the spelter bends then – boom, boom! 'Madonn'! She's as strong as a bull!'

When they made me fall in, a slight kid in a powder-blue suit, she dropped my knuckles to the table like I was so much rag doll and she laughed, embarrassed by her own prowess.

Now, Danny and I could see her through her kitchen window preparing her sauce for Sunday. It was a preternatural process that sent delicious smells throughout the West End.

Danny Boy knocked on the kitchen door and I heard Nonni say,

'*Dio*,' worried about a caller at dark. She peered warily through the curtains. Danny Boy pushed me out in front. Nonni opened the door to the extent of the chain lock and looked at us through the small space.

'Nonni,' my brother spoke. 'I've got the *mal'occh.*'

'*O dio mi*,' she said in her husky voice, and it took her awhile to make a decision. Eventually, she unlocked the door and waved us in, looking out to the street to make sure the carrier of the evil eye, perhaps the hunchback Rosario with her eyebrows that met in the middle, was not lurking.

Nonni's sauce: two five gallon kettles filled to the rims with crushed garden tomatoes and a rich base of onions, garlic, basil, olive oil, wine, magnificent breaded meatballs, chunks of lamb, beef, and mushrooms of monolithic shapes and sizes.

With the blade of a large knife, she moved these things aside and sat Danny Boy at the head of the table. Dimming the lights, she lit a candle and set a small saucer of tap water at the center. She sat down at the opposite head and dried her hands on a *mopine*, a checkered dish towel. Very carefully she poured some olive oil into the saucer and watched its consistency settle. In the candlelight, the oil and water danced and Danny Boy looked over at me knowing that I would be enraptured.

'Pretty cool,' he smiled. I nodded, reverent and silent.

Nonni set her fingers on the surface of the water and took some wetness from it. She rubbed it, like a farmer weighing the merit of a soil, and then she leaned across the table and touched my brother's forehead, making the sign of the cross.

And she prayed in the rural mountain dialect.

This went on for a spell and I was keenly aware that I was witnessing magic. Nonni had cured more than a thousand headaches in her time; once, Zia Concetta was on vacation in Florida and she called Nonni long distance, nearly blind with a migraine. My grandmother did the ceremony over the phone and Aunt Concetta's headache dissipated before she hung up. This had become legend in our family.

'*Fui, fui, mal'occhio*,' she pleaded and she returned her fingers to the bowl, letting the oil and water drip back in. Now she watched what happened in the bowl.

So did I.

The oil and water beaded and changed color, it seemed to thicken and clot. Danny Boy sat staring at Nonni, watching for her reaction. She could read the olive oil and water the way some people could read boxscores or wheat futures.

She carried on a conversation with the spirits as she peered into the mixture and then, after a sweat broke on her nose, and one of the sauce kettles percolated on the stove, she sat back. Her eyes sought me out. 'Go sit on the stoop,' she whispered.

When I didn't move right away Danny Boy stared me down. Then he spoke just like my father. 'What did Nonni say over here? Go sit on the stoop.'

As I crossed the tidy living room en route for the porch, I looked for something to read on the grounds that this was something of a doctor's office anyway. But Nonni and Grandpa did not place much importance on literature. On the coffee table, beside a bowl of fake fruit – the apple still had my dental impressions from seven years back when it tempted me – were the only two books in the house: the old Catholic Bible and the large and ponderous tome that I assumed was a photo album. The choice was not a difficult one.

Inside the old album were a collection of sepia-toned daguerreotypes capturing Nonni and Grandpa at their prearranged wedding; she was a striking young woman with long black hair and the most terrified expression I had ever seen on a person's face since Fay Wray. In every wedding photo Grandpa wore a proud countenance and Nonni looked spooked, her eyes peering at her new husband out the corners.

There was a torn and scotch-taped photo ID from the Saukiwog Rolling Mills: Grandpa as a young man, newly arrived in America. This was inserted over the corner of a yellowed front-page article about a strike at United Brass in 1919 and another, at the Saukiwog Rolling Mills in 1920. I looked for Grandpa in the photo but saw only armed factory guards on horseback, forming a line at the gates. '*Excitable Italian element cause for concern*,' a caption read.

Then there was a well-kept photo of young Grandpa after he had quit the mill, standing beside his Conestoga junk wagon. I could see he was having difficulty suppressing a smile of pride as he stood before a collection of old lamps, restored rugs, old brooms fitted to new handles, repaired radios, untangled and restored trolley wire and sharpened ax-blades. On the opposite page was a clipping from the *Republican* dated September 1942: a gang of neighborhood kids who resembled the Little Rascals sat atop a pile of salvage with a handmade sign that read *Doing Our Bit – Scrap a Jap* and there was my young grandfather near his wagon below, rummaging through their pile.

On the following pages were shots of my Uncle Louie posing with a prize-winning *zucchini*; a man who may or may not have been Grandpa pitching a *bocci* ball; news clippings of family items: births, marriages, deaths, my brother's football notices and an old *Saukiwog Republican* clipping of someone in an ill-fitting uniform with his head ripped haphazardly from the paper. I turned the heavy plastic sheets to my own fourth-grade class picture then flipped back, intrigued.

There he was.

My father's second cousin, Angelo. The one Nonni called *Il Mamone*; the man whose very name inspired anarchy at the Sunday table. The one whose ass my father was always praying a tire iron up when he couldn't loosen a wheel lug.

It was him, Goomba Angelo; from the neck down anyway.

The caption beneath the yellowed photo said Angelo Volpe had received certification as a member of the Pinkerton Security Agency out of New Haven. It was dated before I was born.

'Pinkerton,' I whispered, awed by the name that conjured images of men in black suits on saddlebred ponies, pursuing Jesse and Frank James across the Missouri breaks.

The thought grabbed me like a treble hook. We not only had an ex-cop in the family but a one-time Pinkerton detective. A real trained and certified Eye Who Never Sleeps. A 'Pinkerton Man' as the notorious outlaws referred to the agents. Maybe there was some family bickering in years past and Nonni referred to him as dead, but he was still family, and still alive, far as anyone knew.

I felt an almost desperate need to find my father's second cousin Angelo. Was he somewhere in the city? Did he still keep a gun and nightstick in his top drawer? I kept flipping back to the caption about the Pinkerton Agency and wishing I could see the man's face. His head was removed almost recklessly, sometimes at the cost of somebody else's shoulder or an ear, as if Nonni had done it all at once and with superstitious fervor. But what could have happened to garner this awful ostracism? I had always thought that in families, if there was a disaster – a house fire, a car accident, a liver transplant – bygones became bygones. Especially in the so-called tight-knit Italian family. I believed in *Il Destino* as my grandfather called it – God charts the course, even if by dead reckoning – but I couldn't imagine turning my back on a blood relation, no matter his trespasses.

'O *Santa Maddelena*!' Nonni rasped from inside the kitchen, and I slapped the tome shut. I sat tense, until I heard my grandmother announce, '*Va bene*. Good, maybe okay now.' And then, second-guessing her own witchcraft: 'Maybe not, I don't know.'

I returned the family album and hurried back in. Danny Boy gave me the results like a sports commentator recapping the knockout punch at the fights. The oil had begun to spread, which was a bad sign. But then it settled and stopped spreading, a good sign. If it spread through the water – like it had with Gooma Rosario – my brother would have been incurable, a tortured *mal'occhio*, walking the floor all night like the hunchbacked woman from Genoa Street. He let out a breath and Nonni, too, was relieved.

Danny Boy and I watched, intrigued, as our grandmother then carefully lifted the saucer and brought it to the kitchen counter. She rummaged around some empty cans and glasses and settled on a clean Hellman's Mayonnaise jar. As carefully as pouring some explosive glycerin, she spilled the *mal'occh'* into the jar then capped it tight.

She lifted the small candle plate and spilled hot wax along the mouth of the jar, sealing the cap in place. Satisfied, she handed the bottled curse to my brother and gave further instructions. 'The *mal'occh'*, it's in the jar now.'

Danny Boy held onto his jar like he had just been trusted with a live grenade. He appeared reluctant: he would rather have it flushed down the bowl. But this, Nonni told him, could wreak havoc on the sewage systems and leech fields and, perhaps harm the gardens. Tilting the jar in the light of Nonni's porch afterward, Danny Boy studied the tincture inside and wondered aloud if the spell had been cast by the guy who was with his ex-girlfriend Cheryl at the Green on Sunday. She had probably told the guy what an animal he was in the sack, he said; he could see the guy staring at him with the cold blue eyes of a sea-coast enemy. So, Danny took the jar and wedged it in the glove box of his AMC Hornet, and locked it.

The Little Boot was quiet but for the toads my grandfather had not yet exterminated with his spade. As we crossed the lawn to our house, Danny Boy gave me the prognosis. 'Headache's gone,' he said, and he opened a hand so I could slap him some skin. We questioned the old Italian medicine no more than we would antibiotics, and off he went for the Swizzle Stick in his Hornet, and I went off to bed, exhausted from a long day of man's work.

With my head on the damp pillow, I turned over four times to conjure the benevolence of St Rocco. But I was unable to keep my eyes closed. That music was in my head now, those five or six piano notes played over and over like soap opera music. I turned on my lava lamp and reached down under my bed. I brought up my salvaged Lionel steam engine and the shoe box full of archaeological finds. Rummaging, I went to the small token and ruminated on Lady Fortuna. I wished that when Savin Rock Amusement Park had closed down, they had junked her at our yard. Maybe then, I could've dusted her off and dropped the token in, and waited to find out what my future had in store.

CHAPTER SEVEN

Super 8

More gods had battled there than on all the high plateaus of Olympus and Vesuvio. Like giants they shook the earth with their footsteps; it could be felt far across Route 8.

The Rebel had been there, sometimes with a cause, sometimes not, but my mother and father had lent their support and Dad even adopted his walk. The Living Dead had spent two weeks there, hacking people with sheet rock knives and making my Cousin Frannie wet his pajamas. Apes who took over the planet had stampeded through on horseback, dispatching humans with lobotomies, and Bruce Lee had cooed like a wild cat while knocking a lot of little Chinamen (with dubbed voices deeper than James Coburn) straight through wooden walls, leaving their cutouts in the knotty pine.

Bonnie and Clyde were ambushed there by the redneck law and shot through like Swiss cheese, and, in the low times, Marilyn Chambers had chowed down on an elephantinc appendage from behind a green door while my friends and I watched from the edge of the junkyard, marveling at the wonders of special effects.

But with Suburbia spilling in from one side and the nine-screen cinema coming to town – what they called the multiplex – few families parked their stationwagons at the speaker posts and sat back for a triple feature under the stars. And so, after thirty years of wonders and horrors, *The Thing from the Surf*, heavy petting and the best hot-dogs in the city, the Mattatuck Drive-In Theater was being demolished.

It was an eerie place now with the rusted swing set beneath the massive screen, and the rows of headless speaker stalks like a cornfield in winter; tumbleweeds of old French-fry boxes rolled and little white napkins floated high over the barrens. With the city renaissance there would be changes. Mayor Longo had promised us this. But it was hard to accept that a shopping plaza would be built on the hallowed grounds of the last drive-in on the East Coast.

'I guess it's not hard for guys like Zuraitas,' Danny reminded me. 'People need jobs.'

On Friday the big screen would come down via a wrecking ball and the speaker posts uprooted. The lot would be plowed under and smooth-harrowed, and the moist earth dug for new buildings and generators. A security guard outside a tiny trailer near the entrance had phoned Dad and told him that a car had been sitting in the center of the drive-in lot for a very long time, no one was sure just how long; according to the former owner Mr Lucheski, he couldn't remember when it was not there, a speaker clipped on the window and an unfinished cup of Coca-Cola on the dash. It became, to the owner, a kind of set-piece, a landmark; like the dollar a barman puts in his jar to start the tips flowing, there would always be, no matter the attendance, a 1959 Fairlane with New York plates, parked as if watching the show. Big Dan had a crasher Mercury already on the hooks, so after we dropped it at the yard, he sent me and Danny to hunt down the buffalo at the old drive in. This was a gesture of faith in his sons, and we enjoyed the freedom.

'I don't see why they have to knock it down,' I'd lamented as we set out on Route 8.

For all his defending the unemployed, Danny Boy was equally distraught. 'I know, man. This is like tearing down a church,' he said. 'De Niro's been on that screen.'

As we got closer to the condemned outdoor theater, I brought up a more serious quandary. 'That Pontiac's going to be shipped out in three weeks, Danny. We've got to do something.'

'We can't go to the cops,' Danny Boy said. 'Dad could end up in jail for some kind of complicity or some shit like that.'

'I know. But we gotta find out who the guy is, where he came from, who his family is.'

'And how we going to do that, Nunzi? Without rocking an avalanche in the family?'

'*Keep* it in the family.'

'How so?'

'Goomba Angelo.'

If my grandmother was there she would have clutched her red plastic horn; Zia Concetta would have picked up the nearest infant and made a sign of the cross with the child's body; my dad would have made a disparaging sound out the corner of his lips. Danny Boy just looked at me as he drove and then he turned a crazy laugh toward the road. 'The *Mamone?*'

'We've got nowhere else to turn.'

'What are you – nuts? He's not a cop no more, he got fired. I don't know what he is or where he is—'

'He was a *Pinkerton*,' I said firmly.

'Nunzio. A Pinkerton is a fucking security guard.'

'The Pinkertons caught John Wilkes Booth.'

'And the Jets won the Superbowl in sixty-nine. You heard Nonni. Angelo is dead.'

'Yeah, well so is the guy in the trunk and we're not forgetting about him.'

'How about Father Vario? How 'bout you go see Father Vario?'

'Can't do that, I won't get confirmed.'

'Why? You didn't kill the guy.'

'No, but I kept it secret for four weeks. It's a mortal sin to keep a secret like that from Father.'

'It is a sin,' Danny Boy said, scanning the drive-in. 'I can't believe they're tearing it down.'

'Maybe he can find out who the dead guy is,' I kept on. 'A Pinkerton Man knows how to do that. If we can just find out who the guy in the Pontiac is, we can get the body back to his family without anyone ever knowing.'

'Right,' Danny said. 'We unload a ton of ferrous scrap onto somebody's lawn in the middle of the night. "Lucy, I'm hooooome".'

He had a point. We were in as tight a space as the dead man himself.

Danny Boy sat there, looking out at the giant screen. I knew him well enough to know he was calling on St Bob; invoking the great De Niro, twenty-three feet tall and sitting in a deer camp with a rifle, awaiting my brother's request.

'One shot,' Danny Boy said, confirming my suspicions.

'I'm really scared,' I finally said.

My brother turned a look on me, his eyes narrowed. 'We got one shot, Nunzio,' he said. 'Let's make it count.' With this, he bailed and began assuming our father's role, ordering me around as he circled the abandoned Fairlane. 'Good mirrors,' he said. 'Windshield's got a crack. How's the rear rubber?'

I crouched and stuck a quarter in the tread. 'Sweet' was my assessment. Danny Boy went inside the car and began digging around. I joined him from the passenger door, and like raccoons in a galvanized can, we raided and rummaged and ransacked the floormats. Whoever owned the car was immaculate and there were no papers in the glove box.

'No keys, no registration. Somebody just left her here.' Danny Boy went around to the back and grabbed a tire iron from the wrecker bed. He went to the trunk and started to wedge and pry, but something made him hesitate. I watched him, feeling the same uneasiness. The drive-in was still and gray and across the lot an old newspaper slid like a grounded kite at the mercy of a slow wind. The security guard was gone, his trailer a tin shell near the old marquis which now read *Mattatuck Shopping Plaza Site*. Clouds were working up a damp brew overhead.

'New York,' I said, looking at the orange plate which had no registration sticker. Danny Boy handed me the tire iron. 'Check it out, I'll lock up the wheel.'

'No way,' I said.

'What's the matter?'

'I'm not popping it, Danny. No way.'

Danny Boy looked around the area: the old snack bar was a ghost shack and the projection booth an empty eye socket on the roof. He forced the iron under the trunk lid and put his weight on it, pushing downward. The lid popped then creaked an inch like trunks do when they haven't been opened for a long while and rust has sealed the lip.

Danny Boy worked his hands under the trunk lid and tried to draw in a covert breath. But I saw it. And he knew I saw it. So he said, 'Dad'll shit a *bracciola* if we go in the trunk before him.'

'Open it,' I said. But I took a step back.

'Okay, but it's your ass,' he said, sweating.

'Open it,' I said again, looking to the wrecker to make sure I had a clear path for the frontseat. My brother lifted the trunk lid. Our faces went sallow. Together we yelled out. Then we went silent.

'What's in there?' I asked, looking toward the snack bar.

'Nothing.'

But there was something: a small leather case with a rusted latch. Danny Boy leaned in, popped the case with the head of a Phillips screwdriver.

Inside the box was a gun.

Not some old-time revolver, but what appeared to be a space gun, large and hand-held with an eye-like barrel and long vertical trigger grip that dropped below the chamber. We both went for it at the same time. Somehow, in the ensuing struggle, I came away with the box and Danny Boy had the space gun. I could see by his face that it felt awesome in his hand, and that's when we could both see it was not a weapon but something else altogether and with a magic all its own. Danny Boy whispered in near reverence.

'Super 8.'

'Wow! Does it work?'

'I don't know.'

Danny Boy walked away a few steps and looked at it in better light. Along the side of the camera were the words *Bell & Howell Trigonometric*, promising all kinds of sci-fi wonders. Above it was a small hot shoe for sound.

'Dad's going to want it,' I stammered.

'Dad can go piss up a rope,' my brother suggested. 'I found it.'

'What you going to do with it?'

'Make a movie.'

CHAPTER EIGHT

Napoleon at St Helena

'You're very special boys,' my mother said when we called her from a pay phone on Willow Street and told her that we wanted to bring a cake over to Dad's second cousin Angelo for St Jean Baptiste Day. She never brought up the fact that St Jean Baptiste Day was an obscure Canadian holiday we found on the little calendar in the tow truck. Nor did she enforce the family decree that we were forbidden to go anywhere near the *Mamone*.

'Pity is akin to love,' Mom said and she had proceeded to go through her big flowered address book to find Angelo Volpe's number. She agreed that it would be best not to tell Dad and then she suggested we take the man a Boston-Creme pie.

I had bartered with Danny Boy; I would hold fast to the secret of what was in the trunk of the Fairlane at the drive-in if my brother would take us to Goomba Angelo's for the half-hour we were to have lunch. I didn't get the sense that I was twisting his arm however: for all his callous talk, Danny Boy was in as tight a moral corner as I was and he knew we had to turn somewhere. He just made sure we exhausted every avenue, the last one being total apathy.

The man whom Nonni called the *Mamone*, but whose real name was Archangelo Volpe, lived in the Dunn Apartments close to the North End. It was a sad four-story affair on the corner. Not that it was in disrepair; it was constructed of new cheap brick – the kind that is too red to be authentic – and big cement moldings. It just didn't seem to fit in with the seasoned squalor around it; the sordid tenements seemed to have more class in their honesty. A fake stone sign read:

DUNN CONVALARIUM
ASSISTED LIVING RESIDENCE

There were a few parked cars in the lot, a failed water pump away
from our family wrecking yard, and most of the people we saw in
the street were black or Hispanic. They looked at our wrecker with
diffidence, but a few ogled the Fairlane in tow.

We parked with our flashers on and went up the four flights of
steps, looking for apartment 4-D. 'D as in David Niven,' Mom
had said.

I wasn't certain, but I thought 'convalarium' was some kind
of asylum and 'assisted living' another name for a Rest Home.
The residents we passed however, did not look as elderly as they
did angry. A woman in a crash helmet came down the corridor,
squinting at my brother as she passed us and then stopping to turn
and watch us walk on.

'What kind of place is this?' I asked my brother. He shook his
head in response as we continued down the long hall which was
red all-weather carpet peppered with cigarette burns and the small
castings of a lapdog.

At 4-D as in David Niven, we hesitated and studied the plain
brown door. Like the brick exterior, it was sensibly economical,
a notch above plywood. We could hear music from inside: 'Roy
Orbison,' Danny Boy whispered to me as if this made things
legitimate. I wished we had taken my mother's counsel and brought
a Boston-Creme pie, something to have in hand. Danny Boy began
to knock, thought better of it but knocked anyway. There was no
response for a time and Danny Boy rapped harder.

The Roy Orbison music stopped. 'Fuck is it?' a voice resounded
from within. I feared I was going to pull a Cowardly Lion and run
the corridor distance before crashing out the far window. But this
place had no window at the end: just sheet rock.

'It's your cousins,' Danny Boy said but apparently the man within
did not hear.

'Mrs Moynihan? Is that you, you *miserable* old *bag*.'

'It's your cousin Dan Paradiso's sons: Danny and Nunzio.'

There was only silence at this. Danny Boy tried the door. It was
locked. 'Fuck you *want*?' the voice said, half angry, half pleading.

He graveled out something else but it was inaudible, maybe in Italian.

'Let's go, Danny,' I decided.

'Yep,' my brother said, turning quickly on his heel. But then there was a sound as the door unlatched from inside.

'Well?' the voice beckoned, full of vitriol. 'You going to come in?'

Danny and I stared at the door. I glanced over my shoulder and saw that the woman in the crash helmet was still standing in the corridor, looking back at us. It was like opening the trunk of the drive-in car all over again. But finally, my brother seized the knob.

We couldn't see him at first; the place was dark and looked like construction was never completed even though someone moved in, but never completely unpacked. It was a one-bedroom flat with a kitchenette full of dirty crockery and empty cans. As we stepped in deeper – me behind my brother – I could see, in the vents of sunlight coming in through metal Venetian blinds, a man in a wheelchair. He sat there, a wilted figure with hair Arab-black that had once been cut brutally short but had grown out revealing some flecks of steel wool at the temples. He was staring at us with fierce hawk-like eyes – one brow encircled by a quarter-moon scar – and there was no doubt that he was related to us because he had the *Mezzogiorno* eyes, the heavy, lazy Valentinos. In fact, it seemed to me I had seen him once and long ago at some family wedding or funeral, or maybe even at one of our Fourth of July gatherings on the beach. He wore a bright and gaudy shirt with a flowered pattern and a wide late 1960s collar; it was unbuttoned down to his solar plexus, revealing a concave chest under a lewd patch of hair and he wore, on a gold chain, the *corno*. My grandmother must have gotten to him years back, I reasoned. Near his head was an eight-inch long horizontal tube and a small control stick, connected to his wheelchair. There was a terrible scent in the room, like that of a wet animal. I tried not to look directly at him as my mother had taught me to do in the presence of the handicapped.

'We weren't sure you still lived here,' Danny Boy marked time.

'Who'd you say you are? You ain't with Easter Seals?'

'No, I'm your Cousin Dan's son. Dan Junior – Danny Boy.'

A silence swallowed up the room and Angelo's eyes went through several changes, never once removing them from my brother.

'Holy Christ, Dan's kid?' the quadriplegic said. 'I haven't seen that cheap fuck in seven years – you were just a baby.' He jerked his chin toward me. 'Who's the pipsqueak?'

'My brother Nunzio.'

'What, are you selling pecan sandies for Little League? I don't get it.' He was wire-high, my father's cousin, an explosive man confined to a chair with a tube to move himself about.

'We wanted to talk,' Danny said.

Angelo Volpe raised a dark eyebrow and cast a suspicious gaze back and forth between me and my brother. His Adam's apple went taut and for a moment it looked as though he was going to wing a hawker at us. Instead, he smiled and made a little sarcastic chortle in his throat.

'You want to *talk*?' He turned his head toward nobody and made a sound like bitter laughter. 'How do you like my pad? Go home and tell the old man about my palatial suite. Mayor Dunn, the drunk Irishman, had the place built for old Social Security people, but he couldn't get them in. You know why? Because he built the place near the *Zootzoon* section. So what do they do with a four-story building put up with Social Security funding? They funnel in the handicapped like me, funnel 'em in, Dunny! Spill in the overflow from Middletown and Southbury training school – the fucking nutcases, the screw-loose,' and here our distant cousin pursed his lips and looked hard at us as if to make sure we registered his point. 'This is the dumping ground, boys. Have a *seat*.'

I was impressed by this man even as he frightened me into a tremble. One thing was for certain: no matter what kind of sleuth Angelo Volpe may have been years past, he was in no condition to chase a killer, and we would do well by ourselves to sign out – fast.

'You're lucky to be alive, I guess.' Danny Boy prodded the silence.

'Seven stories down, ass-over-teacups, straight through the roof of a Le Mans, you bet your ass I'm lucky – still got a piece of sheet metal in my spine. What do they tell you at the junkyard? 'Bout how it happened?'

'They say ... you jumped,' Danny Boy said. This was the first time I heard this, and Angelo smirked and squared his eyes on my reaction. He jerked his nose upward toward me, his eyes smiling, but not his mouth. I noticed then there was a spread deck of playing cards on the tray attached to his chair.

'He jumped, bad Angie. Got caught up in dirty deals and tried to do himself in, now he's in a chair. Did they call me the *Mamone?*'

'Yeah,' I volunteered and wished I hadn't. But Angelo nodded, satisfied.

'Nobody knows the truth cause nobody ever came to see me. No flowers, no nothing. *Uguatz,*' he said. 'Nothing.'

Now I really wished we had brought him a Boston-Creme pie. Pecan sandies, even. Because Cousin Angelo was working himself purple in the neck.

'Lights went out at the site, five, six guys get a hold of me. Now, I'm not a small man,' he said, but looking at him there, I could see he was never a big man. 'I'm giving them the, you know, the business over here, and they drag me across the room, bring me to the window and out I go, seven stories down, no parachute, not a prayer, Mother*fuckers.*'

'Who?' Danny Boy asked. 'Who did it?'

'The *cops,*' Angelo said as if my brother had asked an inane question.

'But *you* were a cop,' I said.

'That's right. But I wouldn't take no payoffs or nothing like that. And I was going to blow the whistle on the whole city department, all the fucking Irish pricks.'

'Why'd they throw you off a bridge?' My voice sounded too young, too high to be involved with the big boys.

'I just told you,' he snapped, showing no clemency toward my age. 'And it wasn't a bridge. They threw me off the cupola of the Big Clock where I did night patrol. I bet that Le Mans is still up your old man's junkyard with my C-1 vertebrae in the roof.'

We were silent and Angelo could see Danny wasn't satisfied. As for me, I could not remove my eyes from the man's wilted legs and rigid arms, hard as I tried.

'They had to get rid of me, I was a walking fucking cherry bomb.'

'Like Serpico?' Danny Boy asked.

'Fuck Serpico,' Angelo said bitterly, and then he grew pensive as if thinking back on better days. 'Can I get you a glass of water or something?' he asked, halfheartedly and with a breath of resentment.

'No,' Danny Boy said firmly.

'I'd like one,' I said before my brother could give me an eye. My mother had taught me that it was impolite to refuse an offer of food or drink.

Danny Boy fidgeted. 'I'll get it.'

'No, you're my guest. I offer you a drink, I bring the fucking drink to you. You're my fucking guest.'

Danny Boy squinted at him and Angelo seemed to challenge him with a fierce stare. 'You got a problem, kid?'

'No, no problem,' Danny Boy said, growing testy himself. 'It's just that you—'

'I what, Danny? I can't move? Is that what you're trying to say?'

'Yeah.'

'How's a fucking quad going to get me a glass of water? That what we're saying over here?'

We had been Dutch-uncling enough and it was time to shake some fruit from the bough however withered. Because something was troubling me, too. 'How did you unlock the door for us?' I asked.

Danny Boy cut a quick look at the door, stared at it like trying to unscramble a puzzle.

'Ah,' Angelo said. 'How did I unlock the door?'

'Yeah, how *did* you?' Danny said, baffled. 'You'd have to get up.'

'How did I unlock the door, Danny Boy?'

Surely my grandfather hadn't sold him some electrical door-lock invention – Grandpa despised the *Mamone*. And now my eyes fell onto the playing cards again: they were arranged in ten neat piles, face up. He had been playing a game my mother liked, one she called 'Napoleon at St Helena'.

'Do you believe in magic, Danny?' he pressed my brother.

'You mean,' Danny Boy finally said, 'you can *walk*?'

Angelo winked quickly, almost imperceptibly.

'You can get up out of that chair, can't you?'

I took a step closer to my brother. 'You're playing solitaire. You can move your arms.'

'No,' Angelo said. 'I'll never walk again. But I can dance with Ruby Lee!'

What ensued was so startling, both my brother and I yelled out like we had taken a tandem leak onto an electric cattle fence. Goomba Angelo yelled, 'Ruby Lee!' again, and now from out of the dark bedroom there was a skreak and a rattling metal sound as a small animal burst forth on four legs and entered the room. At first I thought it was a cat, but it moved too quickly. And when it launched itself onto the arm of Angelo's wheelchair, I saw that it wasn't a puppy either.

It yawned then scratched its ear with a back leg.

It was a small monkey.

A real, genuine, white-crested capuchin monkey, calico with a yellowish crown as brushy as an outgrown crewcut.

'Jesus!' Danny Boy remarked, watching the capuchin twist its lithe little body and begin licking itself clean with a tiny red and furious tongue. Its movements were quick and restive; one moment it was on the left arm of the wheelchair, the next on the headrest, its tail groping like a fifth limb; and then onto Angelo's lap where it sat as attentive as a bird dog.

'What is it?' Danny Boy asked, backing toward the wall.

'A squirrel monkey,' our cousin said, clearly delighted by our reactions.

'It's a capuchin,' I corrected. 'That's a real capuchin monkey.'

'Who the hell are you? The monkey expert over here?' the man spit. 'It's a squirrel monkey. Now: watch this.'

Angelo tipped his head back to see his pet. 'Ruby,' he cooed to her. 'You ready, Rube? Papa's thirsty. AQUA!' Angelo yowled and the capuchin flung itself to the linoleum, slid a few yards and climbed crablike with dexterity and skill, up the kitchenette counter where it turned to study us with its clever face, its tiny human eyes, watery and shining like polished Formica slivers.

Angelo took the long tube in his mouth and half-mooned his chair so he could see the monkey take up the cup in its small black hands and feet and descend into the sink basin where it turned on the water, filled the cup up to a marked line, then slid down a small chute, doing a strange front-heavy skitter on its hindlegs and chattering. The monkey brought the cup to Angelo's tray. It was half-empty now, but still a cup of water.

'Wow,' was my response.

'Holy shit,' was my brother's.

'Where'd you find it?' I asked.

Angelo told us, with a touch of pride, that every nurse he'd had quit on him, finding him too difficult to tend to. Finally the state sent a woman from Easter Seals who informed him about a program out of a Boston research center that trained and utilized capuchin monkeys to aid the disabled. They felt he was a perfect candidate.

'A blind man gets a seeing-eye dog,' he said to Danny. 'An old guy gets a cat to calm his nerves, a quad like me gets a service monkey. I hate fucking animals so I tell the woman: "*Get the thing OUT.*" But she leaves it with me. So I'm trapped in here with a goddamned *scimmia*, a monkey. It starts combing my hair. I say, "Get a book," it brings me a book, turns the pages. Alls a sudden, I got hands again. You want to talk about man's best friend? This fucking monkey is my *life*.'

The monkey went to his head and put her face in his ear as if looking for a trinket in a conch shell. The crippled man pursed his lips toward her and talked softly. It was a pleasing change of tone. Angelo told us she was female, and although she came with the name Number 9, he named her Ruby Lee after a 1956 B.B. King record. He said it was the first song he got lucky to, and when the monkey came, he felt it was the last time he might ever know luck again.

'Ruby Lee combs my hair – don't you, Ruby? She washes my face and feet, feeds me, puts 8-tracks in, cleans my ears, and she's getting very close to making what I consider the finest Harvey Wallbanger in the city. But don't let Easter Seals know that.'

I was breathless; I had never seen anything like this and neither had my brother.

'Klondike,' Angelo said to the monkey suddenly. In an instant she was on the tray, working her tiny black fingers on the tableau of playing cards. She freed an ace from the stock pile and pushed it into a row above the other cards. The monkey had been trained to deal solitaire for the quadriplegic.

'Mrs Moynihan comes a few times a week with her orderlies, two big dykes, to give me a fleet enema. I'm going to scare her off though, the tight broad. I been training Ruby to jump on a pair of slacks and bite it in the ass.'

Angelo laughed for the first time and I saw that, aside from a faintly discolored incisor, he had excellent teeth like my dad.

'She gets ruffled, old Moynihan, but believe you me that's the most affection that broad gets all week. Now what the fuck is it you guys want, now that you know how the *Mamone* survives in this mean ol' world?'

He had the most musical way of speaking I had ever heard in my life, though it wasn't a sweet music: it built to staccato tempos and crescendoed, thundered almost, like Beethoven going deaf I imagined, and attacking the keys so God would hear his fortissimo. Only *fortissimo* wasn't the F word Goomba Angelo used like a tambourine.

'Klondike!' he yelled, hoarse, at the climax of his diatribe, and Ruby Lee turned over another card, a three of spades that displeased our third cousin. 'Spade motherfucker,' he cursed.

A silence hung in the room as we tried to gather our bearings.

'Come on, boys, spit it out. No one's come to see me in seven years and all a suddens you're knocking on my door. What you selling?'

'We need help,' I said.

'*You* need help?'

'We have a family problem,' I said.

'What is this, a joke? What fucking family?'

Danny Boy was trying to quiet me. He stepped in and said, 'We need a little advice, that's all. From somebody with connections to law enforcement. And it can't go out of the family. That's why we're here.' Danny Boy had one foot angled to make a move for the door if necessary.

'And what is this family problem?' said our crippled blood relation.

'We think we know where there's a dead body, and we want to know who it is.'

'Dead body,' he said. 'Where's this?'

My brother and I looked at each other. This was it: fish, cut bait, or run for the wrecker.

'In the junkyard,' Danny Boy quietly allowed.

Angelo smiled. The monkey, sitting on the arm of the wheelchair, was staring at his face and she seemed to be resisting an urge to finger the cripple's eyebrows, like picking lice from one of her own kind.

'You're shittin' me,' said Angelo.

'We think it's in the trunk of a '73 Pontiac.'

'Four-door, hardtop,' I amended.

'Uh-huh. Why didn't the old man call the police, have them come down and take a look?'

''Cuz he don't believe me,' I said.

'Do you fucking blame him?'

'And because,' said Danny, 'the body's not exactly . . . accessible right now.'

'How so?'

'It went through The Crusher.'

Angelo did a take. Danny Boy fidgeted then lit himself a Kool.

'We don't want some big public foofooraw that gets our dad in trouble with the Motor Vehicle Department,' Danny said. 'We just want some help to find out who the guy is.'

Angelo ruminated for a few seconds. 'Motor Vehicle Department?'

His laughter made Danny Boy tighten his lips and glare resentfully at me.

'Did your old man send you up here to fuck with me?' Angelo said.

'No way.'

'There's a body in a crushed car? A compressed dead guy?'

'Look,' Danny Boy said. 'Nunzio saw the body, I found some evidence. I found a, uh, what do you call it, a bullet casing.'

'Numb Nuts saw him, you found some evidence – and what the flying fuck does this have to do with *me*?'

'You were a cop.' I broke the static.

'Yeah. Traffic. Could've made detective. But they had to hire so many *zootzoons* a year.'

'You would have made a good detective,' I observed. 'Having been a Pinkerton Man.'

I half-expected Angelo to regard me with pride, but instead he looked at me like I was wearing Mickey Mouse ears.

'I was a *what*?'

'You were a certified uniformed officer with the Pinkerton Agency. I saw it in Nonni's scrapbook. Your head was ripped off but I know it was you.'

'Oh, yeah, Pinkerton. I did a little security job before I got in the Academy. Why the fuck you so interested in Pinkerton?'

'They caught John Wilkes Booth,' I said.

Angelo looked at me with his mouth slightly agape and suddenly he appeared to be the one finding *us* strange. He struggled to get his mouth to the long tube then took it in his teeth and blew steadily. He motored himself slowly across the room to the window. Sitting there with his back to us, he said, 'Okay, you want my assessment? You got a problem, fellas. Well, *several* problems. One: how do you ID a body that's been through a car crusher? Two: how do you solve a murder without putting your own father in the slam for stowing a stiff, leave alone get him a citation from the DMV? Three: you want to keep it in the family. *Che famiglia*? What family? Now you want me in the family alls a sudden, and finally, number three—'

'Number four,' I corrected him.

'Number four: DOORBELL,' he yelled and Ruby Lee scrambled to the door, scaled a little stepladder and fumbled with the chain. We were being invited to leave.

'Get the fuck out. And if you come back, you're going to see what I'm teaching Ruby Lee to do with a .38 Chief Special.'

I did not take this lightly. There were, indeed, what looked like fist-shaped, black powder impressions in the sheet rock. Embarrassed, bewildered, sick from the scent of primate and cheap cigar smoke, I followed my brother toward the door.

'Kid,' Angelo called after me. When I half-turned, he put those eyes on me again. 'Tell your father, "Fuck you. Love, Angelo".'

The door locked behind us. Fuck you; Love, Angelo.

The man, like Mayor Longo, was terse and to the point.

Out in the hall I considered the manure on the carpet again. It was not the castings of a small dog as I had thought: it was monkey scat. I wondered what the other residents thought of our cousin's live-in aide on loan from Boston, loping out to get the *Saukiwog American*. But I didn't stick around to speculate too long; the woman with the helmet was starting back the way she came, her jaw set like a bull terrier.

'Are you satisfied now, Nunzi?' Danny Boy said when we reached the curb. He looked equal parts angry and frightened. 'There's your Pinkerton Man, your Eye Who Never Sleeps. Goomba Angelo.'

I said nothing. Hands in my pocket, I looked up at the building, afraid this cousin of my father's was going to be peering down his big crow's nose at us, winging more verbal abuse and obscenities. It was raining and some black children were running with a large sheet of cardboard over their heads, laughing. Danny Boy and I wasted no time in boarding the wrecker. Dad was going to be looking for us and so we hammered our way toward Route 8, desperate to get our new buffalo home.

As I double-checked the Fairlane out of habit, I saw a car parked behind us, back some thirty feet. It was a two-toned Plymouth and someone behind the wheel was watching us. A black man, just staring. Danny Boy upshifted and moved us south. Thankfully, the Plymouth didn't follow.

Up on the highway, I could see the Big Clock on the skyline and I tried not to imagine a man falling from it, years ago, in the dark of night. 'Hey, Danny,' I said. 'Whose godfather is he anyway?'

Danny Boy looked at me, surprised for a moment.

'Yours.'

Driving home with Dad later, things were more quiet than usual. No philosophy. No radio. No sparring with Danny Boy.

We just drove along, the three of us, and I wondered if Dad had suspicions about what Danny Boy had in the brown paper bag between his army boots. I also wondered if Big Dan was suspicious about our whereabouts earlier in the day. We were gone for three hours just to tow a car and have lunch. Danny Boy told him we'd stopped for donuts. But Dad was distracted and he appeared in the same state now as he fiddled with the radio knob and stopped on a Pink Floyd song.

'That's good,' Danny Boy said.

Dad listened for a time and his brow began to furrow. 'I don't want to say nothing, but that is very depressing music.' He turned it off and looked at Danny as if to see if there'd be protest over who controlled the AM airwaves. The case was closed. No radio today.

'I seen Cheryl on the Green,' Big Dan said, after a silence.

'Yeah,' Danny said, looking off at the river. 'I seen her, too.'

'Home from Yale.'

'That's right.'

'Yale.'

'I can't wait for Yale to play Colgate, man,' I proffered. 'That should be a freaking war.'

They both ignored me.

'Pre-Law,' Dad said. 'Class. She's got what they call *class*.'

'Who's *they*?' Danny said.

'You gonna call her?'

Danny reached over and turned Pink Floyd back on.

Dad switched it off.

In The Little Boot, where the sun was still high like a long Arctic summer, some kids were clustered street side between the church and Crocco's Market. They were sitting on old lumber and cinder blocks, their bikes parked in a neat row. Holding court before them was Monica Lafontaine. She had on her standard cutoff denims and her legs were sun-browned; her Grateful Dead T-shirt was a plain beige but what was inside seemed to move like water balloons every time she plowed her fingers through her brown hair and licked the run-off from a toasted almond ice cream bar.

Eddie Coco was the only Italian kid amongst them, and being a strict Catholic, he was the only boy not looking at Monica Lafontaine. Instead, he tinkered with a combination lock for his bike and looked embarrassed. Tom-Tom Renkunis, a Lithuanian, and the Doyle Brothers, although Irish and Catholic, too, had no qualms about where they rested their eyes.

When we drove past in the wrecker, Eddie looked up and one of the Doyle Brothers yelled something to acknowledge my passing. I only heard my last name shouted and Monica dipped her head so her hair fell over one eye and she inserted the empty ice-cream stick, like a tongue depressor, into her mouth.

And then they were behind me in sunspots and cigarette smoke. But they hadn't made five bucks like I had. They hadn't found a box of old Nick Savage comics, they hadn't gotten a last look at the Mattatuck Drive-In, nor had they been served a cup of cool city water by a state-certified capuchin monkey trained to assist a handicapped ex-Pinkerton officer.

But I wanted to be with them.

A terrible thought jumped me in the shower: what if Monica Lafontaine was giving hand-jobs and I was missing out? What if Eddie Coco had been sitting there, looking guilty as he rolled his combination lock because he had been in his bedroom with Monica, showing her our caterpillars molting and pupating. I went through a metamorphis myself: I changed into some Sears Toughskin jeans that once belonged to a smaller kid than me; aside from some battery acid holes, they fit like a catcher's mitt, and I tucked the cuffs inside my used Puma Clydes; I tried on a tank top but I looked painfully scrawny, so I settled on a baggy black T-shirt with the legend *S.W.A.T.* after the TV show.

'Are you okay, laddie?' Mom was standing in the door.

'Sure,' I said. 'I'm fine, Mom.'

'You don't look yourself. You didn't eat a bun.'

'I'm okay,' I said. Mom lingered a moment, arms folded. She sniffed with an allergy then started away. 'Mom?'

She stopped in the doorway, deep in thought as if ruminating on my problem. If there was anyone in the world I could trust, it was my small, rosy-cheeked mother who was the first daughter of the seventh son of a seventh son, and who had seen the Loch Ness Monster as a child, and didn't care a hoot who laughed at her claim.

'Do you believe me about what I saw in the trunk of that car?'

Mom removed her eyeglasses that she wore on occasion, cleaned them carefully on her red apron. 'Nunzio, I want to. But I canna.'

'Why not?'

'I just don't believe that the world is as bad as the news makes it out to be, or these new movies. I just don't believe anyone around here would have that kind of wae murk in their hearts. And I don't want to see you become distrustful of people, like your father is. I want you to get on your skateboard and hurry over to the school lot and play a guid-willie game of kickball with the other boys.'

I was sitting at my box of archaeology finds, busying my hands with trinkets. Mom sat beside me, tucking her apron. She looked over her glasses into the shoebox and nodded thoughtfully. 'Your brother Danny was the same way,' she said. 'From the time he could walk in the backyard, he brought home bottle caps that caught his fancy, or a blue jay's feather, or an old cork. What is it about boys that they collect dried dragonflies and old spark plugs and snake skin or rusty keys to doors they'll never open?'

Her voice soothed me as it always had; I was an Italian kid, but the first voice I ever heard was the Scots burr of a Lowlander. 'Curios and bric à brac and tackets and twalpennies, and rigwoodie wonders seen through the bottom of an old Kickapoo medicine bottle the color of amber. I don't think it's just bric à brac, son.'

I nodded even as I held the brass token and divined its magic.

'Talismans,' she said. 'Things that are real and certain in an uncertain world. Lucky charms. That's what they are, your red cigarette packs with yellow dragons and your brass coins and plastic tiger heads. Lucky charms, aye.'

'Cool,' I said, and Mom's face crinkled into a grin that could soften a boar's bristles.

'Cool, aye,' she said again. 'It will all come right in the wash, love. Hold fast to your talismans and they'll protect you from the bigger world outside this room. And never stop looking at the sky through the bottom of an old Kickapoo medicine bottle the color of amber.'

'I won't, Mom. Never.'

She gave me a hug and kissed the crown of my head. When she left, I dug through boxes of 1950s can openers, old broken watches, cut-plug tobacco containers, a pocketful of gravel I took from the old Drive-In, and four dozen rare and assorted gems and salvages. I found a talisman: a pair of Wayfarers in fair condition. I put them on and started out. Then stopped. Something was troubling me. I went back to the box, dug in again and found the small hat pin I had salvaged from the Pontiac. I lifted the little worn brass globe that said Chicago. My heart did a roll and I had to sit on the edge of my bed to examine the brooch. Under lamplight I could see the faded words *Chicago Teamsters* set over a cryptic number. Danny Boy's voice was running through my head like an Amtrak: *Jimmy Hoffa was a gangster or something from Detroit or . . . Chicago.*

I had believed what Mom said about talismans and lucky charms, but this curio took on the tepid feel of bad juju. So I dropped it, just let it go back into the shoe box of spark plugs and golf tees and used eyeglasses. It was a crazy thought – like Danny Boy said, it could be Elvis for all we knew – to think that someone would drive a guy from Chicago, dead or alive, to a small mill town on the East Coast. But there it was: *1973 Chicago Teamsters* and the number *24182510.*

Out in the garden I touched the ceramic hand of the Blessed Mary then set off across the verdant yards with my skateboard under an arm. The sun was starting to die back somewhere off near Maple Hill and the big cross, and as I boarded down America Street a slender crescent moon gathered low and the air felt like it may have cooled a full degree. I crossed America and did a rowdy slalom around some younger children playing on the sidewalk, then skitched the rear bumper of a small Honda and let it carry me two miles down to one of the Renaissance Projects where I expected Eddie and the others to go before dark. But they'd come and gone. All that remained amongst the rust-hulk ridges for any archaeological dig was the wooden stick from Monica's toasted almond, licked clean and bearing a series of teethmarks where she let out some tension.

I circled the old metalwork's building as it got dark and the air cooled, but I found no further trace of the brown-legged girl from Genoa Street. Not even a scent of Breck for Oily Hair which is what I saw her mother buy at Pathmark once. A lonely funk came over me and I felt the need to pick up a stone and break one of the windows that the kids hadn't hit yet.

So I did.

And then I felt guilty.

This was one of the last mills to close and it still had a big cut-and-draw press on the floor, albeit dormant and rust-heavy. They used to make the shell for diesel injector tubes in there, Dad had told me on more than one occasion when we drove past it.

I coasted down the alley between the press mill and one of its outbuildings to slalom around small heaps of removed asbestos and piles of old rotten spruce; during the days while I labored in the junkyard, demolition crews were laying the wrecking ball to the Old Fort as we kids called it, just as they demolished the Drive-In and the beautiful ruins of United Brass. I looked up at the broken windows from another angle, from the west side where the lowering sun gave the bricks the soft pastel look of my Cousin Pina's rouge. They used to make the shell for diesel injector tubes. It sounded ludicrous to me: so many people sweating and leaving fingers behind to manufacture such a tiny and abstract piece of the machine that made the country run.

Mr Paternostro, who could be seen every Saturday pushing his granddaughter in a baby carriage up Mary Street, was one of the people who had worked the cut-and-draw press. If we caught him in the right mood, he would take a delight in showing us his right hand: it had only the last two fingers, but the scar tissue where his thumb once was had a heavy callous and gave the impression of a lobster claw. He told Eddie and I once that the shop paid him eighty dollars for his loss. He did not seem bitter however, using his lobster claw to push his granddaughter down St Mary and up along America. I was thinking of him now as I studied the shell of the dead mill. We kids looked at old folks like him, the erstwhile mill hands, as historical curiosities wandering our neighborhoods; like veterans of some long ago war, all wounded.

And then a car stopped at the opposite mouth of the alley. I looked back and saw it slowly reverse; I knew the car, a big land barge, but from where? As it reversed into view I made the connection: it was the green and white Plymouth Fury with some rust on the rocker panels that I had seen in the North End. I knew it was the same car; my stomach shilly-shallied.

The Fury dropped back a pace and negotiated a careful turn down the alley. I did not like the way the big gas-guzzler was easing in behind me. And that's when the gravity of the moment kicked in. I was being followed; the car slowed when I slowed, gassed it when I picked up the pace. I pushed off hard and got my board moving, but the Fury kept stride, 4-barrelling and knocking. The engine sounded like it had carb trouble and I considered the possibility that it was one of the death cars from the yard, stalking me. Indeed it looked like it had been through hell and bumper cars; if the *Strega* and *mal'occh'* could follow emigrants from the Old Country, why couldn't a ghost car follow me home from The Bone Yard?

I abandoned my board, began to run.

The Plymouth laid rubber; the motor, my trained ear decided, was 275 horse – a race I was sure to lose. And when I turned on my Clydes into a defunct loading area, it fishtailed in with me, straining so hard it sounded like it was going to drop its transmission. I stopped hard, had to see it for myself.

The driver was a black man.

This filled me with dread. Perhaps I stuck my nose where I shouldn't have and I was going to be trussed and driven to Maple Hill and shot four times at the plaster feet of *The Three Wise Men*.

Running blind, I slammed into a rusted fence. The Fury skidded sideways, lost a hubcap, and lurched hard on its torsion bar when the driver jammed into park.

I scaled the fence like a cat but whoever was chasing me ran faster than I could climb. A hand grabbed the waist of my Toughskins and another hand, black as the night, wrapped around my leg. Whoever it was had a vicious grip. I came down on my backside.

Hard.

It was not a man standing over me, but a large dark woman who wore her hair in a crewcut. Closer now, I saw an earring in each lobe. She was no man, just big. Her windbreaker was maroon and she wore tight blue jeans that looked like they had been fitted over the rear legs of a draft horse.

The fact that she was a woman did not ease my fears. She had wide shoulders on her and I wondered if she, too, had hauled bags of peat moss like my grandmother.

'I didn't do nothing,' I stuttered.

'Talk to the hand,' she ordered me. And when I tried to speak again she held up one of her big pink palms like she was going to straight-arm me. 'Talk to the hand.'

This, I deciphered, meant she wanted me to remain silent.

'My father's waiting for me, I—'

'Don't even go up that road,' she snapped.

'What road?'

'Into where you're going with this Daddy and Mommy story.'

'What do you want from me?' I shivered, and I had crawled as far against the fence as I could.

'What do I want? From you?' Here the muscular woman bent close to me and looked into my face. Her eyes were as serene as Mother Cabrini's. But then she shrieked so loudly, I felt my eardrums go.

She began to sing.

'R.E.S.P.E.C.T!' she belted out and I knew they must have been hearing her all the way over at Crocco's Market. With one hand held out in a limp hang and the other pointing a long finger down at me, she sang for what seemed to be a full-bore minute. I held my breath through the arcane event, praying for rescue. There would be none. Now when the song came back around to the R.E.S.P.E.C.T part, she wagged that long finger at me in a gesture of admonishment. When she finished, she seemed to expect me to comment on her facility. But all I could do was hyperventilate like a hunted dog.

'That's what I want,' she said. 'Respect.'

'Okay.'

''Cuz I know who you be, little man,' she said, catching her own breath. 'Be the boy who seen too much of something he shunt never ever seen. Now get up and get your skinny ass in that car.'

I just stared at her, knowing that an ice pick was next. She tried to read my eyes. I lowered them. And then, after a silence in which she chuffed hard from running, she grabbed me by the T-shirt and yanked me toward the Plymouth.

'Get in the car, Blue Eyes,' she ordered.

'Okay,' I said. And as she marched me toward the Fury I wondered if I was going in the trunk. Just as she loosened her grip, I made a move like Mercury Morris and bolted. She tripped me. Then pulled me, by my hair, to my feet. 'Respect,' she whispered.

'Yes, ma'am,' I said.

'She work hard for the money,' she added.

'Yes, ma'am,' I said again.

She opened the rear door of the Plymouth and shoved me in. And there was Cousin Angelo, sitting like a wilted plant, strapped erect by the safety belt. 'Oh, man,' I breathed, relieved. But angry, too. I wanted to threaten them both, tell them they could get in big trouble for this. But neither looked like that would mean much to them.

Ruby Lee, the capuchin, was on Angelo's lap and I could see, out the rear windscreen, that the trunk-lid was half opened and his wheelchair most likely folded inside.

'Don't let Johnny scare you,' he said as the big woman shut the door and got in behind the wheel. She sat back against wooden massage rollers and I could see some kind of meter on the dash. 'She's a gypsy cabby. She's my wheel-man.'

'Wheel-*woman*,' she corrected.

'She's a hot-sketch, you oughta hear her sing.'

'I did,' I assured him. Johnny the gypsy cabby sat idle, looking at me in her rearview. Aside from being a woman of size she was handsome with strong bones. With her butch cut and wide shoulders I wondered if perhaps she didn't, like Holly, shave his legs and then he was a she.

'She's going to be singing up the Swizzle Stick someday, watch.'

'You know it, too,' she said with a touch of bitterness; she was putting on some lipstick the color of blueberries. And then she made a sudden movement. A sound went off like a gun: the Plymouth Fury had electric door locks and she kicked them all in. We were going nowhere, parked like lovers in the loading area between the mills and old clockworks. The last traces of sunlight were coming through one of the boarded-up windows on a building. It would be dark in minutes.

'I was hoping to find the other one. Your brother.'

'He's at an audition,' I said, and this made Johnny look at me in the mirror again.

'Where he auditionin'?' she asked.

'We went by your house,' Angelo said. 'I seen your father. You know what he was doing? He was standing in the grass with a garden hose looking up at the clouds to see if it was going to rain so he wouldn't have to waste any water. Cheap cock-knocker.'

This type of talk against my father would get anyone a punch in the chops. But I didn't think it was a good time lest I raised the ire of man, woman or capuchin. I just sat there, heart going like a hummingbird.

'You go to the cops yet?'

'No.'

'Good boy. Smart. He smart, Johnny?'

She sucked her teeth, checked them in her mirror.

Angelo watched my eyes as they fixed on the monkey, the interior of the Plymouth, the Judge's Cave cigar sticking out his front pocket. 'Light me,' he said. And so I did. 'No offense before, kid, all right?'

'No, there's no . . .' I couldn't find the word I wanted because I was still looking at the locked door and worrying.

'What you and your brother paying? For a dick?'

'For a *what*?'

'A gumshoe. Private dick.'

'Oh, I don't know. You gotta talk to my brother.'

'Look,' Angelo sounded slightly irate now. 'You guys are Pop Warner League. You want to pry dentalwork from a crushed Pontiac, you better cough up some incentive here.'

'I'll talk to Danny Boy.'

'You tell Danny Boy I need three hundred bucks.'

'Three hundred bucks?'

'Half up front.'

'Where are we going to get three hundred dollars?'

'That's for you to figure out. *You* came to me, right? You want a Pinkerton Man? I'll do the job. Three hundred bucks.'

Johnny the gypsy cabby shook with a silent laugh. I didn't like this at all.

'Three hundred bucks,' Angelo repeated, 'or a coach ticket down to South Carolina. Myrtle Beach.'

'Myrtle Beach?' Johnny turned. She wasn't laughing any more. 'I thought you wanna go to Nag Head.'

'Yeah, well maybe I wanna expand my horizons.'

I needed to stop them before they got too far ahead of themselves.

'I make five bucks a day,' I confessed. 'Danny Boy makes ten. That'll be our whole summer's pay.'

'You don't have to do this, kid. You can go right down to the station and tell Chief O'Brian about the body in your father's salvage yard. Or, you can forget about it.' Angelo pivoted his head and set that inflamed eye on me, heavy with bags and traces of scar tissue. 'Cat got your tongue?'

'No. Your monkey's got my sneaker.'

Indeed, little Ruby had unraveled the laces on my Puma Clyde and was chewing on the small plastic doo-hickey on the end of the laces. I wasn't sure what Angelo Volpe was staring at until he lowered his head and squinted at my T-shirt. 'SWAT?'

'Yeah.'

'Are you on a SWAT team?'

'No.'

'Sure you are, you're on mine. Me, you, Danny Boy and our wheel-woman here, the chanteuse herself.'

'Don't throw my name in the hat, Motherfucker,' Johnny said to her mirror.

'Do you know why I'm taking this case?' asked Angelo. The sky was near dark now.

'You need three hundred bucks? So you can go to Myrtle Beach.'

'No, Smarty-Smarts, ain't the money. Ain't Myrtle Beach. It's the *case*.' When he had my full attention, he glared hard with those eyes, black and shiny as the oil-cured olives behind glass at Coangelo's Market. 'First I thought you guys was a couple nut balls. But you had this look in your eye when you left, see. I *know* that look. When you work traffic, you get called to a lot of accidents. I seen dead guys. I seen guys with guardrails that were – never mind. But I *know*. Look at me, Numb Nuts. I *know* when someone else has seen a dead guy, *capisce*? So I put the feelers out to Ginny down the station. I ask her what they got in terms of active Missing Person reports. There was an old guy ran away from the Rest Home—'

'Papa Coco. They found him.'

'That's right, they found him. And they found a sixteen-year-old runaway girl at her stepfather's in Naugatuck. But who haven't they ever found? Who's still missing?'

'Jimmy Hoffa,' I said, certain I had the right answer.

'You a wise ass?'

'No.'

'Then answer me over here. Who's still missing in the city?'

'I don't *know*.'

'A guy from the South End – Puerto Rican named Diaz – went on a fishing trip to Maine two weeks ago, never came home.'

'Really?'

'Yes, really.'

A lull settled in the Plymouth. Johnny's eyes lifted onto the rearview.

'Show him, Johnny,' Angelo said.

Johnny handed something back to me, a flyer with a Xeroxed photo and uneven handwriting across the top. The photo was of an old man, caught by flash as he turned with a fish in his hands; it was a poor-quality photo and worse quality Xerox.

'That the man you seen in the trunk?' Angelo asked, his oil-cured eyes out on the alley.

'I don't know,' I said. It could have been, sometimes one old guy looked much like the next. Maybe the guy in the trunk had a little more hair – I wasn't sure. 'What's this say?'

'Spanish,' Johnny said. '*Spañol*. It says "missing".'

'Johnny got it off a phone pole in the South End last night.'

I said nothing, just stared at the flyer.

'So,' Angelo said, 'I call back Ginny in Records and says "Why didn't you tell me about the MPR?" That's Missing Puerto Rican in cop speak. And she says "'Cuz we're investigating the wife. The guy had a big life insurance policy through the Brotherhood of Carpenters".'

'See?' Johnny said, turning in her seat. 'He may have never left for Maine.'

'The wife,' Angelo said, 'may have paid a couple of niggers to shoot the fuck and get rid of the body.'

When he used the N word I looked up at the back of Johnny's crewcut, concerned. But she was laughing, undaunted by the crippled ex-cop's tongue. She seemed almost entertained as Angelo went on: 'So she could collect on the policy – are you following me? The insurance company's got Jew appraisers up in Caribou, Maine while the guy might be deader than the Pope's nuts in a crushed Pontiac just over the fucking hill, over there. Follow me?'

I was filled with terror but also a surge of hope. Maybe we were getting close to burying this dead man. Maybe this abrasive man, my father's second cousin, knew his stuff after all. He must've been a good Pink in his walking days, and chances are, he would have made a fine detective with the city.

'Goomba Angelo,' I said, and I wished I could stop making every word curl up at the end like a third grade question, but I could not. I was terrified.

'It ain't Jimmy Hoffa,' he said. 'This is Saukiwog. It's a dead spic carpenter whose old lady is banging the grocery boy, or the landlord or something. That's real life.'

'Whoever it was,' I said. 'It was awful to see.'

I helped Angelo with his cigar again. Johnny turned in her seat and regarded me with an unnerved eye like she was taking me serious for the first time. 'I mean,' I stammered, 'I seen dead frogs. I seen dead cats. Dead birds, you know, when they fly into the window. But I never seen—'

I noticed then that Johnny was staring at Angelo in the same restive way I was: she looked at me for a moment, turned around, then came back around again with her big shoulders, her eyes searching the backseat floor.

'Is that little motherfucker making whiz in my cab?'

'No, she's just scratching the floormat.'

'Yeah, well, when a cat's going to make whiz, it be scratching like that.'

'She ain't a cat! She starts scratching when she's nervous.'

'I'm the one nervous! It make any kind of whiz in my car, that Curious George motherfucker going to be more than nervous.'

'I told you before, Johnny: blind man's gotta be allowed to bring his dog in a restaurant and I'm allowed to bring my monkey in a fucking taxi cab. I got the papers.'

'Good. Put them on the floor so monkey piss on 'em.'

'What's your problem, Johnny?'

'Tell it to the hand, Angel. That chipmunk make potty in my backseat, he's going back to the Man with the Yellow Hat. Now tell the boy about the rest of the deal.'

This concerned me.

'The rest of the deal . . .' Angelo rummaged in his memory. 'Oh, yeah. Johnny here gets a new pair of tires.'

'Radials,' she said into the rearview. 'Radial ply.'

'Radial ply,' Angelo repeated slowly as if the words were delicious.

'Let me talk to my brother,' was my answer and I could see that this garnered the respect of both Angelo and the gypsy cabby.

'You know where to find me,' Angelo said after a time. 'I'm going to need the ID number off that Pontiac, and I'm going to need that spent shell. Toot sweet.'

'What's the little Dago's name?' Johnny asked the ex-cop.

'Numb Nuts,' he answered with his cigar in his teeth and I tried not to take offense at either of them. But maybe my name had finally been Americanized.

'Okay, Numb Nuts,' the black woman said. 'Mr Volpe gotta go. He need his medication.'

As I started out, Angelo said quietly, 'Hey, kid.'

When I hung my head back in the door and looked at him, he put his tired eyes on me and gave me a look that hinted at sympathy. 'We Never Sleep,' he said.

I hit the loading area, found my skateboard and kicked off, holding my cap on against a wind; I felt solace in the knowledge that we had a family sleuth on the case but I was uneasy in the gut. If the man in the Pontiac Bonneville *was* some Puerto Rican carpenter from the South End, someone had turned him into trunk drums and laid two bullets in his head, and that someone was waiting for our scrap shipment to leave the docks in three weeks. And if anyone got in the way of the plan, what kind of eruptions would occur? More murders? More bodies in trunks? If I hadn't gone to work that day would anybody know? Or would some barefoot woman in Japan be putting bread in her new toaster a year from now and suddenly see a man's ear pressed inside the metal?

A Puerto Rican carpenter named – *Diaz.*

The name stopped my mind from whirling while my board kept going west. *Diaz.* Was that what the old man in the trunk tried to say? Diaz, not *Dio.* Was he trying to tell me who he was before he died so his family would know? It made more sense than I wanted it to.

These were my thoughts as the night grew humid and The Little Boot took on the wet scent of squash blossoms and new mushrooms and Nonni's home-crafted sauce.

I sat on the porch, waiting for Danny Boy but he didn't come home before midnight.

*   *   *

'If I didn't get this part it's not about acting, it's about politics.'

Danny Boy was alive and ardent when I saw him in the morning. 'I nailed it! I'm Captain Lombard, man! And the chicks who read for the part of Vera? All college chicks. No skanks. Saukiwog Community *College* chicks. I smoked it, Nunzio! I gave the character a limp, put a stone in my shoe like Dustin Hoffman. The place went so quiet you could hear a fucking pin drop.'

He was limping in my room now, putting on his work clothes, looking out the window at the brimming gardens of a new day. I told him about the traumatic encounter near the Old Fort, about Johnny the gypsy cabby and Cousin Angelo's story about the missing man from the South End; I told him about the three-hundred bucks our cousin wanted.

'That's a lot of cash,' he murmured as he fastened his belt.

'He'll find out who's in the car, Danny. He talks like a real detective.'

As my brother fretted, he noticed something out the window. 'Oh, shit. Nunzi, go out to my car, get that off the dash.'

'Get what off the dash?'

'Just go, do it.'

I slipped on my work jeans and ran out barefoot to the driveway. Even from a distance I could see Danny Boy's concern now: on the passenger side dash, adhered to the windshield by some kind of gravity were a pair of tan panties. He had often sent me out to dump marijuana roaches from his ashtray or shove beer cans under the seat, but this was a new attraction. I slid into the Hornet and hesitated for a second before snatching his *goomare*'s plain underwear and stowing them in the glove box. It was there that I saw the Hellman's mayonnaise jar and its evil contents.

The canned oil and water was yellowish days before, but now it was taking on the hue of a brackish pond. It was brown and turbid and when I shook it like a snow dome there was a strange roiling within. I cradled it gingerly and was alarmed to find the jar warm to the touch. I turned it in my hands and tilted it, watching my brother's exorcised affliction slide murky like low tide at Milford Beach. There appeared to be a slug inside the jar, attached by suction. I wished my brother would get rid of it; driving around with the thing in his glove box seemed to me as risky as the guys carting explosives through the mountains in the old black-and-white foreign movie *Wages of Fear*. If the jar smashed, what Old Country evils would be unleashed? The thought alone made me bobble the container and I relieved myself of it, wedging it safely between Danny Boy's registration and the stray undergarment.

When I slid back out, Nonni was in the window next door, dusting under Little Tony.

She watched me down the length of her nose, moving her head slowly to the side as if trying to make sure I wore the horn. I gestured toward it and said, '*Il corno.*'

She closed the curtains.

CHAPTER NINE

Another Man's Treasure

I don't know when the idea to design a composite automobile egged at my grandfather, but as I entered the tarpaper shed and beheld the mechanical fusion I recalled a rainy day back when I was five or six and Danny Boy was fourteen and already a freshman football standout. It was after a lavish Sunday meal at our home and Grandpa had sat back on Dad's easy chair for a brandy, a good fart and a catnap. My brother and I were sprawled on the carpet watching a recycled episode of *Batman*, keeping the volume low so the old man could doze. But when Bruce Wayne drove the Batmobile out of his subterranean garage, Grandpa let out a little puzzled sigh as he released the heat of his brandy and said, 'This car . . . she's 'a strange.'

'It's the Batmobile, Gramps,' Danny Boy laughed, almost patronizingly.

Grandpa narrowed his eyes and studied the long black machine as it blazed through Gotham City. 'She's the Ford,' he said. Both Danny Boy and I chuckled – it was amusing, the old foreigner calling the Batmobile a Ford. But then he went on in his soothing, quiet timbre, 'She's'a five'a different Ford. The Ventura. She's'a five'a' different Ford'a Ventura. Five'a different year.'

Danny Boy lying on his back, looked upside down at our grandfather and I remember it was a look of amazement. And when the Batmobile roared down a back alley after the Riddler, Grandpa closed his eyes like he was tasting a new batch of wine and said, 'Ah. V-8. Three hundred'a horse.'

Grandpa may have been a peasant from the Old Country but he could dissect any man made machine just by listening to its parts work as a whole. Big Dan, in one of his more charitable moments, once said, 'If man made it, my daddy can fix it.' That claim remained lodged in my mind because I never heard my father call his Pop 'Daddy' before or since.

I wondered now if Grandpa drew any inspiration from that afternoon watching us watch *Batman*. Whatever the genesis, it was an impressive machine: salmon-pink with a vinyl roof, it was armed with bold gull fins from an eighteen-foot-long 1959 Impala. Set into the fins by some mechanical genius, and just below three fancy tail-lights from a Dodge Lancer, were big and angry twin exhausts. Grandpa had created his own rear-end modification, and Danny Boy said it was a variation on the old four-wheel drive Dodge Power Wagons with a PTO-type hitch in the rear axle, the kind once used in the war. It was the pinnacle of Donato Paradiso's inventions and he knew it.

We knew it.

Grandpa was creating his own Thunderbolt, his own amazing amalgam of salvaged parts. This was his dream machine, the evidence of his merit.

Danny Boy ran his hand over the smooth hood that appeared to have been cannibalized from an old Buick Le Sabre because the headlights were concealed behind a rotating central panel just above the DeSoto grill, a snarling shark row of vicious teeth. Rear quarter windows were obviously from a 1970s Pontiac Grand Prix; the mirrors were big and luxurious lifts from an old Mercury Town Sedan from the 1940s; the interior was not attractive but very practical and featured turquoise memory-powered seats from a Cadillac; the sporty rim-blow steering wheel came from a Mercury Cougar we had all known and loved, and many of the toggles and push-buttons on the dash were not from cars at all but from the wreckage of a single-engine plane that the state police had dumped in our yard; the engine was a Pontiac 455 Superduty from a '74 Firebird.

'Four-hundred horse,' Grandpa said as he revealed the powerplant. This explained the somewhat bizarre vents in the hood. But the most astonishing extra of all, one that puzzled my brother and left me breathless were the two aquatic propellers welded perfectly under the bumper. I knew instantly that they came from the 1967 faddish

Amphicar we had out in back. With front wheels serving as rudders, the British amphicar was capable of 5 mph in water. Grandpa's international melting pot of a car was not only well-muscled and stylish, it was amphibious!

Danny Boy knelt at the props and shook his head in awe as he traced the output shaft, and then he and I were inside the car again, trying to figure out how he turned an in-put shaft into an out-put shaft. Danny was down on the floor near the pedals. 'Jesus, Nunz, look,' he said, whispering, incredulous. The clutch operating system was from a Russian Belarus tractor Dad had retired out back years ago.

'Fan-frigging-tastic,' Danny Boy could not help saying.

'We might be the next Ford family,' I bragged and this made Grandpa smile with his underbite.

'Screw *Ford*,' Danny Boy crooned. 'We're talking *Bugatti*.'

'What are you going to call it?' I prodded.

Grandpa drew back a stiff pace and cleaned his hands with a rag, looking the composite machine over. And then he said it, the name rolling off his tongue like sweet country butter: '*Il Proletario*.'

We stood on each side of our grandfather and shared his view, his moment of glory. *Il Proletario* had a certain ring to it. I found it cool, and my brother's smile betrayed the same sentiment.

'She's'a no done,' he finally confided. 'She no have reverse and she no have the power steer.'

'Grandpa,' I said. 'It's the *balls*.'

Grandpa allowed Danny to sit behind the wheel and fire up the big power plant. It revved and roared like a blast furnace as four hundred horses ran wild and filled the shed with coarse smoke and the scent of mystery oil, and Grandpa smiled like I'd never seen him smile before.

Maybe we were fueled by our grandfather's adventurous heart and the reminder that his resourceful Paradiso blood ran through our veins, but we pulled off the crane job like seasoned cat burglars; I straddled the giant magnet and Danny Boy lifted me high and within four inches of the crushed Pontiac. With Dad's idle cousins, Zi Bap and Zi Toine, frowning at the operation from the shade of the garage door – I waved from on high at them – I was able to coon my way onto the flat hood and pry away shards of glass with a tire iron. It took some shoehorning but I got in at the little strip of number-punched tin and popped it free. While I was up there, I paused for a moment of silence and quietly prayed for the dead man. I felt something between us at that moment, like he was depending on me to get him out of there before he was shipped to the processor. I smelled nothing that would suggest a decomposing body. Just stale gasoline and oxidizing metal.

I had the ID number in my hand, and though it didn't feel all that much like a SWAT adventure, we were in business; Danny Boy placed a call to Cousin Angelo and gave him the number.

'Friggin' monkey answers the phone,' my brother relayed, disturbed.

'What?'

'The *monkey*. I could hear her knock the phone off the hook, pick it up and bring it to him, to Angelo. I could hear Angelo telling that Ruby Lee to bring him the phone!'

Angelo had instructed Danny to stay cool and let him 'work the bush'.

At fifteen minutes to five that afternoon, just as we were getting tow trucks locked away and Primo Canero fed, the sound of a gas guzzling barge with no muffler drew our attention out front. Pop bass throbbed at tempo with the knocking four-barrel, and I could hear singing. The familiar car rolled up, Johnny the gypsy cab driver engaged in a helium-high duet with Donna Summer: '*She work hard for the money. So you better treat her . . .*'

Johnny shut the big land barge down and got out. She was wearing her standard maroon windbreaker, tight faded Jesse Jeans and black high-top tennis shoes. My throat tightened as Big Dan stepped out of the garage to intercept her.

I could see that Tony the Barber had gotten a mirror for his Buick because Dad had a fresh haircut and his neck and ears were a bit raw. 'Yes, sir?' he offered.

'I ain't no Sir,' Johnny protested and I could see my Dad blush.

'I call everybody sir,' he said, fast on his feet. 'What can we do for you, Ma'am?'

'I need some radial ply,' she said and I was relieved she didn't start singing at him. Dad directed her to the tire bunker and when she found us in there, she smiled. 'Oooh,' she said, looking at Danny Boy. 'This him? This the bro?'

'Yes,' I said, and I did my best to make introductions.

'You're the taxi driver?' Danny Boy asked. Johnny nodded and my brother relaxed. 'It's lonely, isn't it?'

'Better than food stamp.'

'You see what's out there at night. The scum, the pimps.' He was doing De Niro and its effect on Johnny was notable: she arced her eyebrows, uneasy. Then Danny said, 'I bet you drive because you can't sleep nights.'

'No, honey,' said Johnny. 'I drive 'cuz I need the green.'

Danny Boy seemed to accept this as some kind of password and he handed over the smashed bullet casing in a small plastic bag. She gave it a cursory look then zipped it in a pocket on her windbreaker.

'I'm going to tell you somethin' about Angel,' she said. 'Man got his ass a death wish. That's how I come acrost him. He flag me down in his wheelchair one night on Willow Street. Want me to take him to the reservoir so he can look at the water. I help him in the car, strap him up, I take him to the reservoir. He want to sit in his chair outside and look at the water and smoke one of them guinea stinkers and have me play his Roy Orbison tape, say he'll pay the fare for my time. I'm sittin' in my car, readin' my book and listenin' to that old "Dream Baby" shit when Motherfucker blow in the tube and the wheelchair start rollin' down the boat ramp. I jump out and catch the fool half inch from the deep end. Strap his ass in the car and take him back to the nut-house. That how I met your cousin. I start taking him to the strip bars on Fridays. I'm like his motherfuckin' chauffeur and I can't do it no more. You know why they give him a monkey?'

When neither of us answered, she said, 'Same reason they send a monkey up in space that time. 'Cuz who crazy enough to go up there? Apartment 4-D. Ain't no nurse go up there.'

'Then why you do it?' Danny Boy asked.

She threw a look at him as if questioning his manners. ''Cuz he got *nobody*. Follow me? And that's why I'm tellin' you this: the man want to *die*. You his only family and you just gave him somethin' to live for. So don't play no games on my Angel. He gets three hundred bucks or a bus ticket to Myrtle Beach, South Carolina. We cool?'

The tire bunker was filled with the kind of silence that only occurs at five o'clock when the wrecking yard is all but shut down. 'Yeah,' Danny Boy said for the two of us. 'We're cool.'

'Angel got news,' she said, walking away, and we both dogged behind her. 'Meet him tonight, after eight, Thirsty Turtle.'

On the way home Big Dan, smelling of hair tonic, grilled us on why we couldn't find a pair of snow tires for the colored woman. We told two different fibs over each other and Dad just shook his head. 'You know, I've got a good mind to just get in my Bel Aire and drive the fuck away.'

'Why don't you?' Danny Boy said.

'What'd you say?'

'Nothing.'

'He didn't say nothing,' I vouched.

'What's the matter?' Big Dan said, working a thumbnail back in his molars. 'You couldn't find any last night? You try the Rest Home up on Park Street?'

'Well, if it isn't Clark Gable,' Mom burred as we shuffled into the breezeway in our grease-caked boots. 'Saukiwog Players called,' she sang out.

'Did I get the role?' asked Danny Boy. My mother need not answer. Her face burst into the aurora that was her smile and my brother whooped.

'All right!' I celebrated, and even Big Dan, for all his diatribe against my brother's lark, gave a little smile.

'He got it? He got the play-acting role?'

'Yes, he did,' Mom said with a touch of Lowland defiance.

'I'm Captain Lombard,' my brother said, already transforming. 'I'm going to grow my hair for it. And I got this limp down. You see, he was in the war in Africa—'

'Daniel,' Mom cut him short. Something was not as rosy as we thought.

'It's not Lombard.'

Silence was broken only by Dad setting down the cash box on the bench.

'What did I get? Who am I?'

'Who is he?' Dad asked, almost suspicious.

'Who am I, Mom?'

'The house parlorman,' Mom announced, buoyant. As quickly as Danny Boy's face went sallow, Mom smiled bigger. 'Jason Robards started out playing butlers. The butler's a good role. Butlers know everything about everybody. And I don't see why a house parlorman can't have a wee limp.'

'He's the *butler*?' Dad said, making matters worse.

Danny Boy pushed roughly past Big Dan and just as gently past our Mom, touching her shoulder as he went. I watched him disappear down the hall toward his room and I was overcome with a painful vision: my brother, the ex-football hero with the key to the Brass City, standing on stage in a walk-on role as the butler, holding a tray of drinks with hands permanently darkened by junkyard grease. No matter how he would scrub before the play, he would have to show his grease monkey hands to the city. Of course, he could always turn it down but I knew he would not.

I had seen my share of driftwood that summer and it was only late June; cast-off cars and obsolete steam engines and old men with missing thumbs and fingers, sitting on porches at midday not sure what to do with their time now that time had been stolen. I had met the notorious Angelo, a broken prince in a wheelchair in an apartment complex for people cast off by their families. I had seen Dave Zuraitas drifting on the Green with a lottery ticket, and I had heard Eddie Coco's mother arguing with her sister over who was going to house Papa now that the Rest Home was raising its rent.

Driftwood.

And I saw my brother Danny leave the house in a hurry that night and pull away in his rattle-crate Hornet.

Where does the spirit of a boy go when it's been knocked from a man's casing with blood and snot and wind, and he's laying there on the thirty-yard line, staring up at the sun and seagulls and strange faces, trying to breathe?

Doctor says there's nothing wrong, maybe slight concussion. You ain't quitting, are you? You quit here, there's nothing left. Don't quit on me, kid. Where's your spunk?

Coach says you keep dropping punts, says you ain't hitting, says

*you're hearing footsteps. What do you mean, you lost it? Che fa?
Lost what? What about UConn, Danny? Don't you quit on this
family. You're going to be the first Paradiso to go to college.*

Don't you quit on us, Donato.

'Does Danny have brain damage?' I asked my mom one night;
Ray Beans was telling kids so in the church parking lot.

'*Och*, no,' Mom had said. 'Your brother tore something, some
cartilage or tendon or some such. He tore something inside, something near to his heart.'

In the middle of the night, I woke up and went to my window.
I knew where it was. My brother's spirit was loping up and down
Kirby Field like a lost dog on the dirt margin of a highway far
from home.

We'd go back for it, me and him.

TWO

The Dogs of Jerusalem

Electric Jamaica – Ten Little Indians –
Tutto de Mare – The Lost Tribe – Hoffa's Hat Pin
– A Christian and a Soldier – Three Teardrops –
Don Gustavo Martone's Amazing Time Machine –
La Forza del Destino – Mr Mojo Risin'

I don't even know what the American Dream
is anymore. Maybe it means picking up
the pieces we've left behind.

Frances Scala
(Interviewed by Studs Terkel)
American Dreams: Lost and Found

CHAPTER TEN

Electric Jamaica

'The monkey's cool, but Beaver Cleaver waits outside.'

Two Lane greeted us at the door of the Thirsty Turtle on Hawthorne Avenue, the well-lighted row of hamburger havens and little dark enclaves like the one we were trying to breach now.

'I gotta let the fucking monkey in,' Two Lane griped. 'You got state papers for him.'

'Yeah, well I got federal papers for my little cousin, so get your fat ass out of the door, Two Lane,' said Goomba Angelo.

He nodded to my brother and Danny Boy fanned out five singles. Two Lane, a casual member of the Diablo Motorcycle Gang, folded the notes in his big fingers but he continued to stare at me, suspicious. He called me Beaver Cleaver again, and I resented it. But I never met his gaze; it was the first time I had been that close to a real motorcycle man and I was intrigued by his smell, a heady stink of beer, smoke, motor oil and urine – all of it absorbed into leather and air-dried like a Parma ham.

'You know, Two Lane,' Angelo said. 'you still don't have a handicapped access ramp in this joint. I can get the state on your people's ass.'

Two Lane chortled dismissively, but he waved us through just the same. Goomba was wearing a long, gray raincoat of a dubious material, but he wore it draped cape-style like some crippled European count, and Ruby was perched alert on the arm of his wheelchair, adding a strange touch of majesty.

Danny Boy walked shotgun into the smoke and strobe lights. His new *Deer Hunter* goatee and stone-washed army jacket almost blended in this place where men sat the bar hunched, their faces low over cigarettes and highballs; a few turned our way, and I wondered what our improbable SWAT team looked like as we made pilgrim's progress through the place to K.C. and the Sunshine Band.

'There are two things in life, boys, that give us sustenance,' Angelo was saying now, adroit in his element. 'Two basic principals that you must always return to, like a starfish to the rocks, and never let go.'

'What two principles?' I said, wheeling him into the inner sanctum. He didn't just answer the question, he yelled it to the whole room as if he were some street preacher in rapture: 'DAGMARS!'

The sight of the naked woman on stage punched the breath from me like the time my Cousin Franny hit me in the midsection with a wiffle bat. Only harder. I felt blood beard my face and something electric volt through me; I was in the presence of some dark and verboten miracle and I didn't belong there.

'Sit down, Boy Wonder,' Angelo ordered me. 'Behold the golden fruits of Athena.'

The dancer's name was Doreen and she was old, almost thirty I guessed, her blonde hair sculpted up like a tiara. Across her belly was a long magenta scar only half-concealed by a spare bikini bottom.

'*Bella, bella!*' Angelo yelled over the music and I felt embarrassed when everyone looked our way. Doreen, hard-faced when we entered, was now smiling at Angelo and singing with the music: '*That's the way, uh-Huh-uh-Huh, I* LIKE *it.*' There was a noticeable rapport, and Angelo informed us that he knew the woman back when she was making brass garden hose couplings at Saukiwog Metalwork. Laid off now, she made her living with couplings of another kind, both of them in her hands now, working one left, one right, like shammy cloths on a waxed car. Few could see me in the dark, but I knew I was privileged; all I could think about was what I would tell Eddie Coco and the Doyle brothers.

Danny Boy shielded me. 'Okay, what are we doing here?'

'Having a highball,' Angelo said. And on the tail of this he yelled again, what sounded like 'MAYPO!' or 'MAYPOLE!' and Ruby Lee raised up on her little brown legs and posed rapt, showing her teeth. 'Give her a dollar,' said Angelo. It took a moment but my brother finally held out a crumpled bill. Ruby took it in her tiny velvet hands. 'GROCERY BOY!' Angelo shouted.

If I thought I had seen wonders in days past I was about to see spectacle six-ways-from-Sunday. To a great wave of laughter and applause, and a stoned biker somewhere yelling, 'What the fuck?' Ruby Lee threw herself onto the stage and scrabbled up the woman's bare leg, clinging to her waistband even as she did an awkward dervish. When the monkey tucked the dollar bill in the little blue bikini bottom, the place erupted like they were ringside at a pro wrestling match. Some folks seemed familiar with Ruby Lee, others appeared stunned. But no one looked away.

When Ruby returned, Doreen smiled and winked at Angelo, and that's when I became aware of a man sitting at our table. In the strobe flicker and smoke he looked like a ghoul, maybe six feet four and gaunt, his neck long. His hair was graying and matted and he wore his sideburns long like the guys in my father's High School yearbook. Peeling the wet label off a beer bottle and smoking a cigarette, he engaged in conversation with my brother and Goomba Angelo, mostly my *goomba*. How long this discourse had been going on I did not know; I was too busy following Angelo's creed and meditating like a Shaolin monk on those two principles.

'I thought you wanted me to hotwire some wheels,' the guy said, lisping through a gap where an incisor had been.

'No, man,' Angelo said, looking unusually poised for a man with no movement south of his collar bone. 'There was a '73 Pontiac, blue, stolen from Margolis Used Car Lot near the Plaza. Three, four weeks ago. My sources at Pinkerton tell me that's your home range. You and Margolis got a deal. He lets you steal one every six months, he collects insurance and you do the chop-chop.'

'I don't know what you're talking about.'

'He don't know what I'm talking about,' Angelo said to my brother. 'This is one of the car theft capitals of the north-east. Ichabod here is the reigning duke, and he don't know what I'm talking about.'

The storkish man peeled away his beer label and smiled at my *goomba* like he was no more than a pesky mayfly. But Angelo dug in. 'Listen up, Ichabod, because this might be the last night you get yourself some jelly roll for about six to ten.'

I didn't understand why not having a jelly roll for ten years would weaken someone's resolve, but Ichabod's smile went slack as Angelo moved his head closer to him. 'There's eleven and a half pounds of pure French vanilla in the rocker panels on that Pontiac. It's sitting in the police car pound with Guess Whose fucking fingerprints all over the fucking wheel, *capisce?*'

My eyes met my brother's in the strobe-lit corner. His hands were clutched tight as he leaned into the conversation and I could see him nodding off of Angelo's cues.

'What the hell you saying?' Ichabod growled under the music.

'Look me in the eye, Ichabod.'

Whatever the *Mamone* was saying had an undeniable effect on the alleged car thief. He twisted a little Thirsty Turtle napkin into a paper screw and his crooked smile returned, a smile that gave him the stiff cast of an animal that had fallen into the hands of an inept taxidermist. 'What's this got to do with *you*, Volpe?'

'I'm working this case, private security.'

'You're blowing smoke up my ass. You been in a wheelchair for six fucking years.' He leaned across the table and looked straight into Angelo's eyes. 'What would you say if I told you ya were full of shit?'

'I would ask you why the Saukiwog Police were sitting across the room, watching every move you fucking make.'

We all looked across the room at the same time: me, Danny Boy and the reigning duke of car thieves. There, sitting at the dance stage in uniform, talking with Two Lane Monroe was Chetty Kelly's father, a city cop with a red brushcut and arms like a marine. He was drinking a soda and staring at our table with a vigilant eye.

'Maybe you want for me to call Sergeant Kelly over here and have him limber the lumber on you, Ichabod?' Angelo said.

Ichabod gave in, lighting another cigarette like it was salvation. 'I drove the car to the salon,' the gaunt man finally lisped, ribbons of smoke going up in strobe light. 'Parked it behind the Plaza, alongside the dumpster like she says.'

'Like who says?'

'I don't know. Broad.'

'Broad. What fucking broad?'

'Broad on the phone. She named a few niggers who work the

North End for me. Nothing fancy she says, low-key Detroit like a Chevette or Polara or some shit. I picked her out a Bonnie-top, you know, Bonneville. Drove it behind the Plaza like she says, left the keys and picked up an envelope from under the tree there, the palm tree.'

It occurred to me then, that this was a man with no interest in trolls, otherwise he'd have taken the rubber trophy off the rear window.

'Palm tree. Where you taking us, Ichabod? Honolulu?'

'Jamaica,' he said. 'Electric Jamaica, it's right up near Burger King. It was your basic hotwire deal. I got nothing to do with no heroin.'

I must have flinched when the ghoul said the H word because he suddenly squinted at me out of the corner of his small eyes and Angelo covered for me: 'He's cool. He don't speak English. He's from the Old Country.'

I would look back at this strobe-lit experience as a defining moment in my future as a casual poker player. I sat on tenterhooks staring straight ahead and sipping the flat Dr Pepper Angelo had ordered for me, trying not to look terrified as I pieced things together.

'Call your dogs off my ass, Volpe,' said Ichabod, 'or this shit can get real ugly. I know people, too, asshole.' He removed a pack of smokes from his shirt pocket, tapped one loose. I searched for a picture of a Chinese dragon on the box, but saw only a camel.

As Doreen left the stage and a big-boned, redheaded woman in lingerie and high-heels climbed up, Ichabod inhaled smoke, stood tall and went to the men's room. When he walked he made a clanking, jingling sound; he must have had thirty sets of keys on his belt.

'There's heroin in the rocker panels?' Danny Boy inquired.

'No,' Angelo said in a clipped whisper. 'But there's a load in Ichabod's trousers.'

'Is Officer Kelly really helping us?'

Danny Boy's question was answered when Chetty Kelly's policeman father approached our table, looked each of us over and then said to Goomba Angelo: 'I thought I'd never see you again, Angie.'

'Physical rehab, Ed. Only with a view.'

'How old's this kid?'

When Angelo didn't answer, Kelly laid down an edict, told him to get me out of there and quick. With the cop gone, Angelo said, 'He was staring at *me*, not Ichabod. But Ichabod don't know that. That's pool. That's playing the bumper without sinking your eight ball.'

To my relief, Goomba Angelo was now prepossessed by something else.

'Freeze the lasagne, I'm going to heaven,' he whispered.

The smoke spread thicker and the big-boned redhead, chestier than the scarred woman, walked up and down to 'Crocodile Rock' up and down with no sense of theater. She looked as if she was punching the clock and doing her half hour. She grabbed her own breasts and moved them around and I had to look away.

'The Towering Inferno,' Angelo said, looking her over. 'What ya think, Nunzio? You wanna bring the next dollar up?'

'No.'

'No,' Danny Boy enforced. And then something traumatic occurred. As she let her lingerie drop away and struggled to pull a high-heel free, she looked right at me. Our eyes met and I wondered what she thought about the minor sitting there in Sears Toughskins and Puma Clydes. I felt myself blushing but I could not look away. If Angelo was right about those two things being lodestones in times of trouble, I was going through a form of ascension. Her legs could have used a stop at the tanning salon up the road, and her belly was a little round, but her breasts were dead doubles for Miss Bettie Page, December 1952.

'Look at that,' Goomba Angelo said into my brother's ear over the music. 'If those things were *zucchini* she'd be queen of the fair. Blue ribbon stuff up there – forget about it.'

Her hair was red, teased wild. Her lips were full, painted orange like Tang. That's when it hit me. Those lips. Orange like Tang. She turned away and continued to do a cloddish rock-around-the-clock to the 'Crocodile Rock.'

Those lips.

Liver lips.

I shot up out of my chair and yelled: 'MISS GRABOWSKI!'

I don't remember who screamed the loudest: me, my fourth-grade teacher, or Ruby Lee.

'No, it wasn't,' Danny Boy said. 'I had her in fourth grade, too. That wasn't Grabowski, but you scared the shit out of whoever she was.'

'Her hair was different, but that was her, I know it was.'

'Liver Lips?'

'She has that mole on her neck.'

Angelo thrust his head forward from the back seat: 'Will you two cork the *fuck up* about Miss Grabowski?'

Danny Boy admonished me with a glance as Johnny pulled into the tiny strip mall that rented space beside Carpet World, Tire World and Color My World house paint-outlet to a small tanning salon with a big pastel and neon sign that summoned passing traffic to Electric Jamaica.

Day-Glo palm trees lit up the plate-glass window from where they nested in plastic coconuts; behind one of the trees was a large poster of Farah Fawcett sitting in the surf.

'All these white people go in there and lay under them machine,' Johnny observed with curiosity. 'They come out lookin' like motherfuckin' pumpkins. I tell you what: I'm glad I'm a black woman.'

The rest of our assembly sat like solemn Argonauts in a two-door Argo, looking for danger in the Straits. Angelo instructed Johnny to drive around back, 'nice and slow'. The gypsy cab's headlights washed over the back wall of the Plaza where some-one had spray-painted names and numbers and vulgar artwork: it gave me the same hollow-bellied feeling that Holy Hill USA did.

In the lights from Electric Jamaica we could see a large green dumpster, packed to the gunwales with cardboard boxes and assorted trash, and a bold decal on its lid read: *Are You Having a Hard Time Finding a Place To Dispose Of Your Bulky Waste?*

Apparently somebody was, on a rainy night in early June when they deposited a blue '73 Pontiac Bonneville in the car park. Sometime between the hours that Ichabod made the delivery and we towed away the car from Maple Hill, a man with horn-rimmed glasses and a white shirt had been shot in the head and stuffed in the cargo space.

I held my breath until we passed the dumpster and circled back to the front of the salon. Inside we could see a woman sitting on a tall stool behind the counter, phone trapped behind shoulder and ear, painting her fingernails. Her hair was magpie black and permed into a wild cascade that may have reached her hips behind the counter. Her skin was light brown, and she chewed gum and snapped bubbles as she coated her nails delicately.

'I know her,' said Danny Boy. 'Desiree. She went to St Mary's. Cheerleader. Vega – Desiree Vega.'

'She know you?'

'She should. I sacked their quarterback on a safety blitz. In the end zone. Those two points won us the city title my frosh year.'

'Good. That's good. Go inside and say hello to Miss Vega.'

'Just go inside like that?'

'No, go in and get a tan.'

'Are you kidding me?'

In the frontseat Johnny spit laughter with her lips pressed in her palm.

'Go with him, Nunzio. Talk to her. Feel her out,' Angelo said.

'Maybe Nunzio should get the tan,' my brother suggested.

'Why me?' I was terrified.

'I can't get a tan,' Danny Boy argued. 'I'm playing a butler. Butlers can't have tans. They don't have that cushy life.'

Goomba Angelo looked over at me. 'Go ahead, kid. Go in and get a sun tan and let the butler talk to the girl.'

Inside Electric Jamaica, Desiree Vega was done with her phone call but not her nails and she was doing some kind of incantation in a foreign tongue:

> '*Voulez-vous coucher avec moi ce soir?*
> *Voulez-vous coucher avec moi?*
> *Getcha getcha ya ya da da.*'

The chant must have been ancient because it aroused in me a pulse I couldn't explain; there in the room of neon sunsets, papier mâché palm fronds, and dozens of dark brown bottles filled with mystery creams and oils, she moved both arms out like an Egyptian while her shoulders each went in their own direction, a black, spaghetti-strap Danskin clinging to her like skin on a seal.

'*Mocha chocolata ya ya.*' She sang, oblivious to us as she lay out plastic goggles, creams, and a towel, careful with the freshly-painted nails on her left hand as she turned the music down.

'What's up, guys?' she said. 'You want a book of four, or just one?'

'Desiree, right?'

She looked at my brother, tried to place him. When she squinted, I thought I saw mascara smeared like she had been crying.

'Where do I know you?'

'Football,' Danny said. He smiled and his dimple caught her eye. 'Kirby. I was—'

'Wait,' she said. 'I know you. Donny.'

'Danny.'

'The Backyard Dog.'

'Junkyard Dog.'

'Yeah, man, that was it. The Junkyard Dog. Meaner than a junkyard dog – Danny Pelligroso.'

'Paradiso.'

'I'm like "where do I know this guy?" You were bad, man. *Bad.*'

'No, he was good,' I said. 'All-City twice.' They both looked at me, then smiled at each other.

'Bad is good,' Danny Boy said.

'Yeah,' she said. Her eyes met my brother's. 'Good is bad.'

'Bad is bad,' my brother said, smirking in the manner of his hero.

Desiree smiled. 'I thought you was going to go play for UConn or something.'

'He got hurt,' I said.

'Just one shot,' Danny Boy said and I couldn't tell if she knew it was a De Niro line but she smiled anyway. I had to look away; she reminded me of somebody but I couldn't nail it down. With a counter-height craftiness I watched her profile in the mirror behind her. Her teeth were straight as a Cheyenne's and her lips were full and as high-gloss red as a candied apple; her eyes were large and deep root beer, set under thick lashes. There was something randy in her eyes, something almost crazy. When she tucked her long hair back to reveal an unusual earring, a long silver fairy holding a tiny spoon, I realized then who she made me think of: the gypsy dancer on the cover of my paperback version of *The Hunchback of Notre Dame*. Yet there was something strange near her left eye. A black teardrop had been tattooed at the corner, and another one just below it, so even as she smiled she appeared to be sad.

'Who's this boy?'

'My brother,' Danny said. 'Nunzio.'

Her eyes had me: those two teardrops. She leaned forward on her elbows and studied me, manufacturing a small gum bubble like a craftswoman blowing glass. As the bubble expanded, Danny Boy and I both watched it with an equal intrigue. When it snapped, Danny took a measured step back as if he felt the concussion.

'How old are you?' she said to me.

'I'm going to be thirteen next spring.'

'He needs a tan,' Danny said.

'Yeah, he does,' she said. 'He looks like he seen a ghost.'

It wasn't so much what she said as how she kept my eyes held in hers like she was reading the secrets of a boy too young to know how to conceal them from gypsies.

She helped me ready the sun bed in Booth 4 while my brother stood in the doorway, hands on his hips, seemingly enamored of her blue leopard tights and black high-heels and the hair that fell to her fanny. Like a schoolteacher she showed me how to insert the token and she insisted I wear the small oval safety glasses so I wouldn't sear my corneas. She closed me in the room and the machine went on in an ultra-violet blaze. I panicked, fearing I would go blind. I pressed the small goggles to my eyes and stood there in the dark, watching the capsule glow and make a ticking sound, but I went nowhere near it.

Outside the door, I could hear some playful badinage and I resented my fate – them out there, me in here, in the dark.

'So what you doing, sucker? What you driving?'

'I'm working,' my brother said. 'Heavy metal.'

'Where at?'

There was a pause that did not surprise me.

'My dad's.'

'Your dad's. The junkyard?'

'The salvage yard, that's right.'

'Are you the Junkyard Dog up there?'

'You could say that.'

'You watch out for the bad guys?'

Desiree was laughing in riposte with my brother now and I wanted to open the door a crack so I could see those teardrops crinkling at the corner of her moist, black lashes, but I was suspended like Alan Shepard there in the dark cosmos while the tanning bed glowed like something radioactive.

'That's what I'm doing tonight,' Danny Boy said, teasing. 'I'm out looking for a bad guy.'

'Oh, yeah?' Desiree was laughing in a manner that would have made my Cousin Giustina label her a 'flirt'. 'What bad guy? Who you going to bite on the ass?'

'The one who picked up a '73 Pontiac Bonneville behind your shop, sixteen days ago.'

Desiree stopped laughing and I no longer heard snapping gum bubbles. The cassette tape she was playing had ended. There was a terrible silence out in the lobby. I held the towel to my chest as if to muffle my heartbeat.

'What *is* this?' she asked Danny.

'You recall seeing that car out back? Blue Pontiac.'

'Do I recall? What is this, man? Why you talking like Columbo, sucker?'

'Somebody dropped it off. Then somebody picked it up.'

'What you *doing*? Moonlighting for the Motor Vehicle Department or something? I don't know about no junked car. What are you, an insurance adjuster or something? Do I *recall*? I don't like the way you're talking.'

'I'm a junkyard dog, Desiree. That's all. I'm a watch dog.'

I wondered how long that token would keep the ultraviolet machine buzzing, how long I would have to stand suspended in the dark. It would be the longest half-hour in my life. But when the tanning bed finally kicked off, and the lid yawned open, a thought occurred to me.

The brass token.

My heart drummed at a march beat as I dug down into the pocket of my Toughskins and pinched out the brass blank that Mr Carmella said resembled the tokens at the old amusement park. What if the killer was a sun-worshipper? Or the dead man? Was this the connection to Electric Jamaica?

Tempting the Three Sisters of Fate, I approached the coin slot and knelt. I touched the token to the slot and held it at the abyss for a moment. Then I let it go.

It didn't fit.

I turned it, spit on it, like my dad always did at Coke machines. I buffed it with the towel, tried again. But the brass blank did not fit. I was in total blackness now with the purple goggles on. I fumbled for the door knob and came out into the main room, my towel still under my arm. In an effort to sell my ruse, I toyed with my belt buckle.

Desiree Vega was staring fire at my brother. And Danny Boy, as was his way, let his facial muscles give as he manufactured the De Niro look, eyes squinting. She drew back a step, frowning. 'You got sinus problems or something?'

'I'm protecting you from something you don't even know I'm protecting you from, Desiree.' This was once again a clean steal from *Taxi Driver*, a homage lost on the gypsy girl. She wouldn't know, I reasoned; she was from another world in which she danced the meringue in a whirling white dress while her goat performed in the Square.

'I need protection?' she asked my brother. 'From who, you son of a bitch?' *Charamanbiche* was how she said it.

'There's a lot of bad people out there.'

Desiree clawed at her countertop, clearing paperwork and *People* magazines and bottles of Ultra Glow. She grabbed a large, sagging rattan handbag and began digging through it.

'You going to protect *me*?'

Lipstick came out, a coin purse, a pack of cigarettes, more tanning solution and then something metal and imposing.

She had a black can that said SPRAY AWAY on a key chain. She aimed it at my brother and his face withered. She was walking him backward to the door while I tagged the two of them, nervous.

When she had him pressed against a big travel poster of Cancun, she smiled and chewed her gum for a time, aiming the Mace at his eyes. 'You're barking up the wrong tree, Danny,' she said.

Danny Boy backed against the door until it opened and deposited him in the car park, shuffling backward. He was smiling, as if not to be bested, not to give her an upper hand; but he wasn't about to be blinded with Mace either. I remained, for a moment, alone with the dark beauty.

'Here's your towel,' I said, politely. She was staring at me. Entranced, I stared back. And then I realized what I must have looked like standing there in a Mao cap and purple tanning goggles. She removed the glasses, took the towel, then held the door open so I could go. She was in no mood for formal goodbyes. But as I began to slip out she grabbed me by my sleeve and I could smell the bite of her nail polish.

'Is it true about him? He got a steel plate in his head?'

'I don't know. I don't think so.'

'Well, Home Boy sure acts like it.'

She let me go and secured her salon with angry latching sounds and the jamming slide-crack of a dead bolt. And then she yanked down a bamboo curtain that had a silk-screened sunset on it.

Driving toward the South End, Johnny explained the black teardrops. 'Be a Puerto Rican thing,' she educated our crew. 'When a Puerto Rican woman gets her heart broke she gets that teardrop tattoo. Stand for lost love. That girl had two, see. I do that, they be runnin' down my arm. Man, I been mistreated.'

'She knows something,' Goomba Angelo said. 'She's got angst in her walk.'

'Hoo!' Johnny laughed, casting a glance my brother's way. She was in awe of Angelo. 'He know his shit. Motherfucker like Baretta.'

I wasn't so sure about his analysis; it seemed to me that anyone wearing high pointed heels and pants that tight would have angst in their walk.

'She got pretty,' Danny Boy said. 'She used to be too skinny. All eyes. Damn, she got pretty.'

'Never mind that shit,' Angelo said.

'Yeah,' Johnny said a moment later. 'Don't even get on *that* interstate.'

As we stopped at a red light I looked out at the car beside us and saw the bold white and teal colors of a city police car. Officer Kelly was at the wheel, a partner beside him. They were staring over at us. Before I could alert my team, they turned into Bonanza steak house and were gone.

'They still got that poor woman they turn into a pile of salt and pepper up there?' Johnny asked as she guided her big land barge up Maple Hill where plaster seraphim held night vigil. Danny Boy just stared ahead. Angelo shrugged. But for me, this was a clean coup:

'Yes, they do. Lot's wife.'

'Who wife?'

'Lot's wife. She was punished.'

'For what?'

'For looking over her shoulder.'

'I like this man,' Johnny said. 'I have faith in this man here. Man who read the Bible got no grass growin' under his shoe.'

I felt emboldened as the adults offered up a respectful silence. The Big Clock read five after midnight, and we were walking into the fireweed of Jerusalem at dawn, me pushing Goomba Angelo with Ruby on his shoulder and Johnny and my brother walking ahead, sharing a morning smoke and Burger King coffees. 'Now who that kneeling down over there?' Johnny slowed a pace to ask me.

'The fishmonger,' I said.

Danny Boy circled the plaster Christian and slid on his heels down to the gravel lot where the blue Pontiac once sat, ghostlike.

'Crime scene,' Angelo announced. 'Stay out of it.' He then motored himself with his tube down into the lot and began a slow reconnoiter. 'Clean the table, Ruby,' he said. Ruby Lee slid down his slacks – which seemed to hang on bone – and scrambled about the area, picking up a gum wrapper, a spent pack of matches, a bottle cap, and what looked to be a washed-out fossil of a Dunkin' Donuts coffee cup.

'Save it,' he ordered. Ruby carried the booty up onto her master's lap and stuffed it into a Glad Bag. The nimble capuchin could turn book pages, deal Three-Card Monte, scratch the Daily Numbers, spoon-feed yogurt, and although I doubted it was any different than her daily chores, bag evidence at a crime scene.

When Ruby struggled a little with the Zip-Loc, Danny Boy started to move in helpfully but Angelo stopped him with a hard look; he was adamant about keeping his nurse disciplined and his independence intact. Eventually the monkey sealed the bag, pulsing her lips at us and making a clicking sound in her throat. She pushed the bag down into what looked like vinyl saddlebags on the wheelchair. I crept closer, intrigued. Baretta had a parrot; McCloud had a horse; Mike Longstreet had Pax the dog; but my father's second cousin Angelo had a capuchin monkey that could bag evidence.

'That John the Baptist over there with no head?' Johnny asked me. No, I told her, it was Ishmael but someone had laid a baseball bat to the poor son of Abraham.

Angelo circled the area several more times and seemed interested in an oil stain. He had Ruby pat at it then bring her delicate velvety hands up to his nose so he could identify the scent. 'Diesel,' he said.

Into Jerusalem he motored and we followed his wheelchair into an area that was all but engulfed in ferns. A weathered plaque there read:

CEMETERY OF VICES
Let Us Bury Forever: Hate, Gossip, Avarice,
Prejudice, Jealousy, Malice, Animosity

Seven candles were set out on a long cement girder that had once been part of a street curb. There was shadowed movement around them. This seemed strange in a place that was so static. As we drew closer to the candles, we could see some were burning. Angelo stared down at them and I watched him, waiting for his read. Somewhere in the squalor of the surrounding South End a dog barked itself hoarse and I could smell the scent of frying blood sausage and propane. But Angelo Volpe seemed stumped.

'Okay, baby,' Johnny finally said to him. 'This shit way too Catholic for me. Let's go.' Angelo, it seemed, was onto something like a hunter on a track, and Ruby was as attentive as a tiny bird dog. We climbed the hill of miniature plaster mountains where a little marker read:

IS THERE NO BALM IN GILEAD?

No, there was not: only wilted fern and fireweed, and we stood knee-deep in it, all of us gazing across the Dead Sea, a big sandpit strewn with cigarette butts and an outcropping of dog waste. There on the edge of Gaza some kind of tenement sat shingled in black. The only signs of life were four cat bowls on the porch, but this was sign of life enough.

'Who lives there?' Danny Boy asked.

'The penguins,' Angelo said. 'The nuns who watch the place.'

'We gotta go,' I announced suddenly, looking at the Big Clock in the distance. 'Our dad's going to go berserk.'

This didn't mollify Angelo, and Danny Boy was too piqued to quit now. Both were set on going to the small convent on Maple Hill. As I rummaged my mind, back through the memories of going to Holy Hill, USA on Easter, I vaguely recalled something about nuns taking over the place after Deacon Flynn disappeared – I think I saw one greeting tourists years back – but that was easier to accept in the days when the place was a going holy concern and the city was still rolling in brass. 'What do they do up here?' Danny Boy inquired.

'I have no fucking idea,' Angelo said, staring off.

'We perpetuate the word of God,' a voice said and Johnny let out an alarmed little whoop. There, in the ferns and fog between Gossip and Avarice, stood a nun in a habit and frock and high-top tennis shoes. She emerged, hands folded behind her back, trailing her boxy cloth; she was perhaps as old as Nonni but her eyes – magnified like large azure marbles behind bifocals – were bright and childlike. Her skin was Celtic ruddy and she had an overbite that propped her lips into a smile.

I stood terrified as Johnny broke away from us and hurried down through Moab, trying to hurry without running – her torso was swinging but her big draft-horse backside was set still and she was covering her lips to stifle a hushed laugh. 'Oh, shit,' she spit into her hand, escaping like a schoolgirl caught soaping the windows of the gymnasium. She threw a look over her shoulder then vanished down in the area of Lot's wife.

'I thought I heard the dogs,' the nun said, looking down into the area that represented the Dead Sea. 'They come through here at night and look for garbage. Feral dogs. They take my cats.' She nodded warmly to me and then saw that I was fixed on her large sneakers. 'Corns,' she said, and then she introduced herself as Sister Racine. Her eyes fell on Angelo and she studied the cripple in the unabashed way of a holy servant. 'Years ago, a man made pilgrimage here in a wheelchair,' she said, almost at a whisper. 'He sat in Jerusalem for two days waiting for his legs to be healed.'

'Did it work, Sister?' Angelo did not seem daunted by the nun.

'No, it did not work. The man did not come here to empathize with Christ. He skipped Nazareth and went straight to the Peace Cross and parked there like he was in the checkout line at Pathmark, waiting to ring up his miracle. God bargains with his Own children no more than any other father should.'

'Well, with respect, Sister,' Angelo said, his voice hoarse but strong, 'I didn't come here to bargain with God, or Jew down Moses, or Lot's wife or the Cardiff Giant, or anybody else you got up here on the hill. I'm a cop.'

When he said this I felt safe for the first time all night; I had been waiting for him to admit to being a blue knight, even if we had pulled him out of mothballs. 'What I'm looking for, Sister Racine,' he went on professionally, 'are some answers about a motor vehicle that was abandoned here back in June. A car that may have had a deceased individual in the cargo space.'

The nun's blue eyes held fast to their gleam. 'Our Holy Hill is dying, Officer. Developers have targeted this site for the Maple Hill Mall. A woman from some folk art institute came here in May and chained herself to the Cross in protest. But we Sisters of the Filipini Order are not here to save folk art or kitsch. We are here to perpetuate the word of God.' Gawd, was how she said it.

'I'm losing you, Sister,' said Angelo.

'Vote for the Mall,' she said. 'There's nothing left here but shards of wishful thinking. A place to take drugs, scrawl obscenities, have sex, dump garbage, draw in vermin and perhaps now, as you suggest, commit the worst mortal sin of them all. When the vote comes up again in October, vote for the Mall. We Sisters plan to open a religious bookstore. What old Deacon Flynn wanted here years ago was to perpetuate the word of the Bible. He lost hope, but we cannot. We must adjust to the changes like everyone else.' With this she walked away back toward the convent on the edge of Gaza.

'Who lit the candles?' Angelo said.

Sister Racine stopped in the ferns and ran her fingers through the crowns of the taller stalks. Angelo's eyes were half-lit in the candlelight. When no rejoinder came, he tried another angle: 'These candles were lit about three hours ago, Sister. And they appear to have been lit the night before, too. And all this . . . wax,' he said, making wax sound like it was something repugnant. 'This tells me the candles are lit night after night.'

'And so they are,' said Sister Racine. 'And so they have been since Michael Flynn began the practice in 1959.'

'And so they were on the night of June the sixth when somebody drove a '73 Pontiac up here and dropped it like a hot *bracciola*.'

Sister Racine just stared through her large magnifying glasses, smiling bucktoothed.

'Can you read, Officer?' she said, and her habit trembled with a touch of palsy. 'You're standing in the place where Gossip has been forever buried.'

'Well, guess what, Sister Racine? I'm here to dig it back up. Like the Roto-Rooter man. We've got a missing Christian in the city who deserves to be waked by his family. I've got a twelve-year-old boy over here who seen something no one should ever have to see. He's living with it night and day. And in the interest of our good citizens, we've got a killer loose in Saukiwog. I need some help over here. With respect, Sister, I'll settle for gossip.'

'Goodnight,' she said.

'I need some help over here,' Angelo sang out to her again, beginning to lose the composure he had marshaled through the long night. He rolled his head like he had chills down his neck, and he said a little Italian thing I didn't understand. 'Fifteen years later and I still get anxious around them penguins,' he said. 'Just like what's-his-name's dog.'

'What dog?' Danny said.

'What's-his-fucking face? Oh, shit – you know. It's a Polack name. Somebody's dog. When you have a reaction to something—'

'Pavlov,' said my brother, distracted.

'There you go,' Angelo said, distracted himself. 'Pavlov's fucking dog. I see a nun, my ass hurts. From Mother Superior's fucking ruler in third grade.'

A moment later, the screen door on the convent clapped shut. Sister Racine was returning, only now she had a second nun tailing her. I glanced at Angelo to see if this worsened his phobia. At fifty-six years old, Sister Giselle LaBow was the baby of the convent. Her eyes suggested a Chinaman and were set too far apart. We were all standing – except, of course, for our wheelchair-bound shamus – at the Cemetery of Vices. It was dark, and the only light came from the flickering candles. The Day-Glo peace cross was losing its glow. We were going to pay for this all-nighter, I knew it. Mom was probably up, phoning St Joe's Hospital to see if there were any AMC Hornets involved in a car wreck.

But when Sister Giselle spoke, I was startled back into the moment by her voice, deep and raw. Sister Racine began sign language, and I realized that the second nun was deaf.

'Sister Giselle is the youngest of us,' she said. 'It's her duty to light the candles nightly.'

Angelo began to speak, but Sister Racine cut him off, her hands still working in sign. 'She saw the old blue car parked here a week or so ago. She assumed it was teenagers parking.'

'Bingo,' Angelo said, angling his chair so he could look off toward the crime scene. Sister Giselle worked her hands upward and out in a kind of graceful ballet.

'She says that as she was lighting the last candles, a shadow appeared across Egypt. She feared the stray dogs at first but then saw that it was a man walking toward Moab.'

We all looked at each other – me, Danny Boy, Angelo – and a lull settled for a moment on Maple Hill as if the mention of the killer conjured his shadow here and now in the soft strobe of the burning wax. Angelo prodded, wanting to know what the man looked like. Sister Racine signed the question, running a finger down her face and accidentally bumping her glasses. Sister Giselle made some sounds from her abdomen, and Sister Racine deciphered slowly.

'She says the man was in the dark. He appeared. Large. Blue jeans and a jacket. A wool ski cap.'

'A wool ski cap in June,' I said, and Danny Boy nudged me quiet.

'He was heading out of Moab, smoking a cigarette. Threw the butt down, but then stopped, went back and picked it up. Sister Giselle thought what a fine man to correct himself so in the presence of the sacred. But then, there in the light of the peace cross, Sister saw something . . . something on his jacket.'

'What?' asked Danny Boy.

'Beelzebub,' Sister Racine translated off a slight gesture and then Sister Giselle crossed herself.

'Beel-ze-baaaa,' the deaf nun said in a struggling voice that would haunt me.

'What's Beelzebub?' Angelo asked.

'Lucifer,' I volunteered. And when I said it, Sister Racine looked at me, pleased.

'Well,' she said. 'Beelzebub is actually a devil of the First Hierarchy, in charge of the sin Pride.' When Sister Giselle signed further, Sister Racine watched her, then translated. 'His jacket was black and shiny,' she relayed. 'And on the jacket, on the back, was the head of the horned devil. Red as fire.'

'Oh, man,' Danny Boy said. He let a breath from his lips and shifted his weight.

When Sister Giselle frowned as she recalled, I knew why she made me think of China: she was a ringer for a South East Asian farmer in my sixth-grade Social Studies book, an outdated tome published in the late 1940s.

'He picked up the cigarette butt then walked back to the blue car,' Sister Racine translated. 'Sister Giselle saw headlights on the Dead Sea, but when she looked up later, the blue car was still there. It was another car this man left in.'

'Chevy?' Angelo asked. It was apparent that the Pinkerton Man had researched the make of Mr Diaz's missing vehicle.

'She said she didn't see it,' Sister Racine snapped, vinegar-lipped. 'And she didn't think much of it.'

Here, Sister Giselle looked down at her rounded black shoes, and then lifted her face with a rapt expression and she gestured with struggling motions.

'There was nothing that unusual about that blue car,' Sister Racine translated.

Again there was a silence, but for distant sounds down in the South End projects, joyful voices carrying on a breeze. Latenight partying. Or it may have been dogs, setting each other off.

Angelo remained motionless, his eyes darting in the glow of the peace cross. But there would be no more gestures from Sister Giselle LaBow. The two Sisters walked back to the convent, hand in hand.

We retraced the route of the man the deaf nun had seen that June night, and it took us down the far side of Maple Hill where knee-tall goldenrod told Goomba Angelo no one had come that way in years. He dispatched Ruby into the brush while Danny Boy worked a flashlight over the earth.

There were footprints in the hardened mud of Moab. We hadn't had more than a drizzle of rain since the day I opened the trunk of that Pontiac, so Angelo believed we had cut the track of the killer.

'Work boots,' he said. 'Steel shanked.'

'How do you know they're the shooter's?' Danny Boy questioned.

'Did you hear the penguin?' our cousin retorted. 'She seen the guy turn back and pick up his cigarette butt. An act of penance? Or a smart cock-knocker not wanting to leave anything behind? Look at these tracks. The guy heads down the backside of the hill then comes back up, stops, pulls a one-eighty again. And then he walks faster down the hill. At this point over here near the old chicken wire, he breaks into a jog. That's when he saw his back-up car coming by.'

My pulse was going at hummingbird wing-speed as I watched Goomba Angelo, Ruby's silhouette on his shoulder.

'Let's go get a cocktail and talk this over,' said Angelo. He was, after all, an Eye That Never Slept.

'I have to get Nunzio home,' Danny Boy said. But I could tell it was he who wanted to leave the holy place.

Driving out, I could see the lit windows and Sister Giselle was watching us go.

*   *   *

I had not been up past midnight in the four years since I had seen *The Night of the Living Dead* at the drive-in and my Cousin Franny had wet the back of the family stationwagon right down to the beige carpeting over the spare tire (no shampoo could save that Torino and it, too, was sacrificed to the junkyard Crusher).

Now a Thursday was dawning, and off to the east a trace of jasmine streaked the sky. But there was hope that we could gain some coasting speed on America Street and roll motorless into the driveway. If Mom was up there'd be no cause for panic. To the contrary: she would buy the story wholesale, maybe even put some toast in for a snack before bed.

Danny Boy was an expert at coming and going, unseen, at all hours – 'a Ninja bastard' my father had called him one morning. So I followed his cues like a rapscallion in training. But as we rolled the Hornet in beside Dad's tow truck, I felt like a Christian about to be tortured for his faith. The house was dark, quiet, and as we stepped out, silently latching the car doors, I saw a strange flickering light in the basement window. A soft light, changing the shapes of the cedar hedges.

Danny Boy saw it, too.

Carefully, we crept toward the back porch, Danny sliding along the wall, his army jacket scraping. At the basement window, he took a knee, peered in. I was at his shoulder, clinging to him, trying to see the source of the basement light. Who could be up at this hour?

On the far cellar wall images danced in faded color. Football players, running in the peculiar speed of 8 millimeter; boys in green slamming helmets into boys in orange. And there was number 44 in the defensive backfield, helmet turning left then hard right, black cleats digging in, moving backward, picking up his man, number 86 in orange. The ball coming high and short, a dying duck of a pass. Number 86 turned, but not as fast as Danny – he picked off the pass and held the ball tight even as Number 86 grabbed him in a sloppy tackle and brought him to the grass.

Then the images went backward in the quick and silly manner that used to make us laugh. The same play ran again: Danny turning his helmet left then hard right. Cleats digging in. Sitting by the projector was my father. He was in a T-shirt and boxer shorts, his thinning hair unkempt like he had been sleeping earlier. He was eating cheese doodles. The flickering light from the projector cast his shadow large on the opposite wall as he leaned his elbows onto his knees and watched the play in concentration. He stopped chewing a cheese doodle until Danny intercepted and came down with the goods, then he resumed the munching, reached over and reversed the play again.

I was afraid to, but I moved my eyes onto my brother. They held the flicker of 8-millimeter light. And something else. I heard him make a swallowing sound if such a sound could be called swallowing. He pushed back against me, his shoulder softly scraping the cement wall; he seemed desperate to get away unseen. He grabbed my arm and led me toward the front porch. As I left the basement window, I saw my father sitting rapt, bent forward, like he was watching the game for the first time. He let the play run longer now, young Danny getting to his feet, turning with the ball and offering it toward the camera, his mouth going, teeth guard slipping, jabbing the ball at the camera, at my father who was filming. I remembered that Saturday in Watertown: Danny yelling, 'That's two, Dad. Two for you, Dad.'

I remembered Big Dan, shouting back, 'Nice job, Danny!' And then glancing quickly at the other parents and townfolk around him in the bleachers, catching their eyes on him, the father of Danny Paradiso, the Junkyard Dog. I remembered him sitting there smiling, from kick-off to the final gun, never taking his eyes, or the camera, off number 44.

And then Danny Boy and I were inside, moving like Ninjas across the carpet and to our respective bedrooms. Even in his high-topped army boots, Danny could do a moccasin creep.

Army boots, fashionably unlaced.

I watched them move over the linoleum and leave behind a soundless print made from the black soil of our flower garden.

Steel-shanked boots.

I watched them go panther-pawed into the dark of his bedroom, and I slipped into the hollow of mine. At twelve, a boy begins to sleep with his door closed.

But not tonight.

*   *   *

In the morning I did my best to sell our tale over forkfuls of peppers and eggs. Danny and I went to see *Kramer Vs Kramer* because they were running a preview of the upcoming De Niro film *Raging Bull* at the Colonial Plaza Mall. When we'd returned to the car we were exhausted from working all day and Danny Boy felt he should nap for a half hour before driving us home. The next thing we knew, it was past midnight.

'You boys are doing men's work,' Mom covered.

'You fell asleep outside the movie house?' Dad queried. 'Like a couple of *moo-moos*? Nobody falls asleep in a parking lot – what are you, anemic?' And then as Danny Boy sat at the table, his hands splayed in apology, Dad turned and looked him up and down, nostrils open as if to sift the smell of booze from gasoline. 'Let me see the tickets,' he ordered.

Danny Boy had a pocketful of movie stubs in his army jacket and Dad examined them. 'The movie was good,' Danny Boy said, 'but you ought to see the preview of the new De Niro movie. You should see Bobby, Dad. He gained forty pounds for the role. He's the King. He's God.'

'That can't be good for his heart,' my mother worried.

'Don't say somebody's God,' Dad snapped as he went through the stubs, unsatisfied. He laced up his work boots, his face straining. 'This kid is twelve years old,' he indicted my brother. 'You don't keep him out all night.' And then he gave me a polygraph test with his eyes: 'Where'd he take you? The laundry mat? That's where he finds women.'

If Dad knew where I had been, and with whom, the refrigerator would have been bear-hugged and hoisted across the linoleum. If he knew I had been in the South End, walking around the ruins of the shrine at midnight, he would have driven the ice box through the sheet rock and then the massacre would have begun. 'No, Dad. We weren't at the Swizzle Stick.'

'You know,' Mom injected helpfully, shuffling about on slippers, 'Danny did test positive for that Mediterranean Anemia gene when he was eleven.'

'Yeah, it was jeans,' Dad said, tying his work boots. 'Did you get in them, Danny?'

'Stop it,' Mom said, her face going ruddy.

'Okay,' Danny said. 'You want the truth? We were at Holy Hill. Up at the big cross.'

I looked at my brother, stunned by his confession.

'I took Nunzio up there to talk to the nuns.'

'You what?' Dad said.

'For his Confirmation. He wanted to ask the nuns about the Stations of the Cross.'

'There's only ten goddamn stations. You got home at three o'clock in the morning.'

'Fourteen stations,' I said.

'Very good, Nunzio,' said Mom, pouring Tang.

'Bullshit,' Dad said. 'That's a dope den up there. That's the P.R. section. You could've been zooked with ice picks up there.' Big Dan stood up with his coffee and looked directly at my brother while giving me an order. 'Nunzio,' he said, sipping his coffee as a means of suspense: 'Hook her up.'

I knew what this meant.

Mom did, too.

Most of the neighborhood knew as well.

It had happened before, several times in the last two years, but Danny Boy was particularly fond of his green Hornet, so this came as a harsh condemnation. I was being ordered to hook my brother's car to the family tow truck.

'Oh, no, Dan!' my mother protested but my father aimed a finger at her, stopping her in her skidding slippers.

'Quiet, Nancy. I've had it with the movie actor. Now he can walk to Hollywood.' He turned on his heels and swept a hat off a kitchen chair, a yellow ball cap with bright red letters that said *We're here to help!* Under this slogan was the name Pete. Dad loved that hat because customers who did not know him would call him 'Pete' and he got a charge from this, like he was pulling one over on them. But now he pulled the yellow brim over a knotted brow and started for the door.

'Hook her up,' he said.

On the far north face of Paradise Salvage, on a flat plateau of black dirt and crushed-glass diamonds, sat the only baled cars that would never be shipped to Bridgeport. There were three:

the small red Chevette, a black 'Cuda and a little Chevy Vega
– all of them compressed into flat wafers of metal; all of them
the former cars of Danny Boy Paradiso. Big Dan, often given to
charitable moments, would tow in an old car, do his two-pinkied
whistle to get my brother's attention and say, 'You like it? She's
yours.' The two would then go to work on the vehicle, sandblasting
rust and slapping on Bond-O, rebuilding the motor if needed, and
arming the rig with the best steel-belted Firestones to come out of
the bunker.

'You put a little sweat-equity into her, she'll be a cream puff,
Danny Boy.'

Singing along to Jim Croce on the car tape deck, my father would
appear light of heart and optimistic, and seemingly over the past
conflicts with his son. Seeing my father and brother in those rare
days made me feel warm inside, but those were also the fragile
moments when I would twist the collar of my T-shirt up and chew
on it, nervous. I was forever fearful that Danny might take a verbal
step onto a landmine or get too close to Dad and smell like a roach
clip, and then the family peace would erupt like Vesuvio. But often
it coasted easy and Danny Boy would cruise the city in his new
used car with dealer license tags like some kind of prince, blaring
his 8-tracks and visiting his night haunts.

But as unexpectedly as Big Dan gifted a vehicle, he could just as
quickly renege and order it through The Crusher. The flattened
ferrous hulks were assembled up at the back fence as a kind of
memorial to my brother's delinquent behavior and Danny Boy was
often encouraged to take a walk out back and ponder his learning,
smell his sins oxidizing under the sun. The Chevette was for the
time he got caught with a forty-six-year-old woman in his bedroom.
She and Danny Boy had been so loaded when they snuck in, that
in the morning, the woman, a cashier at King's department store
in Naugatuck, got up and rummaged through the kitchen looking
for coffee. She collided with my father as he made his way to the
bathroom in his boxer shorts and it was a moment I was glad I
didn't see.

'Do you have any Sanka?' the woman, wearing beige panties and
my brother's Jets T-shirt, had asked my father. According to the
legend, he ran for his trousers then pulled Danny out of bed and

threw him and the woman off the front porch; she attempted to run back in for her clothing, but my father locked the screen door and told Danny to get her off the premises. My mother, to her credit, ran to Danny's bedroom, gathered up the divorcee's blue jeans, blouse and sandals and ran out the breezeway door in her night robe, arms full. The woman, so hungover she didn't appreciate my mother's valor, took inventory of her clothing and then said, 'Hey, where's my stockings?'

'I'll send them UPS,' my mother said in her brogue as Danny Boy backed out of the drive and gunned it out and away.

That was the Chevette.

The Vega was for the Sunday morning Dad went out to move it from the path of the tow truck and found a roach in the ashtray that just wouldn't stop burning. The entire car was filled with thick Costa Rican smoke and Dad claimed he got a contact high, began throwing things about the garage and telling Mom to hold him back because he felt like he could fly and might jump out a window. When Danny Boy laughed and said, 'The shit wasn't *that* good. It's only cheap homegrown,' Dad had yelled, 'Hook her up!' so loud, all of Coangelo's Market knew they'd never see the Vega again. The 'Cuda was for a Friday night in the winter when Danny Boy and three friends closed the Swizzle Stick then hot-rodded on the football field behind the old Kirby High School, ripping the grass into ruts and furrows and taking out the wooden goalposts. It was rumored that he drove the exact same route he took on a state record 104-yard interception return. He was giving his friends a tour of the famous run, or so it was said.

Now, with the green Hornet being drawn into the rusted jaws of the wrecking machine, there would soon be a fourth carcass on the north face and my big brother would have to look at it through the course of the summer and repent. Dad sat high up on the two-pronged Caterpillar, face shaded by Pete's hat, watching the car go through while Danny stood by, holding some 8-track tapes and his Samuel French playbook under one arm, the black jar under the other. It was always the same: Dad's face was set grim and he appeared almost sad that it came to this. Grandpa supported the punishment in most cases. It was instructional, he argued. 'He'll learn to be a man.'

I stood on a pile of tires, my hands resting atop my cap as The Crusher bit down on the car we were just riding in less than two hours prior. Under the jack hammering diesel growl, Danny Boy was yelling something to my father, something defiant, encouraging him to crush the car. 'Go ahead, crush that piece of shit!' he yelled. 'I'm devastated. It was such a muscle-fucking car! It was such a street peach! Go ahead, crush it! Crush the fuck!'

My father, sitting on the throttling payloader, could not hear a word Danny Boy shouted. He just sat on high with a white dishtowel draping his neck from under the salvaged cap, looking like an Arab on a yellow dinosaur as he watched the Hornet come out the back end, flat as a mattress. He forked it and trundled away with the remains.

Grandpa arrived moments later, moving as slowly as a trout in warm shoals as he unloaded some refrigerator wire from his car trunk, and what appeared to be a discarded golf-cart canopy. Danny Boy ignored his request for help. Masking his hurt with a liverish smile, my brother retreated inside the dark tire bunker. From my perch atop warm rubber, I watched him through a window as he stood before his shrine and put on his work gauntlets. He faced a stack of bald tires and began to do a shadow box dance before them. He fired a right jab, another, then garrisoned a left uppercut and a wide swinging right. He spun and faced the mirror, watching himself throw a fusillade of punches just as De Niro had done in the *Raging Bull* teaser. He fired punches until he appeared all but spent, and with the last of his energy, he hefted a tire onto the hydraulic rim separator. His wide back rose and fell and I turned away out of respect.

When I did, I saw that Grandpa was watching Danny through the window, too.

CHAPTER ELEVEN

Ten Little Indians

My *Old Farmer's Almanac* promised the next day to be a halcyon one and blessed with a breeze, an angel's kiss. Instead, the sky brooded and took on a yellow aspect and thunderstorms pounded the neighborhood, washing down hot asphalt; it almost hissed with the sound of relief. Mama Orsini's tomatoes, although still Granny Smith green, were well on their way to blue ribbon size and the *zucchini* were stretching themselves into wonderfully grotesque shapes along the back wall of the Garatonis' cinderblock garage.

In my grandparents' garden, sugar-and-butter corn was high but too young. Still, I broke one off and tasted it raw, drawing the ire of Nonni. Gooma Rosario, the hunchbacked *mal'occhio*, had a witch's way with beans: they grew a full foot up their poles over a weekend, dwarfing her as she crawled on hands and knees in her elaborate terraced jungle.

Fourth of July was just days away, and while a Satanic killer walked the streets of our city in steel-shanked boots and a wool watch cap, thoughts of the Paradiso family gathering on the shore began to fill our home with some much-needed levity. Big Dan had even pulled the twenty-two foot dragnet from the basement and set Grandpa to mending it and repairing the floats. Nonni began taking down canned eggplant and olives and packing them with boxes of pasta into empty California Grape boxes. This bodement of happy times rekindled my faith in the sanctity of summer and I felt determined to salvage what was left of it.

Johnny the gypsy cabby became our only means of transportation and my brother and I would walk out to America Street to meet her, usually with Goomba Angelo buckled in the corner of the backseat, torturing the poor woman with cigar smoke while his pet monkey toyed with the wooden rollers on Johnny's massage backrest while she screamed out vintage Pointer with enough volume to be all three sisters, maybe a fourth.

It was just after supper when she retrieved us at the corner off St Francis and America and taxied us to the Saukiwog Community Playhouse on the east side. Angelo was not with her, but the smell of monkey and Judge's Cave cigars was heavy in the upholstery. Johnny had found herself serving as something of a liaison and Angelo sent messages through her: Mr Diaz's widow wasn't talking; woman be scared of something; we had to get through to her; we would go there tonight and talk turkey, plain deal and get down to bid'ness.

And, of course, there was the request for what our cousin called seed money – a few dollars to stuff into garter belts and buy some vodka and Galliano. You never knew when a dancer at the Thirsty Turtle might drop a bombshell, he said.

At The Playhouse, the former home of the local VFW, Johnny parked and dropped her hand upside down for her fare. Danny Boy slapped a five into it.

'Who sing in this show?' she asked my brother.

'It's not a musical,' he informed her, and she made a little disparaging sound from her belly.

'I've got some questions about this butler's motivation,' Danny Boy told the director, Mr A. Richard Pembroke, from across a small desk. Mr Pembroke was an English teacher from Saukiwog Community College and he wore his red-framed glasses at the end of his nose. Although he wore an informal sweatshirt to rehearsal – and what looked like Kung Fu slippers – he spoke in a manner that would have made Big Dan nervous. Sometimes my father confused excellent diction with being a *mangia*.

'Motivation. Go ahead, Donald. Quickly now.'

'There's something in there,' my brother said, clutching his playbook and appealing to Mr Pembroke. 'There's something about the way he's always in the pantry. Why is that? Why is Narracott always in there while everyone's out mingling?'

'We need to keep him offstage,' Mr Pembroke said with frankness. 'The butler only enters to bring the tomatoes and lemons. Narracott is what we call a secondary player. A sacrifice character, Donald.'

'A sacrifice character.'

'That's right.'

'Right, right,' Danny Boy said, thumb-flicking the pages like a deck of cards. 'But I'm thinking of doing something with this, this always-in-the-pantry-thing. The loneliness thing. I think loneliness has followed this guy his whole life.'

My brother was too fervent in his reverie to notice the look Mr Pembroke bounced off him; the man seemed eager to marshal his performers onto the stage. 'I don't think our Agatha meant the butler to be too deep, Donald.'

'Danny,' my brother corrected, and then he said, 'I think that this guy Narracott, always being in the pantry while everybody's out onstage, he's harboring things. And he's a little . . . I don't want to say depressed, but maybe, maybe lonely is the right word. And this is his motivation.'

'He's lonely,' the director said impatiently.

'Yeah. And so he eats a lot. You gotta figure, he's in there with pancake mix and onion dips and things like that. These are fancy people so there's all kinds of finger foods and salsa, and so, he finds himself eating. A lot.'

Mr A. Richard Pembroke was half-standing now, already having side chats with other actors, but my brother, nothing if not focused, remained anchored to his aluminum folding chair.

'Can you get to the crux, Danny?'

Thrown only for a second, Danny Boy opened his playbook and looked at a stage diagram. 'From stage left?'

'Your *point*, Daniel. What is your point here? This is a small role – an important role, but we can't spend the entire first night of rehearsal discussing the subtleties of the butler.'

'Okay, well what I'm saying is, and what I want to get your support on, Mr Pembroke, is what Stanislavski says about preparing.'

Mr Pembroke arced his brow above his red-framed specs. 'Oh, are we reading Stanislavksi, Daniel?'

'I really want to prepare for this role, Mr Pembroke.'

'In what way?'

'I think I should gain forty pounds.'

There was a growing silence in the former VFW dance hall and Mr A. Richard Pembroke abandoned all his interest in the other actors to look square at my brother and sit again. I was proud of Danny Boy. He wasn't going to phone this one in.

'All you need to do,' Mr Pembroke advised, 'is learn your four lines and wear a clean white dress shirt and dark slacks like a domestic. If you feel compelled to gain weight for the role, fine. That's between you and your mother's grocery bill.'

'Okay,' my brother said, nodding his head and looking off at the wall as if he was accepting a rescue mission over Iran. Relieved, Mr A. Richard Pembroke clapped his hands once and started for the stage.

'One more thing, Mr Pembroke.'

'*What*? What is it *now*?' Mr A. Richard Pembroke fingered his red glasses up on the bridge of his nose and stared impatiently.

'Can I improvise? If I feel something going on, can I—'

'Absolutely not,' the director said, and now as he scuffed in his Kung Fu slippers for the stage, his consortium of community players laughed at his mock escape; I had the feeling these people had done this sort of thing before and my brother and I were newcomers. At center stage the college professor pitched his excellent diction off the cavernous walls and called everyone in to sit in a circle.

Danny Boy went up and took a seat between a pert back-to-school housewife and a thin, balding man with an earring and a beret who was playing Rogers. Danny was going to be, along with Rogers, the first to enter the stage, 'Center from Left,' Mr Pembroke read aloud, 'carrying a market basket filled with packages. Props? Make a note, Props.'

Danny Boy's would be the very first line of the play: 'First lot to be arriving in Jim's boat,' and then something about, 'Here are the lemons, cream, eggs and tomatoes.'

I noticed his hands were darkened from grease and they trembled a little but he read the line without a stammer and the rehearsal was off and running. Although his character disappeared by page 18, he remained focused. I was focused myself: here was a play in which the players were murdered one by one and the survivors began to suspect each other. *Ten Little Indian boys going out to dine, one went and choked himself and then there were nine.*

Somewhere in the middle of the play, Mr Pembroke sprung to center, flapping his scant yellow playbook and uncapping a pen with his teeth. 'No! No, no!'

A lull came over the rehearsal hall as the director raised his excellent diction to an unpitying volume. 'There is a murderer amongst you!' he yelled at the girl who was playing Old Emily, and I could see Mr A. Thomas Pembroke imagined himself On Broadway. 'You don't know who it is, people! Is it the guy next to you? Is it Judge Wargrave? Is it Lombard? Is it the house parlorman? Is it *you?*' he asked, pointing at the thin balding man in the beret.

'Is it you, Vera?' He swung a finger at the young college girl playing Vera and then at my brother. 'Is it the butler who we haven't seen in an hour?' Danny Boy perked up and seemed to favor this possibility. Mr Pembroke chewed his pen again, gyrated to make his point, and spun a finger across the hall at me. 'Is it him? Is *he* the killer?' The players looked at me and they must have seen the warm rush of blood run through my face because several chuckled and it made a hollow sound in the old VFW, and I lowered the leather brim of my Mao cap.

'We don't know who the killer is, do we? We're trapped, people. We're trapped and we don't know who's going to be shot or chopped up at the woodpile next. The little Indians are falling off the mantel. Who is going to be cut in half with an ax, who is going to be strangled in the foyer, who is going to be found poisoned in the woodshed – for God's sake, people! There's a killer among us and it may be the person next to you.'

The words echoed in the hall and they sent a chill through me. 'Which one? Say it with loathing, Wargrave. Which one?'

Which one? Somewhere out there, he was driving alone in the night, whoever he was, thinking he locked a trunk on the perfect crime.

While all the community players laughed with coy and artsy delight, having fun behind their masks, I could only think of the face of the dying man, alone in a car, up there in the dark like the bones of a raven cache in a high rookery.

*　　*　　*

Although Big Dan would undoubtedly take me to task if he knew, I had always felt a kinship to our Puerto Rican neighbors. They were similar to us Italians in many respects: hot bloods, they had their superstitions, their own evil eye and their own talisman (a glass sphere with an eyeball), long-ago arranged weddings, regional rivalries, a deep love for music, and a thing for salted codfish. Like us, they were the only group who were as close to their cousins as they were to their own siblings, and often, much closer. If someone gave a Latino kid a snow cone, you could bet a dollar he'd ask for another seven for his cousins. We were the same way.

As me, Danny Boy, Johnny and Angelo walked through the South End – me pushing the Pinkerton Man – Hispanic elders were sitting out on the walks and stoops, playing cards and dominoes at eight o'clock and calling each other *boricua* in the same manner that our old men called each other *guaglione*. A few craned to eye Angelo with curiosity or sympathy, and a few stopped dead in their game when they saw the small monkey in his lap. But most paid us no distraction.

I had been raised to fear the Puerto Rican section almost as much as the black North End, but Goomba Angelo coasted through with a certain peace and any trepidation I had fell away with each step into the neighborhood. The only music in the air was the sound of some Spanish mountain music from inside a little shop: percussion, string, and what sounded like a gourd. It soothed me. We passed a Botanica where herbs and roots hung in the window. We went up a side street where the old Caribe Movie Theater had been restored as a Catholic Church. The marquis read *Our Lady of Lourdes* on one side and *Saturday Night Fever* on the other.

These people were at peace with the traditions of their Old Country, just like our Lithuanians in the hill section and the Irish and Scots and blacks and Italians. Our city was no melting pot, my mother once argued with Cousin Giustina of the Associate's Degree.

'Oh, I'm sorry,' Giustina had said through her nasal chamber. 'We're talking about a microcosm of the country. All cities are America in miniature, and America is one big melting pot.'

No, Mom had asserted in a rare moment of contention, yet maintaining her pleasant voice. It was like a good sauce, she'd said:

dozens of ingredients and spices stirred and simmered together all adding to the taste but each maintaining its own unique flavor.

I was comfortable with this thought now as we passed the domino-players, drinking cold beer and smoking cigars and laughing from their bellies at tales told in both English and Spanish; their kids and grandkids rode bikes or sweat out the final innings of wiffle ball and a clutch of women came down the walk, dressed up from a visit to Saint Cecelia Church on Taino Street. Nobody paid us any mind as we approached the first floor of the four-story Diaz tenement.

Some fake flowers sat in the window and a fan inside made them rattle every ten seconds. We knocked on the door and a small dog barked from within but no one responded. And then, as the churchgoing women passed by, one of them broke off, saying her goodbyes in Spanish, and came up the walk. She was carrying a brown grocery bag in one hand and leading a small child with the other. When she got halfway to the door and found the strange Argonauts assembled on her porch, she froze and gave us a look, at once frightened and suspicious.

'Mrs Diaz,' Goomba Angelo said, surprisingly soft. 'We've come to offer our condolences.'

'Why? Who are you?' She spoke in broken American.

'My name is Angelo Volpe. Private security.'

'Where from?'

There was an uncomfortable hesitation for only a moment. 'Are you familiar with the name Pinkerton, ma'am?' he said with authority and nobody blinked.

'The police already are here. I no call for no help from nobody.'

'No, Mother, you did not. But these young men here did. You see, ma'am, they may have information on the whereabouts of your husband.'

Her eyes went straight to me. I could see she was a woman who trusted the young. For a moment she looked like she was going to lose composure, maybe cry. Then she glanced down over the sidewalk where men laughed as they played dominoes, and this seemed to distract her.

'So many people make the trouble on me. The *polizia*, the insurance. The newspaper. The women who come and tell me to wear the black. I no wear the black!' she said, shouting it over the railing at her neighbors.

'Ooh, easy now, Mrs Diaz,' Johnny said, and she stepped down to take the woman's arm. 'Jesus made the blind man see.' This she quoted straight from a plaster marker on Maple Hill. It was not exactly appropriate but it had a cathartic effect on the woman.

'My grandson,' she wept, indicating the child beside her. 'Little Joey. I raise. He is only sixteen month. He say "Where Poppi-Pop?" I don't know. What do I say? I don't know! I have to raise up this boy.'

Seeing this lady cry over the disappearance of her husband – and fairly certain that I knew the truth – dug at something inside me and I felt my strength flag; I had been able to maintain a straight face at the Thirsty Turtle, I only blushed in the presence of the nuns on Maple Hill, but here on the stoop of the small yellow house in the South End, my bottom lip went as tight as an overwound guitar string and then everything came up and out like I was having a good barf. I began to cry. Not a full-fledged cry but a quick escape of sound that startled everyone before I could suck it back in. The Hispanic woman drew back a pace and observed me, her fingers at her lips. Angelo, on the other hand, could not have been more pleased by my timing.

'Terrible things this boy has seen,' he said. He wasn't lying, just being resourceful. 'Can we speak with you, Mother?' he asked as she kept her troubled eyes on me.

'*Si*,' she said finally and she removed her house keys from her purse.

When we entered we found that the barking dog was a fuzzy, battery-operated terrier that yapped whenever anyone touched the door. The boy, Little Joey, took it in his small arms and toddled off to a corner of the room where toys were splayed like they had dropped from a busted pinnate. Mrs Diaz noticed Ruby on the investigator's lap and adjusted her eyeglasses. 'Where you are finding this alley cat?'

'It's not an alley cat,' he told her. 'It's a squirrel monkey.' He looked right at me when he said this, as if challenging my Natural History again. Mrs Diaz meanwhile seemed nonplussed by the primate in her kitchen, but she attempted to be the gracious host that I could see she was.

As Ruby chewed on Little Joey's leftover baby biscuit, Mrs Diaz poured me a lemonade in a coffee cup and I said, 'Thank you, Mrs Diaz.' But as I lifted the porcelain I saw something disturbing: printed on the cup was a grainy black and white photo of a man who must have been Mr Maximino Diaz; it was sepia toned and faded by time, and his face was just a blur, but he wore glasses and the mouth looked familiar as he yowled in mock fear from inside a spinning teacup at Santa's Village. Under the picture were the words *World's Greatest Poppi-Pop*.

The more I stared at the transfer the more he fit the man in the trunk. The *World's Greatest Poppi-Pop* was not lost in Maine. *The World's Greatest Poppi-Pop* was dead, and Angelo told her so, straight across the kitchen table.

Mrs Diaz removed her glasses and massaged her eyes and began slapping a hand on the table and saying something in her own tongue. Repeatedly she did this, and with each slap of the table, the battery-operated, sound-responsive dog barked and Ruby Lee limbed on the wheelchair with the wet biscuit in her teeth and arched her back. Little Joey clapped his hands in delight.

'Let the woman cry some,' Johnny said. 'Don't stare over the lady.'

Johnny lowered her eyes and folded her hands respectfully on the table top, but one eye kept rolling up like she couldn't stop looking. When Mrs Diaz composed herself, she told us why she had purchased the battery-operated dog at Caldor department store. She had been the victim not only of a family mystery, but of a brutal tug-of-war between the women at Our Lady of Lourdes – who had been urging her to don black – and the *Yoruba* woman who wanted to light four candles for her and summon her husband back from the dead. And more. There was the city police, telling her to stop faking and confess the truth about her husband. They even sent a cop who spoke Spanish, but he was one of those recent Guatemalan immigrants and he came to the house with a little Lebanese man named Charlie from Nutmeg Insurance. Her son, she told us, a good man, had already been to the insurance company inquiring about the policy on his father's life in the event he never returned.

This responsible act by a good son created suspicion and a *parrada* of trouble up and down her front stoop.

'They come on m'house and knock – boom-boom, boom-boom – all night, see? So I buy the dog, see. No real, because they make piss.' Another common link to the Italians I observed: Nonni often talked about cats or dogs 'making the Ka-ga' or 'do the *peeshad*.' These oldtime immigrants liked to keep their linoleum spotless, it seemed.

'STARBOARD!' Angelo suddenly shouted and Ruby levered the wheelchair in reverse then angled it until her master said, 'Hold.' There before the refrigerator our cousin sat staring at the door on which there were a half-dozen Polaroids, Little Joey's crayon explosions, and several news clippings from a Spanish-language journal.

'Who's the handsome cowboy on the motor bike?' Angelo asked her. She didn't understand the question so Angelo jerked his head at me and I went to the ice box. I pointed to the photograph of a big, dark man with long flax hair straddling a chopper. I didn't know why Angelo called him a cowboy. He was dressed in a black leather vest, blue jeans and military boots. The little boy Joey, younger in the photo, was sitting on the handlebars.

'Tino,' she said. 'My son.'

Angelo asked me to bring the Polaroid over to him and so I did, holding it a few inches from his face.

'Little Joey's father?' Angelo said.

'*Si*,' whispered Mrs Diaz, her eyes darting from my cousin to my brother as if trying to read their minds.

Angelo angled his chair back toward the table. 'Nunzio,' he said, and I was grateful that he didn't call me Numb Nuts in front of the old woman. 'You can put Tino back on the fridge.'

When I went back to the ice box and pulled the little watermelon magnet off, I lingered to look at some of Little Joey's crayon drawings. They reminded me of the ones I did at his age, the ones Mom kept in a tin box in her bottom drawer.

'Your husband came to this country in what – the late 1940s?' Angelo said after letting a silence press into the woman.

'Nineteen fifty-two,' she said with a hint of pride under her plaintive voice. 'He worked in the brass mill.'

'Didn't we all,' Angelo said.

'Overtime,' Mrs Diaz said. 'Always the overtime. The Saturday, the Sunday. When the mill shut down, no benefit, *nada*. But he saved twenty-nine year and so he make his own construction business. He build the house, see. He turn the old movie house into the church. He build the shopping center over here, see. Save all his life. And he buy the old rolling mill so they no knock it down.'

Angelo studied the clippings and then, with a command, had Ruby give him his tube so he could guide himself back to face the woman. 'Ambitious man, your husband,' he said.

'He want to make the old mill into the housing. For the poor people. Even the state say they will give some money into the housing.'

'So why did he go to Maine? Find some cheap pine or what?'

She hesitated, and I wished Angelo was not staring at her in the relentless manner he was.

'He is upset,' she said, beginning to weaken again. 'He have the high blood pressure.' *Predjoor*, she pronounced it.

'Upset about what? You two have a little spat?'

The woman frowned at him, wetness at the rims of her glasses.

'A little fight?' Angelo probed, patiently. 'You know, like husbands and wives do.'

'He can no get the permit,' she said. 'Can no get the approval for the engineer.'

'He couldn't get an engineering permit. From who – the zoning board?'

'*Si, si*. The Aldermans, the Housings. He was so *mad* – he have the high blood predjoor,' she said, revealing some blood in her own face. 'His life for saving he put inside this rolling mills and he can no get the permission to build his apartment for the poor people.'

'Little Five Card Draw,' Angelo said, turning his head toward my brother. In moments like this during our investigation, my *goomba* reminded me of a doctor and my brother an intern being instructed on the job with the unfortunate patient standing by.

'But *si*,' Mrs Diaz sighed, '*Si*. Yes. We have the fight. The spat.'

'Ah, the spat,' Angelo sighed in turn.

'He have so much trouble making this building, I tell him to sell the lands. He can make a lot of money just to sell the lands. He get mad, take his gun and the fishing pole and go out. Mad.'

'To Maine?' Danny Boy wanted to confirm.

'He like Maine,' Mrs Diaz said. 'He go up there to fish, to hunt. To think. Always to go think.' And then, burdened by the weeks of worry, she dropped her head in her hands again and groaned, 'But never this long.'

'I'm sure he had a lot to think about,' Angelo said. 'He invests his life savings to buy an old factory then can't get city approval to do anything with it? He's stuck with an old mill and no money.'

Mrs Diaz did not respond for a time. Her face was set like old brick. 'The police, they even look in my closet,' she said. 'They rip up the floor because maybe I am hiding my husband someplace.' She laughed at the absurdity even as she wept.

And there had been other vultures knocking at her door: an Italian who made tombstones; a nephew who brought a cake and then asked if he could have her husband's toolbox; some developers who had offered to take the old mill ruins off her family's hands and make payments to her; Tino, a good son, admonishing her for not protecting herself by taking out a larger policy; even her landlady, a fat Spanish spinster who suggested maybe she go someplace smaller to free her responsibilities – 'and the rent control,' offered Johnny Mae who said she had been through that one before. With the scent of death comes vultures, Angelo commiserated.

She had told them all to leave her alone. Her husband would come back, she shouted at the landlady. Max would return as he always did, maybe with some pheasant-back mushrooms and a new resolve. A fighter, he would apply for the approval again, go to Mayor Longo himself if he had to. Put on his banquet suit and march up the steps of City Hall with his plans rolled under an arm. He had come to this country a *jibaro*, a greenhorn, with nothing but his hammer and square, and he built a bridge from sheet rock and faux brick for a new generation of Diazes. He would prevail.

This is what she told herself.

As the grown-ups talked over strong Spanish coffee, I removed a little Mass card from an ice-box magnet and a business card that read *BCD* beneath a logo of the Saukiwog Mills clock. I brought the items to Goomba Angelo like an eager bird-dog and set them on the table before him. He gave me the kind of look my dad often gave when I brought him the wrong-sized wrench.

'Senora,' Angelo said, nodding a cue to Danny Boy, 'do you recognize this at all?'

Danny Boy half stood to get his hand into his jeans pocket. He came up with a fist, set it on the table, and let some loose rosary beads click on the Formica. They rolled to the center. 'O Dio,' Mrs Diaz choked. 'He keep the rosary bead on the mirror in his Chevy. Oh, my *Jesus*. Where are you finding this?'

'We can't tell you right now, ma'am,' Danny Boy said. 'We're working on it. Just trust us and please don't say anything to anybody. We're here to help you.'

I felt spurred to move in. I pulled the brass token from my pocket, and then the Chicago Teamsters hat-pin, holding both out in my open hand. The Latina elder looked at the trinkets over the frames of her glasses.

'Have you ever seen this?' I asked, my eyes coursing the table to make sure Angelo or my brother weren't laughing at my effort. 'It says 1973 Chicago Teamsters and it has some kind of number on it.'

She stared. For a long spell, she studied it like a jeweler, then shook her head. 'He never go Chicago,' she said. And then she took the brass token from my fingers and angled it in the light of a bare bulb. 'This is maybe the subway coin? Sometime he go into New York to the Spanish Harlem. His cousin have a botanica store over there,' she said, hopefully.

'That's what *I* was going to say,' Johnny put in. 'Look like a subway token. Or one of them coins you put in a Coke machine to cheat out a soda pop. What you call them – plug?'

'Slug,' said Angelo, sucking his teeth.

Mrs Diaz shook her head, not quite understanding.

'What about Savin Rock Amusement Park?' I asked and suddenly everyone looked at me again. 'Did he ever get his fortune told?'

'I don't understand,' Mrs Diaz said.

'Maybe he should have,' said Angelo wryly. 'Maybe he should have had his fortune told.'

'I no understand what you say,' the widow lamented.

'No, it's okay,' Angelo said, keeping his eyes on her. 'We've got

Chip and Ernie working with us over here. Just don't make a deal
with anyone, Mother. Don't file an insurance claim yet, don't give
away his toolbox, don't move out and don't wear black. Not yet.
It ain't over till the Fat Lady sings.' He looked at Johnny with that
dark oil-cured glimmer in his eye.

'Don't even get in that lane,' she said.

Mrs Diaz picked up one rosary bead and enveloped it in her
hand. She held it there and tightened her shoulders. For a moment
it seemed she was going to cry again. But then she took air in
through her nose, and more air. A web of veins became visible at
her neck. She had survived a lot in her days, I could see that. 'Who
kill my husband?' she asked and there was rage etching grooves
about her lips.

'We don't know, Mother,' Angelo said. 'But keep your doors
locked.'

Down at the Plymouth cab, as Danny Boy and I helped Angelo's
lifeless frame into the backseat, I heard something up on the third
floor of the Diaz apartment, a kind of muffled music. TV music,
it sounded like; the mind-numbing piano theme of a Spanish soap
opera. It gets our minds off our own troubles, Mom once told me
when I tried to sit through five minutes of one of her soaps.

I couldn't imagine any soap character having more troubles than
the Widow Diaz. As we pulled away from the curb, Little Joey
waved to me from the porch.

Driving back to The Little Boot, Johnny's Fury III resembled not so
much a cop cruiser as the backseat of a school bus on the morning
after a *Kojak* episode. Johnny shouted her murder theories over
Angelo; Danny Boy was twisted around in the front seat, pitching
his voice at our cousin, wondering about the son Tino; I was
determined to have my say about the man I saw on the coffee cup;
Angelo was intent on relegating all of us to 'dumb cock-knockers'
or 'marginal morons' and he lamented his involvement in such
penny pool.

'If assholes could fly,' he said, 'this car would be an aircraft
carrier.'

I was beginning to regret my involvement as well; I felt a terrible
guilt, as though we were performing open-heart surgery with the Dr

Kildare kit I found in the trunk of a '63 Dodge. But there was no one else in this city investigating this brutal murder. It was our property now, just like the car itself, inside the Paradiso fence, crushed metal yet to be redeemed. It was ours whether we liked it or not. There was also, as my mother would say if she were there, 'no tree but bears some fruit'.

Over and over I had to remind myself: if we went to higher authorities than Angelo, my father could end up serving time in some cement prison. Even if he had no knowledge of the trunk's cargo, he could find himself in a Hitchcock scenario, trapped in the correctional center in Danbury. 'I didn't know what was in there, fellas,' he would plead with the guards. 'I thought it was dead puppies.'

'I know Motherfucker ain't in no Maine,' Johnny wailed into the rearview mirror. 'She had his Spanish ass *kilt*.'

'Easy, woman,' Angelo said. 'Not so fast.'

Danny Boy took our cousin out mid-sentence with actor's projection: 'If that's a Harlem subway coin, maybe he was into some shit down there. In New York.'

'Woman had the man *smoked*,' Johnny insisted. 'Ya'll see that purple candle burning in the living room? That be voodoo shit.'

'That was him, the man on the coffee cup,' I said, more to Ruby Lee than to anyone. '*The World's Greatest Poppi-Pop*. He liked spinning tea cups.'

'What was that Savin Rock shit?' my brother said, and everyone joined in to drill me.

'Mr Carmella at the bank said the token looked like the kind you put into Lady Fortuna.'

'Woman did it to Sam Cooke,' Johnny threw in. 'Woman took down James Brown. Hell got no fury like the woman when she know you been sticking it somewhere else. What if he was messin' with the suntan girl? What if that why she wearing the teardrop tattoo?'

'He was refused his building permit,' Angelo said. 'He was depressed. Wanted to go to Maine, get away. He drives down over here to the river and looks at the old brass mill, makes him *sick*. Can't even look at it. Got to get away from it. Far away from it. Right, Danny Boy? Like the way you got to get far away from your old school: it reminds you of your . . . you know what I'm saying.'

My brother went stony for a second, then turned a look on our third cousin, but Goomba Angelo allowed no derailment. 'He drives off for the interstate. Now that takes him right past the big peace cross – keep in mind the guy is down. He's Old Country P.R. Superstitious, Catholic, keeps rosary beads on his mirror – so he drives up Maple Hill to pray. He parks. Goes into Jerusalem. Prays for holy intervention. Ain't that the time we pray? When we need our plumbing permit passed? Or we need a raise? Or we need to win the Daily Numbers?'

No one in the car answered the question, but we all looked at each other, as if trying to see who appeared guilty of such depravity.

'The Shooter pulls up,' Angelo said. 'Not in his own car, but a stolen Pontiac Bonneville to cover his tracks. He walks up to Max Diaz, puts a gun to his forehead and says, "I put all my fucking money into your apartment scam and now I'm shit out of luck. Where's my money, *Jibaro*?'

'"Gone," Diaz says. "It's all in the rolling mill."'

Angelo went quiet. We waited, but he didn't finish his hypothesis.

'So what happens?' Johnny asked, turning around as she drove.

'Ask Nunzio,' the ex-cop said. 'He saw the results.'

Danny Boy flipped down the sun visor and found Angelo in the mirror. 'Where's his Chevy then? Where's Diaz's Chevy?'

'Chop shop. History. Remember: we live in the car theft capital of the world.'

'Who is this Shooter?' I asked, clinging to Johnny's headrest, aware that my voice was quavering.

'We better ask Lady Fortuna,' Angelo quipped, '"cuz I ain't got the answer. I say we go to Public Land Records and find out who had any liens on the rolling mill.'

'Or maybe,' Johnny said, 'be the Shooter givin' some to Mrs Diaz on the side-order and he took out the husband. Maybe that little boy over there really belongs to the Shooter. Ooh! I don't even wanna think about this shit no more!' she said, shaking off the chill she gave herself.

We pulled down along the Mattatuck River and followed its

green, percolating ooze past the ruins of rubber shops and defunct brass works that sat like beached whaling ships long after the whalers' era. Further we drove, down toward an old building the color of sun-baked red mud where a cornerstone was inscribed with the date 1899. In the long shadows of the old brass mill we parked and looked at Mr Diaz's lifetime acquisition. The notion of his dream, to transform the defunct factory into affordable housing, made me think of my own grandfather's passions and I felt a terrible darkness come over me as the sun sank low and a light wind rapped at a loose board on the fourth story of the old mill. The large plastic letters bolted across its face were still intact: YANKEE BRASS. All but three of the windows were broken and those three were opaque like smoked plastic. It was as much a ghost adrift as Max Diaz himself. The fine hairs on my nape bristled under the touch of cooling night air.

'Why do you think they wouldn't give him his permit?' I asked, looking at the place as perhaps Mr Diaz would have – or the way Grandpa would – envisioning its potential. 'He was going to turn it into apartments for *poor* people.'

'That's right, Nunzio,' Angelo said. 'Affordable housing. Huddle fever. Pregnant colored women with six kids on the balcony and twins in the crib, drug dealers moving in, selling dope off the seventh floor to the father of the kids on the third floor, some Cape Verdean guy on welfare. Or a Uruguayan – one of the new arrivals coming late for dinner. Or freeloading H-caps like me who you have to throw a bone to. Costa Ricans crowding in on Puerto Ricans, more stress on schools. That's not what the city wants. They want to see industrial parks, malls. Shoe outlets. Self-Serve ready marts. By the time Diaz saved enough money to build his great vision, it weren't so great any more. By the time the poor bastard saved enough money for the American Dream he found himself up to his asshole in an East Coast nightmare. Man got stuck with a pile of old brick.'

'I'll bet you dollars to donuts,' Danny Boy said, 'that he's up in Maine. Fishing and hunting like she says.'

'No, he ain't,' Angelo said.

'If he's in Maine, then who's in the Pontiac, Danny?' I said.

Angelo said something to Ruby Lee that sounded like 'SNAKE

EYES' or 'SHAKE ICE,' and the monkey went into his jacket pocket, burrowing and making a sound like a rusted water spigot. When she came up, she was shaking something like dice in a cup. 'Drop it,' Angelo ordered. She did. Right on the seat between me and Angelo: a tiny vial, dark amber. I picked it up and held it for all to see.

'Would he go to Maine without his blood pressure pills?' Angelo said.

The little sticker on the vial was all in Spanish, but I recognized the name M. C. Diaz. Danny Boy looked back at it, took it from me, then turned an eye on Angelo that betrayed something close to amazement.

Johnny was looking, too. 'Damn.' She smacked her lips, astounded by her Angel's talents. Then she bent low to the dash, straining to look at the roof. 'I bet Motherfucker's ghost is runnin' around up in there, hammering nails and shit. Puttin' up wallpaper.'

'No,' Angelo said. 'His ghost is up in a junkyard, trying to stop that shipment of scrap from going overseas.'

Angelo was right. There were a lot of ghosts at Paradise Salvage; Mr Diaz was amongst kindred dead.

'When's that load of crushed cars go out?' Angelo said.

'Two weeks,' Danny said, glancing over at me for verification. 'Goes to Bridgeport on the truck, then gets shipped out from the docks by the gross ton. To Japan.'

'Japan?' Johnny said in the rearview. 'You mean this dead man might be going to Japan?'

'If we don't nail the killer in two weeks,' Angelo said.

'What they do with that shit in Japan?' Johnny sang high.

'Shredded,' Danny Boy said. 'Then melted down. Recycled.'

'Say *what*?' Johnny said, fixed on this now. 'That man might come back to this country as a Honda Civic?'

'See, Johnny?' Angelo said. 'There *is* such a thing as reincarnation.'

'Yeah,' she chortled. 'My ass comes back, she gonna be a Lincoln. With radial ply.'

CHAPTER TWELVE

Tutto de Mare

The tradition was as sacrosanct as any festival of saints. It was a ceremony entrenched in our family lore, one that may have begun on the shores of the Adriatic centuries ago; one spoke of it in the same breath as Easter, Christmas Eve, Columbus Day and the Festa di San Donato. It had been going on long before my brother Danny was born and years before the invention of Tupperware or Zip-Loc bags.

The procession of family cars, six or seven, were loaded down with coolers of shrimp and *calamari,* used grape boxes of *fusili* and *ziti,* great vats of Nonni's sauce and carloads of fresh garden vegatables, and of course, as Angelo reminisced, the *baccala* – salted codfish in a thick oil. The family cars, a diverse cavalcade of junkyard keepers, parked in an orderly row at the coast. Tailgates dropped. Arms bucket-brigaded the crates and bowls, and laughter and song and *Ponti* language carried on the salt air. The men of the family, most wearing nothing but floral print Bermudas and black loafers with no socks, did less hauling of the food but carried most of the umbrellas and chairs. Two picnic tables, claimed by our clan, were laid out with the feast; umbrellas quickly speared into the sand for the old women and my mother whose Celtic skin burned easily; lawn chairs creaked into position and my young cousins and I wasted no time in moving a pigskin up and down the surf.

'Never'a mind the basketball,' Grandpa would say to us. 'Come on over and work the net.'

Grandpa, for as long as I can remember, had sat himself in his favorite lawn chair – the one he repaired with long strips of rubber inner tubes – and his salvaged straw hat shading him, thick brown arms folded across his chest. Like the king of a gypsy caravan, he would sit for hours watching his progeny, seemingly evaluating each member's place in the pedigree and their potential. Only when the feast began did he stir. Or sometimes, maybe after a few cups of wine, he would play *morra* with me, Little Vinnie and the other young cousins. Of course, at high-tide he joined in with the core ceremony that marked this event: the Great Net Ritual of the Paradisos.

All of us: Nonni, Zia Concetta, Gooma Rosa, Goomba Rocco, Giustina, Lena and Pina Maria, and everybody in the family plus their godfathers who we could not physically accommodate in our kitchen on Sundays; the entire *gumbaraggio* took their places along the thirty-foot bait net and walked it slowly into the ocean. Corked on top and weighted at the bottom, we dragged the net as far out as Big Dan directed us. There was a broom handle attached to each end and these were the skill positions: Danny Boy took one end, Big Dan the other. Out beyond the breakers with joyful Italian language and laughter all about us, we dipped and swept, and hauled the net back in.

Other families on the beach, the people with skin that always burned before it tanned, encircled us and looked in at our magnificent sunlit catch. As always, I marveled over the Medusa's head of eels and snails and unidentified wonders that lay flapping and croaking in the net: flatworms and jellyfish, sea spiders and hermit crabs and an array of starfish; leatherfin lumpsuckers beating their gills in the harsh sun, greenbanded gobies and flamebacked angelfish thrashing amongst silver-black eels and chalk bass and shining little bolts of vibrating bait fish; what looked like a sea cucumber came to life when poked, revealing itself as some toothed exotic with sharp gills; a black drum had been making a croaking rumble in its throat and triggering great curiosity amongst the other kids surrounding us. And there were seashells galore, and old All-star Kola bottles, flying fish and pisser clams – and flotsam from afar.

Nonni, her black slacks rolled up, walked in amongst the catch with a stick and a bucket. Anything that looked poisonous was clobbered; anything that looked like it would add some flavor to her sauce, bucketed. Out of the Great Net Ritual came a most exotic and delicious *tutte de mare* – everything of the sea – even though we couldn't identify half of it. My brother referred to this particular July sauce as 'the red tide'.

Only one member of our family did not participate in the netting, but this was due to a talent of his own and he was respected as a most-gifted piscator. Zi Toine, eyes shining with his own potent wine, had slipped off his black loafers soon after his arrival. Year after year the reaction was the same: a great gasp and expressions of awe as Zi Toine displayed his neglected toenails. As long as jack-knife blades, they were a frightening aggregate of shapes and lengths, yellowish and curling up in places. 'Clam diggers,' my father said with a kind of familial pride, and Zi Toine started his slow long-strided, head-bobbing, blue heron walk into the surf. Out past the breakers with the ocean up to his neck he drifted in a very slow, methodical manner, his feet probing the silt and seaweed below. If one did not know the nature of his sea dance, they would think it a floating head with a thick mustache, adrift on the changing tide. Whenever his remarkable toenails dug out a cherrystone or a quahog, he submerged and stayed under until he secured the clam. After three or more hours he returned to shore with his neck sun-dusky, blowing saltwater from his nostrils with a mulish honk; his gathering basket was his swim trunks and they bulged and sagged, clams rattling with every long stride.

This, I'm sure, seemed a foreign ritual to the other kids, but to me, it was as normal as making sandcastles. A fine moment it was when Zi Toine stepped onto a spread bedsheet, inserted his thumbs in his waistband and tugged as he shook his legs – first the left, then the right – and clams dropped to earth with a sound like castanets. These too, found their way into Nonni's pot that night, and the following day at the table Zi Toine would be acknowledged with a *saluti* and a mention of his tusk-like clam diggers.

For us *Pontelandolfesi*, these were times of emotional and physical solace. But they were also, for me, times of strange displacement. While we feasted on magnificent crocks of *maccherone*, Nonni's sauce and its meaty wonders, and great jars of olives, slabs of sharp *provolone*, other kids at neighboring picnic tables ate hot dogs with relish and quaffed Pepsi.

Sitting there, between my father and Goomba Rocco, lost in the passionate Italian conversations, I felt like an American kid trapped in the camp of a foreign faction – like Will Mummy from *Lost in Space* time-traveled to eighteenth-century Europe. Nonni looked at the *Americani* children at the next table and whispered with compassion. A hot dog was child abuse to an Italian – you were starving the poor freckle-faced kid. A little redheaded girl in a green one-piece and matching flip-flops, flapped her way over to our table and stared down at the spread, wrinkling her freckled nose.

'They're eating squids, Daddy,' she announced to the entire beach. But when her father came to the table to apologize and retrieve her, he glanced down, froze in his step and began an awkward discourse on the tides, his eyes crawling over thick slices of lasagna. 'Sit down,' Zia Concetta said. 'Eat.' I never saw a man shove his daughter toward the waves and take a seat so fast in my life. Maybe, I reasoned, there'd be an extra hot dog left over at his table.

Danny Boy ate a quart of everything and placed the blame on Stanislavski; preparing for his role of Narracott, he explained to Cousin Pina. He then sat alone on a blanket, his belly turned toward the sun and his thoughts hidden behind RayBans and his Super 8 camera. He was filming the beach event. Watching him, I noticed he had that snake-bit look again, hungover and oblivious to the comments being made about him by Gooma Rosa. Nonni defended him, saying that the *mal'occhio* had done a number on him and he needed time to rest.

'*Nunzi-oooooooh*,' Grandpa sang to me from his lawn-chair throne. He was wrapping netted fish in the Sunday paper as quickly as my father cleaned them and Nonni inspected them. I came over in my skinny jaunt – nothing on but colorful baggy swim trunks and my golden horn fetish. With the sun browning my back, I knelt at Grandpa's sandals and helped him wrap our bountiful catch. My father seemed at peace with the ritual, far from the junkyard and whatever secrets he may have been harboring. And so, I too found peace in it, not daydreaming for once, but making a true effort at wrapping fish for the family food cache. However, an allotment was made when we got to the comics and I scanned a little Beetle Bailey as I encased a black drum.

'Nice job,' Big Dan said, handing me a fresh sheet from the Local

News section. Grandpa lifted his eyes onto me when he heard this approval from my father. He smiled. I could tell that he was feeling secure in his belief that summer labor would make a man of me. As I slapped an American sandlance on the newspaper, my eye caught a bold headline: INDIANS TO STAGE CLAIM.

'Hey,' I said. 'Hey, Danny.' I shook sand from the page and waved it for all to see. 'It's about the play. You're in the paper!'

This prompted a loaded silence, but Danny Boy lowered the Super 8 and reached for the local section.

'Never'a mind,' Grandpa said to me. 'When you work you work, when you read, you read. Too much read, you go blind.'

'Ah, *si, Jesu Christa,*' Gooma Rosa said from under her umbrella.

But Danny Boy was piqued. At Mom's egging he read aloud. 'Saukiwog Mayor Frank Longo—' he looked up at Dad's reaction, as if the mayor's very name validated the performance.

'Frankie baby,' Cousin Giustina said from her chaise longue where she painted her toenails casino pink.

'He's like'a my son,' Nonni said softly. 'Frank. He's nice boy.'

'Mayor Frank Longo announced late Friday,' Danny Boy read, 'that he will initiate a hearing to draw local support for the remaining members of . . . the Mattatuck-Saukiwog Indian tribe . . . who claim to have once owned lands in Saukiwog Mills and . . . ah, this isn't about the show.' He dropped the sheet of paper. Grandpa reached for it, intent on wrapping a sandlance, but I pulled it free and footed into the open sand.

'What show?' Pina Maria asked glibly, picking cream from a *canoli* with her long fingernails.

'Indians in Saukiwog Mills?' I asked. 'Real Indians?'

'Not that I ever heard of,' Lena said.

Big Dan looked up at Goomba Rocco. 'What's Longo want to do? Give them the land back?'

'They were here first,' Mom said, always defending the underdog. 'We stole the land from the poor people.'

'*I* didn't steal any land, Nancy,' Big Dan made a retort. 'I'm not responsible for taking any Indian's land. What are they coming out of the woodwork for now? Why don't they go to work like the rest of us?'

This set off a debate in English and Italian with my mother and Cousin Giustina of the Associates Degree backing the Indians. 'It's all stolen land,' Giustina said as she gingerly painted her crooked little toe.

Grandpa even got in. 'I like the Indian man. He make the garden, some good thing. The bow and the arrow, the tepee'a house, he no bother nobody. He use all the part of the cow.'

'Yeah, Pop,' my father cut in, 'but that's a long time ago. We going to go back in time now?'

Nonni did not know what American Indians were. She thought we were speaking about gypsies, *Zingara*, and so she crossed herself. Being well-read on the subject, and an Indian at heart and hair, I stood and faced the picnic tables. 'This was their beach,' I said. 'And their fish.'

'What?' Dad asked. Our picnic area grew quiet.

'All of it. We came in and killed women and babies and poured boiling soap inside them, and just took it.'

'Wait a minute,' Dad said, turning from his squat over a blackfish. 'Who is *we*? What's this *we* took the land?'

'Columbus,' I said. And I wished I hadn't.

'Columbus? He was Italian. He founded this country. He's a great Italian.'

I could feel something happening that day between my father and I. Something that happens between all fathers and their sons when the boy reaches a certain age. Dad and I were having a stare down, and for the first time in my young life, I was giving no quarter.

'You look at me like that, mister, I'll cut your hair right off,' he said.

'Oh, leave him alone about the hair, Uncle Dan,' Giustina said. 'It's cute.'

'Columbus was a crook,' I shot out, and then I ran for the dunes. That's when I saw the two-toned Plymouth Fury in the car park, Johnny behind the wheel.

'Oh, I'm glad you're here,' Johnny said, slapping down a magazine when my shadow fell on it. 'This pain in the ass back there got me watching a bunch of I-talian eatin' rigatoni on the beach.'

'What are you doing here?' I said. 'You're going to start a lot of trouble.'

'Eat me,' he said.

The smell of sour highball mix knocked me back a step. 'Is there a law against me sitting in the parking lot? It's the Fourth of July and I wanted to get out for some sun – look at that cheap bastard,' he suddenly hopped track, referring to Big Dan. 'Look at him wrapping fish over there. He's wrapping up carp and bottom suckers, I bet he don't throw nothin' back.' And then, as if to taunt me, he extended his head out the window and yelled as loud as he could, 'Hey, you cheap prick!'

My father, bent over the fish, looked up at the sound. I held my breath. Dad's thinning hair lifted on a breeze and he searched the picnic tables and umbrella. He must have thought it was kids playing because he resumed his work and never looked up again.

'Don't do that,' I pleaded with Angelo.

Johnny came to my aid. 'Why you doin' that to this man? I like this man. You do that again, I'll drive your handicap self right back to the booby-motherfuckin'-*hatch*.'

'Look at Nonni over there. Ain't she beautiful? You ever see pictures of her when she was young? Hair longer than Cher's, cheekbones, man. What she make – the *baccala*? How about the sauce? Who made the sauce – your mother? That woman could make a sauce so good, that after I ate it, I wanted to kill myself 'cuz there was nothing left to live for.'

'Ain't sayin' much,' Johnny quipped. 'You always wanna kill yourself.'

'I oughta send Ruby Lee running across the table. Can you see Gooma Rosa? A fucking squirrel monkey jumping in the *calamari*. She'd fall over.'

'Grandpa might stab it first. And marinate it.'

'Nunzio,' he said, and his tongue seemed heavy and numb in his mouth. I searched the backseat for Ruby Lee and found her curled and sleeping down in the shade. 'Take me in the water.'

'I can't.'

'Please.'

Johnny angled her broad shoulders and slapped the magazine off the headrest. 'Yeah, go ahead, drown your sorry ass.'

'Nunzio,' Angelo pleaded with expressions that went from wistful to overwrought, like a Vaudeville actor's. 'You and Danny Boy each take an arm and let me buck a couple of waves. That's all I ask. I won't bother nobody, I promise. Let me body surf.'

'I've got to go.'

'I won't bother nobody.'

'I have to go, Ange, really – I'll get in trouble.'

'Forget it. You're just like your old man.' The sun was beating on the car and Angelo looked like he was baking in there. 'You really think I came all the way out here to the beach to beg my way back into the family picnic? Warm people, ain't they? Big, warm-hearted Italians. How they love their family. Everybody's there. Every-fucking-body in the family is there, Nunzio.'

'Do you want me to get you a soda up at the snack bar?'

'I came to tell you boys there's going to be a fireworks show tonight. The best view is from the Turtle. After dark.' He let his Wayfarers slide down on the bridge of his cockatiel nose to show his eyes in an act of confirmation; they were red-rimmed and bleary but nevertheless sincere.

Johnny started her Plymouth with a four-barrel knock and gas draw. She drove Angelo out onto the sandy stretch and I watched the gas-guzzling land barge drive away. Ruby was up in the rear window, toying with a rolling tennis ball.

When I returned to our camp, a great round of applause made me self-conscious and I turned, cringing with a grin until I realized the ovation was for Zi Toine as he walked in from the water, each hand filled with clam shells and his flowered shorts sagging with two dozen more; his notorious diggers made claw marks in the sand like the Creature from the Black Lagoon. Zi Toine tugged at the waistband, shook his trunks and let a landslide of clams clatter in piles at his feet.

'O *Dio!*' Nonni cried out at his crude presentation.

'Charming, Uncle Tony,' Cousin Giustina moaned.

'Clam diggers,' my father said, both repulsed and amused.

I tried to pretend life was perfect; I kept scratching my dad's massive back through the day – something he enjoyed – and I think I said, 'Isn't this the best Fourth of July?' one time too many. But no matter how I tried, no matter how many times I said St Rocco's name or prayed to Grandpa MacLeish, this was a summer of secrets and skeletons that didn't let my mind rest long. The entire way back to the brick crib of the city, silence filled our old Bel Aire. I looked up at the Big Clock to see how much time we had before meeting Angelo. What would this night have in store for us? Would we get closer to the answers? I glanced at my brother to see if he was eyeing the Big Clock, sharing the obsession. He was.

Dad drove slowly down Mary Street where our neighbors were beginning to take seats on their front porches and fireworks were being prepared in the lawns. The peace cross on Maple Hill was just beginning to glow, promising a night of rockets' red glare. Eddie Coco ran alongside our car, scuffing in his corrective shoes and yelling something to me about some cherry bombs. But my attention was fixed on our driveway. So was my brother's.

'Who's here?' Mom asked. Dad was silent, studying the car parked at our house. It was a white Oldsmobile Cutlass with chrome wheels and fuzzy dice hanging from the mirror.

My brother and I exchanged furtive glances. Strange cars were something foreboding at this point in time; perhaps someone was lurking inside in work boots, a Jennings .22 in his waistband. We all stepped out, barefoot and sandy and sunburned, cautiously eyeing the vehicle.

'Whose car?' Dad asked Danny Boy.

'How should I know?' he quipped back.

'You should know,' Dad said. He picked up a little ceramic frog near the house and came up with something small in his hand. He tossed a single key on a paper tag to Danny. 'It's yours, kid. A little wax and shammy and she's a cream puff. What do you think?'

'Hey, Dad . . .'

My mother stood beaming by the birdbath and Big Dan walked into the garage, his tight lips losing a tug of war with a mischievous smile. Danny Boy did not move. He stood there, key in his hands, looking at his new used car. 'Cutlass,' he said with a smile digging dimples at his left cheek. He hurried to the car, going through it with unbridled glee. 'Thanks, Dad,' he yelled from behind the wheel.

'Isn't this the best Fourth of July?' I shouted, holding a bucket of sea shells.

Far off in the hills, fireworks rumbled, making the city sound like a war zone.

On the porch, Big Dan turned and watched Danny admire his new car. 'Take her for a drive, Danny,' he said. 'She's got a full tank.'

Danny Boy's newly acquired Cutlass Supreme Coupé had some Bond-O coloring and was not much to look at from the outside, but the seats were a plush corduroy and we exchanged self-conscious smirks as we motored along. We were kings, I imagined, seated in velour while the rest of the world squirmed on sticky vinyl.

Taking the Cutlass for her maiden voyage was a seamless ruse to get us to the Thirsty Turtle where we were to meet Angelo. As we parked between a phalanx of motorcycles and Johnny's piebald Plymouth, I could see my large friend asleep behind the wheel and I was careful not to slam my door even though the music thumping from the bar was enough to wake my dead Aunt Nicoletta.

Inside sat the early birds; strange men and women, hunchbacked at the bar, watching *Laverne and Shirley*. Here at the Turtle they gathered, drinking in the dark and staring at the TV, but not laughing, not even smiling at the canned guffaws while outside the sun was still up. It gave me an eerie feeling. What kind of people sat in a dark topless bar and drank beer from plastic cups and watched *Laverne and Shirley* at six o'clock on the Fourth of July? Where were their families?

'Hey, you *Mamalukes*!'

As often was the case, Goomba Angelo's hoarse timbre preceded him and we found him Stage Left of the bar where he sat making a nuisance of himself by use of his little capuchin. Ruby Lee was turning three-card Monte and performing tricks while thinking she was serving the handicapped. A hard-faced woman screamed when the monkey four-footed it across the bar, and a few bikers growled in base approval as the monkey fished a pickled egg from a glass bowl and then rolled it in her black velvety hands while making a score of faces and cricket sounds in her throat. Tricks like this were apparently footing Angelo's tab. His sippee-cup was full with vodka and Galliano.

'Over here!' he summoned us, his plastic straw in his teeth. I ducked under the biting scent of urine and Lysol and pickled eggs and went straight to Ruby; in the same manner that I hurried to her for comfort, she lunged at me, mounted the vinyl arm of my letter jacket and began grooming the seams. With the monkey retiring now, the patrons turned their faces back to the TV, and my brother and I huddled with Angelo to learn the news.

He was as drunk as Zi Bap on San Donato Day, and his eyes glistened like a roguish child's. Danny Boy took in a long breath and angled his chair to put himself between Angelo and two girls who were sitting at a back table, watching the monkey show and getting drunk on cocktails.

'How long you been in here?' Danny Boy said.

'I'm the Eye Who Never Sleeps,' said Angelo. 'We always get our man. Right, Nunz?'

'What's the deal?' Danny Boy said.

'You bring money?'

'You bring news?'

'I need some seed money.'

Danny Boy looked around the place before nodding; there was a clutch of bikers at two tables, their voices rolling like gravel in PVC pipe; Two Lane Monroe was there and I watched him in the bar mirror when he stood to act out a story for his cronies, his black vest making a sound like sun-hardened saddle leather. Danny Boy was paying for another Wallbanger before he knew it, and I was lighting a Judge's Cave for our besotted cousin.

'We're going to see some Dagmars tonight, Boy Wonder,' Angelo said with the cigar in his lips. 'See them two girls? They come up from Bridgeport. They're class. They do nice clean dancing.'

Danny Boy scuffed his chair closer. 'You said there were going to be fireworks. What do you have for us?'

Goomba Angelo turned a gaze on Danny that made me go warm in the face. It was a terrible look, the kind a cat gives a shrew in tight quarters.

'Can I give it to you right between the eyes?'

'Shoot.'

'That dancer we seen in here two weeks ago? It *was* Miss Grabowski.'

'See!' I shouted. But Danny Boy was fuming; he did not set out on the road less traveled by, nor was he forking over money to Angelo Volpe to learn that one of our former schoolteachers was making summer cash removing her blouse at the Thirsty Turtle.

'Ruby Lee!' yelled Angelo suddenly, and the capuchin left my arm, scrambled onto the wheelchair. He kissed the monkey's tiny ear and said something that sounded like, 'PAPER BOY'. Ruby launched herself from wheelchair to table to floor, and she crabbed toward the bikers. One of them, a tall Hispanic man with an earring and a goatee like Genghis Khan, was firing a cigarette and that's where Ruby Lee was headed. No sooner did the biker set his pack of smokes down than the monkey hopped on the table, snatched his Camels, and bolted back to her master in two great bounds.

Danny Boy and I watched dumbstruck as the biker lunged at Ruby's long tail. But he was no match for the monkey's agility. Angelo now owned a half crumpled pack of Camels. Some of the other bikers laughed and taunted their friend as he fell to a knee in an effort to catch the animal. He made an awful *psst* sound like when one tries to scare a cat.

'Good girl,' Angelo said to Ruby as she stuffed the Camels in the pocket of his flamboyant late 1960s shirt. The huge Latino biker stood over us, grinning at our cousin.

'That's real fucking cute, man,' he said, bringing his cigarette up to his mouth and sucking at it hard. 'Give me the smokes or I'll wheel your ass down the service stairs and flush your monkey down the fucking hole.'

Ruby Lee found her way to my shoulder again as if sensing the long-haired man's wrath.

'My monkey's been performing in here since four o'clock this afternoon,' Angelo said, 'and you haven't so much as looked up from your own fucking tattoos. Maybe we were just trying to get your attention, Cowboy.'

The biker's eyes waxed and waned as he focused on the cripple; he seemed stunned by the man's bravado. And then Angelo nodded to me and I pulled the Camels from his pocket and sheepishly returned them to the big man. He grabbed them without removing his eyes from our cousin.

'Keep that fucking monkey on a chain, hombre.'

'No offense,' Angelo said to him as he started away and then he added, 'Chills.'

The biker stopped. He cast one eye on my cousin, squinting through his own cigarette smoke.

'You *are* Chills, right?' asked Angelo. 'Cool Chill?'

'Who the fuck are you?'

'Alias Chills, alias Chilli-Dog. Mama calls you Tino?'

The name made me and Danny Boy look at each other and fidget. It was, indeed, Tino, the stepson of the missing Mr Diaz.

'My bro's call me Chilli-Dog,' he admitted, squinting at the cripple and his monkey. 'You at the VA hospital? That where I seen you?'

'Yeah,' Angelo lied. 'I stepped on a land mine outside Poon Tang.'

With Chilli-Dog still squinting at him, Angelo glanced up casually and said, 'I'm not trying to be an asshole, Tino. Just wanted to say something to you.'

'Spit it the fuck out, soldier.'

'I'm sorry.'

'About what?'

'The old man.'

Chilli-Dog took a step back on his boot heel. He glanced over at the barstools for a second then adjusted his studded belt.

'What you know about it?'

'Good carpenter. Hard worker. Missing in action. I know it's hard on Little Joey.'

Tino looked back at where his cronies sat, and then back at our strange group. 'They'll never find him,' he said, and it seemed for one fleeting second he looked straight at me; maybe he saw something in my eyes. 'He hung himself on a fucking oak up in Maine. You would, too, if you lost three hundred grand.'

He told the bartender to fill Angelo's sippee-cup and then, tucking his Camels in his vest, he turned and walked back to his corner. Chilli-Dog, like Two Lane Monroe, sounded like creaking saddle leather and smelled like leaded gasoline. It was hard to imagine him being Little Joey's father, or anyone's father for that matter.

Angelo did the thing he did with his eyes that meant for me to come near. 'You want your shooter?' he said in a soft, relenting voice, then he tipped his head toward the bar.

When I stood and looked at the bar, there was nothing but bottles and their reflections in the mirror; my own face beneath my cap, chin on the wood; the glowing heads of cigarettes and faces angled toward the TV.

And then I saw something that ran a charge of terror through my body: over my shoulder in the bar glass was the reflection of Tino's leather jacket and the visage of a red horned devil.

What the Filipini Order of Nuns did inside their dark convent up on Maple Hill, no one knew for certain; it was unholy to speculate. As the ceramic block said, *Let us bury gossip forever*. No one with the exception of the propane man had ever seen the interior of the small, chocolate-brown dormitory set on the edge of Egypt. And now, with Danny Boy knocking for nearly ten minutes it was likely to remain a mystery. There was a muffled music playing somewhere within, in some back room on the second floor, and I suggested to Goomba Angelo that the Sisters might be in some kind of meditation. Johnny was waiting in her car, parked down at the gate while I stood off near Nazareth resting my elbows on the back of Angelo's wheelchair.

'Is it locked?' Angelo asked my brother.

'Ain't finding out,' Danny Boy whispered. 'I bet that Sister Racine keeps a gun for those dogs.'

Just then, a light went on and Sister Giselle LaBow appeared in a window. Just as quickly, she was gone. But then she came to the door, unlocked it, and stood in the screen, staring blankly with her wide-set eyes. The music was louder now and sounded like a record on a turntable, some religious piano music. Danny Boy seemed unsure as to how one might speak to a deaf person so he cast a look back at Angelo.

'Show her the picture of Tino and the matchbook,' instructed Angelo.

The Polaroid I knew of – it was snatched from the Widow Diaz's kitchen – but the matchbook was news to me until this moment; Ruby Lee had taken it, I would soon learn, from the biker's table. Danny Boy showed the nun the Polaroid and she just stared, vacantly. After a moment, she looked up with a definite shrug. Danny Boy then held up the matchbook and she bristled for a moment. She made the sign of the cross then opened the screen door to get a closer look at it in yellow porchlight.

I moved in now, too, hoping to get a look inside the nunnery. But what I saw was the matchbook in the porchlight. On the front was a cartoon graphic of a devil, the same one I had seen on Tino's black leather. On the back of the matchpack was the name *Diablo Motorcycle Club* and a Chapter address.

Danny Boy turned a palm upward in question.

Angelo studied the Sister from a distance.

I watched her wide-set eyes as she stared intently at the graphic.

Jerusalem was static, the only sound perceptible coming from the record-player somewhere in the building. Sister Giselle leaned out and stared harder at the matchbook for a time. She shook her head, casually. A moment later, Sister Racine came to the door, wiping her mouth with a checkered napkin.

'You again,' she said, looking at Angelo.

'Seek and ye shall find – right, Sister?'

Sister Racine looked at the matchbook in the impaired nun's hand. 'Ah, the motorcycle gang,' she said, pushing her glasses up on the bridge of her nose.

'You know them?' Danny Boy said, surprised.

'They've been here.'

My brother looked at Angelo, and so did I. Our cousin almost smiled, confident in his progress.

'They came here once, a few years back in December,' Sister said. 'They drove in on those loud motorbikes looking like a motley crew if there ever was. They circled the convent and shut off their motors. We locked the doors. They were in a kind of formation. What they did next . . . well, let's just say we did a novena right through Christmas.'

Angelo stared, nodding slowly. 'What did they do, Sister?'

'They began to sing "We Three Kings". For fifteen minutes they sat there on their motorcycles and sang Christmas Carols – and at a choir group standard, mind you. Then they drove away. I read in the paper that they then went to several Rest Homes and to the Children's Ward at St Joe's to do the same. Judge not that ye be not judged.'

Angelo appeared thwarted, in no mood for Psalms now. 'What's the deaf Sister say about the devil head?'

Sister Racine signed with the matchbook and Sister Giselle made a sound from down in herself as she touched her ear then pinched her nose as if something smelled foul.

'That is not the emblem she saw. It has no ring.'

'Ring? What ring?' Danny Boy said.

'A pierced nose, Sister says.'

'The guy or the devil?' Angelo said.

'Beelzebub,' Sister Racine answered hard.

'So, Beelzebub's got a pierced nostril now,' Angelo sighed.

'The Diablos sang Christmas carols?' Danny delved.

'Never mind the carols, Danny. It ain't Christmas. And it ain't Tino.'

Sister Giselle LaBow was not finished and what she had to say with her hands made Sister Racine laugh, grackle-like.

'What now?' Danny Boy said.

'Sister Giselle has an opinion on your investigation, Mr Volpe.'

'Please,' said Angelo.

Sister Racine puckered her lips over her ample teeth and said, 'It's bull.' She laughed and mussed Sister Giselle's habit like an amused older sister, which she was.

And she was still laughing when she returned to the kitchen.

'That's some strange-ass shit,' Johnny said on the way down the hill.

'The devil with a pierced nostril. Sounds punk,' Danny Boy puzzled. On a corner, in front of a Spanish market, some Hispanic children ran out in front of us with sparklers. Johnny leaned into her horn and scolded them in a high-pitched wail that I knew was more about the murder than the young pranksters. We were all on edge, and Angelo told us more than once to stay composed.

That's when Johnny screamed.

'Oh, shit!' she wailed, her eyes in the rearview. 'It the Man!'

'What man?' I said, terrified.

'Don't stop,' Angelo said.

'What you mean don't stop? He pullin' me over!'

'Keep going,' Angelo said. 'Just don't stop. Fuck 'em.'

'She has to stop,' Danny Boy hissed, surprised at the demand.

'Shut up,' Angelo shot back. He was leaning his head against the window to use the side mirror.

'I'll lose my cabby license!' Johnny yelled back at him, but she didn't stop. Now a siren was screaming right up behind us.

'Lose him,' Angelo said. 'Pull a U-ee.'

'I need this job, you motherfucker!'

Finally, Johnny pulled over to the side of the interstate and Angelo sighed in resignation.

I turned in the backseat and was blinded by a stark white light: the kid inside me felt relieved, safe even. But the mannish-boy I was becoming felt distrust. I couldn't even trust a police officer right now and that scared me. It was the police, after all, who had thrown Angelo off the Big Clock tower.

Angelo cast an eye on me. 'Don't air the family wash,' he said.

He need not worry about that: if I let a breath free, I feared I would also let my bladder go slack, and so I sat as rigid as one of the plaster figures in Moab while Johnny fumbled for her license in her huge white purse and Danny Boy combed his hair. Angelo stared ahead at the strobe flashes in the dark.

As instructed, I did not breathe.

When the police officer appeared, he moved along the rear windows, cautiously, then to the driver's port where he bent low and revealed himself as Officer Renkunis, a clumpish, pink-faced Lithuanian cop who had once given Dad a ticket for towing a car that had no title.

'What were you doing up on Holy Hill?' he said to Johnny, but his eyes were in the backseat with me and Angelo. 'It's closed at night.'

'We wanna see Lot Wife,' Johnny said.

'Who's wife?' the cop asked.

'Lot wife. She was punished for looking over her shoulder so they turned her ass into a pile of sugar.'

'Salt,' I whispered from the backseat but the cop heard me and aimed his flashlight at me.

Now a second policeman appeared on the other side, shining a flashlight into the backseat with an arm that had a bulldog tattoo. No one else saw him but me.

I could see the back of Johnny's crewcut head, her black neck taut, her tension palpable. Danny Boy appeared fairly relaxed, but when he looked up to motion toward the cross, his body jerked, alarmed by the second cop in the passenger window.

Officer Kelly took a step back and crouched, aiming the light beam on me and then on my godfather. Angelo sat crumpled in the back corner, chewing on the soggy end of his Judge's Cave and looking up with those larkish eyes.

'You're getting around again, Angie,' the brushcut cop said, directing the light down onto Ruby Lee whose pupils dilated in the beam. 'What kind of scam you running now? You selling bonds to the nuns or something?'

'It's the Fourth of July, you stupid mick. Where's the best view in Saukiwog?'

Kelly was not amused. 'What you got these kids doing? Running numbers for you?'

'It's none of your business what I'm doing, Eddie. I'm in business for myself.'

Kelly laughed. 'What business, Angie? You and that monkey?'

'That's right.'

'Organ grinder? Barnum and Bailey? What?'

The policemen laughed from either side of the car and I noticed that Danny Boy and Johnny were both smiling in the same disquieted manner; they weren't waffling, they were just afraid not to smile at the policemen's jokes.

I wished Johnny would start the car and go, but her Plymouth Fury was her livelihood and she wasn't risking a citation at any cost.

'So is this your detail?' our cousin finally said and he winked at the Irish cop. 'All these years in the Department and you're on Holy fucking Hill. I thought you'd have a shield by now, Kelly. You missed your chance when the Irish ran the city. You know who's gonna run it next, don't you? The writing's on the wall, Kelly.'

'Renaissance City, Ange. Holy Hill's a drug haven. Kids dealing coke up there, smoking shit. We're on ass-kick detail. I'm up there to find the bad boys.'

'You couldn't find your ass with both hands, Kelly. That's why you're up there,' Angelo said, and I held my breath in. 'Renaissance City?' he mocked. 'If this is a Renaissance city, then I'm the fucking *prince* of North Main.'

Kelly smacked the back door of the gypsy cab and looked up and around as if wanting to share this with Renkunis. When he came back down and looked in at me and Danny Boy, his eyes were hard. 'Do you boys know the prince here? You know who this is you have in the car with you?'

'Let's go, Johnny,' Angelo said. 'Start the car.'

'He's my little brother's godfather,' Danny Boy said.

'That right? He tell you how he got gimped?'

'Start the car, Johnny – you deaf over here?'

'Which story? Vietnam? Formula One racing? He flipped a race car and went up in flames, he tell you that one?'

Johnny started the car but she didn't go anywhere. Kelly was blinding her with his flashlight. 'He tell you about the little girl?' Now he blinded Danny Boy. 'He tell you the truth about the little girl?'

'Fuck you,' Angelo said to the officer.

'Ask him about Romeo's Tavern. *Ask* him. Ask him why he jumped.'

'Johnny – fucking *now*.' Angelo spit his dead cigar. Kelly ran the flashlight down over our paralyzed cousin like he was tormenting a chained dog.

'You got a bad actor here, kids,' Kelly said, and Johnny punched the gas, lurching and skidding forward in roadside gravel, and I couldn't hear Kelly laughing any more but I could see him, grinning like a seventh grader at the back of the bus. He was standing under a street-lamp with his somber partner, laughing, shaking his head.

As we merged with traffic and drove on relieved, Angelo said, 'Mick bastard. He's pissed off because the blacks are getting all the suit jobs.'

'Well, nobody giving *me* one,' Johnny said. 'I don't want the police on my ass. No more of this murder shit. I want these boys outta my car. *Out.*'

Danny Boy spoke without turning. 'What was Kelly saying?'

'He was blowing smoke up our ass. Did you know those cops carry little .22's in ankle holsters? Did you hear him say they're kicking ass up there? Maybe we should start looking at the city police.'

'What was he saying – about Romeo's Tavern? About a little girl?'

Angelo grunted a sound of derision. 'He's the reason I'm a quad. I told you's: him and his crooked crew threw me off the tower because I was going to blow the whistle.'

'He said you jumped.'

Maybe it was the callow ring of my voice, or maybe there was truth to it, but Angelo turned a glare on me that revealed, beneath the fierce black eyes, a sorrow that was unbearable to consider. 'You can believe an Irish-Democrat pig or you can believe your own flesh and blood,' he said.

Danny Boy had him in the visor mirror and was watching him in silence.

'Fuck you *looking* at?' Angelo spat.

Danny Boy flipped the visor back up and let out a flustered breath. He took in my gaze, nodded, turned away and fell quiet; he pretended to doze off.

When we returned Angelo to the Dunn Convalarium and escorted him up the service elevator, everyone was tired and more than a little vexed. We set him before his window, and I cleaned up Ruby's cage, checked the monkey's cat food dispenser. Johnny fingered a half-dozen medications into his mouth, and when she refused to mix him a Wallbanger he simply gave the monkey orders and the damage was on its way to being done.

'If assholes could fly,' he grumbled, 'this place would be Bradley International.'

There were no goodnights.

Sorting out my family history was like digging through the piles of detritus at the salvage yard. I had to take whatever parts I could find, sand off the rust, bang out the dents, and then assemble the metals by grade, weigh them, check them against book value. Some parts of the pedigree were interchangeable, like my father's and Zi Toine's Korean War experiences – they borrowed each other's tales for so long that neither was sure which one really happened to who anymore. Some of the family tales had to be stripped clean and shredded, smelted down then recast into something that stood to reason, even if it stood on one leg. But trying to revamp an accurate history from the story of Angelo Volpe was like my grandfather's weed-whacking invention: the pieces could be welded into a fundamental order, but the product in the end was barely practical and no better off than the sum of junked parts it came from.

Some of the Angelo Volpe *storia* came from Nonni, but to her, scandals were secrets to take to the grave. She attributed the man's condition to the devil; some threads were woven in the form of Grandpa's fables and I had to humanize a scorpion or a fox to shake out any truth; my mother felt the Beatles should have let Charles Manson join the band because he had a hard childhood, so in her telling, Angelo was a handsome man, a fine dresser, and the best fast dancer at weddings before he wound up in a wheelchair.

'Aye, he could move like Gene Kelly,' she told me. 'At the family weddings he would take out his wallet and let the wee children touch his police shield. He was always telling everyone he was up for a suit job, he'd be promoted to detective, and no one believed him.'

Of course Mom did.

'He drank the highballs a little too hard at the family weddings, but who didn't?' she said.

'He's not really related to us,' my father said when I asked.

The stories went around and around in a maddening *tarantella*, me in the middle like I always was at those big weddings, trying to link a face to a name, and a name to a story as I got stomped underfoot in the folk dance until one of my cousins pulled me to safety under a table. But here is what Danny Boy and I assembled from the used parts:

In the winter of 1973, Angelo was working his beat as a street cop near St Joe's Hospital when he responded to a dispatch in one of the more sordid neighborhoods out in the backsettlements: an after-hours problem at Romeo's Tavern in the North End. So Angelo went over to lend a presence.

A young girl – though my mother couldn't remember if she had been fourteen or sixteen – lay dead of a Bacardi and barbituate cocktail in the bathroom. Romeo was known for letting under-age girls into his bar and feeding the prettier ones shots of tequila and pills. Angelo covered for Romeo by dragging the girl's body out to the side of the road and reporting the death off-premises. Officer Volpe claimed he found the girl lying at the roadside on his routine visit. There was evidence that Romeo had paid Angelo 1400 dollars from the register that night. Their official story – the cop's and the tavern owner's, and the one that first appeared in the *Saukiwog American* – was that the girl was left in the snow by scared, unidentified friends.

'No one knew if it was the bouncer or one of the patrons in the wee hours who betrayed Romeo,' Mom said. 'But the truth came out and shamed your daddy's family.'

Angelo was suspended pending an internal investigation, one which began to unravel a reckless quilt of graft and unsavory abuse of official privileges. Angelo was branded a dirty cop, a bad apple. His dream of ever becoming a city detective was over; at best, he'd go back to the brass mills, but the mills were all shutting down. What was left?

Two days before the hearing, Angelo Volpe consumed a fifth of Boodles gin, put in an old Roy Orbison 8-track and drove over to the Big Clock tower. He climbed the stairs to the cupola and stepped out onto the precipice of the historic clock and, as Mom said, 'cast his lot to the wind.'

His body pierced the roof of a parked Le Mans head first and his spine was cut by sheet metal at the C1 and C2 vertebrae. But to his dismay – and moreover, everyone else's – he survived. The state board and the girl's surviving family felt his self-inflicted quadriplegia was punishment enough. For all intents and purposes he was a dead man – worse than dead, many could argue: up in his little apartment in the North End, he was like Prometheus chained to a rock as the vultures pecked at his liver. But Goomba Angelo hadn't stolen fire from the gods. He had padded his pockets with dirty money and helped exonerate a tavern-owner who subsequently served a year in prison then went into the vending machine business in West Haven.

If the scandal did not fully alienate the family, the capuchin monkey he began displaying on his shoulder did. When he appeared downtown in his wheelchair, having Ruby Lee chase pigeons on the Green or mount *The Soldier's Horse* and defecate in the fountain, the word spread like the germs in the water and relatives gave the cripple a wide berth. While Nonni found the mere image of him viral, my father found the monkey sheer lunacy; others made jokes about him, and still others, like Gooma Rosa, claimed that he was not really a blood relative but had been left on the steps of Our Lady of Mount Carmel by Albanians. And so Angelo Volpe's head was torn from every family snapshot and his very name made taboo. He was the *Mamone*, the family outcast.

Angelo's own story about being thrown out the window by cops was just that, a story. According to my father there were also tales of childhood polio, a faulty staircase in the home of a Jewish lawyer, some workman's tale about being caught in the rollers at United Brass, and even an encounter with a wild boar at a canned hunt on a ranch in Delaware which most of us knew had happened to Zi Toine only recently.

The deeper we dug into the mystery of the dead man in the Bonneville, the deeper we seemed to slide into the piled bones and empty bottles of our own *storia*; and when we weren't, we were digging in the wrack and ruin of our vocation and helping Big Dan hunt buffalo.

Driving home on a Friday afternoon, I sat between my father and brother while each of them wore 3-D glasses they had found in an old Plymouth from the 1950s.

'We put in a good day, boys,' Big Dan said. And then, as we passed beneath another Renaissance City banner on Willow, 'we're a part of it, too. We're the sandpipers in the surf. We're the beachcombers, we comb the streets.'

I wondered how he could read the banner with his 3-D specs, let alone stay in the lane. As I looked up at my dad, smiling from behind the funny glasses, I felt something like I had never known – a biting stitch akin to a hunger pain, but I wasn't hungry. I wanted my dad to be happy; I wanted him to go home at night and sit and watch TV with his feet up, not hiding in the basement with his coin collections or taking midnight drives to the junkyard alone, to check the gate, worrying about his license, and our survival.

I wanted to protect him.

That scared me. I was hardly capable of protecting anybody, even myself. But if some dark secret was eating at my father's insides, I wanted to free him from the hold. I just didn't know how.

CHAPTER THIRTEEN

The Lost Tribe

'Bring a jacket, might get a wee bit chill.'

She was wearing a new dress of a 1966 vintage that Dad had found in the trunk of the Plymouth. It was yellow with small swirling stars on it and the entire garment was made of paper. 'You can scoop a neckline or raise the hem with a quick snip of the scissors,' Mom had read from the tag with all the excitement of Mother's Day.

'No more dry cleaning bills,' was Dad's observation as my mother unfolded it. 'Nice and light for the summer. It gets dirty, you use an eraser,' he had said, watching her model it. The dress made a rustling sound.

Mom matched it to a pair of cream-colored high-heels that had come from the Yard and then through two steamings at Zi Bap's dry-cleaning shop. If they seemed to pinch her a bit as she walked she never mentioned it. Dressed in fine ephemera, large white pocketbook over her shoulder, she looked light of heart and spirit. 'Angels can fly because they take themselves lightly,' she used to say if she caught any of us brooding.

We were heading to the car, just Mom and me, when Big Dan came out of the bathroom whistling 'Wichita Lineman' through his teeth. To my surprise he was wearing a short-sleeve dress shirt, slacks and some buffed penny loafers. He smelled like Aqua Velva as he drew near, checking the money in his wallet, then tucking it in a back pocket.

'You got the keys, Nancy?'

'Aye, I have. Look at you, Gorgeous George.'

My surprise was clear to see, for Dad had to egg me out onto the porch as he locked up.

'What'sa matter, Nunz? You don't want me to go see the Injuns?'

'I didn't think you wanted to.'

'Mayor Frankie might give them my land. You bet your ass I'm going to be there. Like Custer, I'll be there.'

As we backed out of the drive we all could see Grandpa at work in his garden. He had his weed-chopping invention with some modifications and he was trying to get it started. 'He better not bring that thing into my yard,' Dad said as we left The Little Boot.

Seeing Big Dan in his dress clothes was another strange experience on the order of Sister Racine's sneakers: no matter how hard he scrubbed his working man's hands and forearms, they remained dark with the residue of his labors. Not that they were dirty, they were just permanently tattooed. He flattened his hair with a little black comb, and Mom's dress rustled in the wind as we gunned the Bel Aire up Grand Street toward City Hall.

The magnificent Art Deco building was one long football pass away from Union Station and the Big Clock tower. I could not imagine the White House being anymore majestic; with carved marble, big brass doors and manicured front grass encircling a stone fountain, it was a veritable Taj Mahal.

It was hard for me to tell how many citizens were assembled for the hearing or how many were just enjoying a summer eve in the neighboring library park, but when Mayor Frank Longo came out onto the steps, conversation faded off and all eyes went to His Honor. Within seconds my view was obscured by a clutch of girls trying to get a better look at 'Frankie'.

'I spend too much time inside,' Mayor Longo said into a standing microphone but it wasn't turned on. Off behind him was his group of older city men, and Mr Campobosso moved in to adjust the microphone. Alderman Sforza handed him a folder.

'I spend too much time inside,' Mayor Longo tried again and now his voice was plangent, like Oz over Grand Street.

'What'd he say?' Big Dan wanted to know.

'I figured all of you are working hard, and summer's too short to sit inside a school gym. Besides, I always wanted to make a speech from the front steps over here like Mayor Dunn used to on St Patrick's Day. But I'll be damned if I'm gonna kiss the Blarney Stone.'

Laughter drowned him; my mom's little hen-gobble of a laugh soared.

'What'd he say?' Dad wanted to know again. But the mayor was rolling now.

'Politicians are big quoters. They quote Plato and Aristotle, Shakespeare and Ben Franklin. But it's summertime and I don't feel like quoting the Greeks. Because what I really want to say to you all this evening is: We are F-A-M-I-L-Y.'

The throng went into a roil; the young people, especially the blacks, responded to the song refrain if not the political message, while the older folk missed the song refrain, but appeared in favor of solidarity. I swore that I heard Johnny, somewhere toward the back, belt out, 'I got all my sisters with me,' in refrain to the mayor's quote, and this triggered a lot of voices from black women: laughter, whistles, and clapping.

'The Italians, the Latino community, our black community, Irish, Portuguese, Lithuanian, we share this house. All of us, pulling together to rebuild this house. But I'm afraid, people, we have forgotten the original tenants of this house. The American Indian people.'

The assembly grew quiet now. As Mom once said to me, mystery begets mystery. Now another mystery was upon us.

'If we're going to recognize and honor each other, if we're going to respect all the threads that make up this quilt that is our city . . . we must acknowledge the native peoples who our great-grandfathers . . . who our great-great-grandfathers encountered here on the banks of Ol' Matty and slowly steamrolled over.'

'What's he going to steamroll?' Dad said, and Mom sorted it all out for him with a whisper. I could not be more pleased: the young mayor defying tradition and speaking on behalf of the Native Americans. If I could have done a two-pinkied whistle like Big Dan, I would have let one fly right then and there, but all I could do was look around at the faces, the threads of the quilt that made up our city – everyone hanging onto Mayor Frankie's every word. Another thought crept in as I scanned our good citizens: Which one? I was thinking of Mr A. Richard Pembroke across town, directing my brother. *The killer might be standing next to you.*

My eyes worked the gathering. I looked at the larger men, examined their shoes. Many wore work boots – guys like Dave Zuraitas, the laid-off machinist and my brother's former teammate. He caught my look and nodded at me, a strange far-off glaze in his eye; and Mr Couto, a Portuguese mason who kept one of his work boots together with a strip of duct tape; and two dozen or so men who had come straight from work to the hearing. I began to drift away from my mother and father and search the faces of the crowd as the mayor spoke over the P.A.

Somewhere in the middle, I got lost and tried to collect my bearings, and that's when I saw it. Between a rail-thin black man and Andy Tibbets's mother was something that sent a chill of terror through me. It was the face of a horned devil.

It was on the back of someone's shirt, red on black, red as fire. I jostled my way to the person, going low and excusing myself between bodies. But when I came up through the crowd, he was gone. I was closer to the steps now, the mayor's voice louder.

'What were our grandfathers looking for when they came up the Mattatuck River? They encountered a people who offered them companionship, sanctity, wisdom. Wealth in wisdom. But that's not what they wanted. They wanted gold, silver, pearls, slaves. Let's face it, it was greed, people.'

We could have heard a bobby pin fall from my mother's hair at that moment.

'Our Indian peoples in Saukiwog were not only exploited: their numbers were so decimated that today they are not even recognized as a *people*.' Mayor Frankie sent his voice like a spiral far across the city to where it might be heard on the Green. 'Hey, go figure.'

Mayor Longo often used Italian-American urbanisms like 'go figure' or 'forget about it', and this made him our mayor, one of us. Now, as he let a silence press against us, I moved past Mrs Tibbets and started toward the outskirts of the gathering, searching for that black jacket, that red symbol.

'As we form our rainbow coalition,' Mayor Longo spoke clearly, 'as we move with cautious optimism out of the industrial era and into a new arena, let us make room at the table for the first peoples, those who once offered us true wealth.'

And there it was. The head of Beelzebub on the back of a man who had shoulders like two rocks set on either end of a two-by-four plank, and a neck as thick as a transmission housing. I looked down at his shoes to see unlaced work boots, clean, jeans tucked in the shanks. I couldn't see the man's face, but I heard him shout something to the mayor. And when he turned, slightly, I saw a profile I knew. It was Ray Beans, the bodybuilder with the silver Camaro. He looked right at me and my face went warm.

'Hey, *Goomba*,' he said and he shifted his weight, took a playful jab at me. I saw then, on the front of his T-shirt, flaring red letters that said GO BULLS.

It wasn't a devil, it was a sports logo, a cartoon bull, and I felt myself blush. The inevitable had occurred: I was seeing the killer behind every fire hydrant. 'Watch yourself,' he said to me. 'You might get scalped. The Indians are coming. Woo-woo-woo.'

Someone grabbed me by the back of the shirt and twisted me nearly off my feet. I made a sound of alarm, but it was lost under the mayor's speech and the public soundings.

'Hey, Little Big Man,' Johnny said, twisting me around. I was happy to see the large woman.

'You come to see the Indians?' I asked.

'Shit no, I come to see the mayor,' she said, putting on fiesta pink lipstick. 'He can ride in my taxi cab anytime he wants. Where he get his suits?' Johnny amended. 'Man must take the 6:10 to New York. That shit's tailored. Mmm. That's a classy man right up there. Class act. Them ain't no Buster Brown shoes on *his* ass.'

'Removal, relocation, reservation – these are words we have long forgotten,' the mayor went on. 'A house without a foundation will eventually collapse in on itself. Is it time or is it not time that we recognize the Mattatuck-Saukiwog Indian tribe as the foundation of this land? Is it time, or is it not time, that we come together and pass a bill to give these native people recognition in their own house? State recognition and federal status – like the Sioux, the Cheyenne, like the Apache.'

Some folks clapped, others grumbled, but most, like Dave Zuraitas, looked confused and too hot to think in the throng of bodies. It was, I had to admit to myself, a strange setting to be talking about the Sioux and Cheyenne, about Indians in general – here in the car theft capital of the world. But it also filled me with hope. If there were still bona fide Indians in a place like this, how many steps were we really removed from paradise?

'Recognition, people,' the mayor said again. 'The Mattatuck-Saukiwogs belong in the books as a living, breathing, Native-American tribe. Not as feathers in the Saukiwog Mills Museum!'

The word 'tribe' echoed, and the hair nettled on my arms. Mayor Longo had impressed me with his Brass Balls speech weeks earlier. Now he gained my respect as a man coming to the aid of the disenfranchised. In the mayor's first term, when I was in second grade, it rained for a week and our school was flooded. Mayor Longo had been the first one on the scene that day, wearing a Civil Service helmet and directing the rescue efforts. He'd made me feel secure in his presence then. I could talk to him if I had to; I knew I could.

'He looks so much like Tyrone Power,' my mother cooed again.

Mayor Longo stood at the microphone and scanned the crowd. 'As we move forward in this period of renewal and renaissance, let us right the wrongs of the past so we can build a future with integrity. But I can stand up here and shout till I'm blue in the face. I can quote Ben Franklin. God forbid, I can quote Mayor Dunn.' He gave a clever pause, allowing some laughter. 'But I cannot speak for the Mattatuck-Saukiwog people till I've walked a mile in their moccasins.'

A mumble of intrigue began to spread as Mayor Frankie looked over his shoulder and gestured toward the brass doors. *Moccasins*, I was going to see moccasins. Johnny went quiet, craned to see. Ray Beans lifted himself an inch on his work boots. I went to Johnny's left and found a corridor that allowed a view.

The brass doors opened.

I stood as rapt as a cat.

A great hush fell over the City Hall grounds and spread far out beyond the library park. Three Indians emerged from City Hall and walked proudly toward the silenced congregation. A great gabble spread through the assembly.

They wore feathers; one of them, the War Chief, had long twin braids and carried a staff. They walked with heads held high and everything about them was noble. Their very deportment restored a quiet across the grounds. But there was one incongruity that made Dad knot his brow. In fact, the entire crowd seemed to be puzzling.

I had always believed Indians were red. The three men on the steps of City Hall were black. There was no mistaking this; the three Saukiwog Indians, albeit handsome and regal, were obviously black men.

'Wait a minute – who's this?' Big Dan whispered through his teeth and this triggered whispers throughout the crowd.

'My name,' said the man in the center, 'is Reginald Whirlwind Fire Keeper. I am the War Chief of the Mattatuck-Saukiwog Nation.'

There was not a sound for two square miles around City Hall as Mayor Longo stood off with the coterie of his elder council, hands folded behind his back, listening heedfully as he watched the Mattatuck War Chief on the steps.

'This over here is Uncas Fontenot, councilman. To my right here is Tyrell Sun Dog, our elected Chief for Life.'

War Chief Reginald Whirlwind Fire Keeper spoke in an ardent manner similar to a Baptist reverend I once saw on Channel 10. His braids were twisted long and were not so much braids as they were dreadlocks; his outfit was a faux Navajo print bathrobe that Johnny swore she had seen on sale at Sears the previous winter. He wore gray sweatpants and Adidas running shoes, unlaced. And he smoked Pall-Malls.

'The sufferin' is done,' he said. 'That's what I say. The sufferin' is done – a new cycle of life has begun, for the Saukiwog and the land. We want our sovereignty before we disappear like . . .' here he consulted some notes, 'like the sun before the snow, as long as the grass grows, and the river flows.'

'You want a weekly check, you sonuvabitch,' Ray Beans suddenly megaphoned through his hands, and this started a domino drop of grumbling and grousing.

Johnny bent low so she could whisper in my ear. 'If that man's a Indian chief then I'm Miss Idaho.' She straightened her back again, tried to get a better look.

The War Chief turned the microphone over to councilman Uncas Fontenot who wore military fatigue pants. 'I hear the sound out there,' he said. 'The sound of genocide.'

The crowd began to mumble amongst themselves and Johnny tried to press her laughter back in her lips with her hand. 'Shit,' she whispered. 'I seen that nigger down the Five-and-dime.'

I stayed focused: I had seen white kids in school claiming to have Indian blood after *Little Big Man* came out, and even Monica Lafontaine supposedly had some Indian in her French blood. Why couldn't these black men have Mattatuck-Saukiwog blood?

'Manifest destiny' was a phrase Uncas Fontenot kept reading from some paperwork. The story came forth in statutes and old land deeds: there were only fourteen members of the entire tribe left, scattered on the outskirts of the city. The oldest member was the ninety-eight-year-old mother of Tyrell Sun Dog and she was in a Rest Home in Torrington. For years, their status was managed by the state Welfare Department who did little more than ignore them. They were an endangered people, and without federal, state and local recognition, they would soon be a memory and a black mark on our city history.

'We will be gone for ever,' Reginald Whirlwind said grimly.

'I never knew you were here,' Dad quipped above a whisper and my mother shot him a look. Genocide was a word Uncas Fontenot used repeatedly, and once he referred to Custer which I found exciting.

After Tyrell Sun Dog, the elected Chief for Life spoke – a speech that began with a Sitting Bull quote and ended in a statement about tax-free cigarettes – Uncas Fontenot beat on a drum and the three lowered their heads and prayed. Mayor Longo, a Catholic, appeared slightly uncomfortable, but when it was done, he returned to the microphone and asked everyone to attend a hearing the following week and vote in support of federal status for our local Indians and the return of their rightful lands, a mere four acres on which to establish a reservation even if symbolic.

As Dad fell into a conversation with a confused Tony the barber, I slipped toward the front of the stage to get a closer look. I swore that Uncas Fontenot was wearing the pluckings of a feather duster attached to an earring, and the T-shirt under his Naugahyde jacket said INDIAN, but had a picture of a red vintage motorcycle. I wondered if maybe the horse culture had adapted to motorbikes and that maybe, dusting feathers were used in the effort to spare endangered eagles and osprey.

The War Chief and his party sauntered back through the brass doors as swiftly as they had appeared. I saw no horses, nor any red motorcycles. The mayor came to center, meeting the incoming tide of city residents; he was jostled from all sides and I admired his composed manner. Many citizens felt we had more problems to deal with than ordaining three mixed-bloods as official city Indians; some citizens hammered him about the tax base, about job training, the inter-racial basketball court, and the proposed Mall. The mayor nodded, delivered terse rejoinders, or slapped shoulders as he looked from face to face, and that's when his eyes caught mine shaded by the brim of my cap, standing diminutive amongst the adults.

Mayor Frankie lowered himself to the step and sat, signaled for me to come forward. I had the feeling that he viewed me as a godsend at that moment, freeing him from the grip of the cynical adults who were now farmed out to Mr Campobosso and the aldermen.

'Paradiso, right?'

I nodded.

'You look just like your brother. How is he? How's my man, Danny?'

'He's good.'

'Number 44. I used to love to watch him do a safety blitz – guy was an assassin. They called him the Junkyard Dog. I called him the assassin.'

'Mayor Longo,' I came close to interrupting him. 'I like Indians, too. I'm glad you're doing what you're doing.'

'Maybe you're the only one,' he said quietly and he had to hold up a hand to keep people at bay. 'Maybe we're the only two, Nunzio. It's not an easy thing, juggling people's needs and demands. But I'll tell you, Nunzio, if the keystone's not laid, the future won't hold during frost heaves.'

'I knew we had Indians once,' I volunteered. 'Podunks and Pequonnocks. The Mattatucks were a long time ago. They used to fish in the river when it had fish. I looked them up in my Eastern

Woodlands Indian book. They were supposed to have disappeared in the 1700s. Wiped out by the Mohegan.'

'Maybe I should put *you* on the council.'

Some citizens had wriggled past the mayor's advisors and invited themselves into our conversation, but they did no more than grin or report what was being said to the people behind them. I grinned, embarassed, and toyed with a lace on my Puma Clydes. 'Mayor Longo? Can I ask your help with something?'

'Fire away, Chief.'

'Me and my dad, and my brother, we towed a car off Holy Hill last month.'

'Okay.' The mayor was being pulled at by the circling crowd and the old men tried to appease them.

'There was this '73 Pontiac-Bonneville, two-door, and . . .'

When I looked up at the mayor, Big Dan was staring at me, incredulous. The mayor did not see him.

'Go on. You towed an old car. What about it?'

'I saw something horrible.'

'Nunzio,' Dad said at the very moment his molars crushed a pair of Tums. He stepped in, crunching the tablets. 'We have to go.' He smiled at the mayor.

'What, are you still taking the Tums over here, Big Dan? You got the *agita'* in the belly?'

'Yeah, Frankie, how you doing?' Dad tried to shove me into the crowd with one hand while Mayor Longo stood and shook the other.

'My hands are dirty, Mayor,' Dad said. He always said that, had gotten used to it.

'What, are you kidding? I'll shake your hand before the Bishop's. You're a working man.' And then he spoke Italian and Dad spoke it back and they laughed some. 'You got a good kid over here. It's all about the kids, Dan, isn't it? Just give us a second.'

The Tums seemed to turn into dry mortar in my father's mouth as the mayor turned back to me, placed a hand on my neck. He gave me his ear.

'What were you saying? What did you see that was so horrible?'

'The Blessed Mother,' I said. 'Her arm was busted off.' I could hear Dad send a breath out his nose. Finally, his crushed Tums went down and he wiped his bottom lip with a hanky.

'Nunzi don't like how people treat the shrine up there.'

'Neither do I,' the Mayor said firmly.

'They spray-paint bad words on Moses. They dump garbage in there,' I started ranting like Uncas Fontenot. 'They knocked Ishmael's head off. It's not right.'

'I'm working on it,' he said. 'Part of the Renaissance. I won't stand for that stuff.'

I wanted to thank him; for saving the Indians and for restoring *The Soldier's Horse*, but Big Dan said goodbye and pulled me along. Then the mayor called me back. Big Dan looked nervous. It seemed he just wanted me out of there; I could see that, and it troubled me.

'Hey, Nunzio. This is for you. Never forget where you come from.'

I didn't get a good look at the cold round thing Mayor Longo tucked inside my hand until we made it through the crowd and to the street. It was one of the round and polished brass weights the mayor carried with him. Two years ago he had presented Danny Boy with a brass key. Now he was giving me, Nunzio, a brass ball.

CHAPTER FOURTEEN

Hoffa's Hat Pin

'No one will ever steal the Big Clock,' Big Dan was fond of saying, ''cuz you two guys are always keeping a close eye on the bastard.'

'So is Willie Loman,' Danny said on this day, shortly before the Big Clock surrendered the cherished 5 and a train hissed diesel spray beneath it in Union Station. Dad shut down The Crusher, and Grandpa dead-bolted the door on his shed in Area 51. Me and Danny Boy fed Primo Canero, scrubbed clean, changed, then raced off in the Cutlass for The Playhouse.

Danny Boy was late but it did not matter. He would not get to practice on this night. Mr Pembroke was intent on the pacing of the second act which had nothing to do with Narracott the butler. Still, we sat beside each other in metal folding chairs and watched the mystery blocked out, stiff actors shuffling along with playbooks in hand.

Even though my brother was not on stage, I was impressed by his transformation: he had gained six and one-half pounds in fourteen days. It was not a difficult achievement in The Little Boot. He visited Nonni and was stuffed with olives and *soprasatta* and great slabs of fresh-baked bread swabbed in olive oil; he made certain to cut through Mrs Orsini's backyard and say hello in Italian: she would feed him heaping bowls of *gnocchi* or *tortellini* with a thick cream sauce, peas and *prosciutto;* one day I saw him sitting in Zi Bap's back lawn with a towering plate of fried squash flowers which were the size of pancakes, sharing a glass of home-made red with our relative. Although this was a work-related challenge it did not seem an ordeal. When he would come home from these missions, he'd quaff two big Foster Lager beers for bulk.

'You better get me home,' I said when rehearsal ended late. 'We don't want Dad to smash this car.'

'We've gotta go someplace first,' was his cryptic answer. And then he added, 'Eggs, cream, tomatoes, butter, mother*fucker*. We have everything.' It was not how I imagined a butler on an Indian Island speaking, but I considered the possibility of this being a good thing – what my mother called 'playing against type'.

'Where do we have to go?' I asked him. Headlights washed over his face. I had to ask him again. I feared we were going to the Thirsty Turtle because he gunned the Cutlass up Eat Street into the queue of neon signs and golden arches and factories-turned-shoe-outlets.

Danny Boy put on his signal light near the entrance of the little strip mall where Electric Jamaica flickered in ultra-violet light. I felt something odd down in my chest when I saw Desiree from afar: it was a sweltry night and she wore a little lime-green tube top, her cleavage glossy with sun creams and mystery oils, her arms thin and tawny. We were up close now, parked right in front and I could see the black ink at the corner of her striking left eye, the black tears in a frozen cascade.

'Get me the Super 8,' Danny said.

When I opened the glove box, my hand touched the *mal'occhio* jar and I withdrew it fast. It was hot. Not warm from being in the car but hot, like chicken soup, and black as motor oil.

'Danny? You going to bury that jar?'

'I don't know what to do with it,' he said, combing his hair back. 'It's like I'm carrying a nuclear bomb.'

'But the headaches are gone, right?'

'Yeah. Next time I'll take some Bufferin. Like the rest of America.'

He looked at me and suppressed a smile. I could see my father in him as a dimple sunk in his cheek and his eyes reflected neon. And then he let the smile open his face and he reached across and mussed my hair. My heart lifted a bit; just to see him smile like that. If he wanted to get fat, that was his choice, I just wanted him to be happy. I passed the small black box to him and he sat behind the wheel, looking through the viewfinder at Desiree. He lined up a shot, switched on the car's interior light and checked the shot again. 'There she is,' Danny Boy said, lowering the camera and watching Desiree through the blue-lit plate glass of the tanning salon.

'She going to be in your movie?'

'She's got to be,' he said. 'She's Iris. She's the one.'

My brother was capturing Desiree in motion now, little movements collected in his small secondhand movie box. I loved the sound of a Super 8 camera, the feathery clicking that promised magic on the wall. This Bell & Howell had sound; Danny Boy was speaking softly into the hotshoe in a kind of narration: 'I'll get you out of here, Iris.'

Danny Boy would always have Desiree in her tube top and teardrop tattoos, moving in mysterious silence behind the glass with an exotic backdrop of papier maché palm trees and glow-in-the-dark poster oceans.

'I'll get you out,' he whispered as if she could hear him. When he was satisfied with his work, he lowered the box and switched off the interior light. He sat, cradling the camera, watching Desiree do her job.

'How's she fit into your movie?' I asked, cautiously.

'I cut from the knife cleaning fish at the beach. To her, in the window.'

'I don't get it,' I confessed.

'Symbolism,' he said.

'I still don't get it,' I said.

Danny Boy suggested that I wait in the car; I convinced him that the presence of a kid would defuse any tensions. The truth was, I wanted to get my chin on the counter and smell the punch of nail polish remover and Maui Wonder Cream.

She was my Iris, too.

'Someday a real rain is going to come and wash all the scum off the streets.'

When Danny Boy said this, I could tell Desiree had not seen *Taxi Driver* twenty-seven times.

'A rain's going to come, Desiree, I promise you.'

'You know what's going to come, Danny?' she said. 'A cop car. In five minutes, sucker, you don't get out of here.'

'Call the cops,' my brother said. 'They might ask you what you know about a '73 Pontiac. Blue. Four door, hard.'

'I don't know nothing.'

'I think you do, Desiree. I think you're in some kind of trouble. And I only want to help you.'

'You're my watch dog? That it?'

'I'll pay you for the time. I don't need to go in the back room and get a tan like these other people. I'll pay you the five bucks just to sit and talk. About you.'

Desiree stared him down for a time, slow-working her gum. Without looking at me she said, 'Blue Eyes. Go outside, okay? I need to talk to your brother alone.'

I started for the door, watching her reflection in the plate glass; she made a fist and gingerly tapped on the crown of my brother's head. 'Is there a steel plate in there, you?'

'Very funny,' he said.

'Stop playing games with me,' she said, suddenly hard.

A foot from the door out, I saw him.

In the parking lot, stationed right beside Danny's Cutlass was a silver Camaro. Behind the wheel, just staring, was Ray Beans. Although he was short, Ray Bonacascio was swollen with muscle and blood, his arms like pork hocks bursting from his shirt.

When he climbed out from behind the wheel, he looked like a de-iced primitive in a tank top tucked into wildly painted California pants and unlaced work boots. The way he carried himself was terrifying. He was yelling something in the parking lot to no one in particular, like some bear roaring at the moon as he marched toward the salon and the muscles between neck and shoulders – what my brother called traps – were descending like small mountains.

'Danny,' I said.

He ignored me. Desiree could see Ray Beans coming, but she seemed to reel my brother in like a trout; he was leaning on the counter speaking an inch or two from her ear. She smiled, let him closer.

'Danny,' I said again, tugging at his shirt.

Desiree leaned toward my brother with a smile that made him oblivious to everything else around him. Her dark eyes flitted casually toward Ray as he came through the door, sending me into the wall. Danny turned to see the short but powerful Ray Beans doing exaggerated inhales and whale-like exhales, blowing his back out wide, crooking his arms into a kind of pose and gorging blood into his face.

'Hey, Ray, what's up?' Danny did not alter his relaxed stance at the counter. Desiree sat down and tied back her Samurai tail of black hair, watching intently. Ray gathered in his breath.

'Why don't you tell *me* what's up, Paradiso? You trying to move in on my woman?'

'I didn't know she was your woman, Ray. I was just asking her something.'

'Asking her what?'

'Just some questions.'

'I heard you. About what?'

'Hah?'

'About what?'

'About what?'

'That's what I said, Danny. About fucking *what*?'

'A junk car.'

Ray Beans narrowed his eyes in what appeared to be confusion. Then he smiled and shook his head. 'What are you, peddlin' your junk over here, nine o'clock at night?'

'It's eight-thirty,' I said from behind him.

'Shut the fuck up!' Ray wheeled, thrusting a finger at me.

I knew Danny Boy wouldn't allow this. He removed his hands from the counter and faced the raging bodybuilder. 'Yo, Ray. Easy, man. That's my little brother.'

Ray Beans stared at Danny Boy, still breathing like he had been underwater for five minutes. He stared at Desiree who watched the whole thing, rapt, that crazy Francis Farmer thing in her eyes. Then Ray Beans walked away. He walked past me, to the plate glass, looked out, and just as I began to calm, he turned and charged. He hit my brother square in the face with a jab and Danny Boy's head rocked back. He gave two heavy body punches, grabbed Danny's thick hair and flung him across the lobby into the wicker sofa where he fell amongst *Travel* and *Leisure* magazines, his eyes wide with shock, one leg over a sofa arm in an unflattering state of repose. Desiree screamed as my brother clamored to his boots to defend himself. Ray Beans kicked him with an unpolished karate move and knocked him against the glass. Danny Boy threw a wild punch, but Ray batted it down and struck him hard in the midsection.

'Drag ass,' he hollered as hoarse as a drill sergeant. 'Drag ass and don't ever come back here, you faukin' loser.'

Desiree was screaming and trying to pry her boyfriend off, and I found myself scrambling toward my brother and wedging between him and the enraged muscle man. Ray shoved me out of the way and Desiree's fingernails got caught at my neck when she tried to catch me and pull me clear. I felt something pop: the chain of my gold horn medallion opened and small tin beads scattered across the pink linoleum.

Ray shoved Danny Boy against the front door then forced him outside. 'Don't scratch the faukin' Camaro!' he bellowed as Danny fell against it. Desiree and I followed, as if watching Danny Boy get clobbered would somehow help.

My brother was bleeding at the bottom lip and he was trembling – something he never would have done two years earlier when he was the All-City Junkyard Dog. Ray Bonacascio had him trapped in the tight alley between the old Cutlass and the new Camaro and he was gut-punching him. I lunged again but Desiree pulled me back and swung me, and I fell against the front of the silver muscle car.

Desiree gently took my arm and whispered, 'Don't scratch his car, honey.'

Ray Beans sent an uppercut to Danny Boy's newly plump middle but to my surprise my brother remained on his feet, buoyed by his Oldsmobile.

'You didn't get me down, Ray,' he said, dazed and tottering, blood welling at his teeth, as he mustered the salvaged piece of the *Raging Bull* preview. 'You never got me down, Ray.'

Ray Beans and Desiree both stared at him, puzzled. Ray took a step back and cocked his left arm. 'I did now, asshole.'

My brother's eyes told me that he saw the punch coming in slow motion, a wide, meat-saw roundhouse, and when it landed, sweat sprayed from Danny's head and blood welled in the bilge of his mouth.

And he went down.

My magic horn was lost. I knew well what would happen on this night:

It would come back for the vulnerable as predators are wont to do. Like Grandpa's tale of the old country fox returning to the chicken coop night after night until nothing was left, or the fox was killed, one or the other. She would come back, the Daughter of Lilith.

Like the Komodo dragon who inflicts a bite on an island deer as it runs away and then tracks the weakening animal by the scent of its infection, it would not relent. The *Strega* had made several visits to The Little Boot in the past days, terrifying Eddie Coco by squatting on his chest and sucking his breath away. Word was around that his dog, Barnaby Jones, scared it off. And Gooma Rosa said it appeared at the foot of her bed, paralyzing her but then fleeing and leaving behind a foul smell. Nonni had another strand of plastic red peppers in her windows and she kept her broom close by. So it was only a matter of time before Lilith's Daughter returned for me, Nunzio, an unconfirmed Christian, and a frightened soul adrift.

This was a summer of fitful dreams, but on this night, with Ray Beans' walloping fists coming at me each time I edged near sleep, my bed became a torture chamber. With my lava lamp on, I sat up and rummaged through my salvages, looking for the talismans my mother spoke of, the certain things in an uncertain world. I sorted and restacked *Police Gazettes*, I ran clay poker chips through my fingers and studied the rubber troll. I canvassed the few pennies and the brass pin from the Pontiac, the Chicago Teamsters button. So much could be learned about people from what they leave behind, but I felt as far from resolving our dilemma as Papa Coco was from the Atlantic and his lost son.

Maybe something would break.

Or maybe, better still, I would wake on a sunny August morning and find that it was all a nightmare and I would experience the rush of renewal like when you dream your mother has died and you wake to the glorious revelation that it was an illusion and you hear her say, 'Would ye fancy some Tang?'

I burrowed my head under my pillow and thought of the family gathering at the beach: the rhythmic wash of ocean waves and gentle laughter.

In the dream, I walked with the family out into the surf, manning my place along the net and drifting with the ebb and tides; I saw my father smiling and sharing some Italian joke with Goomba Rocco; I saw the other beach children closing in on us ocean gypsies as we dragged the net in then opened it to reveal the mysteries of the ocean gods. And there in the net, lying amongst eels and crabs were the remains of Max Diaz. '*Diaz*,' he groaned as he reached for me.

I slammed the trunk shut.

I woke, tried to sit up. I could not. I knew what was coming next. I tried to call out, but my lungs were decompressing as quickly as the shadow formed near the window. In the light of a quarter moon she did a slow dance, hair moving in the wind that played in my curtains.

It was a figure I had seen before.

La Strega, I had been schooled, could shape-shift and play a host of tricks on the victim but this was macabre; she peeled off her top and swung her breasts, left larger than the right, both to and fro, scarred belly jiggling as she came toward me, smiling just as she had weeks back in the evil den of the Thirsty Turtle. There were sounds of voices, some kind of singing, and in my crippled state I grabbed for logic and wondered if it was not a radio from a car parked over on Lucia Street.

It was that song, some kind of Creole disco – 'Lady Marmalade' it was called – and as it thumped louder, Doreen whirled, letting the weight of her bosom throw her into a pirouette and when she spun back on the next rotation her hair was longer and darker, and in the changing light, she was Lilith's Daughter, laughing, hungry for a celibate monk.

> *Voulez-vous coucher avec moi ce soir?*
> *Voulez-vous coucher avec moi . . .*

She was coming for me, the spawn of Adam gone bad, the evil thing that had come over from the Old Country on a tramp steamer, and she was now taking on another form: a tall demon in a short and glossy black windbreaker, half-zipped over a tiny Danskin, leopard tights and black high heels. As she sang along with the music, she swept a rogue strand of hair from an eye in ghostly slow-motion and danced like she was center-stage at the 10 competition over at the White Parrot, and she danced the meringue, and she danced the magic of Esmerelda in the square of the Notre Dame.

And she danced for me, in my bedroom at 11 Mary Street, filling my room with scents from the Caribbean. She danced like no one I had ever seen: some movements were fluid, like a river moving in a deep channel, but then she would freeze in a pose like a mannequin, only to explode into furious, controlled bursts of movement so intense I could see muscle fibre quivering under the blue leopard print. Then she was on my bed, crawling in exaggerated big cat movements, all a part of the Creole ritual. She was like a South American Jaguar shaman who could transform into a panther and devour a boy. This was the way of *La Strega*.

Only this violation I wasn't sure I wanted to fend off at the moment.

She undid her hair and let the black curly mass topple forward, brushing me lightly. Her cheek was against mine, I felt one of her fairy spoon earrings, and then I felt her lips brush my face. Just my cheek. Her breath was in my ear. I wanted to touch her but I was paralyzed.

'You're pretty, *coqui*,' she whispered.

As she leaned over me I could see, on the left breast pocket of the black windbreaker, some red cursive stitching forming a basketball and some slogan about NBA Champs. I looked the demon square in the face. She was no longer tormenting me with the visage of Desiree; Lilith's Daughter had taken on the form of Bettie Page from *Vue* magazine, 1952, dressed as a topless she-devil. Shadows engulfed shadows and I struggled against them, forced my head back so I could see her in the dim yellow of my grandparents' porchlight.

But again, like a prism slowly turning, she had changed from Bettie Page into another female creature, now wearing a tie-dyed T-shirt and cutoff denims. She had taken on the shape of Monica Lafontaine and she was pinning me down in a tomboy wrestling hold. 'Say Uncle,' she said.

'No way,' I whispered.

She slid her mouth over mine and I felt the warm probe of her short tongue. I could smell a cigarette and the faint scent of Breck for oily hair.

She was crushing me. I could not tell her to count the straws on the broom. I wasn't exactly sure I wanted to. I was breathing hard, and she raised a finger alongside her nose and silently mouthed, 'Sshhh.'

And then I woke up, a cool breeze freezing the sweat on my face. The *Strega* was gone, just a wind in the curtains and a pungent scent in the room. It smelled faintly of Chlorox and salty sweat, and where she had sat, the sheets were damp and warm. I lifted my head cautiously and touched down there. Something had happened; my God, the *Strega* had not only stolen my breath away, she had invaded my dreams and stole from me like she had from celibate monks for centuries.

I collapsed into my pillow and took in a breath. Maybe it wasn't a sin, I reasoned. *I* didn't do anything. It wasn't *my* hand. I said a Hail Mary anyway, rolled onto my knees, and then rose up with a sudden thought.

Desiree's windbreaker. The one she put on outside that night: Ray's jacket. With a basketball on the left breast.

A basketball.

The hat pin; I needed to see Hoffa's hat pin. I grabbed for it and held it in the light, so close to the bulb my hand grew hot. It was not a relic from some Chicago World's Fair; it wasn't a hat pin from Jimmy Hoffa's teamster days like I once fantasized. It wasn't even a globe.

It was a ball.

1973 Chicago Teamsters. *Why* teamsters? Why 24182510? The Chicago what – Bears? That was football. The Bulls, the Chicago *Bulls*. The brass pin was a tiny basketball.

I found myself standing in the center of my bedroom while the walls seemed to revolve around me.

I went to my steamer trunk and dug in, pulling out old copies of *Dandelion Wine* and *The Hunchback of Notre Dame*, my stacks of *Police Gazettes* and Chilton auto-parts guides and the Old Testament, and then my football record books, my baseball cards and a huge, rat-eaten tome called *The Basketball Bible*.

I hefted it onto my bed and craned the gooseneck lamp over it; I licked at my thumb and fingers and turned pages, going from the Celtics to the Lakers too fast, so fast I was tearing the flimsy, yellowed sheets. I took a breath. Turned the pages gingerly. And there it was: the horned devil with a head as red as fire.

The Chicago Bull that was on Ray Beans's T-shirt at the Indian hearing. Only this one, this '73 logo, had a ring through its nose, snorting in aggression like a mythic bull.

I had to wonder: was that what Sister Giselle LaBow saw that night up in Holy Land? Was it Raymond Bonacascio, wearing a wool cap down over his face, who fired two .22 caps into Mr Diaz, then hefted him like a 150-pound curl bar, rolling him into the trunk?

I thumbed through the year summary pages from 1968 to 1972 and when I found 1973, I traced a finger down the team roster. The players' numbers were listed and I tried to find a match between active jerseys and the cryptic number. 2: Van Lier; 4: Sloan; 18: Boerwinkle; 25: Walker, and 10: Love.

24182510: the best defensive back court to ever play the game, the book opinioned. The arcane number wasn't a teamster ID at all; it was the five best players on the '73 Bulls. The stars.

The team . . . *stars*.

Chicago Team*stars* is what it must have said before it was scratched away in the seven years Ray Beans wore it on the cuff of his windbreaker, before it popped loose behind him in the front seat of the Pontiac.

My God; I had the *Shooter*.

Me, Nunzio Paradiso.

But I didn't have much time.

Danny Boy angled the Chicago Bulls pin in his hand like he was trying to make a flame with a magnifying glass. 'I don't know, Nunz. Hanging a guy on the basis of his being a Bulls fan is a little thin. I mean,' he kind of whispered, 'I'm a New York Jets fan – I should be euthanized, for God's sake.'

I had been going like Charlie Chan all day at the junkyard and hadn't let up on our way to The Playhouse. Danny said that what occurred the night of the brawl was a separate issue – he had been touching tomatoes in another man's garden and he had to pay the price.

'But he was there,' I said. 'He was there at the tanning salon where the Pontiac was dumped. Desiree's his girlfriend. Did she call Ichabod for him?'

Danny was quiet now as he drove the highway, smoking a Kool.

And then he flipped the gold pin back into my lap. 'Whoever killed Max, arranged to have that car sent through The Crusher. That's called premeditated, Nunzi. Ray Beans isn't smart enough to premeditate. And another thing: the deaf Sister saw the guy throw down a cigarette then go back for the butt. Ray Beans is a bodybuilder. He doesn't smoke. He wouldn't.'

'Maybe not, Danny. But I want to go see Goomba Angelo.'

Danny Boy pulled up to The Playhouse, braked hard. 'You want to go see the Eye That Never Sleeps? Go see him. I've got to get in character and I can't have this shit in my head right now. Okay? I can't own this shit.'

He got out of the car and removed his props, a paper bag of tomatoes and lemons from the trunk. He was safe into the skin of a large butler. I wished I could slip into another character, too; I just didn't know who to be.

Just me, Nunzio, I said into the black pay phone.

Johnny hung up on me.

But she was there inside of twenty minutes, looking harried. She called me a pain in her black ass and basted me through the fast ride, but still, she was there. She could have left me at the phone booth. 'I only have an hour,' I told her. 'I have to be back by seven-thirty to do the sound effects.'

Somewhere in her diatribe, as she cut off a car here and honked her horn there, Johnny mentioned Myrtle Beach and her wish that Angelo would just go so she could get on with her life.

'He ever been there?' I asked.

'Who, Angel? No. He never been out of this city.'

The stories about Myrtle Beach came from her, she told me. Her mother and father had migrated to Saukiwog Mills from South Carolina in 1951. Not that the Sisson family frequented Myrtle – in those days they had separate beach showers for the coloreds – but she had been down south since: two funerals and a summer vacation with her Carolina cousins during which she first went to Myrtle. Her folks, she said, 'Wanted to get away from all that racism down there.' And then she turned a look on me, holding back a smile. She saw my look and let the smile burst free, nodding her head and laughing her slow laugh. 'Oh, yeah,' she said. 'You get it, Nunzio. You get what I'm sayin'. Fryin' pan into the fire.'

Her father went to work in the Saukiwog Rolling Mills. 'So did my grandfather,' I said as if it were a grand happenstance. Johnny just shrugged. 'Them Italians was happier than shit to see some niggers come in. That knocked their asses up a big notch. And then when the Puerto Ricans come over? Hoo, my daddy got bumped up to the casting room.'

We were deep in the North End now and Pope Street held some old water from the prior rain or an open hydrant. 'Shit roll downhill,' Johnny epigrammed. 'But I tell you what. I'm gonna win my ass the Lotto. And when I do, I'm gonna go to New Haven and cut me a record. My own record.'

'Hey, neat,' I said.

'Yeah, neat,' she sniffed. 'You know what I call it?'

I studied her, shook my head.

'Too Hot For You, Baby'.

'What?'

'That's my record. "Too Hot For You, Baby". With my picture. My big ass in a sequin dress. Them long white gloves. Screaming into a microphone, you see all my teeth. All of them, all the way in back, like when Donna Summers screams her ass.'

She caught me staring and she did a take.

'I'll buy it,' I said. 'I'll save up and buy it.'

'You mean that?'

'Yeah.'

Johnny drove along, her thoughts somewhere deep.

'Your father have spelter bends?' I asked.

'Say what?'

'Spelter bends. From breathing in zinc in the casting shop. My father's Goomba Rocco has it: he shakes all the time.'

Johnny stared at me with her face pinched for a full block, and then she braked at a stop sign and let both arms sag over the wheel. 'That what that shit was?' she said at a high decibel. 'My mama think the man have the DDT's from the drink. All them years, she say "watch old man shake from the drink".'

She remained at the stop sign, digesting this. 'Damn,' she said.

'Spelter bends,' I confirmed.

'Spelter bends,' she repeated, then she dropped the car into drive and motored on, deep in memory. I couldn't help but feel an affinity; she was black, I was Italian-Scot, but we were related by zinc fumes, spelter bends and the migrations of our ancestors.

'I knew the man weren't on no bottle,' she said to herself quietly, like an afterthought.

We found the apartment dark; the smell of the place a heady mix of Lysol and animal urine. We could not see him in his corner but we could hear him giving orders to Ruby, and the capuchin was cheep-cheeping back like they were some long-married cantankerous couple.

'Now,' Angelo slurred, and so I assumed the monkey was dealing out a little Demon Patience or Napoleon at St Helena.

Click, I heard. A metallic sound.

'Now,' Angelo said again.

Ruby chattered back and then – *click*. Again. Dry metal. Johnny tugged a light cord. A bottle of Galliano sat on the dresser, all but empty. Half a Wallbanger remained in a plastic sippee cup on the floor, not far from Angelo who sat with Ruby Lee perched on his shoulder like a sailor with a parrot.

It was not his drunken state that disturbed me nor the appearance of his face, ashen and tubercular. And it was not the fetid scent of the apartment, the playing cards scattered in no order.

It was the task he had set Ruby to, making her sit on his shoulder and clutch his .38 Chief Special with the barrel against his temple. Johnny and I stood abreast, me hugging myself against the chill, Johnny afraid to remove her hands from her hips lest she startle Ruby.

'You stupid mother,' she said. Then she adopted a more maternal tone albeit stern: 'Put that down *right now*.'

'Now,' Angelo said again and Ruby Lee pulled both her small hands toward herself, dry-firing the gun. Me and Johnny flinched as the hammer kicked and the barrel rocked slightly against Angelo's temple. The monkey convulsed a pace and did her coo and *neet-neet-neet* chatter as if in protest. She was an obedient companion, and pulling the gun's trigger must have been no different than turning the water spigot or sliding the chain lock.

Ruby was his hands. He had said that. She was his arms, his legs, his lifeline, and now he had her carrying out a game of Russian Roulette as he sat drunk and medicated, clearly bereft of reason. Or was this what sold him on the idea of accepting a trained monkey in the first place?

A way out.

'Get down, Ruby,' Johnny said. 'I mean it, now.'

Ruby Lee jerked her head toward us and showed her teeth. Angelo, keeping his head daringly still, lifted an eye on me.

'What are you doing here?' he asked, a slight slur evident.

Johnny dropped to a knee and summoned the monkey. 'Drop the gun, Ruby. Come here, come on.'

When Ruby obeyed, Angelo acted as if we had interrupted some intimate moment of romance; he cursed us and he cursed the monkey's disaffection, and in the light of the stark 45-watt bulb, I saw traces of tears on his unshaven face.

Johnny picked up the gun and rolled the chamber. There was nothing in it. I heard a breath come out of her as she composed herself then set the revolver down hard on the dresser. Turning, she grabbed the arms of the wheelchair and looked straight into Angelo's face.

'If that lady from Easter Seals ever sees shit like that, you're going to lose Ruby. What then, fool? Who going to fetch up your newspaper then? Who going to wipe your sorry *ass*?'

'Don't tell me what I can't do for amusement.'

'This ain't good for the boy to see.'

'Did I invite the boy over? What is it – Jell-O Night? Fucking Hallowe'en over here? The gun was *dry*, Mother.' He tried to lock his eyes with Johnny's but they kept slipping off, sliding about the room, bleary and moist.

'I know what you're doing,' Johnny said, a slight quaver in her voice. 'You practicing to make sure you got a ticket out of town. But look at me, Angel.' She put her face square in his. '*Look* at me. You ain't good at killin' yourself. You never was. So give it up, and deal.'

'And you ain't good at singin', so shut the fuck up and go drive your hack.'

Johnny looked like she might slap him. Instead, she wheeled and went to his kitchenette and poured herself a glass of water.

'Take me for a ride,' Angelo said, and he licked at his teeth like his mouth was arid. 'Let's go to the Turtle. One drink.'

'We've got something,' I said, clandestinely.

Angelo looked up and said, 'Listen to me, Numb Ones. You got junk. Scrap.'

'Salvage,' I retorted.

'And I'm a Pinkerton Man. The cocksucking Bonneville leaves in six days and the case is over, pal. You got *shit*.'

'I've got the Shooter,' I said.

Angelo bent a look on me that bore traces of Zi Toine, my father, Al Pacino, my grandfather, and for a terrifying second – somewhere at the eyebrows – myself.

'Ray Bonacascio,' I drilled. 'Desiree from the tanning place's boyfriend.'

I set the hat pin on his lap tray but he didn't even look at it. I edged closer to him. 'He gets tans at her place. He's a Chicago Bulls fan and I found that pin in the driver's seat of the Pontiac.'

'Wait a minute. You come over here – eight o'clock at night – to talk about fucking *basketball*?'

'Johnny,' I begged. 'Tell him.'

'I ain't tellin' him *nothin'*.'

I pulled the folded, crumpled sheet from my pocket, the page I had torn from the basketball diary, and I spread it before him. He cast an eye down on it. '*There's* your horned devil,' I said.

Angelo looked at the cartoon bull then lifted his watery eyes onto me. A little bit of his tongue showed between his teeth; he was attempting a smile but his mouth seemed numb.

'Lew Alcinder was tops,' Angelo said. 'Then he changed his name to Moslem, like Cassius Clay. I'm going to tell you something, Danny.' Drunk as a bear in crab apples, he was calling me by my brother's name. 'He's still Cassius Clay to me. He's still Cassius Clay to his mother.'

I stared bewildered at his drawn face as he made an effort to focus on me. 'For a minute,' he said, 'try to imagine what it feels like to be in the foxhole and something lands at your feet and you look down and it's a fucking G-banger.'

'Bullshit,' I cut him off.

'That right,' Johnny said. 'Bullshit. You can't fool this boy. He know his Bible.'

'Well, that's good. Stick with the Bible and forget about this other stuff, 'cuz I'll tell you something, kid. I know who did this thing, and you don't want to know, and I don't want to talk about it again. I didn't know it was going to go where the fuck it's going.'

'And where's that?' I said, uneasy. 'You mean the police like you said? Sergeant Kelly?'

Angelo barked out an order that sounded like 'Roy!'and Ruby Lee hustled to a bank of shelves and climbed onto an 8-track player. The capuchin straddled the box like it was having jungle instinct with it and chattered as she slid the fat tape in. The music that came forth was turned to high volume. It was that Roy Orbison music, old and stale as the smoke in the room, and Angelo began singing, 'Shahdaroba'.

Something cold flooded my veins and I wanted to look Mr Volpe in his pallid face and call him a *Mamone*. I glared hard at him, harder than a twelve-year-old relative should. 'They're right about you. I thought you were some kind of hero or something.'

Angelo turned a look on me. '*What* are you sellin'?'

'They were right about you. And they're right about me. I'm a frigging daydreamer.'

Angelo stared for a hard moment then resumed singing, louder, as if hoping to drive us out the door.

Far down the cheap carpeted hall I could hear my father's second cousin singing with a liquored up torment. Johnny looked at me, concerned. 'You want a Carvel?' she asked. Never before had an ice-cream cone sounded like pure salvation, but it did then.

So on the quiet ride back to The playhouse, Johnny Mae and I savored single vanilla scoops in sugar cones. Neither of us said a word, but we did exchange blissful looks during a lick or two and once she said, 'Who need drug when you got Carvel?'

I had to agree.

She sang with Stevie Wonder on the radio, licking at her cone in between lyrics. 'You know what else I'm gonna get when I win the Lotto? Air condition. It's hot out there.'

'"Too Hot For You, Baby",' I said, trying to catch running ice cream.

Johnny looked at me, threw her head back and laughed with all her weight. She laughed so hard, she had to pull over to the side of Route 8. Tears began wetting her eyes and her laughter sounded like a tropical bird that hurt my ears once at the Bronx Zoo when I was four.

I could see all her teeth, all the way back. The Plymouth rocked a little on its springs as her laughter ran away from reason, and mine ran with it. We laughed together like two kids on a roller coaster.

That night I sat in my room reading my *Police Gazettes* and pondering the truth about Jack-the-Ripper. Danny Boy knocked on the doorjamb, but said nothing. He seemed to be surveying the things in my room: the curios and bric à brac and remaining links to a boyhood he once knew well.

'You don't have to go with me, Nunzio,' he said.

What he really meant was: don't let go of the magic.

'I want to, Danny,' I said.

What I really meant was: I had no choice.

At the abandoned drive-in, two yellow Caterpillar bulldozers and a back-hoe were parked for the night near the tilled and tamped area where the snack bar once stood. 'Remember,' I probed, 'the last movie we all went and saw together?'

Danny wasn't listening, so I followed his gaze to a green dumpster that was packed to the gunwales with uprooted speaker stalks and decapitated heads; there was also what appeared to be torch-cut sections of the monkey bars.

'*Walking Tall*,' I said. 'Daddy said it was far-fetched.'

When Danny Boy swept his headlights past the desecration, I could see that his mark was a lone vehicle, parked and facing the screen just like the Ford Fairlane we had found weeks earlier. Only there were figures in this car, one behind the wheel, one in the backseat. The entire cabin was filled with a ponderous mist, a drifting gray smoke. A tiny gargoylian figure perched in the rear window moved suddenly when our headlights caught it. Its eyes glowed like an opossum caught in the trash bins. When it came alive and moved along the rear windshield and down into the backseat, I knew then it was Johnny Mae's Plymouth and Angelo was strapped upright in back.

'It's Goomba Angelo,' I said.

'You were expecting Buford Pusser?'

We pulled alongside them and parked in what felt like a macabre re-enactment of the drive-in's glory days. Danny Boy got in back with Angelo. I sat up front with our gypsy cab driver. She was in a mood, I reasoned, because she didn't even glance at me. Impatient, she rested a hand on her wheel and kept her gaze straight ahead on the big vacant screen. I wondered what movies Johnny Mae Sisson liked and if she had ever brought her children here on a Sunday night in summer, dressed in their pajamas and having pillow fights in the backseat. I didn't even know if she had children but the thought comforted me. On the frontseat between her and me – propped atop her music tapes, last Sunday's newspaper and her Naugahyde tip pouch – were two large curry-yellow folders, spilling over with papers.

'Why'd you call us here?' Danny Boy said, looking uncomfortably at Angelo.

'This place went downhill when they started the fuck movies,' Angelo said.

'Get to it, Angel,' Johnny cut in, confirming her bad mood. 'This place ain't cool.'

'A man,' Angelo said. 'A man with something to lose would walk away. A man with nothing to lose, shouldn't care. But now I got this kid here. My godson.'

I felt everyone look at me as Angelo went on. 'He came to me. Six years, the only one. He comes looking for help, from me. The family might be right about me, but I ain't gonna let them be right about him.'

The Plymouth was so full of broadleaf tobacco smoke, I felt a touch dizzy, like the car was floating off the ground a foot or two.

'What you have?' Danny Boy said.

'I'll tell you, Frosh,' he said. 'But if I do, there'll be no turning back.'

'What do you have, Ange?' my brother said again.

'All right,' Angelo said to Johnny. 'It's show time.'

Johnny pulled her headlight switch and drove her sneaker with a click into the high beam button on the floor. There before us, lit stark in the shadow of the old screen, was a big metal dumpster, half-green, half-rusted and filled with pieces of the snack bar. Emblazoned across the length of the large rust-and-green metal box was the bold decal: *Are You Having A Hard Time Finding A Place To Dispose Of Your Bulky Waste?*

Under it was the business name and address for Testa Refuse, Inc.

I knew the name. Danny Boy did, too. Johnny stared at it as if she was deciphering some petroglyphs on an ancient stone.

Salvatore Testa, the scrap-metal merchant and the man who could turn magic with George Washington's image, was the owner of the demolition company that maintained the green dumpsters. Hardly a revelation, my brother said.

'Testa,' Angelo dug in. 'He's got a contract with his Uncle Guy Valle. Guy Valle owns Valle Construction and Demolition out of Bridgeport.'

'Sally Sheet Metal,' I said.

'You know him?' Angelo asked. 'You know Testa?'

'Yeah,' said Danny Boy. 'But what's he got to do with this?'

'He's got a contract with Valle Construction and Valle Construction's got a contract with Brass City Development. Johnny spent the whole day at City Hall and Public Records, copying zoning permits going back a year.'

'She work hard for the money,' Johnny reminded us.

'There's a pattern here, boys. One company wins a bid, they all get the job. You follow what I mean when I say a pattern?'

Danny Boy nodded, but I was not impressed. Talk about zoning reports and construction bids had the same effect on me as long division.

But Goomba Angelo then dropped a name like a pebble into still water and it woke me from the lull: 'Diaz,' he said, 'Max Diaz was refused an engineering permit for the old mill. After he disappears, some developers approach the widow offering her a pretty penny for the building. Are you fucking *stunods* with me at all?'

'Yeah, but,' Danny Boy said, toward Johnny so he wouldn't have to look over at Angelo, 'how do you know it's the same people? All

Mrs Diaz said was some people came to see her, wanting to buy the mill.'

'Hole card,' Angelo said suddenly and Ruby climbed into his lap and probed about his eyebrows. He said something mean in Italian and the capuchin quickly adjusted herself, dug about her charge's front shirt pocket, removing a small black comb, a one-eyed Jack, a folded Mass card that I recognized as the one from the Widow Diaz's freezer, a King of Hearts, and what appeared to be a business card. Danny Boy took the card and angled it toward the moonlight.

'BCD,' he read and I recognized the acronym instantly as the business card that I had lifted from Mrs Diaz's fridge, the one with the logo of the Saukiwog clock. Angelo apparently had Ruby snatch it just like the blood-pressure pills.

'BCD – Brass City Development,' he said. 'Same investors turning this drive-in into a shopping plaza. BCD bought it, Guy Valle's building it and Sal Testa gets the scrap. In every jungle there's a food chain, boys.'

'*Hmmm*-mm,' Johnny agreed, drumming a thumb on her steering wheel.

We were all quiet now. Angelo took in some more cigar smoke, tasted it for a time then let it out his nostrils. When I told Goomba Angelo that Sally Sheet Metal visited our family salvage yard every other Friday, he said, 'Watch your backs.' When Danny Boy explained that Fat Sally dealt in scrap bridge metal, copper and cobalt, Angelo said, 'Watch your backs.'

When Danny Boy said goodnight to everyone and signaled for me to follow him out of the Plymouth, Angelo said, 'I need fifty bucks,' and Johnny said, 'I need ten for gas.'

CHAPTER FIFTEEN

A Christian and a Soldier

Sunday morning in The Little Boot:

Not long after daylight and the seven o'clock church bells, the aromas began. Down along Mary Street, garlic and onions sautéed in olive oil. The base for the sauce, prepared early. Laying in bed, we stirred, noses so finely tuned we knew when Nonni's garlic was almost golden. I could smell the roasted peppers, six large ones, skinned and seeded and added to the mix. While a block away, aromas spilled from the open back door of Coangelos' where Mrs Pisani was baking *torta con gelato* and anisette cookies, the loaves baking and sending the scent of anise up over backyard grape arbors and cinderblock garages. By the noon bells, a plate of these would be set on a doily on Nonni's table; Mama Orsini was making her own sauce, one she called *paglia e fieno*, heavy with cream and peas and *prosciutto*.

But it was my mother's sauce that filled our little house with the scent of basil and parsley. A version of her mother-in-law's sauce, it would be placed in a smaller bowl beside Nonni's and it would meet the Sunday test once again. As Mom worked a wooden fork in the hot oil and garlic, her leavened Celtic face ruddy from the heat, she pretended not to notice Nonni, coming to her own kitchen window every few minutes in an effort to look in and critique.

And the sound, there was really only one: the slow thuck of a *bocci* ball landing in the clay pit behind the Garatoni house where Mary Garatoni's father was practicing for the game he would hold after lunch. The balls, brought over with the first Garatonis, would land in the clay in a soft and steady tempo. Every third Sunday, a few lawnmowers got going early, too, and the smell of fresh-mown grass added an earthy lust to the baking breads. If I didn't hear *bocci* balls landing soft or lawnmowers choking awake, or my Nonni flattening ants with the heel of her shoe, I slept in because it meant it was raining. That's how connected we were to the smells, the sounds, the tempo of The Little Boot. Me and Eddie Coco often met early to watch Gumby reruns while dunking Stella D'oro cookies in warm *azzupe*, and Eddie might refer to Poky as *stunod* instead of slow-witted. We were a long way from Huck and Tom despite ourselves.

On this particular Sunday, Dad was up, reading the thick edition of the *Republican*. Danny Boy was still in bed, having gone out after depositing me in the drive around nine the night before. It was probably not the most appropriate time to ask my father, but the kitchen was quiet and he looked calm as he bit into a warm, oil-soaked *bruschetta*, toasted Italian bread heaped with an egg and red peppers.

'Hey, Dad?'

'Yes, sir,' he said, chipper. It was part auto-response, part distraction; it always caught me off-guard however, made me laugh uncomfortably.

'You know Sally Testa?'

'Yes, sir.'

'You know him a long time?'

Dad shrugged as he ate. 'Sally Sheet Metal? Too long,' he said.

I wondered what Goomba Angelo would make out of that answer. My mother crossed the kitchen on quick slippers and grabbed a few spice jars from the cabinets. 'He's a nice man, Sally,' my mother vouched. 'He's got a wonderful voice. He sang at the Connecticut Junkyard Association Christmas Dinner a few years ago. What was it he sang, Dan? It was a Tom Jones song, I think.'

'He's an ass,' my father said casually, creasing the sports page. 'Any guy who gets up and sings at a party when there's already a band, is an ass.'

'He talks dirty,' I said.

This didn't faze my father but Mom stopped on her slippers and cast an eye on my father. 'Did you hear that, Dan?'

'What's that, Nance?' Dad said, looking up from the paper.

'He says Sally speaks dirty. Are they speaking dirty with a lad about?'

'Nothing these kids ain't heard before, Nancy.'

'Well,' my mother clucked her tongue. 'Sally should know better. He's Nunzi's godfather, for the love of Columba.'

My orange juice came forth with pulp seed. 'What, Mom? He's my *what*?'

'Salvatore. He's your godfather.'

The kitchen grew still.

'He's your *goomba*,' my father confirmed. 'But when was the last time he sent you something on your birthday?'

'Wait a minute,' I said. 'Zi Bap is my godfather. And so was Goomba Angelo.'

'I told you never to mention that name,' Dad said. 'But, yeah, Zi Bap's your *goomba*, too.'

'How can you have three *goombas*?'

Dad slid his empty bowl off the sports page to read something.

'Well,' Mom said, shaking celery salt into the pan on the front burner, 'Angie was named your godfather when you were born, but he and Daddy had a falling out. Dad asked Zi Bap to be your godfather when you were about four, then *they* had a quarrel. So Dad asked Sally to be your godfather. Then Zi Bap came into his good graces again and we felt it kindest not to offend either.'

And so, after Mass, I set out for a day of Sunday freedom, burdened with information I wasn't looking for. Sally Testa, the fat scrap-metal merchant who may have been in on a plan to make Mr Diaz disappear over a demolition contract, was my *goomba*? I felt uncomfortable, overloaded with godfathers. Having Zi Bap as my Confirmation sponsor was bad enough. Did I have a prearranged bond with a killer as well?

Moreover, I felt small; Zi Bap and Angelo hardly acknowledged me as their godson and Sally Testa didn't even know my name. I puzzled over this as I walked with Eddie Coco down to Our Lady of Mount Carmel School to see if any kickball was going on in the lot. Eddie was telling me a story about how Joey Massi's older brother, Tips, got caught with pot, but my mind was elsewhere. And then, coming toward us up the sidewalk was Monica Lafontaine. She looked delicate in her pink church dress, her hair done up by her aunts. I saw Eddie blush and he saw me blush, and this made each of us go a deeper shade, together.

'Hey, Nunzio,' she said.

Eddie and I stumbled over each other's penny loafers.

'There's a big colored lady looking for you,' she whispered with a fearful hiss. 'You better run.'

And then she hurried off across the street. The piebald Plymouth came up America Street, started to throat its way down Mary then stopped in the middle of the road, carb knocking and throbbing, and making gas-sucking sounds. When Johnny saw me, she leaned on the horn.

Eddie ran.

He spun on his heels and bolted, vaulting the wall behind Gooma Rosario's and scaling her terraced gardens. I ran, too. Up the sidewalk to the Plymouth, stopping four or five feet shy of the driver's window in the event someone saw me and the word got around.

'Man,' she said to me, 'you don't got to leave this city to see the world. I just drive up to this 'hood on a Sunday and I'm in Rome.'

'Well, Naples,' I corrected her.

She saw me looking in the backseat. 'You got to go see Angel. Now.'

'On a Sunday?'

'You think Manix get Sunday off?' she asked me, and she started in with more.

'Okay,' I stopped her. 'Drive into the school, I'll be over on the side of the gym.'

'*Get in this car,*' she shrilled, but I took off running in my loafers. She leaned on the horn once again then set off after me, flustered. Eddie Coco was watching from the Massis' backyard, and when he saw me running, he took it as a signal and spun off onto Lucia Street, running so hard I could hear his breathing.

I whispered St Donato's name twelve times and prayed that I wouldn't start a racial war.

Goomba Angelo celebrated Sundays in his own way.

He sat in whatever sunlight fought its way into his room and listened to Roy Orbison on his music box. Ruby Lee was sleeping, curled at the side of the little stereo and I wondered how many times the tape had cycled since the day began. Johnny did not accompany me up the stairs. A block before Dunn's Convalarium, she caught a fare, a handsome elderly black man dressed to the nines for church, and she all but kicked me out of the frontseat, assuming the voice of a train conductor and announcing, 'You deep in the heart, baby.'

The handsome man in the backseat had laughed heartily and Johnny looked pleased with herself when I scrambled out the door. As I ran, I could hear her and her fare laughing at my bowlegged way of hurrying.

The door to 4-N was wide open when I got there, and Angelo looked as peaceful as a monk when I stepped in. 'Hey, kid,' he said. And then my Sunday garb caught his sharp eye. He whistled through his teeth. 'You look like Johnny Travolta over here.'

'I don't have long,' I said. 'I got to be back for dinner.'

'Come here,' he said suddenly, and he jerked his head, calling me over. I held my distance. 'Come over here, kid,' he said again, using his head to beckon me closer.

I approached slowly and my footsteps awakened Ruby who looked up and blinked her tiny shiners. She showed her teeth and yawned. 'Come on, closer,' Angelo said.

I was up on him now, looking down at his wilted form. He wanted me to bring my ear to his lips. He had a secret to share.

And when I did, he kissed me.

It was a soft kiss despite his sandpaper stubble and the scent of shade tobacco. A gentle kiss with maybe only a tiny smack of sarcasm in it.

And then he said, 'You're a sharp fucking cookie.'

When I drew back slowly, I noticed that he had the Chicago pin on his chair tray amongst cigar ash and a half-eaten peach. He had been up to Holy Hill again, he told me. He had Johnny rouse the nuns and show Sister Giselle the torn page from the *Basketball Bible*, the one with the flaming red Chicago Bull. She was startled by it, or, as he phrased it: she shit a *bracciola*. She spoke in tongues, he said, frightened mute cadences while Sister Racine herself came down the steps to see Angelo in his chair, and said, 'That's your horned devil, sir. The *bull*, like Sister Giselle tried to tell you.'

Raymond Bonacascio *was* the Shooter, he said.

'What about the pattern? What about Sally Testa and Valle Construction and these land deals and—'

'You think those chickenshits would pull the trigger?' Angelo said, his eyes piqued. 'They needed a dumb fuck. A macho man.' His description fit Ray Beans to the letter. But there was even more glue to stick Desiree's boyfriend to the fly strip:

'Ray Beans was employed as a trash collector for Testa Refuse until the Monday after you found the body in the car. And the following Thursday, he registered a used Camaro in mint condition at the DMV. By the way, you guys oughta give me a bonus for dealing with the fucking DMV – I aged in the lines over there. Ownership was transferred from one of Testa's other companies, his demolition company.'

'Oh my God,' I said, dropping into the easy chair near the radio. The legs of my suit were too short and I saw Angelo eyeing my blue socks and penny loafers.

'Kid,' he said, almost amused. 'You did good.' Then: 'Ray has a record down the station,' he said. 'Been busted twice for dealing in steroids. This is a dumb macho fuck with a Napoleon thing. You take steroids to be bigger than the boogie man. What can make you bigger than having people whisper that you're a made man? Ray Beans bought the myth. He thinks he's a Wise Guy, but what he is, is a fall guy for the underclass underworld.'

'The what?'

'The old man Valle. Down in Bridgeport. Ties.'

'Ties.'

'Yeah. Connections. To a guy who owns a metal smelter in Danbury and has ties to a guy named Piccolo. Piccolo has ties to a major crime family in Rhode Island or some fucking place. Sally Testa's tied in with them. Saukiwog's in a real-estate boom. Renaissance City, right? You want to know why Max Diaz was whacked? Follow the bulldozers.'

'Angelo . . .' I was wriggling in my seat.

'Go for it, kid. You got my ear now.'

'Sally Sheet Metal . . .'

'That's right. The Dacron Don.'

'He's my *goomba*.' I didn't just say it; I yelled it. GOOMBA must have echoed down the hall of Dunn's Convalarium. Now the ex-cop was silent for a time.

'Say again?'

'Sally Sheet Metal is my godfather. I mean one of them. I have three, yourself included.'

'Isn't that just like your old man,' Angelo said. 'Naming a child's godfather is supposed to be the highest honor to an old friend. He named me because I was a traffic cop and he figured he might catch a break down the Motor Vehicle Department. Your old man probably asked anybody who he had to pay a bill to, hoping to get a break. I can just see Big Dan writing out a check and his hand's trembling 'cuz it hurts to part with it, and so he says, "You know, I'd be honored if you'd be the godfather of my son," hoping the guy will knock off ten percent. He probably asked the fucking milkman so he could get a break on cottage cheese—'

'He brings asbestos,' I said, 'and drums of stale oil, pieces of rusted bridges, just about anything he needs to dump. And he buys copper, radiators and heater motors and heater cores. He gets all the copper. Man, this sucks the hairy moose.'

Then I apologized for my language.

Angelo told me not to despair, that kids my age had fought in the Civil War, gone over Niagara Falls in whiskey barrels, and played the cello at Radio City Music Hall.

'I've got to go home,' I told Angelo.

'You're a sharp cookie,' he repeated as I left, and I was relieved that he didn't attempt to kiss me again.

'Redemption day,' Big Dan said with a white smile against sun-browned skin.

It was Monday and the sun was unusually high for eight in the morning and Dad was damp with the kind of sweat more typical for noon as he climbed up the steel rungs to his big wrecking crane. Redemption was a word he used a lot when talking about junk. We didn't crush cars, we 'redeemed' them.

I stood staring at the hulk of the Bonneville, thinking of the trunk and all the terrible things I had set loose from it, the least of which was the possibility that we, the Paradisos, might be the last link in the chain that Angelo was talking about. Was our family auto-wrecking yard a disposal pit for some kind of crime family?

Was my third *goomba*, Salvatore Testa, not just *my* godfather but a *godfather* per se – a kingpin like Marlon Brando? He certainly didn't talk like one, did not dress like one. Unless *sotto bossos* favored Pat Boone shoes and green polyester slacks and checkered Dacron shirts and liked to sing Tom Jones songs at the Connecticut Junkyard Association Christmas Dinner.

I thought back to all the times Dad had come home from work, and over his salad and the newspaper, mentioned that, 'Sally Sheet Metal was up today. He brought some ice cream.'

Looking at him now, my father hardly appeared a man with mob ties. He had a new hat on – a salvaged green visor that said *Don't Blame Me – I voted for McGovern*. Not only was it outdated, but I knew he had voted for Nixon. His ancient Mack truck was parked up near The Crusher which meant one thing: a load of ferrous scrap was going to the Bridgeport docks to be redeemed. I made this connection before my brother did, and panic weighted my legs.

'Nunzi, why you standing over there with your thumb up your ass, honey?'

Dad liked me to anticipate a job, and usually I did, but now, even after this admonishment, I stood frozen. 'I don't know where your mind is today, Nunzio Paradiso,' he said, 'but it ain't here.' Dad punctuated this statement by pulling the crane's choke lever in and out several times to breach a coat of rust.

'Dad, maybe you shouldn't go to Bridgeport today,' I said.

'Why not?' he said, working the choke.

'It's going to rain.'

'What? We going to melt over here? Rain, snow, you gotta work. Cars don't go to Bridgeport, we don't eat, Nunzio.'

Guiding a giant electro-magnet over the stacks of crushed cars, Big Dan lifted each square hulk as carefully as antique china and set it neatly into the bed of the semi. Danny Boy and I exchanged glances every time he swung the giant magnet closer to the crushed Pontiac and we breathed sighs of relief each time it escaped the lodestone pull, causing Big Dan to select a flat Ford or Plymouth.

Me and Danny Boy were assigned to 'the ground', a job which

entailed the collecting of any pieces of cast iron or valuable scrap that was left in the black soil.

It took the entire day – with a short lunch break – to load the semi to the gunwales. The flattened Bonneville would put the truck in the overloaded category and Big Dan hesitated. If Danny Boy and I had not been staring at the ruins of the blue vehicle with such obvious angst, perhaps Big Dan would have been satisfied with his load.

'Stop looking at the fucking car,' Danny said to me, edging close.

But he was looking up at it himself. Big Dan was looking there, too. When he rose from the seat of the crane to better calculate the size of the scrap load in the truck, I turned away, hoping to hear the crane shut down. But my father's daring won the day. He dropped the big magnet onto the Pontiac and lifted it high, swinging it up and over the other hulks. He cut the magnet's charge and let it fall.

The crushed Pontiac and its dark cargo was packed and leaving.

Since I was five, Big Dan liked to take me on these junk runs to Bridgeport; it was to me, a long and exotic journey to the mysterious ports on Long Island Sound where old barges lay docked and Barnum was once King of the Yankee harbor town. We always stopped for a grinder in Fairfield. But now I was a working man and Dad told me I had to stay on call with Danny and to make sure Grandpa didn't blow up any acetylene tanks while trying to make something hydraulic.

Alone now, we stood together, listening to the diesel growl of the Mack growing distant, shifting into high as it gathered speed for the interstate.

'We let it go,' I said. 'It's gone.'

When Danny didn't respond, I glanced up at him.

''Bye, Max,' he said. 'Good riddance, you dead pain in the ass,' and he winged a hubcap out over the sea of junked cars. He spit in the dirt, kicked a tire out of his path and sat on a tire stack to light a Kool, something he would never do at the yard in front of Big Dan.

When the phone rang, he stormed for the main building. I hurried to the tarpaper fence, scrambled up a stairway of used batteries and hooked my elbows on the lip of the wall, straining to hear the Mac truck take to the interstate. I felt at once relieved and so ill I had to drop to the dirt and kneel there a moment. My brother was right: our troubles were heading south.

But so was something else.

Something we'd have to live with for the rest of our lives. We let a dead man go.

'Get your bow and arrow, Nunz,' my brother said, hopping into the smaller tow truck. 'We're on a buffalo hunt.'

It was after 6:00 and black clouds were in a holding pattern in the west as we set out to answer a tow call. The city had an odd red cast overhead, as if I were looking at it through a broken piece of tail-light reflector. This got me thinking about some nature wisdom imparted by Big Dan once during a long-ago summer while we were weeding the garden. He had looked up and said, simply and ominously, 'Storm breeder.' And then, satisfied with the trepidation etched into my young face, he told me that if I heard the sound of a freight train coming out of the stillness to run for the cellar and batten down.

Riding shotgun in the tow truck onto Route 8, I listened now for the sound of a freight train but heard only the diesel rumbling under our own butts and some last factory death rattles – a loud bang here, an air blast there – down and across the river.

'Storm breeder,' I said.

Danny Boy looked over at me, but said nothing.

We drove along the river and railroad tracks toward the bucolic outskirts where the highway begins to narrow between layers of schist rock and unruly pasture birch. Within ten minutes we were out of the redbrick innards and trundling along the dirt stretch known as Asa Bean Road – the site of what had been Hudd's, the last dairy farm in Saukiwog Mills, and now a last stronghold for keg parties, necking and shooting rats with Daisy BB guns.

When I looked at Danny Boy, he appeared relaxed, more so than I had seen him in weeks. It was as if the Pontiac Bonneville was not only lifted out of the yard but off his own chest. He quietly sang along with the radio, a casual bass harmony to Elton John's 'Benny and the Jets' falsetto.

'I don't see nothing,' I said.

Danny Boy didn't ignore me, he just didn't hear me as he searched the dust ahead. His hand was gripping the shift and vibrating hard as the tranny slipped and gnashed over the rough road. Several yards from where the lane died back into a garbage dump and sparse wood, I saw a prism of refracted light.

An old car, broken and abandoned.

As we moved in on it I took inventory in the manner in which I was trained: '72 Newport sedan. The windows were opaque and the body, once purple, was gray with dust, rocker panels thick with dry, caked mud. The tires were 'Kojak' as we coded bald ones, and the rear-end hunkered low on spent leaf springs, but there was 'thirty, forty pounds of copper in that animal'. The vinyl roof was layered in dust, fallen leaves and berry-blue swallow drop baked to a cement in the hot sun. It was, for all intents and purposes, a beater: if it ran, however, it could be a potential torch wagon.

Danny Boy killed the tow-truck motor, pulled on his greasy gauntlets.

Silence hovered over the dirt cul de sac, heavy, like the humidity. Cicadas were ticking in the high grass but there was no other sound. We sat for a time in the wrecker just looking at the lone buffalo.

'Dog shit,' Danny said, eyeing the car as he struck a match in a tough manner that gave me security. He lit a cigarette and said,'Windshield's okay. Lot of Bond-O. Muffler's history.'

When we stepped out onto the dry dirt, our boots crunched pebbles and the cicadas stopped their ticking. All at once. The car smelled of warm, rat-nest upholstery and old cigarettes; whoever drove this sedan was a rabid smoker and drank Pabst Blue Ribbon by the caseload. Danny Boy sizzled his belt out through the loops and began securing the steering wheel for towing. That's when he saw me going for the trunk.

'What are you doing?'

'You know what I'm doing.'

He stopped me with a firm grip on my arm, the one that was carrying a tire iron.

'Don't be stupid.'

'I want to look in the trunk.'

'Right,' Danny Boy said, agreeably, and he displayed the keys in his hand, like a magician revealing a palmed card. He was right: I was being foolish in my haste. The keys had been on the driver's visor and opening the trunk would not entail prying and pounding.

Danny Boy inserted the first key but it did not turn. A second and third did the same. As he fumbled with the fourth key I saw that someone had finger-scraped a smile face and the words *Wash me* in the trunk-lid dust. This, for some reason, soothed me.

'Ah.' Danny Boy slid the next key in easily and turned it.

The trunk unlatched with a muffled pop.

Danny Boy turned and I saw a dozen emotions running through him – his eyes were intense, like a man bucking up the valor to pull an arrow out of his own leg. He was breathing in short heaves, and then he began to laugh.

This took me aback.

His laughter was, it seemed, a precarious mix of nerves and bewildered amusement. I feared that he was going crazy, out here on the secluded backroad.

'You know what this is?' He spoke in the same high timbre as his laugh. 'This is fucking ludicrous.' He said 'ludicrous' again, this time his voice as high as Elton John's.

The great knot in my belly came undone and I laughed despite myself, snorting like my mother did at Cary Grant's antics.

Danny hefted the trunk lid. 'See?' he said flatly.

What was in the trunk made me scream out. I grabbed at Danny like a drowning person grabs for anything solid, and he pushed at me like another drowning person trying to save himself, and he was yelling, too.

In the trunk was a tire and two old gas cans.

The cicadas began ticking again, stirred from their repose.

'You asshole,' he shouted. 'There's nothing in there.'

'You screamed, too, dickwit,' I sniffed, backing away.

'Hook her up,' he said, throwing his cigarette down. Then he walked away, mopping the side of his face with an oil rag. I unhitched the two wrecker hooks, threw them to the dirt. I went to my belly and dragged the chain under the car. As I fit the hooks in place, I thought I heard something from under the trunk. At first I thought it was the cicadas making their clicking noise, but it was coming from under the trunk. Not so much a clicking now. A ticking. A slow ticking sound like maybe someone had left an alarm clock in the trunk. I set the hooks and crawled back out.

Danny was standing at the empty trunk with the spare in his grip. He had been examining the tread, but now he was looking at the space where the tire had been. There was a metal box with a short pipe extruding from one end. And it was ticking.

'What is that?' I said. 'Danny? Why's it making that sound?'

The bugs around us went silent again. Danny Boy grabbed my arm and shoved me toward the wrecker. 'Get in,' he said, running for the cab himself. We peeled gravel and rumbled down the dirt road.

'There's a goddamn bomb in that car,' he said.

'Then why we towing it, Danny?'

My brother hit the brakes, jumped out and lowered the boom. He kicked at each hook then ran back to the cab; he got behind the wheel and floored it.

And that's when it blew.

The entire Newport exploded like an aerosol can. Sheet metal went up in a twist and a blue sphere thundered from its shredded roof.

'Jesus!' Danny yelled, throwing the wrecker into third and just outdistancing a great chunk of quarter panel that struck the road with a violent clang. I was turned in my seat, watching the car burn. It smelled like torched copper and melting wire mesh and the smoke from the rubber shop. A section of the rear seat was burning out in the field. Danny Boy punched at the wheel as he drove wildly up onto a side street; he struck his palm off the dash twice and kicked at it, all the while yelling, 'No way, no way, no *way*!'

'Was it a *bomb*, Danny?'

Danny seemed lost in his own panic; he kept striking the wheel as he gunned up onto the interstate, dragging the loose hooks. In the opposite lane, two police cars and a fire engine were screaming sirens and turning lights. Danny Boy slowed down as if considering going back there, telling the police what happened. But then he quickly accelerated and got off the trestle exit.

I knew where he was going.

*　　*　　*

'Say *what*?' Johnny yelled from the little kitchenette where she was cooking some kind of porridge on the hot plate. Goomba Angelo was sitting in his usual station in the corner of his room, Ruby Lee on the arm of his chair, clever eyes blinking and darting.

'Are you serious?' he said.

'As a heart attack,' Danny Boy said. 'And I almost fucking had one.'

'Me, too,' I said, breathless.

Angelo was staring as if in a coma, then he blinked. He flicked his eyes away from ours for a moment as he tried to register what we had come to tell him. He took his head tube in his teeth and puffed himself to the window as if to search for smoke on the horizon.

'What do we do?' Danny Boy said, wringing his hands.

'This is bad,' Angelo said, turning his chair and depositing his monkey onto the sill and hitting my brother with a forbidding eye.

'Danny asked you what we should do,' I stammered.

'TELL THESE BOYS WHAT TO DO!' Johnny screamed suddenly, banging silverware into the sink.

'Pay me,' he said. 'Pay me and get the fuck out.'

Danny Boy rose from the chair. 'If we've got evidence on Ray Beans, we can end this thing right here. We can tell them the body's in a car at the docks in Bridgeport. Let's do it.'

'Tell who?'

'The Feds. The Pontiac's off our land, we don't own it. We can tell the Feds.'

'Yeah, we can,' Angelo said. 'But then we don't get the whole cancer.'

Danny Boy was in the chair again, paranoid. 'What do you mean?'

'We nail Ray Beans for the murder of Max Diaz, and we might implicate these developers for extortion. Your old man might get acquitted with the right Jew lawyer once they trace the scrap. But we won't get all the cancer.'

'I still don't follow you, Ange.'

'It goes *higher*!' said Angelo Volpe. He seemed flustered that he had to reveal this here and now, as if whatever he knew was an inside straight that he wanted to keep face down a bit longer. 'Johnny,' he said. 'Get me the Friday paper.'

Johnny went into the impossibly small bathroom and returned with the local section from the Saukiwog *Republican*. She creased it and slapped it into Danny Boy's hand. Angelo told him to read an article about the new Plaza that would be going up on the hallowed ground of the old drive-in.

'*MALL SITE BREAKS GROUND?*' my brother asked.

'No, *LADIES AUXILIARY HOLDS FUCKING BAKE SALE*,' Angelo spit.

Danny Boy sat in the easy chair to read the piece. I straddled an arm to partake. As always, my eyes went for the pictures first: there was a large one, black-and-white, framed to the bottom right of the article. A group of well-dressed men stood posed around a shovel in the barren acreage. One of them smiled easily as he held one edge of an open site plan while another man, not smiling, held the other. The man smiling was familiar. Peering closer at the photo, I recognized him.

'That's Mr Butterscotch Sunday,' I said.

'*Who?*'

'Carmella,' Danny Boy said, distracted as he read. 'From the bank. Nunzio and his friends call him Mr Butterscotch Sunday.'

'Right,' Angelo said, irked. Then he dropped the mandible: 'Carmella is a principal in BCD, boys. Do you hear what I'm saying to you? The president of the thrift, of the S and L, is a principal investor in Brass City Development.'

'Is that bad?' I said.

'No,' Danny Boy said. 'No, there's no law against that.'

'No, there's not,' Angelo said. 'But look at the seating arrangement at the feast.'

'I'm losing you,' my brother said.

'The building projects in this so-called Renaissance, every project has to get cleared through boards and commissions. They have to get through the aldermen. The soul diva breached the City Clerk's office today.'

Johnny went to the radiator where her purse sat. She opened it and produced a folder of Xeroxed records. 'City Clerk,' she said. 'Black man, but a schoolboy brother with big eye-glasses. Mr Antoine Davis. Well, Antoine took one look at me and them glasses start fogging up and he start stuttering and I just keep turning up the heat.'

'He let Johnny see whatever she wanted,' Angelo said.

Johnny said that out of sixteen major restoration and developments that were given city approval since January, fourteen involved BCD. Which, of course, farmed out all their work to Valle Construction and the bottom feeder, Testa Demolition.

'Jesus, Ange. What are we saying here?' Danny Boy said.

My face, feeling damp, must have been a sight because Angelo looked at me, did a take, then made a chortle from back in his throat. 'Nunzio didn't just open the trunk on a '73 Pontiac Bonneville. He opened the gate to the nest of the fucking vipers.'

Danny Boy cast the newspaper off like it singed his fingers. 'You mean Carmella's paying somebody off—'

'He's rewarding somebody,' Angelo said hoarsely. 'He's got to be.'

'How high up?'

'High enough that somebody wants you two bums wasted.'

'What evidence do we have?'

'It just went to Bridgeport. Other than that, these guys are insulated.'

'Look, we've got to put the Feds on this. Tell them what just happened.'

'We jump now, we'll never get the whole ring.'

'But we don't jump now we could get fucking killed.'

'That's draw poker, Danny Boy.'

'Well, this is *life*, asshole.'

'What's the difference?'

The room had turned static, holding humidity like a terrarium.

'I guess the question is,' Angelo said, 'do any of us really give a fuck about this city? Or do we cut our losses right now?'

Danny Boy stood slowly and crossed the room. Johnny, obviously shaken, excused herself, telling us she had to go pick up a fare at the YMCA. Angelo sucked his teeth, pondering it all. 'I'll tell you something right up front. Me? I don't give a rat's ass about this city or who's getting ripped off. In fact, I got a good mind to call Carmella and tell him I'll take ten grand off the gravy train just to keep my mouth shut.'

Danny Boy struck the wall with the flat of his hand. He turned and looked at me, his eyes bleary, cheeks sunken. I knew he was worrying about me more than himself. He moved at Angelo, his hands going into his hair, his fingers digging into his scalp like they were edging along on a Ouija board. 'This fucking *sucks*.'

'The moose,' Angelo said.

'This wasn't supposed to happen, Ange.'

'Lower your voice, Danny. There's retards sleeping next door.'

'We just wanted to find out who was in the trunk, that's all.'

We could hear Johnny's big gas guzzler start up down on the corner.

'I don't need this in my life,' Danny Boy said. 'I'm not even supposed to be in this shit-hole.'

'Where the fuck you supposed to be at?'

'College.'

'College,' Angelo said. 'I see.'

'You see, do you? Do you see this, Ange?' Danny flipped him the bird.

'Yeah, fuck you, too, Danny.'

'I *am* fucked, Ange.'

'Come here, Danny Boy,' Angelo said with a sigh of resignation. 'I'm going to tell you something I don't think your little brother should hear. Come over here.'

Danny Boy shook sweat from his head like a wet dog and made his way over to our cousin. He stood over him but Angelo would not share the secret until my brother leaned down close to the restrained man.

'What?'

'Come here.'

Angelo tilted his head and put his lips to Danny's ear. I wanted badly to hear what he was whispering. From the corner of the room I knelt beside Ruby and scratched her neck, watching. Maybe, I reasoned, Angelo was going to plant a kiss on my brother like he had done to me days earlier, call him a hot sketch or a sharp cookie. But what Goomba Angelo did made me flinch and spring to my feet.

He bit my brother's ear.

He bit into Danny's lobe and held on like a Jack Russell terrier on a water rat. Danny Boy screamed, tried to dislodge himself from our cousin but the paralyzed man's grip was unrelenting. Danny

Boy could not turn his body to get a hand on Angelo, and it was a disturbing sight, my brother held in place by his ear.

'You crazy *Mamone* motherfucker!' he yelled, finally breaking free and stumbling toward the wall. He touched his ear, looking at the blood. Angelo sat there, watching him reel in shock. Someone, somewhere in the building, banged on a wall and cursed the ruckus.

'Your life is fucked, Dan? Is that what you said?'

The room grew quiet again. Angelo just stared at him. 'Well, let me tell you something, kid: until you got a service monkey from a federal program feeding you Maypo and Metomucil . . . don't talk to me about your broken dreams.'

Danny Boy let the tiny trickle of blood run down behind his neck and he swallowed. Angelo watched him, attentively. 'Until you've got a nurse coming on Tuesdays to give you digital-stimulation and a fleet enema, don't cry about your bad shake.'

Somewhere on the streets below, a refuse truck made a beeping sound as it reversed into an alley. 'You were calling for a fair catch but that big colored kid never stopped. He hit you like a train while you were signaling for a fair catch. A *fair catch*. How fucking *unfair*. Well, guess what, *paesan*? Life ain't fair. You never pulled a ligament, Danny Boy. You didn't get a concussion, you didn't rip a tendon or all that shit it said in the Sports page, this dislocated jawbone shit. You broke *l'uovo*.'

'I broke the *what*?' Danny Boy was against the wall, a hand at his ear.

'The egg.'

'What fucking egg?'

'The egg *inside*,' Angelo said with such passion that I believed for an instant that he was going to find it in him to move his arm and touch himself at his chest, which is what I could see he wanted to do. His eyes looked larger, more alive than I had seen them.

'When you got hit, you broke *l'uovo*. Your confidence, your balls – that's what broke. You got scared, Dan. Gun shy. You hear footsteps, Danny? I remember your old man telling me, the kid hears footsteps now when they kick the ball at him. Junkyard Dog turned into a fucking puppy. Look at you shaking over here.'

'Don't fuck with me, Ange.'

'Get up off the grass.'

'Don't you play with my head, you sonuvabitch.'

'Get up off the grass, Danny. Don't let them write you off. It's what they want. They don't want you to get back up. Because in a place like this, kid, if you got a hope, it scares them. They want to keep you here. We want to see you hurting. Like all the rest of us lifers.'

Angelo was red in the throat from straining. 'Get up,' he said, hoarse. 'Run with the damned ball.'

I was afraid to look at my brother, but I did anyway. His eyes looked like the eyes of a cow smelling fire in a locked barn. They were fixed on Angelo. I feared he was going to charge the disabled cop, strike him even.

'Do we fish, cut bait, or go to Bridgeport?' Angelo pressed.

Danny Boy paced the room. He appeared numb, a handkerchief at his earlobe. He went to the window several times, searching the distance.

'Call it in the air, Danny,' Angelo said, not letting up. 'Fair catch? Or we running with the fucking ball?'

'That car is gone,' my brother said.

'Is it at sea?'

'No,' Danny said, and he lifted his chin to me. I told Angelo what I had learned about the scrap shipments from my long-ago Saturday journeys with my father: the barges shipped out by weight, I told him. By the gross ton to be more precise. That was what my father once told me while we watched a crane transfer our crushed cars onto the flat deck. Soon as a barge tipped out at its capacity, it sailed for Japan. But Big Dan always waited till the last possible slot lest he be charged for scrap storage waiting for the vessel to depart. So my best hunch was as soon as a few more hopper cars of pig iron came in on the train and unloaded, Max was leaving the country without a passport.

Angelo regarded me with what may have been intrigue. 'I guess it's up to the Junkyard Dog,' he said, his eyes avoiding Danny Boy. 'But I want to say one last thing in the event I never see you guys again. I'm in this chair because one fucking night I decided that fourteen-hundred bucks mattered more than if some girl died in the lady's room of a bar or on the side of the road. Don't make the same mistake I did.'

Angelo's back was to us and he was looking out into the rain on the exposed pipe of the rooftops. 'Four days after the little girl dies,' he said. 'Her imprint was still on the side of the road, in the snow. Remember snow angels when we were kids? She was gone, but the fucking snow angel was still there and the department made me take her old man down there, he wanted to see where his daughter was found. He got down on his knees and touched the dirty snow, the angel, all exhaust filth and dog piss. That was the first and last time I ever heard a man cry like a fucking baby. And he didn't even know then that Romeo and his friends had raped his daughter in the men's room till her heart stopped beating. That was the day, boys. That was the day I made up my mind I was punching the clock. That'd be too easy, though. Look at me, Danny. See? This is justice. *Giustizia*. Right here, in this fucking chair. No chance of parole.'

Angelo stopped there, keeping his face turned from us. 'I'm no fucking good,' he said bitterly. 'But you get used to it.'

Danny Boy took my arm and we left him alone with Ruby Lee and a deck of cards.

Mom told us how it happened while swabbing peroxide on Danny's wounded ear:

That night, with Big Dan home from Bridgeport and me and Danny off at play rehearsal, a red El Camino had pulled into our driveway and the city fire chief, Mr Murray, had walked in his long-legged circle around Dad's tow truck. He was a nice man, Mr Murray, even if he wore prescription sunglasses after dark, and Dad thought he was a bit officious the way he wore his fire badge on his hat and looked over the rims of his smoked glasses when you spoke to him. But on that night, Mom said, he seemed friendly as he sat on the porch with Dad, drinking a cold lemonade and petting the neighbor's cat, explaining why he was there.

An old junked car had caught fire down on Asa Bean Road and a tow truck from Paradise Salvage was seen leaving the site. An investigation, using dogs and chemical tests, revealed that the trunk had two full gas cans in it and apparently someone dropped a lit cigarette into the cargo space. It was no real biggie, Mr Murray said. The car burned safely on the dirt road, nobody got hurt, and that was the important thing.

Big Dan told the fire chief that he was in Bridgeport all day and knew nothing about it, but he would take it up with his son, Dan. When we came home that night, Dad was in the garage tinkering with his Bel Aire. When he saw us pull in, he stood erect and made a gesture that brought our pulses up. He straightened his hand into a kind of karate chop, lifted it to his mouth, and bit his knuckle. In an Italian family, this was time to run.

But we were frozen now.

'What the hell happened today? On Asa Bean Road.'

Danny Boy lowered his eyes. 'Dad—'

'You were smoking, weren't you?'

'The car just went up—'

'Was he smoking, Nunzio? Tell me the truth. You guys opened the trunk. Was he smoking when you opened the trunk?'

'Yes,' I confessed.

'Were there gas cans in that trunk?'

'Yeah,' Danny said, 'but—'

'But nothing. You could've killed your brother, and you could've killed yourself. I ever see you smoking on the job again, say goodbye to this car. You hear me? Ever again, it's through The Crusher.'

We both stood there, absorbing, and I could tell Danny Boy wasn't sure now that someone had tried to off us with a pipe bomb. I could see that he wasn't sure about anything anymore. Neither was I. Except for the fact that Max Diaz was now waiting on a barge in Long Island Sound and the ship was going to sail.

'What happened to your ear?' Big Dan said to Danny.

'Oh. Nothing,' he said.

'That's not a hickey,' Dad said. 'You found yourself a vampire broad at the Salvation Army. I don't know who that woman was, but we should hire her to siphon gas.'

The next day was Saturday and I was given liberty. Not that Confirmation rehearsal was anything of the sort – I would have rather spent the day in the junkyard – but I was still able to watch some vintage Abbot and Costello in the early hours, and

I had hopes for some kickball in the church lot following the ordeal.

So I put on my suit, the one Dad had found on a hanger in the backseat of an abandoned Comet. Two dry-cleanings had faded it to the hue of billiards chalk, but I liked it. The loafers on the other hand made me cringe at the mere sight of their flat polish. The two pennies stuck in the tongue were dated 1966 and Dad replaced them with shining new coppers from 1978 and gave them a good buff. Still, these loafers brought a blush to my face whenever I horned my feet into them.

My hands were scrubbed back to their olive hue, my hair combed to the side – like Robert Wagner, Mom said. Dad told me to do good in church and Danny Boy said nothing as he headed out to the wrecker. I felt bad for him, knowing the dark secrets he knew, and envisioning him alone in the tow-truck cab with Dad.

But I seized freedom and cut my way across my grandparents' yard. My mission was simple: go to Zi Bap's house down the street and ride with him over to Our Lady of Mount Carmel Church for the torturous dry run. But sometimes even simple missions can become adventures. On reaching my godfather's there was no answer at the door and I began to grow worried. He was my sponsor for the Sacrament; we were to sit in the pew together as Father Vario prepared us for a pre-Confirmation visit by the Bishop on Saturday.

I went around back to try the cellar bulkhead and I tripped over something that sent me into a grass-staining slide. Zi Bap was asleep against his fig tree, drunker than Bacchus and just as rotund, his hairy belly exposed through his unbuttoned dress shirt and his slacks unbuckled. He had clean white socks on. I didn't need a Pinkerton Man to unravel this stumper. Zi Bap had decided to have a little taste of his new wine batch while he dressed for church. A sip became a *bottiglia*, one *bottiglia* became two . . . and as Dad had said, it only took one glass of Baptiste's home-swill to render a man *stunod*.

I pushed at the slumped immigrant and attempted to revive him, but he snored like a badger down a hole and I was exhausting myself with the effort. My dress-shirt was beginning to turn transparent and cling. Finally, Zi Bap stirred and opened one awful eye, black as onyx, fixing it on me.

'Whadda you do? Soap'a my window? Steal'a my fuckin' fig?'

'We have to be at church, Zi Bap.'

'You go, I come.'

When he didn't budge, I hesitated. Zi Bap wrenched his neck and hissed like he was scaring off a squirrel. I had to take his word on it – we were late now – and so I hit the street in my penny loafers and ran for Our Lady.

Inside, every young anointee, from Eddie Coco to the white and frilly Monica Lafontaine, had a sponsor sitting beside them. I slid into a pew, breathless, looking toward the entrance. What was worse, I asked myself? Having Zi Bap not show or hearing the doors bang open and seeing him amble up the aisle with his shirt-tails out, calling my name?

'Why do we receive the Holy Ghost?' Father Vario asked the assembly. He was not a tall priest, but imposing just the same; a first-generation *Napolitano*, he spoke an educated English that impressed my father, and a *Mezzogiorno* tongue that often made my Nonni weep during the Italian Mass. His hair was black and cut out of fashion, not that fashion mattered to a priest. His eyes were dark and large behind thick glasses that went out of style in the 1950s. But it was his face that gave every sermon urgency: his mouth always appeared to be on the verge of trembling, like he was going to have a tantrum or a nervous breakdown. My grandfather felt no loyalty to the holy man and called him a crook. Many old Italian men like Grandpa distrusted the Church while their wives found sanctuary there.

With his arms folded and tucked in his vestments Father Vario crossed in front of the altar, scanning the young, terrified faces of the anointed. Most of us were Italian kids, but there were still some Irish families going to Our Lady and some of the Puerto Ricans who were edging closer to our neighborhood.

'Young man?' Father Vario was asking Eddie, and I could see my friend's olive skin go deep green; his hands were twisted into a knot at his crotch. His sponsor, his big Cousin Sandro, also greenish in color, had his arm around him and they conferred.

'To become,' he balked when he heard his voice echo in the church. 'To become a strong and perfect Christian and a Soldier of Jesus Christ.'

Father Vario hardly nodded. He kept walking, now toward my section as if on the hunt for a wrong answer. Again I looked back at the entrance.

'To become a strong and perfect Christian and Soldier of the Lord Jesus Christ,' he repeated to all of us. 'And what does the holy chrism signify when the confirmed is anointed?'

He walked past me and for a moment his eyes touched mine. I sat rigid and he walked on, looking at Monica Lafontaine and her Aunt Gwen. 'Young lady?'

Monica's face was scrubbed so clean her small upturned nose had a shine to it. But she, too, was wringing her fingers. She must have been anticipating Confession because she kept squeezing her right hand. She bit her bottom lip and made a little squint and the Father stared at her.

'It means you're confirmed,' she whispered. 'To be a perfect and strong Christian—'

'NO!' he boomed and it sounded like the thunder the pew kneelers made when they all dropped at once. 'You are giving me the answer to the last question. The Bishop will be displeased. Are you studying, young lady?'

Monica nodded and her aunt nodded in support. I heard a sound at the entrance and I turned. It was just a custodian.

'You. You turned around over there.'

I was stuck where I was; turning was death. I looked up at the stained glass image of St Francis and I prayed silently for help – any kind of help.

'Turn – around – this – instant.'

My mind was back inside the wine-dark curtains of the confessional, two months earlier when I confessed to masturbation and Father Vario had laid his ear against the lattice.

'You what?' he had said.

I explained that it must have happened during sleep and he told me to have my brother Danny Boy tie my hands to the bedrails each night. I had convinced Danny to do this even though he howled with laughter; but still I woke to the sin of Onan. Now I knew it was *La Strega* giving me the hand laundry—

'Turn around!'

I did. The Father's face was taut and when he pushed his horn rims up on the bridge of his nose, his big brown marbles horrified me. 'Where is your sponsor?'

I was afraid he would ask that. I couldn't lie, here in church, preparing to be a strong and perfect Christian. But when I began to explain that he was drunk under his fig tree, the words hardened like rubber cement against my teeth.

'He's on his way, Father.'

'He's on his way. Okay.' He smiled, and said it again: 'Okay.' He started walking away but this was just a tease, because he turned toward me again, came closer. That bottom lip was trembling with emotion. 'Okay. Then while we wait for him, please tell me why the Bishop gives the person he confirms a blow on his cheek.'

A blow on his cheek? I had studied my pamphlets, but I did not recall any mention of the Bishop giving anybody a blow on his cheek.

'Answer,' said Father Vario.

'I don't know, Father.'

'What? I can't hear you! Are you going to whisper timidly when the Bishop asks you a question? The Bishop is not coming all the way down from Hartford to hear little mice whisper. Stand up.'

Everyone rose with a hollow shuffling noise and the banging of pews.

'Just him,' the Father said.

Everyone sat again with the same shuffling sound.

I stood and I could feel Monica's eyes on my legs as they trembled. Father Vario walked toward me and I felt blood push at my temples. I was blushing before the whole assembly, all the kids and their sponsors.

'Now,' he warned, 'why does the Bishop deliver a blow to the cheek?' The echo sounded as though Father Vario had allies shouting down from all sides.

Silence fell over the church, but the priest would give no quarter. He stared at me. And then a voice came back that was not an echo.

'To put us in mind, Padre.' It was a husky and raffish voice, as much a product of Saukiwog as rolled brass. 'That we must be prepared to suffer. For the sake of Christ.'

He stood at the back of the church, a large figure in a green polyester suit and white shoes. He made the sign of the cross then continued down the aisle, hiking his slacks up and adjusting his buckle.

I didn't know what Salvatore Testa was doing here or why he answered a question put to me, but I could have hopped into the aisle and kissed Sally Sheet Metal's Pat Boone shoes.

'Mr Testa?' the priest addressed him.

'I'm the kid's godfather.' His voice was gruff but his manner formal as he genuflected before squeezing his great bulk into the pew beside me.

'Very good, Mr Testa,' said the Father. 'But can he answer his own questions?'

'He's a working man, Father. As the gospel says, "Know thy work and do it". He's doing it, Father. For his family, for his moral development. Don't it say in the Bible that work is a form of prayer, Father?'

Sally threw an arm over the back of the pew then pushed his yellow tinted glasses up the bridge of his nose. He crossed his legs and one of his white shoes bobbed casually as if he had just settled in at the movies.

The church was more silent than I had ever heard it and Father Vario was studying the large man over the rims of his spectacles.

'Well,' the Father said, 'in these new days when faith and morals are exposed to so many temptations, work is the touchstone of a developing Christian. Indeed. Thank you, Mr Testa.'

Sally nodded respectfully, his shoe still fidgeting like he had better places to be. Father Vario looked at him a moment longer, considered me again and repeated Sally's answer, 'To put us in mind that we must be ready to suffer. Yes. Very good. Let us all say it together.' With the young anointees and their yawning sponsors making a sluggish, echoing, out-of-synch drone, Father Vario now moved along to the next trembling victim.

Fat Sally never looked at me even though he had his big arm around my shoulders. His eyes were either on the priest or on his watch which he twisted up and around my neck every few minutes so he could see it. And once, during a discussion of the Chief Mysteries of Faith, he wrestled a hanky from his green slacks and worked it at his nose, sniffing like he had an allergy. He blew some loud snot, too, and didn't seem self-conscious. In my periphery, I saw a half-dozen kids looking over, fascinated by the honking of a large man clearing his nose.

My eyes never left Sally Testa.

Mysteries of Faith? Here I was, saved from the wrath of a priest by the man who may have ordered a murder. One thing was a given: it was a sight less disturbing than Zi Bap staggering in, six sheets to the breeze, or Angelo wheeling toward the altar with his monkey on his lap.

Outside, Sally said hello to nearly everyone he passed. It was a hurried hello, a cursory greeting as he coaxed me with his big hand, down the shaded street and across to Crocco's little market on the bottom floor of a three-story house with a flat roof and tar shingles.

'You don't talk much, *guaglione*.'

'I didn't know you were coming.'

'I'm your *Goomba*. Your old man says you were making your Confirmation, right? I'm at Mass every Saturday night so I seen the flyer about this, the rehearsal.'

Inside the market, he purchased two cups of orange Italian ice and as he did so, he took his dollar change and began to fold it. Right in front of Mrs Crocco he asked me, as he did weeks back, if I ever saw the George Washington trick. Hastily, I reminded him I did, and he shrugged like it was my loss. He spoke a southern dialect to Mrs Crocco, and the two laughed easily. She said something about how handsome I looked in the suit and my third godfather set a hand on my shoulder like he was showing me off. But then his hand swept up some of my collar-length hair and he said something captious to which Mrs Crocco clucked her tongue and commiserated, shaking her head.

We sat out on the street and savored the flavored ices in the humid air, me on the curb, Sally sitting on the hood of his Monte Carlo, licking at the kiddy sweet with a child's glee.

'I never bought you a sweater at Christmas-time,' he said. He licked at his ice, gazing across the church lot, seemingly troubled by this admission. 'I never came to your birthday parties. But then again, you never came to the hospital when I had the prostate. Am I right or wrong?'

'I'm sorry.'

'Right or wrong?'

'Right.'

'Hey. Never mind. I'm sorry, too.'

I nodded, orange ice on my lips.

'The thing is, a kid is just a kid till he gets to your age. Now you got hair,' he looked over his shoulder, whispered, 'you got the hair on your balls. You better anyway – you're twelve and you're Italian.'

I felt my face go warm.

'Before that, what am I going to say to you? Have you watched Bugs Bunny? Have you found any cat shit in the sandbox lately? What am I going to say to a little kid? Confirmation is a big step. You're getting confirmed. Now we can talk. You like Italian ice?'

'Yeah,' I grinned with cold teeth.

'Where's your brother?' This question broadsided me, left me silent. And then Sally answered it for me as was his habit. 'Sleeping one off, ha? Romeo over there.'

'I don't know.'

'That kid played some football. *Madonn'*, he played some football.' He pondered sadly for a moment then broke himself from the reverie. 'Whatta ya going to do? Hey. That's life.'

Sally Testa studied me as he lipped some melted ice off the rim of the flimsy paper cup. The moment was growing awkward.

'And you, you play *morra*, the fingers game. You're good. That's a gift.'

'No, I just guess.'

'No, you don't just guess. You know things.'

'I do?'

Goomare Rosario, the hunchback, came hobbling up the walk past Crocco's and Sally greeted her in Italian. When she passed, he crossed himself and touched his horn medallion. Again, he said '*Madonna*.'

I crossed myself, too.

Sally watched the witch admire some bread in the window but when she walked on he let a breath free. 'That woman's still alive? She's like a cockroach, she don't wanna die. She got the *mal'occh* like nobody's business.'

'I know,' I said. 'Her eyebrows touch in the middle.'

'See what I mean? You know things, secret Italian things like that.' Sally didn't budge from the shiny hood. 'When you play the fingers game, you know what the other guy is thinking, that's how come you know how many fingers to throw out. What if I'm your stake horse?'

I was unfamiliar with this term but I thought perhaps he was referring to the horse steak that one of our larger grocers was accused of selling the previous winter.

'Your stake man. I put money on you to play the *morra*. At the Italian Club.'

'Man, I don't know.' I covered my teeth when I grinned because I could feel the cold, orange stain. I was grinning out of downright fear – another one of my tics.

'For a good-lookin' kid, you're shy,' he said.

My silence only confirmed his observation.

'I'm your *Goomba*, you gotta talk to me. See, Father over here is going to have you make Confession. You might wanna discuss with me the things you feel you have to *sfogare* that you might not want to *sfogare*.'

'I'm supposed to tell him everything,' I said.

'Right, I know. But you're not going to tell him about . . .' Sally Testa looked over his shoulder toward the market then leaned closer to me – he waited for a UPS man to pass – then he dropped his voice. 'You going to tell him about the crush? About the man in the squeeze?'

The ice froze in my lungs and a terrible headache started at the back of my neck. I wanted to run but one of my legs had fallen asleep against the curb.

'About the man in the squeeze?'

'Yeah. The one-eyed stiff. The bald guy.'

Foot asleep or not, I stood and looked down the street. I could make it. I could make the corner of Lucia Street and go right down the bulkhead door of Eddie Coco's cellar where I knew the layout of the laundry room and a dozen places to hide.

I bolted. Like Mercury Morris I bolted.

But Sally Sheet Metal grabbed me and held me fast. 'Hey, hey!' he said, looking around the area a bit nervously. 'Don't worry about it. We can talk. *Sfogare*. Let it out.'

'I don't want to *sfogare*.'

'We're *going* to *sfogare*. We're men over here. And no matter what Father Vario says, you know he's boxing the clown, too.'

'Boxing the clown?'

'Yeah, punching the one-eyed stiff. Rolling the *canoli*. Shaking hands with the unemployed.' And here, to my great relief, Fat Sally resorted to a crude jerking fist and my face went flushed; not because I was embarrassed, but because I thought I had come within an inch of being trunk drums. But my sense of relief was about to sail higher.

'He ever try to tell you the Devil's whacking you off at night?'

I nodded.

'Well, he ain't. It's just wet dreams.'

'Wet dreams?'

'That's all. You're okay, kid. It's no sin. You're clear.'

'Really?'

'You're a free man, Nunzio.'

Sally smiled when he heard me let a great sigh go. 'You know what *I* used to do?' he volunteered.

'What?'

'I used to tell Father a few things like – oh, I don't know: I swore at the dog, I ate my sister's licorice, I kicked a kid in the ass – stuff like that. Then when he'd give me sixteen Our Fathers to do, I add a few Hail Mary's to cover what I *didn't* tell him. So God knew, ya see. In the end, kid, it's you and the guy up top, not some fucking crook in a collar listening in on your secrets like an old woman.'

Then he crossed himself.

Sally looked me square as if trying to divine something deeper. 'You don't have to tell Father you put the bald guy in the squeeze.' He leaned off the hood and gave me a soft and affectionate play punch on the chin. Again his eyes went to his watch. He wiped his big hands with his hanky, rubbed it vigorously at his nose, then unbuckled his slacks to tuck in his tails. When he slid off the hood, the Monte Carlo's front end rose up on its coils and the chassis yawned in relief.

'I gotta go, *guaglione*. I'll see you up the yard.' He got into his

Monte and looked at me out the window. 'Tell your brother I'm going to get him in the Italian Club. Then he can bring you over to play some *morra*. You got luck, kid. But someday it's going to run out.'

He started the car and fumbled with some cassette tapes. 'The Bishop's coming. Study up. Stay home at night and read that book.'

It may have been my high-idling imagination, but when he said 'stay at home at night' I saw something in his eyes, something almost imperceptible, but something hard and threatening. Something that didn't go to Tony Orlando and Dawn on his stereo radio as he left a faint strip of rubber behind him on America Street.

As I ran for home, I couldn't help but feel a tickle of ambivalence: the man who may have entombed Max Diaz in metal had just freed me from the fear of God and the left hand of the Devil.

CHAPTER SIXTEEN

Three Teardrops

Tomorrow I'd be going back to work.

But today, I was going over the stone wall.

'Nunzio,' Monica sang out when I landed on my Puma Clydes. Finding my way near to her, I felt my face warm when she smiled at me and tossed the kick-ball my way. When I caught it cleanly, I realized it was not a ball but a shoe. A dreadful brown shoe with a strap and buckle and dull shine.

'Over here, Paradiso,' Tony Massi called out, his hair curly and wet with sweat. 'It, It, It,' the others sang out, and that's when I saw the girl, standing in the center of the circle, forcing a smile with her large bucked teeth.

It was Kim Vu, the little Cambodian girl, oldest child of Mr Thong Vu who arrived in Saukiwog Mills six months prior to go to work as a stitcher in the motorcycle seat shop now housed in one of the old brass mills. In a plain brown dress, the girl stood on one shoe and one sock, grinning so she wouldn't cry.

'Don't touch it,' Monica shouted out. 'It's got malaria!'

'Crotch rot, crotch rot,' the chant became. Kim Vu looked at me, holding her shoe and her smile remained fixed, her Adam's apple high and protruding like she was trying to swallow a plum. In a reflex, I tossed the shoe to Massi and he shuffled in the circle around the girl, juggling the shoe like it was a hot coal, and finally winging it at her in the same sidearm he pitched with in Little League.

The shoe struck her in the side of the head and she stood there, touching her temple but still grinning against tears, the knotted thing in her throat rising a little higher. 'Chink, Chink, Chink,' they sang.

'Watch out,' Massi croaked in his changing voice. 'She might know Kung Fu!' And with this, he curled his hands into his notion of some Chinese fighting stance and hurled a kick in her direction. I felt a terrible heaviness inside and suddenly felt small and mean, dancing in the circle with the other kids. The shoe was kicked about in a flurry and it skidded through my legs. 'Get it,' hissed Monica. So I did.

Monica told the Asian girl that she smelled like a Kotex. The kids howled with laughter, together a community. I jostled in the swell, toward the girl who was still holding her head where she had been struck by her own shoe. There was a faraway look in her eye, like the way my *Time-Life Book of Mammals* described the manner in which a zebra hypnotizes itself while being eaten by a lion, actually numbs itself to the torment and accepts it. Still grinning with her large and crooked teeth, Kim lowered herself to the asphalt, sitting on her hip and tucking her dress ladylike.

It was enough.

I entered the circle and handed her the shoe.

The circle stilled, tightened around us.

'What the frig you doing?' Massi said.

'He's one, too,' someone said, I didn't see who it was. A girl, I think. And then the chant began, directed at me. 'Chink's lover, Chink's lover, Chink's lover.'

That didn't bother me. I had to end the bucktoothed girl's agony. Just give her the shoe back and let her go home. It had nothing to do with Father Vario's Seven Spiritual Works of Mercy. It was just wrong, that's all.

Kim Vu grabbed her shoe and scrambled onto her feet, hopping on her one Brownie into the circle and falling in, fairly breathless. Desperate, even. She began to chant with the others, pointing toward me as I knelt in the center.

Dump digger, dump digger, dump digger.

I felt my mouth go slack as the ring of kids now put me in their sights and attacked; I watched only the Cambodian girl. Her grin was enormous, her eyes still welling but showing relief as she moved on one shoe and a pink sock, trying to become one of the circle. Saliva made a string in her mouth as she chanted *Dump digger, dump digger, dump digger*, and I knew she had no clue what she was saying. Monica was chanting it, too.

Tony Massi, nearly delirious with cruel joy, came forward, yelling like a fighting cock. 'Look at those sneakers!' he shouted. 'Right out of the dump! Find them in a trunk?'

Dump picker, dump picker, Kim sang with her new neighbors, rolling left in the shuffling circle and delighting in all the smiling faces, the fun she hadn't known all summer. Though, as I stared at her, I knew she wasn't really having fun. She was surviving.

Massi lunged at me again. 'Them are faggot sneakers,' he said. 'Your old man pulled them out of the dump. Your dirty old man with his dirty old hands, and his dirty work shoes.'

That's when I knew – deep down and no matter how I had challenged the fact all my life – I was a Paradiso. I stepped up and punched Massi square in the eye. Massi stumbled back a pace, stunned for a second. The church lot went quieter than Our Lady Herself. I hit him again, in the same eye. He swung a wide punch, but I hit him with my other fist under the chin. He fell onto his buttocks, hands splayed, mouth open like a beached fish in the sun. I was on him; every punch landed harder. The Paradiso was loose, like Primo Canero snapping his chain. And I kept on hitting him.

I hit him for my lost summer.

I hit him for Max Diaz who had met bullies of an older kind.

And I hit him for the thing my brother tore near his heart.

Just for the hell of it, I hit him once for the zebra in my *Book of Mammals*, too.

His eyes were walled and bleary and I could see him taking in the crowd of kids in his periphery; Tony Massi knew his summer was over, too. He knew he would never be able to walk down America Street again without kids looking at him as the boy little Nunzio beat the tar out of in the church parking lot. I felt bad for him. I felt his fear and his humiliation as strong as I felt my own rage.

That's when I knew, for sure, I was a MacLeish, too.

And that's all the hesitation Massi needed. He drove a knee up into my crotch and sent me backward. Tom Bernota and Lonnie DiTullio fell on me and held me. Massi got to his feet and lumbered over, snot and blood on his chin. With everything he had left, he hiked his leg back and kicked me square in the belly.

Someone, some adult, must have been fast approaching because I heard kids running. I didn't have the wind to even look up, but someone was hurrying toward me in the quick, clicking sound of a woman's high heels and I hoped it was a neighborhood mother coming to my aid and not Mother Superior. I felt a hand on the back of my head and I smelled sweet grapes.

'Oh, my God,' the voice said. 'Nunzio. Nunzio, look at me.'

When I unlocked my torso, Desiree Vega was beside me, squatting on her haunches and platform sandals. She wore a bright orange tube top and tight jeans the color of a ripe guava. Her eyes were hidden from the sun by cat's-eye sunglasses and the black brim of a red Chicago Bulls ball cap, her hair pulled high and through the rear band in a tail of wet, dark ringlets.

'Here.' She offered me a cold can of Tab, helped me tip it and drink. 'You okay, honey?'

As she looked me over for scrapes, I saw the teardrop tattoos at her left eye just beneath a dark lens. Only now, she had three. Three teardrops forever. I sat wounded, drinking the soda and savoring her attention.

'Let's go, you,' she said.

Her yellow Le Mans was parked behind the church and we sat inside, the two of us alone. The car was not well-kept but it held the scent of Bubble Yum and baby powder, clove cigarettes, and grape Bonne Belle Lipsmacker.

'Does your bro still want to protect me?' she said, her eyes on her rearview mirror.

'He said so, didn't he?'

'Yeah, he did.'

She flicked her lighter and I stole a glance as she got a fuschia-colored cigarette burning. 'You have another teardrop,' I observed. Desiree nodded slowly and brought her cigarette back to her dark lips. She looked into her mirror, angling her face to study the ink job.

'That's right,' she said. 'Raymi broke my heart. And maybe my ribs, I don't know.' She inhaled these words with smoke, held them in.

'This is a nice car,' I said.

Desiree finally let the smoke out her nostrils. 'The lady in the grocery store said you was playing kickball in the school lot.' She reached across and touched the scrape near my chin. 'I didn't think I'd find you getting your butt kicked.'

'You were looking for *me*?'

'Yeah, I was looking for you, *coqui*.'

'Me, not Danny?'

'Danny wasn't the one who seen something in the blue Pontiac.'

'Oh.'

'Yeah, oh. Tell me about the car, this blue Pontiac.'

'What about it?'

'What the hell was in it that everybody's going crazy on me?' She fixed her eyes on mine even as she tapped some ash off her cigarette. 'What did you see, boy?'

'I don't want to see it.'

'You already seen it.'

'I mean, I don't want to say it, I don't want to see it.'

'It's okay, honey,' she said. But it seemed like I had answered her question already.

She took her time putting out the butt in the ashtray. I looked at it, saw grape lipstick prints. 'Ray Beans had you call that guy Ichabod, didn't he?' I said. 'He had you get Ichabod to steal that car.'

Desiree looked out the driver's window, away from me. 'When you love somebody, you'll do anything for them. Ray says "call Ichabod and get me some wheels". I know Ichabod because the girls at the Turtle know him and they all get tans at Electric Jamaica. Ray needed me.'

She drew fierce on her cigarette. 'But then after that shit at the Plaza that night, with your brother, I finally says, "Ray, what the hell, man? What did you put in the trunk of that car?" He says if I ever mention it again, he'll have to kill me and then kill himself, because he took some oath or something. That's when he shoved me and I put the curse on him.'

'You put a curse on him?'

'Worse. I put it on his Camaro.'

'Cool.'

'I'm Puerto Rican, Nunzio. You don't talk like that to Puerto Rican women.'

'I'll remember that,' I said. One of my penny-loafers was tapping a nervous tattoo on the floorboards.

'What's that noise?' she said, uneasy.

'My foot,' I confessed. And she reached suddenly for my knee, stilling the tic. When I stopped tapping, she retracted her hand. She reached for her sun visor, ran her fingernails the length of it and came away with a pack of smokes – a small red pack with Asian characters on the back. She tapped a blue cigarette out, started to put the pack away, then noticed me staring.

'What?'

'Can I see those cigarettes?'

'You shouldn't smoke. You too young.'

'No, can I just see the—' I saw it then as she turned the pack: the yellow Chinese dragon. 'Does Ray smoke those?' I asked.

'No,' she said.

'Then you were in that car,' I said. 'In the Pontiac.'

'Ayy, watch what you say, sucker. I never got near that car. Raymi took my smokes. See, he cracked a front tooth at the gym a few months ago. The juice gets him crazy and sometimes he bangs his head off the weight bar and shit like that. He has this busted tooth from biting the bar, so I turned him on to cloves for a few weeks. Numbs the lips. They're Indonesian cigarettes. Cloves.'

The last piece in the puzzle set firm. In my mind, I saw Ray Beans walking in the dark of Jerusalem, sucking on a clove smoke to kill the pain, taking in just enough to numb his teeth, dropping the smoke, then thinking better, coming back for the butt. My Chinese dragon had more value than a lucky charm now; we were going to put Ray Bonacascio in prison before summer went out. Desiree would never have to worry about him killing her.

'Raymi was such a big talker,' she went on. 'All his ties, you know.'

'Ties?'

'Yeah. You know, to the Big Boys, that kind of shit. Some of the Puerto Rican boys they say they in the Latin Kings and it's all talk. So I think, he's giving me another dog for that bone, you know? He had all these codes of silence and things and I thought it was all talk. When he drove away in that stole car that night, he says he was going down to Bridgeport, to the Old Man's house. He used to drive me by that house and say, "That's the Man, the boss of bosses," and all this shit. He used to drive by and make the sign of the cross.'

'Wow.'

She bunched her thick bottom lip and blew some stray hair from her eyes. She looked at herself in the rearview and lightly fingered one of her long fairy earrings. 'Once the old guy was out in his yard and Ray pulls in and goes up to him and takes the old man's hand and kisses it. He *kisses* the old man's hand. Well, the guy looks at him like he's *nuts*. And he says, "Get the hell out of here." So I don't know what to think. I think Raymi's a bullshitter, but sweet, you know. Maybe he got hisself caught up in his own bullshit and can't get out. But *I* want out. I do, Nunzio. Your brother said he'd get me out.'

'I know, I heard him.'

'I remember him in High School, he wasn't afraid of nothing. I seen big *Jibaros* and blacks on our team not want to go out for passes where your brother was. They knew if they got hit by that sucker, they was going to St Joe's for a day at least. Something really bad happened to him, didn't it? I mean, I know he got hisself smashed up, but it's like he ain't the same boy.'

'I know,' I said. I would never confess that to anyone. Why I did to Desiree was a mystery to me. But as my mother said, mystery begets mystery. And then I felt her staring.

'He's going to be okay,' I said. 'He's going to be an actor. Like Pacino and De Niro.'

'Yeah, but come on.'

'What?'

'It ain't practical.'

'Why not?'

''Cuz it ain't.'

'Maybe that's what's wrong with him.'

'What?

'Everybody around here saying that to him. Telling him to give up and go apply for a job at Toys'R'Us, go take night classes at the Tech School. Just because he didn't make it in football doesn't mean he still can't make it, somewhere.'

Desiree grew quiet. She seemed to be pondering what I said, and I hoped it wasn't too stupid. 'You're young, Nunzio,' she finally said. 'You'll find out about the real world someday. Oh, you will, little sucker.'

'I have to go to the bathroom.'

'There was a body in that trunk, wasn't there?'

I thought I just stared fixed, but I must've nodded because she did, too.

'I'm scared. Is that what your brother wants me to say? Go tell him I'm scared.'

'I'm scared, too,' I said. She looked at me for a moment then reached across the seat and took my hand. She held it. Her hand felt warm and her long fingernails pinched my wrist.

'Your brother said he was my Junkyard Dog, right? Said he'd protect me from the bad people. I'm asking for his help. Go tell him.'

'He'll be home from work around five.'

'I'll meet him right here. I'll be sitting right here. 'Cuz I'm afraid to go anyplace else. They going to kill me, Nunzio.'

She was in the Cutlass with us, three feet from Danny, and my brother seemed aware of little else. She told us where to go – south on Route 8, just keep driving. She told my brother everything she had told me, and I put in the shades she left out, including 'You never talk to a Puerto Rican girl like that,' and when the tale was told, Danny Boy looked like he needed to pull over and collect himself. But to his credit, he kept his eyes on the dark highway and nodded every now and then, said, 'I hear ya.'

'So how?' Desiree asked, a quaver in her voice. 'How you going to protect me from Raymi and whoever he's in with? With your movie camera?'

Danny turned his eyes to her. I could see he was doing everything in his power not to look down at the hint of dark rings showing through her orange top. I tried to cue my brother.

'You told her someday a real rain will come.'

'Nunzio, shut up. I know what I told her.'

'Don't get down on Nunzio,' she said. 'He's my bro.' Then she turned around, finding me behind the driver's seat. 'What's that mean, Nunzio? Someday a real rain will come?'

'*Taxi Driver*,' I said. 'De Niro. He says that before he gets a gun and—'

'Before he gets a *gun*?' Desiree stared at me for a long moment, and then slowly, she turned her gaze on Danny. He was looking straight ahead now, uneasy and seemingly self-conscious about his dirty hands, and the look he gave me in the rearview made me wonder if I'd be hitch-hiking home.

'You wouldn't do that, would you, Danny?' She ran her eyes down along his dirty T-shirt and hard arms, down to his work boots.

'What do I got to lose?' he said in a voice that had no bite to it.

My heart stalled, but Desiree's eyes brightened and she stopped smoking for a moment as she registered this. 'No, Danny,' she said without much feeling, but her eyes held a teasing shine. 'You don't want to kill somebody just for me.'

'Yeah, Danny, man,' I said. 'You don't know what you're getting into.'

My brother was fidgeting behind the wheel now with both Desiree and I looking at him. By the waxing and waning of his facial muscles, I knew he was silently invoking St Bob, but several forces were holding him to the velour, one of which sat beside him with three teardrops forever branded beneath her left eye.

'Who is this guy in Bridgeport, the Old Man?' he said.

'The *bosso*,' she said. 'The *Padrone*.'

I sat in the backseat, drinking a Tab and petting the corduroy velour like a trusted dog and wondering what a Padrone was and where we were going and what was really on my brother's mind. He looked pleased to have Desiree Vega up front with him, but I had the impression I was excess baggage.

'You have any matches?' Desiree asked, turning and trying to locate my small frame in the large backseat. 'My lighter is dead.'

When I shook my head, she foraged in the glove box. Suddenly, she let out a little startled run of Hispanic swearwords I never heard before.

'What is *this* shit?'

I knew she had come across the Hellman's jar with Danny's briny curse sliding about like black salve.

'It's the *mal'occh*,' I volunteered. 'Danny's evil eye.'

Danny Boy looked embarrassed and at a loss for words, but then Desiree told us that she had medicine women in her family, too – what she called a *yoruba*. In fact, she said, the night after she put a curse on Ray's power steering, she'd practiced a little *santeria* to try to bring Ray back. She had hollowed a pumpkin and filled it with marjoram, pepper, an egg, Florida Water, a talon from a chicken, one of Ray's old threadbare weight-lifting gloves, and his name written on a piece of paper. She then drove it over to the old bridge and pitched it out her window into the Mattatuck River where it bobbed for an hour before slipping under green sludge. She also lit four blue candles under glass after Freddie Prinze had committed suicide a few years earlier. She confessed that her first teardrop was in memory of the comedian who was her first crush and whom she still called my *Boricua*. And so she stuffed the jar back in amongst service manuals, the Super 8 and clippings of De Niro; she settled for some lipstick instead, producing from her large purse a Bonne Belle Lipsmacker. It smelled like chocolate. When I watched her apply it in the rearview, putting herself very close to my brother and jeopardizing us all, I could see that it looked like chocolate, too.

'Oh, man,' Danny Boy said with a shy laugh, making no effort to hide his meaning. We were now driving along Port Jefferson which I had never seen at night. The docks were crowded with barges, only a few of them lit. Desiree did not notice my brother and I both looking toward the water. She was busy, leaning over the dash like a navigator, and directing Danny Boy up into the inner-city neighborhoods and onto a one-way street. It was a fine street, lined with shade trees and well-spaced with large homes and stonewalls of the old Yankee variety. It was different from the Bridgeport squalor, but still, nothing my father would call 'big bucks'. We took yet another side road marked by a yellow dead-end sign, and we climbed for what seemed an eternity to a cul-de-sac where a modest two-story house loomed over the smaller Cape Cods and one-family brick ranches. It was made of red brick and the upper windows were double hung. It was the kind of home my father called a ranch, a title that never failed to amuse me. Only one light was lit on the first floor and if anyone was home at the old man's ranch, the vehicles were hidden behind a pair of white windowless garage doors.

There was an elaborate grape arbor in the front yard, well-maintained and watched over by a stone fountain sculpture of the Blessed Virgin. If that wasn't a dead giveaway to the resident's ethnicity, the vegetable garden was: the half-acre plot could support a small population of large herbivores. At the far edge of the yard was a fig tree the same size as my grandfather's.

'This is it,' Desiree said as we slowly circled through the paved driveway. 'The Old Man's. The *Padrone*'s.'

With a basketball hoop over the garage, it was hardly what I imagined a Mafia kingpin's enclave to resemble, but there was no reason to doubt Desiree. She was with us now, and neither Danny nor I regretted it. It was here, she told us, that Ray Beans drove the stolen Pontiac on the night of 4 June to meet with the man and get his assignment, his contract on somebody who needed to 'disappear'.

'Oh, Jesus,' my brother said at a whisper. His headlights were on the white mailbox where a name was painted, but no house number. 'Valle,' Danny said, looking for me in the mirror. 'Valle Construction.'

This mysterious Padrone then, was Guy Valle, the construction king that Goomba Angelo said had ties to men with ties. 'I've seen him picking tomatoes,' Desiree said. 'He's old, man. But Ray says all the guy has to do is pick up the phone and put the black hand on somebody, they disappear.'

Did Ray Beans kneel before the old mob guy and kiss his ring? I wondered. Was there any blood and wine and candlelight?

Danny Boy stopped the car suddenly.

'What you doing?' Desiree said, looking pointblank at him.

'Somebody's in there,' Danny Boy said.

'Well, keep driving,' Desiree insisted.

I saw the shadow, too. It fell across a back wall of stucco and then lowered out of sight, slowly, as if sitting.

'Go, Danny,' Desiree shoved.

And now from the house came a sound, abrupt but pleasant. A piano. I knew the song but couldn't place it. It was slow and haunting, a strange repetitive musical phrase. It made me think of my Nonni, made me think of a wedding reception or two at the *Ponti* Club.

'What is that?' Danny Boy said.

'A piano,' Desiree and I said at the same time.

'No, I know, but what is that song?'

Whoever was playing the piano went up an octave and now the tune became familiar to me. More than familiar. I felt myself grow ill at the sound of the notes, four of them, played in repetition.

'Oh, my God, Danny. That's the music I heard,' I said, 'when I took the call the night before we towed the car. I thought it was soap opera music. *That's* the music.'

'The call came from here,' my brother whispered.

Danny Boy began to search for me in the backseat but then all of our eyes were drawn to a sudden rumble in the drive. One of the garage doors was opening by remote and someone's legs were coming into view.

The piano was still being played passionately inside. Whoever was playing knew what they were doing.

'Will you fucking *go*,' Desiree said.

The garage door raised higher and I could see a woman's legs in pumpkin-colored pants. Her hips were wide and they began to angle. All of her was orange, it was some kind of pantsuit.

Danny Boy drove his heel into the gas pedal. And the Cutlass burped some carb air and stalled. The overhead door rose higher and the woman's hips were still spreading from east to west.

The Cutlass would not turn over.

The overhead rose above the rest of the large-hipped woman; she came into view so that our headlights made her dip her head and she looked out, confused as to who it might be at this hour. She had a dry cleaner's suit bag over one arm, car keys in the other hand. Her color was more *caffe' con leche* than cappucino. On her top lip was a beauty mark though I would not venture to say she was any beauty. For one thing, she was far too old: forty, I guessed.

'*Quien es?*' she called out, shielding her eyes from the headlight glare. It wasn't Italian – that, I knew.

'Bolivian,' Desiree informed my brother as he stomped the gas pedal like it was a lit match in dry grass. 'His housekeeper,' she said, turning to get another look at the wide-hipped woman as Danny's coupé came alive and left a length of rubber on the asphalt.

But I was sure that as we motored away, the woman in orange

saw my face pressed against the rear passenger side window, looking right at her.

'Housekeeper,' my brother said, pushing the Cutlass Supreme back down the steep road. He said it like it confirmed all suspicions of the man's station beyond a shadow of a doubt.

'She saw me,' I said.

'No, she didn't, Nunz.'

'Yes, she did. She looked right at me.'

'She's always there, that *jibaro*,' Desiree said. 'Ray says she's illegal.' Desiree turned and looked at me with her tattooed eye. 'You okay, honey?'

I nodded but made no effort to conceal my distress: if that's what was drawing sympathy from Desiree then I wanted more.

'Who plays the piano?' Danny said, as we came to a red light under a rusted trestle.

'Him,' she said. 'The *Padrone*.'

'He's pretty damned good,' my brother said.

'I have to use the girl's room, 'Desiree said, and so we pulled in to a Merrit gas station off the thoroughfare. Me and Danny Boy watched her walk, under night lamps, to the lady's room. She pulled at her orange tube, making sure it wasn't slipping away.

'I have to protect her, Nunzio,' he said. 'I'm in it now.'

'Me, too,' I said. But only to myself.

Danny Boy let out a long breath then sat in quiet reverie, and I knew then he would not be calling for a fair catch as Angelo said. He proved this further after Desiree returned and we drove down to the pier, up to a small lit gatehouse. A security guard inside was eating a candy bar and staring off into the night whcn we eased up. Danny gave him his best smile.

'What's up?' the guard said.

'I'm from Paradise Salvage up in Saukiwog Mills.'

'What can I do for you, Paradise?'

'See that Number Six Liberty over there? We've got nonferrous scrap onboard. I need to know when she sails out.'

'I don't know,' the guard said, relishing his own dismissiveness, mouthful of Mounds.

'What do you mean you don't know?'

'Liberty ships by weight. At fifteen thousand gross tons, she goes.'

'How much is on now?'

'I don't know.'

'Then check the fucking paperwork,' my brother said. Desiree looked back at me and arced a fine plucked eyebrow.

'Why?' the guard said, looking away as he chewed his snack.

'Because we want to try to load some more scrap before she goes.'

The guard sat looking off into the port lights and lit barge decks until he had carefully masticated his Mounds Bar. Finally, he swallowed, brought a paper towel to his lips and patted. He swiveled in his chair and looked at a desktop. 'Number Six, you said?'

'That's right.'

'Twelve, five,' he said.

'So about two thousand more tons she sails?'

'Good math,' he said.

'What are you waiting for?'

'Train from Hartford. Be here Friday morning. You want to load more scrap, you have to wait till next month.'

'Friday morning. Okay, thanks, pal.'

The guard did not say you're welcome, or goodbye. He swiveled back to his view and worked nuts from his molars with a thumbnail. My brother stared at him for a long moment.

'You a Pinkerton?'

'Yeah. Why?'

Danny Boy winked at him. 'You guys are the best.'

The guard appeared taken aback as Danny Boy reversed slowly, he lowered his head and lifted his gaze onto the stack of ferrous hulks on the barge. 'Hang on, Max,' my brother said.

'I like to move,' she said.

She didn't just say it, like someone might say they like peanut butter and jelly, she said it almost in defense, like maybe she heard a voice in her head telling her otherwise.

We were driving back to Saukiwog and the car had grown quiet. Desiree was staring out at the lights of little houses along the river.

'What's that?' Danny Boy said.

'Four years old, I was doing it. Traditional Spanish, tap, everything. My mama thought it was cute, her little *negrita* all dressed up, dancing. That's what I wanted to do, dance. But when I turned sixteen, they stopped paying for the lessons. She said I was too old now, my mother. Said it wasn't cute no more. I cried, man. I mean, I didn't think it was cute, I thought it was my religion. Mama said she'd pay for hairdressing school, cosmetics, whatever, but the dancing was done, girl. No money in it. So I go down in the basement and rip off all the wallpaper and put up mirrors. I put a sign outside, looking for fifteen girls to start up my own studio. A dollar fifty a girl for lessons. Then my father says we ain't got the insurance to cover a bunch of girls doing isolation funk in the basement. And no money in it. Remember when I was a cheerleader? Funk jazz and all that? I choreographed that shit, man. But they say to me, if that girl Jacinta Cabrera couldn't make it as a dancer, nobody can, and *not'ju*, honey. Do good in school and go see your auntie who work down H and R Block. Learn them tax returns, girl.'

Danny Boy was staring at her so hard, I had to touch his shoulder and alert him to his drifting toward the river. But I saw what he was staring at. The teardrops on her cheek were not tattooes; she wiped them away with the back of her hand, then lit another cigarette. 'I should've listened to my own fucking voice, man.'

'I remember you,' Danny Boy said. 'I wished St Mary's would score just one more time so I could see you do that thing where you looked like you had epileptics.'

'Isolation funk,' she said.

Desiree's big yellow gas-guzzler was still parked in our Italian neighborhood, and Danny pulled carefully alongside it. 'I'm glad your dad didn't tow it away and crush it,' she said, smiling.

'Desiree,' Danny said, his throat sounding a little dry. 'Nobody's going to hurt you, I promise.'

When she stepped out of the car, I heard my brother release a great breath. Her scent was still in the velour. And then, like magic, she was at his driver's window. 'Come to my house tomorrow night, yeah? I'll make you a Puerto Rican pasta you won't believe.'

I saw Danny's dimple hole in, and then he smiled. 'A guy would have to have a steel plate in his head to say no.'

'Can I come?' I said.

'Nunzi,' Danny said, shaking his head, embarrassed.

'Next time,' she said.

The record heat of August showed no sign of waning. Voyager One was still up in space; the hostages were still in Iran; John Wayne had yet to rise from the dead after three days, nor had Maximino Diaz. And I was still in the junkyard, stacking transmission housings and differentials and gathering stray hubcaps and counting backward from Friday. Barring a train wreck out of Hartford, the Number 6 Liberty was heading out into international waters in five days. Big Dan, meanwhile, set to work crushing cars and building his next stack of square blocks. My grandfather was doing less banging and tinkering in Area 51 and more sitting in his ancient lawn chair, observing his *Proletario* from various angles of light, as if waiting on inspiration from above. With his sombrero shading his eyes and his brown arms folded across his chest, he sat pondering the composite vehicle for hours at a time, like a yogi in deep meditation.

'Nunzio,' he said to me on the afternoon following our foray to the mysterious Guy Valle's house. 'No work is'a never done that we no' do better.'

I handed him a frosty orange soda bottle and he pressed it to his bulldog neck to cool himself. 'I think it's great, Grandpa. I think it's the coolest car I ever saw.'

Grandpa drank some soda and air escaped from the bottleneck. He wiped his lips with the back of his hand, seemingly lost in thought. 'She no' have the reverse. Sonamabitch reverse, she no' want to lock, see? But maybe . . . maybe, Nunzio . . . reverse is no' such a good thing. The people today, they like to move ahead, no' behind.'

'I hear you, Grandpa.' The optimistic spin he was putting on his failed linkage could have ranked with my mother's silver proverbs at that moment. But in fairness to the old man, he looked tired.

'Maybe it's time,' he said, 'for the hood'a ornamenta.'

I volunteered my knowledge of several ornament caches about the yard and suggested he might put a Mac truck bulldog on the hood of his creation. But this, Grandpa told me, compromised his patent. 'She need something'a *special*. So when the people see her come they say, "ah, here come the *Proletario*, the only one they ever make. In the Worl'."'

Grandpa returned to his quiet musing and I sat on an old transmission by his feet to admire the invention. Those moments would be indelibly printed in my mind for all my years to come: I was in the presence of an artist, a man who could gather the pieces and parts from the rusted margins of the city's highways and backyards, and manufacture something new and fantastic. I was keenly aware of my grandfather's large callused hand resting on my head now and I felt safe, alone with the old shepherd and his dreams.

'Grandpa,' I said, after a time. 'You know, don't you? You know there was something in the trunk that I wasn't supposed to see.'

My grandfather sat still, took in some air through his nose, his eyes still on his invention. 'Nunzio,' he said softly, 'I make the can-open machine, I make the weed chop. I make the spoon she spin, I make this car. *Allora*: someday, I'm'a gonna show you a machine like you never see in you life. A machine that take you back in time, see.'

'Back in time? You mean, like a time machine?'

'Ah,' he whispered. Grandpa had a way of luring a boy off the course of worry and right to the brink of faith, big a jump as it might be.

'Cool,' I said. 'I want to see it. When can I see it?'

'Someday, I show you,' he said. 'I take you to see the time machine.'

'Can we go to Little Big Horn? And watch Custer get—'

Dad whistled for me, and so I grabbed Grandpa's empty soda bottle and sprinted for the front of the main building. Danny Boy was standing a few steps away from the scrawny redheaded kid with the transparent skin and the Jeremiah tattoo. Sally Sheet Metal was there, too, just as the day's routine dictated. 'Hey, *guaglione*,' he said when he saw me hesitating. 'Come on, we need some muscle over here.'

The redheaded kid knitted his freckles and made a sucking sound as a comment on my alleged muscles. He was a vile thing and I tried not to look at him. I avoided my *Goomba*, too, as I hefted scrap radiators and heaved them onto the rusted tailgate. But I could feel his eyes on me while he stood beside my father, watching us labor.

'You been studying the book?'

'Yes, *Goomba*,' I said, sounding like an apple-polisher. This wasn't lost on the redheaded ghoul because he hissed like a snapping turtle then shook his head repeatedly.

'You better, *guaglione*. The Archbishop's coming and I don't want to be embarrassed.'

'Nunzio knows all his saints,' my father bragged as he counted radiators.

'Good,' Sally said. 'Don't let nobody fool ya. That's good, what he's doing, reading his saints and what not.'

Through the course of a hard twenty minutes of loading scrap, Sally covered a diverse range of topics. He talked about some bad mushrooms going around The Little Boot, about the price of sausage at Coangelo's Market; he shared some arcane wisdom with us about how women have two bones in their vagina that can unexpectedly seize and clamp, doing untold damage to a man's *mingilone* during intercourse. He cursed the New York Yankees and praised the grade of confectionery sugar Mrs Pisani used on her angel cookies; he warned of what happens when the heat gets above ninety degrees and the *zootzoons* get jungle crazy and riot; he ran down a pantheon of 'mick bastards' in the city; he talked about cheese, too. His mother used to make a sheep's milk *peccorino*, and when he mentioned his late mother he made the sign of the cross. When my father mentioned a new tax law, he made a different kind of sign: triangulating his fingers magically into the shape of a small hole and then proceeding to open and close the hole – whatever this was supposed to convey, it was lost on me – and there was some Italian spoken at times, when they looked directly at me or my brother, but we had become accustomed to ethnic code talk around Nonni's table.

He lit a black cigar with a plastic filter, and then, to my amusement, let out a cavernous fart and groaned like an old gelding horse as he let it free. 'Sonuvabitch didn't pay his board,' he said, about the expelled fart. The redheaded kid grinned and pretended to wave away a stink.

And when the job was done and Big Dan went off to negotiate

over a used windshield with a customer, Sally closed the tailgate of the dump truck and said, 'Let's go, Dummy.' But when he was alone with just me and Danny Boy, he grew quiet. Very quiet. He watched us through his tinted glasses as we dusted ourselves off.

'Let's see some, kid,' he finally said to Danny.

'See some what?'

'See some what? Some movie acting,' Sally said. 'Let's see some movie acting. That's what you study, right? Movie picture acting.'

'Come on, man,' Danny Boy moaned uncomfortably. But Sally Sheet Metal was intent on a private show, and so he took hold of my brother's arm, keeping him in place. 'It was you, Charlie,' Sally said in an affected young Brando, 'it was you.'

'That's pretty good,' Danny Boy snipped, trying to free himself from Sally's hand. But Sally wasn't about to submit.

'It was you, Charlie, it was you. You was my brother, Charlie.'

I felt a tinge of embarrassment for Sally, but he didn't notice or didn't care. He stood proud, self-amused. 'I did school plays,' he revealed, fighting back a smile. 'A lot of *mangia bracciol'* though, you know – queers. That's who controls Hollywood: the Jews and the *mangia bracciol'*. They know how to make you cry, the Jews. And the queers, too. Next time you watch a movie and you cry at the end, look at all the names on the TV: Weinstein, Goldberg, Blumenthal. We cry like fucking babies and they laugh all the way to the bank.'

'*Soldi, soldi, soldi,*' my *Goomba* sang, and as he did, he struggled to get his billfold out of the back pocket of his polyester slacks. He pulled out some bills with the nonchalance of pulling a handkerchief. I wondered if perhaps he was going to transform the sixth president into something lewd as he had done with Washington, but he had no such plan. He folded four one hundred dollar bills over each other, found two fifties and put them inside.

'I'll be your stake horse,' Sally said. 'Ain't a gift, *capisce*? It's a loan. Because I think you can be a contender. When you're a big fucking movie actor and the girls are begging you to fuck 'em twice on each side, you pay me back, that's all. Here, take it. Get the hell out of this shit-hole and go catch the 6:10 to New York. Go follow your dreams before you ruin your hands in the scrap business.'

Danny Boy stared at the five hundred dollars. Something knotted in his throat as me, Sally and the redheaded Dummy watched for his reaction.

'What's'a matter?' Sally said. 'You don't want to go? Maybe you don't really want to leave here. Yeah, I know what you mean.' Here, again – as Sally put the money away – he answered his own question and was satisfied. 'It's a fucking rat-race, and the *zootzoons* – they stick you with a Phillips-head down there. You think they're bad over here? Forget about it: I seen in the paper they cut a guy up on the subway 'cuz he asked for a match. And *mangia bracciol'*? By the *thousands*. They have *parades*.'

'I *work* for my money,' Danny Boy said abruptly.

Sally grew still. He pushed his glasses up on the bridge of his nose and then wrinkled it to set his vision square. 'That's good,' he said. 'Do it for yourself. So what if you don't get anywhere? You're pumping gas in fucking Saukiwog – hey, you tried, right?'

The three of us stood in the hot sun and gas fumes in a long and awkward moment. Then suddenly, Sally Testa lunged forward and clenched my brother's arm again, laughing. 'Don't look so fucking *serious*,' he said, and Danny Boy forced a smile. 'I'm just having fun with you, Danny Boy.'

A horn sounded from Sally's red Monte Carlo parked in the shade of the main building. A passenger – I didn't know there was one till now – was leaning across into the driver's seat and putting some elbow to the horn. A woman, irate as a queen bee.

'C'mon, Sal,' she whined from her nasal passages. Sally's wife had black hair, cropped short, which accentuated her crested nose. She wore large baubles in her ears and a leopard spotted blouse. There was an uptown air about her, too well-dressed to step out onto the grounds of a salvage yard. When she angled herself in the passenger window and stared out, I saw she was speaking to someone else in the backseat. A face appeared in the rear window behind large sunglasses. But they did not conceal her identity. It was the woman in Bridgeport we had seen standing in Guy Valle's garage, the Bolivian housekeeper who wore an orange pantsuit the previous night but a white uniform like a nurse today. Mrs Testa leaned back on the headrest, saying something to the other woman who stared at me from the backseat. And then, she nodded quickly, said something brief and sat back in the shadows.

'Hey, hold your fucking horse radish,' Sally Testa barked at his wife. He leaned close to Danny who was staring incredulous at the woman. 'Watch out for these *goomares*,' he advised, gesturing toward the woman. 'They'll run you over trying to get to the fucking Mall for a sale. And watch out for those crossbones.'

Sally Testa made a furtive little gesture, clamping two forearms together while his wife stared at me, cool in her leopard-spots. Sally slapped Danny Boy on the back and started away, mussing my hair and adjusting his shirt-tails all in one movement. With his wide back to us, he said, 'Especially Puerto Rican pussy. It'll get you killed.'

He turned quickly, as if in an attempt to catch Danny off-guard. Indeed he did, and he appeared satisfied. He pushed his glasses up on his nose then smiled at me. 'It was you, Charlie,' he said to me, making his way to his Monte Carlo. The redheaded kid started the motor on the truck. Danny Boy held his ground, watching them go.

'That was her,' I said. 'In the backseat. That was the woman in the garage – the housekeeper.'

'Shit.'

'She saw me.'

Danny Boy held his position as if making certain the Monte Carlo left the premises. And that's when I noticed something else. On my brother's white T-shirt, in the place where Sally had clapped him between the collarbones, was a bold hand-print made of grease. It was a big hand, all the minute swirls of fingers and palm imprinted deep.

A black hand.

It could have just been accidental. We were, after all, lifting radiators in a junkyard. But it could have also meant my brother Danny was going to disappear.

CHAPTER SEVENTEEN

Don Gustavo Martone's Amazing Time Machine

Grandpa's Buick moved along Route 8 like a mule at Belmont. His trunk was held open by rakes and bags of peat moss, boxes of nuts and bolts, bales of wire and a sawed-off olive oil can packed with C-clamps. I tried not to look back at the line of some sixty vehicles trying to pass him when the road narrowed to a single lane. Horns blew and Grandpa said, 'You sonamabitch,' a few times, but he didn't break a sweat. He drove at eleven miles an hour and that was that.

Finally, and to the relief of an angry procession behind us, we parked at a meter on the busy main street of Downtown Saukiwog Mills, just opposite *The Soldier's Horse* on the Green. The aroma hit me before we reached the old and boarded-up Loew's Theater, and it made my stomach groan in need. The scent was venting from a tiny shop at Main and Fourth, the smell of nougat paste and anisette. Grandpa's nostrils dilated and from my low vantage I could see the small hairs in his nose as he snuffed the air. He was looking into an old-fashioned plate-glass storefront where fancy lettering advertised MARTONE'S CAFFÉ – GELATI – DEGLI AMICI and below, on a punched tin sign, TURKISH TROPHIES.

A white cat slept in the window. In the sepia shadows within, I could see a small man behind a counter, working a wooden spoon in a bowl. Whatever it was he was mixing, he tasted a sample on his thumb, seemed to meditate for a spell, then resumed his mixing. The smell was thicker and more seductive than the sleeping gas at the dentist's but it gave me a similar tickle in my stomach.

'What's that smell, Grandpa?'

'Ah,' the old man said. 'You have a nose for the sweet.'

'It smells good,' I said hungrily, pressing my chin to the glass. The white cat lifted an eye and nothing more.

'*Sfogliatella*,' he said, in a gentle music. He repeated the word with a kind of reverence, pronouncing it *sfa-ya-dell*, then he pushed against the door. The vapors of Heaven were released onto the streets. I had not forgotten the time machine, but I saw nothing wrong with tasting a little *gelati*.

'Donato.' The voice belonged to a tiny man my grandfather's age. He had a handle-barred mustache and wore a black vest under an apron. When he smiled at me, his teeth called to mind the yellowish wood on a dead elm that I once saw a woodpecker tapping at.

'Don Gustavo,' my grandfather said, and he said it with an almost affected eloquence I had never seen from the old shepherd and inventor. The little baker, Don Gustavo Martone, gestured toward a table and we sat there, appreciatively, facing the street where we could see heads passing by the letters on the glass. The white cat remained motionless, its lassitude infectious. The aroma came at me like fastballs and change-ups: rich, sweet nougat paste and *pasticotti* dough, cocoa powder and canned pumpkin; fresh-ground coffee beans and baking bread; and the smell of newspapers hot off the mandibles and stacked near my chair.

Behind the counter, a tiny olive-skinned girl who may have been a year younger than me, folded dough and frosted it, and looked at me in between the tasks. Her hair was so black it was almost blue and it was fashioned in a boyish bob. She had a tiny birthmark above her lip and when she smiled, my stomach butterflied and I looked away.

'This is my grandson,' Grandpa told Don Gustavo, his hand fluttering in a delicate circle like he was rolling the thick air in his fingers and surveying its weight. He seemed to be waiting for me to speak or rise or do something respectful in the presence of the old baker. I did both: I stood and said, 'Hello, sir.' Then I looked at the girl – she smiled – and I sat again.

Don Gustavo's dark hands soon slid two plates beneath my nose. On each was a warm, plump pastry on a paper doily that resembled the frilly smock Monsignor Flynn wore during Easter Parade.

'*Mangia*,' Don Gustavo encouraged. 'Eat.'

That would be the last English I would hear for a spell. Don

Gustavo Martone pulled up a chair while his granddaughter manned rising pinoli cookies and sorted tin containers on the shelf, all of them with ancient Italian labels.

What my grandfather and Don Gustavo discussed I could not be sure but I knew it was about me and whether or not I should be entitled to experience something secret; they continued to study me, whisper to each other, glance toward the back room. Once they laughed and the little girl who Don Gustavo called Graciella laughed, too. At eleven, she spoke fluent Neapolitan and this intrigued me. When my grandfather said *docento* I knew he was giving my age. Graciella turned and looked at me as if to see if my size matched my years.

Don Gustavo studied me, too, an amused shine in his ebony eye as he nodded.

For as long as I could remember, Italian was spoken to keep secrets from us kids or non-Italians, and I always felt resentful, flustered. But here, as I ate the *sfogliatella*, I became relaxed in the company of the old men, inexplicably secure.

'*Va bene*,' Don Gustavo said. 'All right then.'

The old baker left the table with a brisk step that belied his age. He slipped behind the counter then vanished behind a dark purple curtain that hid the kitchen from public view. As Grandpa and I savored the warm pastries, we could hear Don Gustavo setting to work on something behind the curtain. I had a gnawing suspicion that perhaps I was about to get my first sip of beer or brandy, or even a Turkish Trophy though I had yet to figure out just what a Turkish Trophy was. There was a clanking of metal and then a hiss like a steam engine, a quiet humming. The curtain opened, Don Gustavo stood there, drying his hands on a small towel and looking at me with that same studious eye. He returned to what I could now see was a magnificent brass machine. He pushed a black knob in, then turned a long brass lever from left to right. He adjusted a dial, checked a gauge. Pistons churned and steam was pumped up through vents, hissing like a snapping turtle as the machine hummed loud and soft and loudly again, more steam coming up like Old Faithful, engulfing Don Gustavo as he worked boilers and valves like a glass-blower making fine adjustments.

'Is that it, Grandpa?' I said. 'Is that the time machine?'

Grandpa never looked over at it; he only monitored my face with quiet amusement. And then Don Gustavo returned to our table with three miniature coffee cups bearing handles so small that Goomba Angelo's monkey would even have a time gripping one. With a hot cup before me I was overcome with the scent of jungle fire. Grandpa inhaled the smell and moaned in delight.

And when he sipped the crema at the top and said, '*Bella, bella*,' I was intrigued. Then Don Gustavo removed his apron and joined us at the table. He watched my grandfather savor the black potion and he showed his termite's den of teeth. Both men ingested the roasted substance and whispered something sacrosanct. Don Gustavo cleansed the beans from his mustache with his tongue. '*Madonn*',' he whispered, pleased with his own ability to brew a cup of black magic.

'*Madonn*',' Grandpa underscored. I had to admit to myself, the old men made it look better than hot cocoa and whipped cream; they made it look more potent than a vanilla Coke on a scalding day, and as they sipped and savored, their eyes glazed over and they seemed to look through each other, into wondrous places. When they finally looked at me, I lifted my tiny cup, balancing the black swill at the brim, and took a cautious swallow.

And that's when the tempo of the day changed.

My heart lurched from zero to sixty-five in a flood of feeling and my focus sharpened the way it does when the eye doctor flips a lens on his vision machine and says, 'How about now, kiddo?'

How about now, Kiddo?

How about I join the Fantastic Four and see through sheet rock? How about I dance The Locomotion on the ceiling? I don't know why, and I was never certain of its translation, but I yelped so suddenly it made the white cat flinch in the window.

'*Madonn*',' I yelled shrilly.

Graciella turned from a *pizzele* machine with a perky smile, her birthmark teasing.

Don Gustavo Martone stopped mid-sip and twisted the end of his mustache. Grandpa smiled, nodded and moved his hand toward me like he was conducting a flute solo.

Don Gustavo's tongue popped free again and mopped his lip hairs; he watched me with his eyes shining like the night sky in winter as I drank the roasted bean oil down to the tart lemon peel and beyond to the light crema in the recesses of the doll-sized cup. Somehow, whether the black magic did witch's work on me or it woke a part of my brain that was connected to my ancestors' collective ways and wisdom, I really don't know.

But I began to understand *Napolitano.*

I began to feel the language. The music. That's what it was: music. Music that made me see stories the way Strauss once made me see Peter and the Wolf. When Grandpa said, '*Buono,*' it didn't just mean good, it *felt* good, but someplace remote. I half-stood, laughed out loud, yelled '*Buono,*' myself and Don Gustavo chuckled, touched his mustache. He spoke in a canto of Italian words and I knew their meaning: 'The great Caruso was here once,' he said.

As he and Grandpa remembered that time, I moved about the counter to touch things, everything. I moved to the far wall to study a framed photo of Old Saukiwog Mills, and I bounced off that wall and found myself in the window box with the white cat. I petted her. Graciella smiled at me. I smiled back, listening to the symphony of soft Italian. I gazed out the plate glass at the streets. This little drink, this tiny cup of black potion that Don Gustavo called *ticino caffe nero,* sent my mind running alongside the old men's swift sentences, jumping on, like riding the rails. I went with them, wherever they were going, and at that moment I didn't want to be anywhere else.

Outside, a rain was coming down in light mist, so light one couldn't hear it as it beaded on the window that said TURKISH TROPHIES. It was overcast outside but not gloomy, just easy on the eyes; colors seemed to fade while the black and whites came to life. The men and women in the square seemed to multiply like pollywogs, quickening their pace, their movements, speaking in the quick and clipped tempo of the Bowery Boys. But the thing that struck me and pulled me to the glass like iron to a lodestone was the unity, as if they all had the same mother who dressed them for the day; the hues were soft as wet wood and the women, with their lips as red as candied apples, walked with straight backs and heads high and looked altogether a different species. The men moved quick and with a fluid grace, removing hats when the ladies passed. Their black shoes fell along in the same soft kiss as the rain. I wanted one of those hats. The way they were cut; you could ride the wind in a hat cut like that. Everywhere out there, it seemed that the people were having fun.

As they crossed and ducked in front of a fruit store, a heavyset man in a white apron stood on the walk, polishing apples and pears. 'Whatta day,' he said to every third or fourth passerby, and they smiled and sent good words his way.

'Whatta day, Jack,' called out another just up from the Loew's Theater which glowed like a great Mecca. 'Everytinga nickela,' an Italian man sang as he traded with folk. An old man with a hoary head and eyebrows handed him a nickel and the vendor tucked a small brown bag into his hands and grinned.

'Everytinga nickela!' he called out across the street. I could smell roasted peanuts and I could hear laughter of a different strain. The old man with the white hair and eyebrows entered the Green where elm trees were tall and full. He leaned on one, tossed peanuts to the pigeons. The sky darkened there were so many pigeons, and women kept floating by with hair pitched high and to one side, and one of them took the arm of a man who had just traded a nickel for an apple and when he bit in, I heard it SNAP.

It was the sound of living.

A tall policeman was standing with the hoary-haired old man now and both were speaking in thick Irish and they laughed a lot. Passing them, the high-haired woman and the man with the apple said, 'Whatta day,' and again the man bit into the apple, and again, I heard a tremendous SNAP.

It was the sound of something I longed for from someplace so distant in me, it didn't even feel like my own longing, but it was in me just the same and it made me lightheaded and happy and sad at once and my heart was pulsing so fast I wished I never drank the black magic. I wanted to tell my grandfather that maybe his invention back at the yard had no reverse, but this brass machine sure did.

I went to the table and sat, another cup before me. The old men were still talking, about how Caruso had come into the café that day, the day following his historic performance at the Loew's, and he had shaken young Don Gustavo's hand with a white glove and thanked him for sending a cake backstage.

And they went farther back than Caruso. On the wings of black magic with a little lemon, they time-travelled back to where it all began and they took me with them to see – to really *see* – things I would not be allowed if I hadn't opened the trunk of that Pontiac in the family salvage yard on a muggy morning in June; down into the belly of a tramp steamer on the docks of Naples where a man named Gaetano Valdambrini paid their fare to go to *L'America* and work in the Brass Mills of Saukiwog where they sweated and sang:

> *Where do you work'a, Bill?*
> *In the Saukiwog Rolling Mill,*
> *And whatta you do there, Bill?*
> *I roll'a, roll'a, roll'a . . .*

Every Friday the man, Gaetano, was there at the mill gates to collect his portion from each 'bird of passage', for he was the Padrone, the labor boss, a man with the peculiar habit of dabbing at his teeth with a white kerchief as if to remove red wine; a man whom the Irish millhands called Guy Valle. A man who never accepted my grandfather's fare as paid, even now in the winter of their lives. But that was *destino*, a man's destiny.

They sang another song, the old men: Caruso doing Verdi's *Forces of Destiny*. They laughed at each other's inability to carry a tune. Don Gustavo chided Taiwan for stealing our industry; Grandpa cursed Columbus for discovering America in the first place; then he set two dollars on the table and said, '*Ciao*.'

CHAPTER EIGHTEEN

La Forza del Destino

The family *storia* that my grandfather brought to America in his goatskin satchel was now burning a hole in the pocket of my Sears Toughskins. I had to tell Danny Boy – and I did so, even before I got seatbuckled into the Cutlass which intercepted Grandpa's Buick at the stop sign on America Street. Danny seemed to be driven by an equal urgency, guiding us north on Highland.

'Have you been sitting in cars with the motor running again, Nunz?' he said when I told him about the brass machine and my time travel and the ancient pact that Grandpa had called the Padrone System.

'No, Danny, listen. It was magic. He told me everything. The true *storia*.'

'How come he never told *me*? I'm the oldest.'

'I don't know. Maybe because I'm the one who saw. And now I know. Or I *think* I know.'

'You think you know *what*?'

'Why they sent the body to *us*.'

Danny Boy glanced over at me, his eyes more unnerved than suspicious. He pulled into the parking lot of Dunn's Convalarium and shut the engine down.

'Guy Valle,' I said. 'Gaetano Valdambrini – The Padrone. He paid Grandpa's way here from the Old Country. That's what he did, he found guys to come over and work in the brass mills.'

Danny Boy just stared at me for a time, a cigarette halfway out of a pack.

But I kept talking. Two cups of espresso had my motor going high; I told him how Grandpa and others, like Don Gustavo, had given half their weekly pay to the Padrone in exchange for being placed in the brass mill, and how Grandpa defied the system by quitting the mill and going to work for himself, collecting and repairing the things Americans threw away, like the special old piano he had restrung and gifted to the Padrone when he couldn't meet his payments one week and the labor boss threatened to get our Nonni deported.

'Guy Valle controls the waste and scrap-metal business in Connecticut,' Danny Boy finally said. 'What you're saying here is that he sent Max to us because he's had our family by the balls since the day Grandpa left the docks.'

'Bingo,' I said.

For a moment it appeared Danny was going to open his door and void his stomach right there in the North End, but he didn't. He lit a smoke, gave me his keys and said, 'Lock the glove box.'

Goomba Angelo was sitting in his favored corner of the apartment, near the west window, Ruby Lee asleep in his lap. Goomba had been playing solitaire but it was obvious that the last hand frustrated him, or Ruby Lee, or the two: the bicycle playing cards were scattered about.

'We don't have much time,' he said, when we let ourselves in. 'There's a shit storm brewing.'

'Yeah, there is,' Danny Boy said. 'You can bank on it.'

'They're already banking on it, Carmella and his thrift – the bank of the hardworking Italians and Portuguese, right? My mother bought stock in that fucking bank with rolls of quarters when Carmella started it up. They all did. But that sonuvabitch has been using their funds to invest in land and building projects that they bully away from smaller contractors like Max Diaz. Take a look,' he said, nodding toward the avalanche of manilla folders on the linoleum.

'Is there money getting kicked back?' Angelo said, looking hard at Danny. 'Kickbacks for greasing the runway on multi-million-dollar developments, while up on the streets, it all appears to be a city revival? And maybe it is. Maybe crime does pay in the fucking long run.'

'If it did,' I said, and I couldn't believe the words were coming out, but there was no retrieving them, 'if it did, you wouldn't be in that chair.'

Angelo stared at me, and for a moment it looked like he was going to impale me with a skewer of Neapolitan curse words. But he said nothing, just gazed at Danny Boy who was sorting through the copied zoning reports Johnny had gathered from the city newspapers.

'The funnel,' Angelo said. 'How is money getting from the bank to City Hall?'

Johnny burst through the door then and I was happy to see her. She was dressed like Martha Reeves and wearing cobalt eye-shadow, a big Dolly Varden hat, a tight sundress, and old-fashioned high-heels. She had been to see the City Clerk again, had asked to see Treasury records which were public. Mr Antoine Davis had been reluctant to open certain records that had been stamped as received but not yet filed, but Johnny sang 'Dim All the Lights' and smoothed him like honey.

'She more likely mashed him like a *polenta*,' Angelo said, and Johnny turned a bitter eye on him.

'That Mr Butterscotch Carmella Motherfucker been leasing the top three floors of the old Kirby High School from the city.' She was blowing high like a tea kettle now, storming Angelo with two sheets of Xerox and the potent scent of cologne. 'I found the funnel,' she said and then she broke into her high-pitched '*R.E.S.P.E.C.T*'.

Angelo sang back: '*B.I.G. D.E.A.L.*'

He said that, like all the other transactions we'd been digging up, leasing office space from the city was no proof of bribery or bank fraud. We needed to find a dummy corporation, he said. 'Forged checks,' he snapped. 'Cross loaning with other banks and whatnot.'

Johnny balled up the lease record and threw it at Angelo, then stormed into the kitchenette area. 'I don't see your gimp ass waitin' in line at the City Clerk,' she said, ripping down assorted vials of medication from a cabinet.

'How far up?' Danny Boy said. 'How far up does it go, Ange?'

I knew then what he was implying. But our mayor was not the dirty type. He was like a young gunslinger riding into a failing town to run the old Irish Democrats out and take the city by the horns.

Indeed, he was already causing a furore in the city by installing an inter-racial basketball court and defending Indian rights. Not exactly a popular guy with the old politicians. And his grandfather, like mine, had come over here from the Old Country and worked in the same mills – who knew? Maybe he even came over on the Padrone System. If Frank Longo couldn't save this city, what was it all for in the end? All the fingers and hands lost, all the spelter bends, all the long hours at a dollar a day.

'Mayor Longo isn't part of this,' I said.

'How do we know that?' Angelo said.

'He wouldn't do something like that to the city. He loves this city. I know he does.'

'I don't know what to think, Nunzio. But Saukiwog Mills is getting raped, and if this Brass Ring isn't stopped, you're going to open the trunk on some old Skylark and find somebody else in there.'

'What do we do?' Danny said, standing now, watching Johnny feed Angelo his meds and cider vinegar.

'Get to the Widow Diaz. *Now.*'

When we climbed the steps to the widow's place, there was no sound-activated dog barking, no Little Joey singing 'Old MacDonald' and no fan rippling the green curtains. The door was bolted and it looked abandoned. All that remained were the pieces and parts of old motorcycles on the stoop.

And then a hand came up from between the steps and seized my leg about the ankle. I yelled and Danny Boy just stood looking down at Chilli-Dog who was beneath the steps boxing old bike parts. 'What are you fucking Weebloes doing *here*?'

When he came to the top of the stoop he was dirty with grease and fluids, and he had a roll of duct tape in one hand. There was no way we were ever going to get off those steps, I could see it in his eyes. He was intent on butchering us and putting us in old Rita's Bakery boxes with his chopper nuts and bolts.

'Corn-Dog,' my brother said.

'Chilli Dog, ass-wipe,' he snapped back.

'Chilli-Dog,' Danny tried again. 'Where's your mother?'

'You even mention my mother I'll cut your fucking throat and hang you over the rail to drain.'

'You have to tell her not to sell.'

'Sell what?'

'The mill. Your father's old mill.'

'What's it to you fucking Weebloes?'

'Easy, man,' my brother said, and he didn't sound anything like a boxer or a taxi driver or even a Junkyard Dog; he sounded like a scared young man. 'What if I told you that my little brother knows where your father might be' – I flinched when Chilli-Dog looked at me and I wanted to run – 'and that we have good reason to believe that he disappeared because of the permit thing.'

'That's fucking news? Of course he disappeared because of the permit thing! He went to Maine and hung himself. He lost his investment.'

'No, they killed him because he wouldn't share the deal with some people in the city who are dirty fucking people—'

'Get the fuck out of here or I swear, man, I'll kill you and your little brother.'

We were on the street, moving, when Danny Boy got up the pluck to turn and shout to the big biker: 'Tell her not to sell!'

'She'll do what she wants.'

We stood there in the South End, looking at the leather-clad figure guarding the apartment like a Doberman. 'She worked all her life in the brass mill – her lungs are green, man. She can make a million dollars now. Payments for the rest of her life for her time in this fucking rat-hole. She can move out of here. 'He stripped off some duct tape and sealed up a box, and while he was bent over, he said, 'Don't be fucking with people's lives, *gringo*. Not in this neighborhood.'

We were too late.

But as we crossed the street back to our car, a small procession of women were coming from the other direction, all of them carrying groceries. All greeted us casually in Spanish and kept crossing. All but one.

Mrs Diaz stopped in the middle of the street when she saw us. She looked directly at me and began speaking under her breath in a foreign lament. She walked toward me in the kind of sore-ankled gait our old Italian women developed after years of ingesting too much salt. She looked down at me, her eyes constricting behind her glasses. The little boy Joey was behind her, a tight grip on her blouse and a Cool Pop in his mouth. In a tortured voice Mrs Diaz struggled to put her words in English. 'He calls me. Every night, he calls me.'

'He calls me, too,' I said.

She let a mournful sound escape as she hurried across the street. My brother yanked me toward the car. 'Why'd you say that?'

'Because he does. He calls to me, too. Max calls to me.'

We got into the car without a second to spare before Tino came across the street at a run, clutching a tire iron and cursing in Spanish. As we laid rubber back toward The Playhouse where Mr Pembroke was undoubtedly cursing his tardy sacrifice character, the Holy Hill peace cross was glowing like a blue beacon in the dark.

The next day was Wednesday and a mid-afternoon rain gave a respite from the heat. My mother said this was a godsend as we would all be gathered together that night in the New Kirby High School auditorium for the public hearing regarding the Mattatuck-Saukiwog Indian land issues.

This gathering (a pow wow I called it in my mind) was a reprieve from more than just the heat for me. I knew that if our Indians had their tribal lands returned, the scales of justice might totter back toward even; God would win a hand against the Devil and perhaps gain momentum in His ongoing match, which seemed to me a battle staged in our city of red brick.

Cars of all kinds, but mostly used tuna boats, were filling the High School parking lot when my mother and I arrived early. At the last minute Big Dan had decided not to go. In fact, he decided none of us would go to see the 'colored Indians'. He was in a god-awful mood, lying on the couch and rubbing his feet together with such velocity I thought he might set his cotton socks afire while he watched *The Price is Right*.

In the end though, Mom wore him out saying that I had been working a man's day and deserved to go see the Indians get their land back.

'They take a vote, you vote no,' he told my mother. When she didn't respond and escorted me out the door, Big Dan called after her: 'You hear me, Nancy? We could lose everything to a bunch of colored guys claiming to be Indians.'

'This is win-win,' Mayor Longo said, 'and I like win-win. I think *you* like win-win.'

He sat in a drab metal folding chair on the gym floor before the gathering of two or three hundred, his suit jacket off and his white sleeves rolled to his elbows. 'If the Mattatuck-Saukiwog Tribe gets their land back, we reap the fruits of restitution.'

Mayor Longo and I seemed to think along the same upstream current.

But seated down there, flanking him to his right, was Mr Campobosso, the former GOP Chairman and the three aldermen, including Mr Sforza. Like always, they regarded the young mayor like fathers and uncles watching their star pitcher hurl from the mound. I watched them closely, especially Mr Butterscotch Sunday who, with other investors from BCD, sat off to the left with the three registered members of the Mattatuck-Saukiwog Indian Tribe: Uncas Fontenot, Tyrell Sun Dog and Reginald Whirlwind Fire Keeper, the War Chief wearing his military fatigues and smoking a Marlboro. The three of them sat with arms folded, Uncas Brown and Chief Fire Keeper scowling while Tyrell Sun Dog looked as if he might doze off. Seated with them were three members of the state's Indian Affairs Council and a bookish woman from the Department of Environmental Protection.

Mom and I were at the very top of the very last row of bleachers and it was difficult for me, even standing, to read body language as Mayor Longo spoke into the PA system about putting milk in our pails, increased tax revenues and, of course, the Renaissance of Saukiwog Mills.

Two years earlier, he had stood in the gym of the old Kirby High and called Danny Boy to the floor. There, he had awarded him the Brass Key and shook his hand and Danny charmed the crowd with a speech that was blunt and confident and refreshingly brief after hours of ceremony.

The public was longing for that kind of brevity now as Bataan-like addresses by Mr Sunday and Chief Reginald Whirlwind Fire Keeper

brought on yawns and peeks at watches. Uncas Fontenot had his
turn again, reprimanding the behavior of not only the white man but
the black man, too. This created a slight rumble through the crowd,
mostly amongst the city blacks. And then someone I could not see
far down in the sea of heads shouted, 'What about the fruit, Mayor?
For us?' and someone else yelled out that allowing a sovereign
nation within a nation, and in our city, was un-American.

Most of the auditorium applauded. My mother clapped, sitting
with her back straight and a smile on her face as if the whole thing
were a production of *The King and I*. She had applauded when the
mayor spoke of past injustice, and now she was cheering the other
side, the people who needed jobs. That's how Mom was – everyone
had their side of the story. If the opposing team scored a touchdown
– well, they had mothers and fathers, too.

Mayor Longo gave the floor to Mr Carmella and something
unfolded that reminded me of Show-and-Tell, with Mr Butterscotch
Sunday unveiling a visual aid board and poking at it with a pointer.
It appeared to be a map of some kind, and when he used the words
'tribal land rights' there was such a chatter in the auditorium Mr
Sunday had to fan his hand slowly to request silence.

'It's all painfully simple,' the president of the thrift and Brass City
investors group said. 'If the Mattatuck-Saukiwog Nation is awarded
federal status, they have the tax-free right to open a business on their
rightful three-plus acres of river frontage.'

A business? What business? some of the more vocal residents
queried from down in front. Well, Mayor Longo explained, look at
the Mohawks over in New York. Look at the way they had created
an infusion of money and a sound future.

'Tax-free cigarettes?' someone asked, and Mayor Longo said,
'Bingo.'

But he didn't mean Bingo like I thought he meant Bingo. No, he
meant, 'a world-class bingo parlor in Saukiwog Mills'.

Bingo?

The word went up the bleachers, and back down, like an open
can of tennis balls.

'A world-class, high-stakes Bingo Palace that will create over
three hundred jobs in the city and bolster the tax revenue. A bingo
hall and entertainment complex that will seat two thousand and

draw visitors from as far away as Montreal. When the state legalizes gaming as they are perched to do, there becomes a great potential for a gaming and entertainment complex that can stand in company with Atlantic City.'

There was applause and when my mother clapped fervently, I did as well. Whatever was right for the War Chief and his tribe of fourteen, was right for me.

'Fred Campobosso has gone to Washington on behalf of the Mattatuck-Saukiwogs and he has returned with an official letter. This letter indicates that the federal status application will be accepted by the fourth quarter of next year.'

A clutch of long-haired men down in the right corner stood and whistled and one of them shook a fist in approval. Others clapped, some booed. I noticed that many of the blacks were frowning and exchanging whispers.

'All *you* have to do is vote yes when this bill comes forth at a city meeting in September,' Mayor Longo said. 'It's your choice, your opportunity. Your city. Our economic future ultimately lies in your hands. The old defense-based world has crumbled. A new one is beginning. Let it begin here, on the Mattatuck River.'

Bingo.

Looking back at his famous Brass Balls speech I remembered how he had peppered his oratory with that word, but I thought it was just an expression then. Now I knew he had something bigger in mind; even back in June he was thinking about Max Diaz's property.

And that worried me.

The applause that swelled in the auditorium made goose pimples run a-tickle up my back and along my thin arms. Mayor Frankie brought the hearing to a rousing end: 'What was once the Yankee Brass Rolling Mill where our ancestors labored, where they lost fingers and the best years of their lives, will now house an enterprise that will put us on the map again and make us a kingdom once more. Let's get people off the welfare rolls and onto the *pay*rolls!'

There was a roar like none I have ever heard, not even when Danny Boy sacked the St Mary's QB for the two-point safety that won us the title his frosh year. The High School auditorium had been transformed into a veritable Roman Circus, all but a handful of folks cheering, and those were down in the vicinity of Father

Vario who quibbled about how an Indian Bingo Palace might cut into the charity bingo games at Our Lady of Mount Carmel School. This made little impression on the crowd.

I stood there on my sneakers, looking down at the officials on the floor and I felt my stomach give. The old rolling mill, he said. Set on three and a half acres along the river, he said. Thoughts of Goomba Angelo filled my head and I wished he was sitting beside my mother and me. This wasn't a hearing in the name of Indian land rights. This was the reason we had a dead man in a '73 Pontiac at the junkyard for most of the summer. The path to the nest of the vipers led not only into the egg crate cubicles of City Hall and the desks of the aldermen, but into the mayor's chambers. The Mattatuck-Saukiwog Bingo Palace, as they were proposing its name, would be a windfall of windfalls for the Brass Ring.

Looking at Mayor Longo, sitting down below, I felt betrayed.

Looking around at the hundreds of city residents, I felt terrified. Was I the only person in the entire hall who knew what was going on? Or did others, who would look away from the facts if it meant a pay check? Around me sat old women like Mrs Conigliaro, on her feet, applauding the mayor, offering him prayers in Italian, her eyes welling; Mrs Doyle, grinning a big hibernian smile and tipping her head near her son, Jackie, an unemployed millworker, whispering something that made him nod, hopeful. *Yes, Jackie, there will be milk in the pail again.* Dave Zuraitas, sitting with his munitions cap in his lap and his eyes fixed on his work boots, not wanting to get his hopes too high up off the tarmac.

Off the welfare rolls and onto the payrolls.

Children, old people, blacks, whites, Puerto Ricans, French-Canadians, Polish, Germans, Lithuanians and the new wave of immigrants, the Cambodians and Uruguayans, whistling and clapping in the name of faith.

The public was allowed to voice opinion and it was one voice of hope after the next: *Hartford has the Jai-Lai, they're getting rich. Why not us?*

That rolling mill stole my father's health. I see this as compensation. Just deserves.

'Bingo,' called out the mayor.

Mr Sunday returned to his chair, and when he sat I saw him let a long breath free. He seemed to have aged in the time he was at the graphics board. I was staring at him and it must have been an ardent look because I felt my mother's hand close over mine. I moved my eyes onto hers, and allowed her to study me more closely.

'If no one else has anything to say,' Mayor Longo closed, 'I'll wrap things up.'

My mother was narrowing her pale eyes as she tried to read mine. I looked vehemently at her. I wanted to tell her, I wanted to let her know everything – but I didn't have to. What I thought then was our gift of the Celtic water deities, I now knew as that mysterious thing between any mother and her son. She had read my soul countless times since I came into this world. She could read my pain under a smile and she knew when she needed to avert her eyes at times as I tried to find my way. She could read my soul like Cousin Pina Maria could read her mood ring.

And she read my soul now.

Because up she stood and said, in her strong lilting brogue: 'I'd like to speak, Mayor.'

Mayor Longo was happy to see my mother. He knew her as the gentle Scotswoman she was, an optimist and homemaker. He leaned back in his chair at the same time he thrust his neck forward and said into the microphone: 'Yes, Mrs Paradiso. Please.'

Paradiso. The name echoed through the new auditorium as it had in the old one on that glorious Saturday morning when Danny Boy walked away with the Brass Key and color in his cheeks. But now all eyes were on my mother, standing there in her flowered dress, holding her large white plastic purse under her arm, looking a little nervous.

The longer her voice remained tucked inside her, the deeper the silence grew and now I felt eyes on me as well. I was terrified, having no idea what my mother would say. Maybe she had not read my soul after all. Maybe she was going to keep her promise to me and speak on behalf of the Mattatuck Indians, and there was nothing I could do now to make her sit.

Then she spoke in her Lowlands burr. 'At length the fox sees the furrier.'

That was it.

The silence hung there for a moment as she smoothed her dress and sat down. Mayor Longo leaned near Mr Campobosso to ask him what the Scotswoman had said. But now a black woman stood three rows down and shouted, 'Uh-huh. Uh-*huh*.'

The black woman remained on her feet. 'The woman speak the truth! There a fox in this here henhouse.'

My friend Ralph Tremaglio's father stood up and cupped his hands around his mouth: 'What will we be now, Mayor? The Bingo Chip city?'

And then old Mr Paternostro grabbed his daughter's shoulder with his lobster claw hand and pushed himself to his feet. 'No casino,' he yelled, for want of a more refined protest. But the people had had enough refined words, and they cheered the former millhand, and they cheered Ralph Tremaglio's father, and they turned again to cheer my mother. The hoots and applause traveled from the front bleachers and cut diagonally across the stands and what I thought for a moment was the sound of people leaving was shoes and sneakers and steel-shanked work boots stomping the bleachers in a heavy tempo.

Now the stuffy auditorium became a full-moon sanitarium and Mayor Longo stood, yanking his microphone free and asking for quiet. But he would have a better chance trying to stop the spring lawn fires in The Little Boot. The citizens began turning to each other like they did at Our Lady to offer signs of peace, only this had nothing to do with peace and everything to do with anarchy. They were shouting at each other, either in agreement or discord, but whatever the hearing had become, my mother did it.

At length the fox sees the furrier.

Mayor Longo looked right at me.

For a second, I heard no sound at all, just blood gorging my ears; my own pulse. His Honor watched me with a curious gaze; maybe it was because I was the only body not moving in the swell, or maybe he, too, read my soul.

I returned the gaze.

It was my night to be War Chief.

'Let's go, Mom,' I said.

The word traveled as words did in Saukiwog Mills.

From garden to garden in The Little Boot, up into Glasgow Row where my mother was an instant folk hero on the scale of Robert the Bruce; down into Little Lithuania, and into the South End where it was translated into the forty-three dialects of Spanish spoken there; it traveled.

My mother, my quiet, crossword-puzzle-loving, Good Samaritan mother may not have been able to make a spaghetti sauce to her in-laws' satisfaction, but she sure could cause a public outcry. Within twenty-four hours pamphlets were going about the Green and fliers were nailed to phone trees, denouncing the gaming hall as selling out our ancestors and our character. There was talk that bone fide Indians in the state, like the Pequots and Paugasetts, sent letters to City Hall requesting proof of tribal registration from the alleged Mattatuck-Saukiwog members; Chief Fire Keeper responded through his lawyer by producing documentation that proved his grandmother had married a man with one-eighth Indian blood. But the black community was angry also. This was a sham, they claimed; political energies needed to go to solving racial issues, not to forking money over to a few brothers trying to hop off the team bus and onto a gravy train. A non-Indian group of supporters appeared in front of City Hall wearing beads and feathers and chanting in support of the Mattatuck-Saukiwogs regardless of documentation. That was just more red tape and broken treaties, they told the newspaper, and they promised to raise money to bring Indian activist Russel Means to the city and start another Wounded Knee.

Johnny Mae Sisson presented a theory about the Bingo Palace that was both intriguing and disturbing: someone in Brass City Development discovered a tantalizing loophole and hit the birth records looking for remaining descendants of the original inhabitants of the river land, so they could seize the site and reap the benefits of a tax-free multi-million-dollar operation. Someone, she said, had groomed themselves some Indians the same way they groomed themselves a young Republican mayor.

'Them brothers never knew they had no Injun blood,' Johnny had said. 'Some guy in a suit do his homework and finds him some Indian blood that go way back. They turn out to be some guys sittin' on a porch, smokin' dope in the North End who wouldn't know if they was related to King Farouk. "Me an Indian? Hell,

yeah, give *me* some land to sell, I'll be *Pocahontas*. I tell you right
now, Numb Nuts: I'm a direct descendant of that sister who showed
Lewis and Clark's lost ass where to go. Now – give me that lot
behind Pathmark and some payback money".'

She laughed at her own waggery till tears filled her eyes. We tried
to laugh, too, but it was a hard truth to swallow and shrug away.
All that the paper said was that Mrs Dan Paradiso of Town Plot
'gave vent to a faction of recalcitrance'.

I liked what Mom said better.

Big Dan, bent over his *azzupe* and Stella D'oros and the *Saukiwog
Republican* the following morning, said, 'I don't believe what I'm
reading here.'

'It was great, Dad,' I said.

'What the hell did you do, Nancy?'

'You told me to vote against the Indians.'

'Yeah, but I didn't know they were putting in a bingo hall. Like
Atlantic City, it says. A tourist Mecca, it says. Hotel and everything.
Jesus, Nancy, what did you do?'

My mother sat slowly, as if numbed by my father's rage. She
dug a rolled tissue from her nightrobe pocket and dabbed at her
morning allergies. 'I believed I did the right thing, Dan,' she said.

'Sixty-five-million-dollar bingo hall and resort,' Dad kept saying
on the way to the junkyard. 'You pay twenty-five bucks for a set
of cards and you can win up to a hundred grand. People will be
coming up from New York and Boston. Christ. *Christ*, you could
get a job there, Danny, racking the chips or something.'

Danny Boy held his tongue and I was proud of his discipline. We
would have to stay calm until we had enough to go to the Feds or
– if the wind turned against us – Max Diaz sailed for the Orient.

'They got Wall Street behind them on a sale bond,' Dad lamented.
'Christ. The mayor's trying to create a Renaissance, your mother
starts a *Revolution*.'

'Feed the dog,' Big Dan said, even before he slowed the tow truck
inside the gate. He and Danny Boy lowered an old Toyota and
began foraging through it, my brother beating my father to a
nice Pendleton shirt behind the backseat. I went off, balancing a
slopping red heap of Alpo on a hubcap, down into the rows of old

cars forever careful not to step past the blue Skylark that would put me in killing reach of Primo Canero. I stooped and prepared to Frisbee the hubcap at the lunging dog, but he wasn't out of his bread truck yet.

I banged a palm on the hood of the Skylark and braced myself for his gnashing jaws and foul scent. But there was no Primo this morning. Stepping away from the Skylark boundary I caught sight of the black dog. He was lying on his side, neck extended, looking right at me with eyes open and fixed. His tongue was so exposed it looked like it had choked on a great length of pink taffy.

Primo Canero, the junkyard dog, was dead.

I didn't call my father right away, but moved in a few steps to make sure he wasn't playing possum in an attempt to shred my testicles. I poked him with a rusted windshield wiper blade but he was as stiff as an old bucket seat. Before him was a dried pool of vomit and a raw, half-eaten steak.

'Poisoned,' Big Dan said when I finally broke and called for help. 'Bastards gave him a steak with rat poison.'

'What bastards?' I said, knowing that in urgent times like this swearing carried no sanctions.

'Kids,' Dad said. 'The fucking kids. Vandals.'

Indeed, a dozen old cars had broken windows, large rocks inside, on the seats and floors. It happened every summer, kids with too much time on their hands.

His eulogy for Primo Canero was brief: 'A good dog as far as junkyard dogs go. Vicious. Brain-damaged. Rejected by the State Police. A killer. He served us well. What's a junkyard without a junkyard dog?'

I went to the Coke machine in the shadows of the main building and wept some.

'You hated that fucking dog,' Danny Boy said.

'Not really,' I said.

'This how they want to do things?' my father said, on his way to The Crusher, popping Tums into his mouth. 'I'm going to buy a goddamned *wolf*.'

I knew that *they* were not kids.

And when the Department of Motor Vehicles hand-delivered a notice to Big Dan one hour before closing, he knew it, too.

*   *   *

Illegal burning of hazardous materials was one violation listed on the pink copy that bore Dad's fingerprints in grease. Oil seepage into the ground was yet another. The Renaissance City was cracking down on eyesores and environmental hazards everywhere within its redbrick limits.

'Bullshit,' my father said, and he was right. I had spent the better part of my summer inside that tarpaper fence and the only burning done was when Grandpa roasted a woodchuck that Primo Canero had killed back in mid-June; sure, there were small residual smolderings that followed the torching of parts and tire burns and so on, but the city DMV was accusing him of some kind of toxic firestorm.

As far as oil seepage, no one was more careful about what went into the earth than my father and grandfather – they had a garden there, for God's sake! But it was the final violation that made my father burn from within and do a magic trick with a roll of Tums, making a half-dozen of the little tablets disappear at once.

Eyesore.

'*Bull*shit,' he said, crunching Tums. 'Me and Pop built a fence around the whole place. Who can see it? Now they say that the fence is an eyesore.'

His junk license was up for renewal on Columbus Day. If he didn't 'clean up his act' his permit would be revoked and he would have thirty days to remove his inventory off the land.

'Why?' he finally cried out as the tow truck climbed the big hill up toward The Little Boot, and his voice broke thin and the sound hurt me inside. I looked at Danny Boy. He was staring out his window at the passing row of little green and pink houses; his muscles were tight where it touched my elbow.

He knew why.

'*You* know why,' Danny Boy said.

Big Dan looked at him then slammed a hand down on his signal lever. He swung the tow truck to the side of the street and shut it down. 'Why?' Dad said, glowering at my brother. 'You want to tell me why?'

I stared straight ahead; Danny studied his army boots.

'*I'll* tell you why,' Dad said. 'Somebody's telling me to keep *you* on a fucking leash, Danny.'

My brother looked up, startled.

'That's right,' Dad went on. 'Sally told me I got a kid who's a loose cannon and I'm thinking he means you got a screw loose which, let's face it, kid, you do. And what's this he says you're going out with a Puerto Rican?'

'That's nobody's business.'

'Okay. I'll tell you what my business is. I get a call from Bridgeport that someone from my yard is down there asking when the scrap goes out. "No," I say. "Must be a mistake." But it was you two guys. Frick and Frack. Sacco and Vanzetti.' Now he stared right at us. 'Twiddle Dee and Twiddle fucking Dumb.'

Danny Boy stared at him in a silence that was as cautious as it was combustible.

'Ever since we towed that goddamned Pontiac, I've got to live with *agita* in my stomach. So I'm going to tell you the truth. I'm going to tell you the truth about that car and why I sent it right through The Crusher.'

My breath caught on Danny's and we both sat with heads turned to Big Dan, waiting for the planet to resume its revolutions. The street seemed suddenly quiet, not a car in earshot.

'What I did was bad. It was wrong – and it was illegal. I knew the story on that car, and so I got rid of it fast. You think it's easy for me to live with what I done?'

'You knew, Dad?' It was me speaking, dry-tongued.

'Yeah. I knew.'

'About the body?' Danny Boy said.

'The body had a lot of damage, lot of dents. The undercarriage was rotted out. I knew it had no title. That's illegal. But the motor looked pretty good and the tires had some life, so I stripped it and fed The Crusher. It was a favor to Sally. He needed to get rid of a junker. I've run a few through for him in the past. Like that old Ford at the drive-in, had to get it out for him. Figure, hey, who's it hurting?'

My father grew quiet now. I could feel Danny Boy breathing again.

'I just wish that bastard would go to Japan so I can sleep nights.'

There was no point in bringing up the cargo contents any more. Nor was there any logic in trying to convince him that those dark contents linked a dozen men to conspiracy, bank fraud and murder. Big Dan had come clean, and he had no clue about what was in that car. He just wanted it crushed and baled before anyone from the DMV might come sniffing around and learn that he junked a car with no title, a misdemeanor that seemed silly in light of what was happening beyond my father's ken. I imagined Sally, or worse, the Padrone, on the phone with Dad, telling him to get rid of the car, just feed it through and get rid of it. The favor was a form of junk tax, the kind my grandfather had been paying for sixty-three years.

My father was no killer. Just a hardworking man trying to eke out a living from scrap metal and used parts in the shadow of his own father's Old Country business arrangements. I knew my brother and I were threatening that living even as we tried to free him. But I wanted to see Gaetano Valdambrini go to prison for ordering a murder. I wanted him to fall and take the others down with him. But like Grandpa had often queried in one of his Italian fables, what mouse had the balls to hang the bells on the cat?

Driving home, Danny Boy remained quiet, his eyes a thousand yards off. Each morning, the look in his eyes told me he was edging closer to doing something of note in Saukiwog Mills. In the tire bunker, I caught him practicing in his mirror. Not just lines now, but the physical routine of pulling my grandfather's sawed-off Italian bird gun from his waistband and aiming at his reflection. 'Suck on *this*,' he'd say. At first, his voice was reedy and unconvincing and he might as well have been pulling a lollipop from a holster. But by the week's end, he was snapping the sawed-off ten gauge into place, and his 'Suck on *this*!' scared me.

I didn't know it then, but he had a target in mind.

CHAPTER NINETEEN

Mr Mojo Risin'

The mayor's receptionist, Mrs Romanski, had put Danny on hold for eleven minutes then returned to say that he could get in to see Mayor Longo in about two weeks, unless of course, he wanted to attend a breakfast at DiTullio's restaurant that the mayor hosted every other Friday for the public.

'This is a private matter,' Danny Boy had said. 'Mayor Longo knows what it's about. He told me that if I ever needed a job or anything, to call.'

Mrs Romanski had put him on hold again – this time for less than thirty seconds – then she told him His Honor could meet with him after five o'clock in City Hall. That, in fact, he'd be delighted to see him.

My hands were sweating when we got there. 'I'll wait in the car,' I offered.

'No, you won't. You're coming in.'

Once again I was being used as 'the kid', a buffer or a witness. I had never been inside the big brass doors and it reminded me of the vast halls and high ceilings of the Peabody Museum. Public servants were leaving for the day and some joked with each other. It seemed a far cry from any evil citadel, and I had to admit to myself that I felt important.

Until Danny noticed what shirt I was wearing.

'Oh, shit, Nunz, did you have to wear that?'

'What?'

'Disco Sucks. You don't wear a Disco Sucks shirt to City Hall.'

'Does Mayor Longo like disco?'

My brother suddenly took me in a walking headlock down the

corridor and laughed at a whisper. 'If he does, then that's enough to impeach him.'

A quarter of an hour later we were still sitting in a large cluttered room that had no more romance than the Motor Vehicle Department. Two women secretaries were working overtime and sweating, even though window fans were flapping at the memos and curry-yellow folders. Mrs Romanski assured us that the mayor would be with us shortly.

Danny Boy and I sat in chairs on either side of the big brown door behind which we could hear the drone of men doing city business. My brother looked slouched, his light green army jacket hunched up almost to his ears and his fingers working at each other. He exuded all the confidence and grace that one might have in the waiting room of an oral surgeon. His eyes moved onto me, only once, and they betrayed a terrible darkness. The thought occurred to me then: what if he had the gun inside his jacket? What if this *Taxi Driver* fantasia had gone too far, and he was set on killing the Mayor of Saukiwog Mills? Was this the real rain he promised was coming?

'Betty, get me Adult Ed on the phone,' Mr Sforza said, coming out of the office in his blue suit, still engaged in conversation with several other men about budget this and budget that, and the sheer banality of it saved me from my own imagination. Mayor Longo hung out his office doorway as if the jamb was keeping him from falling over with fatigue, but he was smiling and as handsome as ever, and when he saw my brother it was as if he suddenly remembered his appointment.

'Danny Paradise!' he said in a voice that seemed more befitting a high school locker room than City Hall. This was a reprieve for the mayor and he seized it with a boyish glow. 'You bring a pigskin? I could use tossing a few in the park.'

He was, as Mrs Romanski had promised my brother, delighted to see him.

'What would they say though, if they saw the mayor throwing a football around in the park?' he asked Mr Sforza. The alderman laughed and winked at me.

Danny stood up with a wan smile, shook His Honor's hand then fidgeted a bit with his hands jammed in his jeans pockets.

'Come on in,' Mayor Longo said, informally. 'It's hot out here.'

'Can my brother come in?'

The mayor looked at me, straightening his mauve tie. 'No. He's got to stay out here and keep his eye on the girls.' When I looked up, confused, Mayor Frankie lunged at me, and laughing at my stoic response, he took me by the arm, yanking me into the air-conditioned inner chambers. In his close grip, I smelled shaving cologne, and it put me at ease.

'Get over here,' he said in mock anger. Inside the mayor's office the air was cold and the brown leather chairs were cool to the touch. We were facing the mayor's cherrywood desk but to his credit, he did not sit behind it like my principal, Mr Mathers, would. He sat on it, so that we were in an intimate huddle, and he gave us each a Coke.

'Disco sucks,' he said, reading my sweatshirt. He raised his Coke can to mine and said, 'I'll drink to that.'

Danny Boy laughed. The mayor winked at him. This was good. Not the climate suited to assassination. My eyes wandered about the large room that reminded me of a library, and my mind wandered with it so that I missed a rather long and informal chat about football between my brother and Mayor Longo. The mayor knew everything about the new wave of Kirby High School stars, the Strazza brothers, Donnie Ensero, and Michael Gonski, and he talked about how he was going to get artificial turf for the new field, and how rough the old field was when Danny played.

'I liked it like that,' Danny Boy said. 'I liked the mud and the chuck-holes. That was football.'

'So what's up, man? You looking for a job – temp work, what?'

'No. I just wanted to talk to you about a matter that has to do with a matter, Mayor, a matter about my father's salvage business and about his junk license and what not.'

'I see. Shoot.'

Something dark swept across my brother's eyes when the mayor said that. I feared that his jacket would fall away to reveal the sawed-off *lupara*. But instead, he appealed to the mayor in a steady voice. 'Mayor,' he said, 'some guys from one of the state agencies are threatening to close down my father's business.'

'Close down the business?' Frankie Longo said, taking a sip of Coke. 'Motor Vehicle, you mean?'

Danny Boy nodded. The mayor stared at him for a very long time and he seemed to be distracted, maybe by the grease under my brother's thumbnail.

'They can be assholes, DMV,' he finally said. I felt a great breath come free, confident that the mayor was on our side. 'But they got to watch out for their jobs, too,' he said. 'My aldermen are breathing down their necks about stepping things up. You're aware of the city slogan we're using—'

'The Renaissance City,' I volunteered.

'Right. Your father's a smart man. He knows what he has to do to be a team player. I'm crazy about Big Dan. And your mother, too. Forget about it – they're salt of the earth.' When he said this, he looked at me. Not a long look, just a glance. Then he pushed a button on one of the two telephones he had on his desk and a secretary's nasal drone came across a speaker.

'Betty Boop,' he said playfully. 'We have any more of those hats?'

'Well,' Danny Boy said, and he was up, shaking the mayor's hand again; we were led to the door with our Cokes which neither one of us had ventured to open, and I felt proud of my brother. Betty met us there, holding a bright red ball cap. Mayor Longo took it from her, punched his hand into the crown, then fit it on my head. The cursive stitching across the front read *Saukiwog Mills, The Renaissance City.*

I felt my face blushing under the brim as Danny Boy stopped shy of the door. 'Mayor, I was hoping that you would – if you had the time . . .'

'What's that, Danny?'

'Well, I'm in a play.'

'You're in a what?'

'A play.'

'A play?'

'I was hoping that you would come to it, to opening night, because I've got a pretty good role—'

'Give Betty the dates,' he said, gently propelling my brother toward the door. But again my brother stopped, as if he was loath to step out from the air-conditioning and cool dark paneling. His eyes moved about the office, taking it all in.

'Mayor . . .'

'Yeah.'

'The business . . . it's only a salvage yard, but it's been in my family for sixty something years. If my father loses his license . . .'

'Your father's a smart man.'

'Thanks.'

'How's this guy in the play?' Mayor Longo said, looking at me with a wink. 'He a good actor?'

'He's great,' I said, trying to see the mayor from under the low brim of the cap.

'You should come see,' Danny Boy said. 'Half the city will be at that play. Everyone loves a murder mystery. They love trying to guess who's really behind the killing and what not. It's usually the last person they'd expect to be behind the murder of an innocent man.'

The image alone was enough to stop my heart like a cold battery: Narracott, coming out from Stage Right with a basket of lemon, tomatoes, cream and butter, to break into a monologue about corruption in City Hall and a dead man in a trunk.

'Is there something else we need to talk about, Danny?' the mayor said. He had dealt with all kinds of men and women, the mayor, and he knew how to look beyond words and handshakes.

'I don't know – is there?' Danny Boy said, holding his ground.

'Oh, yeah,' Mayor Longo said, closing the door and moving over to the big leather chair he had so far avoided for the sake of informality. Now, with a long sigh he sat in it and threw one leg over the other exposing a handsome mauve sock. It was his official mayor aspect and suddenly I didn't feel so comfortable anymore.

'One of two things is going on in this room, Dan,' he said. 'One: you really did get your nut rocked in that football game two years ago, or two' – he looked square at my brother with eyes as black and clear as obsidian – 'you've actually come here, into my office, to take a jab at this administration, or maybe me personally. Which is it, Danny? Be straight with me, man.'

'I'm not a loser, Mayor Longo,' said Danny Boy, and now Mayor Longo looked confused.

'I never implied that.'

'You told me if I ever needed anything, to come see you. All's I'm asking is you come see me in the play.'

'That's it?'

'That's all.'

'You're a funny kid, Danny. I can't promise, but I'll do everything I can to get there.' The mayor rose again and started for the door so we would follow.

'Excellent. Thanks, this is excellent,' Danny Boy said, and I was relieved by his return to politeness. 'But,' he said, 'if my father loses his junk license . . . the city is going to hear a monologue they'll never forget.'

I tried to squeeze through the door, but the mayor wedged it and looked pointblank at my brother. 'What's this?'

'Maybe I got no say, mayor. But for one night, I'm going to have the spotlight. So I really hope that you come see the show.'

'What do you got burning a hole in your pocket, Danny?' Mayor Longo did not seem as concerned as he did curious.

'I've got something,' my brother said, his final words before getting his hand through the door and prying enough to allow his little brother freedom. 'Trust me, I've got something.'

Mayor Longo was smiling the way he did on Public Access TV when he was challenged about police promotions or job training. 'What do you have? Come on, you're across the Rubicon, Danny. What do you have?'

My brother turned at the door and removed his hand from the pocket of his secondhand army jacket, and I flinched.

'I have *this*, Frank.'

He opened his fist and showed the mayor a piece of polished brass, handsomely crafted into an ersatz medieval key. 'Remember what you told me when you gave it to me? You said that now I got the key to the city I can come in any time I want, just don't stay out too late.'

I don't know if Mayor Longo remembered, but I did. It had made the crowd laugh and my brother blush back then. Now the mayor said nothing. He just stared into my brother's eyes, maintaining his smile and a puzzled bend at his brow.

'Leave the porchlight on for me, Frank,' Danny Boy said.

Mayor Longo was still smiling when he said, at a whisper, 'You've made some mistakes in the past, Danny. You can overcome them, get your shit together. But if you fuck with me, Danny, that's a mistake that you'll wish you never made. Because I know you're a good kid.'

'Thanks for the hat, Mayor Longo,' I said. Then I ran.

There was no one left in City Hall but a janitor, and we felt it best not to walk the length of the corridor, but to run. Like holy Hades we ran. We burst out the brass doors and high-stepped down the fifteen or twenty granite steps, not slowing until we were seated on warm velour and racing down Grand Street in the shadow of the Big Clock.

'No turning back now, Nunzi,' my brother said, breathless with his own daring. 'We're inside the Rubik's Cube.'

He meant across the Rubicon, but inside the Rubik's Cube, unfortunately, was not altogether off the mark.

Driving home from play rehearsal in a heavy rain, my brother was a keg of adrenaline. He went on about how, whether or not the mayor even knew it himself, he was in bed with Valle Construction and Testa Refuse who were no better than low-level mobsters. It was all the touching and turning of gears in a machine as well kept as Don Gustavo's espresso fountain.

'Asshole,' he said, feeling in the seat between us for the still unopened Coke, compliments of City Hall, and he popped it with his teeth, took a long swallow.

'Fucking dick wad,' he said in a carbonated hiss, wiping his mouth with the back of his sleeve. I was certain he was speaking of the mayor, but when he punched his horn and cursed into his side mirror, I heard the nasty drag of rubber and the roar of a big power plant behind us.

'Fucking Bozo trying to pass on Eat Street.'

In my side mirror, rain smear made the hood of the tailgating car look like a giant machine. I turned again, got a better look. It was a Camaro the color of a shark.

'Oh no,' I said.

There it was, the blue Connecticut license plate reading: TRI-CEPS.

'Who is it?' Danny asked.

His mirrors were fogged heavy, all he could see were high beams. But I could see the short, bullnecked figure behind the wheel and someone else, much larger, in the passenger seat wearing some kind of hat. 'Ray Beans,' I said.

Danny Boy stomped the gas pedal and shot through a red light, passing the little strip mall where Electric Jamaica blinked in neon and Desiree passed behind the front pane in her perky maneuvers, carrying folded towels. When we turned left, the Camaro turned left. When we pulled into Mike's Texaco, the Camaro waited for oncoming cars in the opposite lane then followed.

We kept driving, neither of us speaking.

Danny Boy got back up on the highway and tried to lose Ray Bonacascio in the fast lane, but the Camaro was playing the Oldsmobile like a cheetah letting an old antelope tire and drop.

Danny Boy got off the exit for the North End and spun a shortcut through the abandoned parking lot of United Brass then drove down a one-way street, rubbing at fogged glass with his palm, his elbow, his Samuel French playbook. We bucked rain puddles, ran a stop sign, almost struck a black child on a bicycle and kept going toward Goomba Angelo's.

Danny's instinct I understood, but the logic left me troubled. What could Angelo do? Send down his monkey?

We wouldn't even get a chance to find out. On the street that led to Dunn's Convalarium, a big early-model Cadillac was parked, blocking the way out. Danny Boy leaned on his horn and cursed, rolled down his window and gestured for the Caddie to move over. Instead, it notched up its high beams on us and the driver stepped out, walking toward us with a slight bounce in his step.

It was Uncas Fontenot, one of the Mattatuck Indians. He was wearing his Chess King Navajo print bathrobe belted over blue jeans and Adidas high-tops.

'Oh, Jesus,' Danny said. But when he attempted reverse, the Camaro was idling behind him and Ray Beans was already out, jogging through puddles to Danny's window while Reginald Whirlwind Fire Keeper crossed to my side to stand in arms with his fellow tribesman.

We were sandwiched, there in the dark of the North End, in the pouring rain. Uncas Fontenot pressed his face against my window so that his nose flattened like he was wearing a stocking over his head. He rapped on the glass, almost politely, but I jammed the doorlock down.

'*Goomba*!' Ray Beans yelled at my brother like he always did, but now it was sarcastic as he plunged his hand into the car and messed up Danny's hair like a schoolyard prankster. He eyed me for a moment as Uncas Fontenot and the War Chief remained at my window, getting soaked.

'Paradiso, you piece of shit,' he said to Danny. 'You won't leave it alone, will you? You won't leave Desiree alone. You're faukin' with the wrong people, man.'

Something dark pressed against my brother's head, right down on top where his black hair was parted. 'Ow!' he said, but when he tried to squirm, Ray slapped his chest, kept him in place.

'What are you doing?' Danny Boy said, shifting his eyes but unable to see the hard thing pressing against his scalp.

'He's got a gun!' I barked and Ray Beans made a little chortle sound.

'After I do you,' Ray said, 'I'm taking your little brother to the club and cut his fucking tongue out.'

'Leave my brother out of this.'

'Why? *You* don't,' Ray said. 'You send him all around town like your little fucking gopher.'

'No, Ray, come on, man, knock it off.' My brother said this as if some bully had him in a headlock at recess, and not as if he was about to have his head blown off, which he was.

'You don't show me any respect,' Ray said.

'Come on, Bonacascio, man . . .'

I felt myself crying but no sound came from me and I feared Danny Boy was going to make a move and Ray was going to pull the trigger, and that's when I noticed that Uncas Fontenot was holding what looked like a ball peen hammer at my window and was gesturing to me; if I didn't unlock the door, he was smashing glass.

Ray Beans did something terrifying then: with his face swollen from steroids and flushed with an insane rage and the rain matting his short hair on his forehead like a pint-sized Caesar, he closed his eyes as tight as he could and strained until large cable-like veins appeared at his temples and he yelled, '*Ciao*, asshole.'

Something popped at Danny's head.

It sounded like a two-by-four broken in half and my brother's head convulsed forward and his eyes rolled. Ray made a sound like a dog getting its foot stepped on as he buckled at the window, his right arm bent at an unnatural angle. The huge club came down again and struck him at his collarbone and I could hear someone screaming so shrill my ears rang.

'You little mother*fucker*!' somebody yelled. It was Johnny Mae Sisson, standing in the pouring rain in her maroon windbreaker, wielding an aluminum baseball bat, the handle wrapped in black tape.

Ray rolled over onto the wet sidewalk, clutching his arm which I could now see had been broken at the forearm. Uncas Fontenot came at the big black woman with his hammer and she met him with a swing of the club that would have sent a softball high over the rooftops and pigeon roosts of the North End. She must've broken the man's ribs because the hammer fell from a limp hand and he collapsed against my brother's car, working his fingers between the buttons of his shirt, unable to draw a breath.

Reginald Fire Keeper meanwhile, was running like a small jackal eastbound along a row of tenement houses, his duster feathers tailing behind his hat. Johnny poked the club into Uncas Fontenot's belly and said, 'Nigger: I ain't even mad yet.'

Danny Boy and I watched it all from the dry corduroy safety of the car. When Ray Beans collected his handgun and aimed it at Johnny, she cocked the club back and hovered over him like an Amazonian tempest. In the downpour and headlights, she appeared mythic; from my side of the rear windshield on this night in August, Thor was a black woman in a maroon windbreaker, yelling: 'Go ahead, Muscle Man!'

'You faukin' *zootzie*,' Ray said, using his regional slang but sounding impotent and pained and still utterly confused as to where the woman came from.

'Shoot me, you little wop. Shoot my ass, they tear you apart in this neighborhood, greaseball motherfucker.'

Johnny's voice jumped four octaves on the last four syllables and it left me trembling at the knees. When Ray looked up, we did, too, and we could see three or four dozen black people gathering in windows and on fire escapes, watching the whole event unfold.

'And if they don't get you,' she said as he considered his options, 'your *goombas* will. 'Cuz you makin' a scene, Motherfucker.'

The Cadillac roared away before we even knew Uncas Fontentot had racked into low and fled, and now Ray was hobbling, whimpering, toward his Camaro, clutching his gun in his weak left hand.

'You ever come near that boy again,' she screamed, 'I'll lay your muscle ass open. That boy study his *Bible*. He never hurt *nobody*. He know all about Lot Wife and Abraham. What *you* know?'

Here's what Ray Beans knew: he knew how to drive in reverse at 45 miles per hour and fishtail in the downpour, leaving us with the cab-driving diva who now looked like she was going to have heart failure. Some folks were applauding from on high, but she was too winded to take note. Some other black woman from a balcony above yelled, 'You go, colored woman!'

Leaning in my window and catching her breath, Johnny Mae gazed in at the two of us, rain beading on her crewcut and a long drop hanging at the end of her nose.

'You all okay?'

'Yeah,' Danny Boy said. 'Are you?'

Johnny kept sucking in wet air like she had run three football fields. 'I been trying to find you boys,' she said. 'I got good news and bad news. Good news be we getting closer to City Hall. Treasurer invested over a million dollar in city pension funds into the damned bingo parlor. On Longo's orders. It's right there in the public records.'

'What's the bad news?' Danny said.

'Get over to the Widow Diaz's house. *Now*.'

She was banging on the trunk of Danny's car and yelling in the rain, so my brother punched fuel and took us out of there. In the side mirror, I saw her standing there, hands on her hips, in her own neighborhood, people crowding her with questions.

Where Desiree Vega lived I didn't know, but I searched the clotheslines for tube tops and Gloria Vanderbilt jeans and black Danskins as we entered the dark streets of the South End. All I saw however, were green towels and pink socks and a lot of bedsheets. As Danny Boy sounded the horn at some children playing in the street puddles, I noticed that his hands were trembling. Bad news, Johnny had said. What were we headed into? Where was Angelo's game of Demon Chance leading us now?

'Look,' Danny Boy said at a whisper.

We were crossing the street to the Diazes' apartment, and there at the curb was a motorcycle covered by a green rain tarp. The TV was on inside the apartment and it sounded like the Spanish channel. Quietly, and in quick bounds, Danny Boy went up the steps. I climbed half of them and decided to wait at the rail. That's when Chilli-Dog appeared, walking around from the other side of the balcony porch. He froze when he saw us. We must have looked frozen, too.

Because Tino was covered in blood.

Shirtless, but wearing his studded black leather POW bracelet, he had blood spots down one arm and his opposite hand was wrapped around the handle of his 16-inch Randall knife with the serrated blade coated in red ooze.

My breath went in and never came out. I was stuck there on the seventh step while Danny Boy stood as still as Chilli-Dog, the two facing each other but saying nothing. Blood was dripping in slow droplets from his left hand, and that's when I saw the thing he held. It was an organ of some kind, a liver or kidney, maybe even a heart.

Who the hell was he hacking up, I wondered, as the feeling returned to my legs and I started slowly down the stairs.

'Jesus Christ,' Danny Boy said.

'Get the fuck out of here, Cub Scout,' Tino said, but he didn't have to. Danny Boy was overtaking me as we ran through the tiny lawn of the apartments, taking a desperate shortcut to where we parked over near the Spanish grocery store.

I looked back at the lit four-stories as we ran. I could see it from the backside now, relieved that no one was pursuing us.

But a strange sight on the Diazes balcony caught my eye. I grabbed my brother's shirt, slowing him. Tino was up there in the porchlight, his long hair pulled back in a ponytail as he ran his big blade down the underside of a white-tailed deer that was trussed and hanging upside down from the fire escape. It had one broken antler and its tongue was out of its mouth in a lewd roll of pink. The Widow Diaz was in the screen door looking out as her son dressed the animal and pulled out another organ to hold over the rail to a gathering of children who grinned at the incongruous sight.

Danny Boy slowly joined the clutch of Puerto Rican children and stood, looking up at the dead buck. The kids were all laughing and speaking in Spanish and I wished I could understand them. I looked at Danny Boy and he appeared intrigued by the sight. Chilli-Dog's eye caught us, he did a take, then leaned his big arms on the rail.

'You want to eat the balls?' he called down.

One of the young children laughed at this, so I knew he spoke English.

'Where'd he get a deer?' I asked, awed by the perverse sight: a deer being dressed on a fire escape in the South End. Though it should not have seemed improbable as we had many a dead buck brought home by the Italian hunters every September, taken in some upcountry wood. Nonni was a good one for venison in her sauce.

'Canada,' the boy said, still grinning up at the bloodied Tino. 'My uncle got it in Canada. He come home last night.'

Danny Boy looked down at the kid in the same instant that I looked up to see someone else on the porch: an old man bent over a card-table and wrapping cuts of meat in butcher's paper. When he stood to take the heart from Tino, I recognized the grayish face, the balding head. It was the man from the coffee cup, *The World's Greatest Poppi-Pop.*

Maximino Diaz was alive.

'Oh, my God,' my brother said, under his breath.

'Yeah, man,' said the kid. He toed something on the ground with his sneaker. 'That's the dick, right there. Tino throw down the dick.'

Tino was now speaking to his stepfather on the balcony and I could see the old man nearing the rail to look down. He was squinting hard right at us and Tino was pointing to my brother and still speaking in soft Spanish.

Mr Diaz removed some eyeglasses from a plastic case and put them on. He seemed to study us for a time. And then he said, in

English and not unkindly, 'Go home, you boys. Mind your own business.'

Desiree's yellow Detroit tuna boat was parked in front of the Saukiwog Mills Playhouse when we arrived, and she confirmed the sighting.

'I know,' Danny Boy said. 'We saw him.'

Talking with Desiree from out the passenger window, I had a better view of her than my brother. 'What the hell, man?' she said. Max had driven into the South End, just after midnight, she said, with a poached deer roped across the trunk of his Chevy and a host of teenagers running behind him like it was the Christmas *parrada*.

The word spread from window to porch, she said: Max Diaz was home. He had told his cousin who was one of the domino players and the story ran from house to house like it had sneakers on: the old builder spent nearly two months hunting and fishing and thinking, and he had considered putting the gun in his mouth once or twice. But he had come to realize many things, up there, in the big woods of New Brunswick. Shooting the deer and tracking it for fifteen miles before it died in a riverbed, made him look hard at life and its food chain.

He calls me, Mrs Diaz had said in the middle of the street that day. *He calls me every night*. Of course he called her, and it wasn't from the grave: standing at a pay phone at some gas station at the tip of Maine, his Spanish as foreign to the air up there as a flock of roseate spoonbills. He was coming home and he was selling the damned Rolling Mill to the big developers. Let them have it, he decided. Why cut off his nose to spite his face? Let the *gringo* wolves fight over the meat: he and his wife were taking the money and moving back to the Dominican Republic. All this, Desiree said, was spreading through the South End and the community cheered Max Diaz's decision. 'Take the money!' they yelled up at his porch from passing cars.

This disclosure pitched us from our foothold, and left us in a fair panic; we found ourselves yelling over each other, not listening to the other and getting nowhere. Danny jabbed his finger into my shoulder. He shoved me, even. Told me to stop panicking. But the panic was only beginning.

'What you been selling me?' Desiree asked my brother, hurt in her eyes. 'There was nobody in that trunk. Ray never killed nobody. You lied.'

Danny Boy didn't have a ready answer, but he looked fearful of losing Desiree. He also looked troubled by Mr A. Richard Pembroke who was now in the lot, squinting at the yellow land barge, curious and perhaps disturbed by the presence of the dark-skinned woman behind the wheel, smoking a clove cigarette and carrying on a heated riposte with his sacrifice character.

While we had been chasing car thieves through the sordid men's rooms of strip bars, digging through land permits, crying murder to a man's wife and son, hunting old men with reputed mob ties, and even rattling the doors of City Hall, Mr Diaz had been driving south on I-93 at thirty-five miles per hour with a dead deer splayed over the back of his Chevy.

Desiree started her car. She looked me in the eye for a moment as if searching deeper for something, something to hold onto. 'Why, Nunzio? Why you lie to me? There was nobody in that trunk.'

She stared hard at me, then dropped into reverse. Her big gas-guzzler throbbed out, muffler scraping on the pavement. Danny Boy watched her go, looking like he wanted to yell out to her. Alone, we watched what was left of her exhaust.

I had a question ripping at me, and I knew my brother did, too. We didn't need to say it, it was there, eye to eye: if Mr Diaz was packing deer meat into his freezer, safe and sound back in the South End, who, for the love of Columba, was in the trunk of the crushed Pontiac up on the Number 6 Liberty at the docks in Bridgeport, the one that would set sail in less than forty-eight hours?

Danny tossed me a handful of dimes and pennies then bailed, hurrying into The Playhouse. I knew what he wanted me to do. The pay phone out front was beginning to look like an old friend to me; I could recite all the graffiti and phone numbers for a free blow job as flawlessly as *The Chief Spiritual Works of Mercy*. I got Goomba Angelo after twenty rings and the sound of scraping as Ruby Lee brought the receiver to her charge's ear. By the ribald tone of his voice, I knew what I had to say was no longer hot news.

'Nunzio,' he said wistfully, 'I built my case around a dead spic. Now the cocksucker rises from the dead after forty days and goes home for coffee? If I could get out of this chair, I'd kill the bitch myself and *put* him in the trunk. *Vafangoolo.*'

'Goomba Ange—'

'We've uncovered a fucking sewer in City Hall – Longo's investing pension funds into this Indian palace and all the king's men are on the gravy train – we've uncovered a brass ring that goes from the mayor to the Mafia, but it was all built around a dead contractor who's alive and watching *My Three Sons* in Spañol. These guys are *insulated.* There's no evidence of a federal crime, and there's *nobody* in that Pontiac. Go home, kid. Go home and play Scrabble.'

'What are you going to do?'

'What, am I punching the clock over here?' Angelo said. 'What do you think I'm going to do? Tell the family I said *arrivederci Roma.*'

'Wait—'

The phone hit the floor, scraped, and several push buttons dialed before the line went dead.

August was coming through the rye, and somewhere a train was clacking between Hartford and Bridgeport, hoppers loaded with pig iron and zinc alloy. A lone maple at the end of Genoa Street held a slight blush, always the first tree to tell us football season was coming. The IGA had Indian corn displayed in the window, the old men were ordering their California grapes by the box and Nonni was beginning to bring more and more tomatoes in from the garden at night.

The name Max Diaz was in the Sunday *Republican*, in an article detailing the plans and struggles of the proposed Saukiwog Mills Bingo Hall development. He was happy to be in business with BCD and to see the Indians have their lands restored, to see the old factory turned into a bastion of Saukiwog Mills' future. He was never quoted directly, of course. It was always his lawyer, attributing words to the immigrant carpenter that made him sound like a Harvard Graduate. *Mr Diaz is delighted to be a pivotal factor in helping an Indian tribe utilize the capital markets to ensure their future while shaping the economic future of the one-time Brass Empire.*

A new hearing was scheduled, and when Mr Campobosso saw

my father at the hardware store downtown, he asked him to bring his 'little tiger of a wife' to the meeting. Dad issued an edict to my mother: she was to stand up at the next hearing and say something good about the Bingo Hall, something paraphrased in one of her little Scots ditties that seemed to have such a galvanizing effect on the city populace. Mom changed the subject whenever she could, or feigned immersion in her crossword puzzles. I began to see something disintegrate between them. Mom was no longer talking to her apron or tuning him out, but facing him now and showing her Lowland peat.

Danny Boy, meanwhile, was growing more despondent. Desiree was not returning his phone calls. And now when Danny saw Mayor Longo at Crocco's Market or driving his little Mazda down Highland, he ducked him, embarrassed. A real rain had come all right: it had come down with a cold front from New Brunswick, down hard on our parade.

Now, Danny Paradiso only wanted to use his key to the city to get out the back door.

THREE

Birds of Passage

Steerage Passenger No. 202 – Three-card Monte –
The Feast of Saint Donato –
– 6:10

CHAPTER TWENTY

Steerage Passenger No. 202

He was a man who had invented a thousand and one novel gizmos of mechanical genius but never filed for a patent. Maybe it was the little streak of anarchist in him, but he refused to trust his electric pasta-turning spoon or his egg-white separator to the government. Thomas Edison was a government man, he told me, and he had stolen the credit and rewards for machines invented by Tesla and his top student, Marconi. Nikola Tesla and Marconi had been to Mars, he claimed, but they kept their flying disc a secret. He understood why.

Grandpa invented things for himself to prove he could do it. He invented the paper clip before some Yankee in Waterbury got rich off the patent, and he was the father of the electric can opener before it became a popular kitchen gimmick. Granted, his can opener was gas-powered and resembled more of a small chainsaw, but I saw it take the lid off a large can of puréed tomatoes once (though they were whole tomatoes before his demonstration). His weed chopper had a few weak links in its construct, but overall, it was an admirable machine in the right hands.

But now, he had reached the pinnacle of his imagination and resourcefulness, and he felt tired. He had built his own automobile, plug by plug, with his own hands. What more could a man do in the automobile age than to create his own car. The *Proletario* was completed.

'The what?' my father said when he finally caught sight of Grandpa motoring around the tarpaper boundaries of the junkyard. But the old man didn't care. He finished it, and just in time. His legs were stiffening more and more each evening, and some mornings, he didn't arrive at the yard until after ten.

He had finished it.

And it was good.

And on the morning of 19 August, 1979, he set out to crown his *Proletario* with the capstone: the final touch. He had spotted the golden object of his desire, high up on a scrap metal butte in the far corner of the grounds. When I saw him at eleven that morning, he was beginning his ascent, using a pick ax to climb the mountain of junk. I volunteered my youthful bones, but he waved me off, saying I would upset my father who didn't know a great invention from a piece of cheese.

I saw him again, some time after lunch when he was nearly halfway up the pile resting on a torn bucket seat from an old Hudson and eating a peach he had carried in his pocket. Ledge by rusted ledge, he climbed, and an hour later he had gained considerable altitude. Dad spotted him from afar at one point and said, 'What's Sir Edmund Hillary doing over there?'

And then, just before five, as Dad was gathering his keys, he told me to go fetch Grandpa and tell him we were locking up. I had to stand back a dozen feet from the scrap mesa to get a decent view of the old inventor, and I spotted him up there in the jasmine sunspots of late afternoon. He was at the very top, an astonishing feat considering he was eighty years old and the pile just over one hundred feet high. Passers-by on the low road outside could see an old man in a tattered sombrero, high above the junkyard fence if they were so inclined to study junk heaps as they passed.

'Grandpa!' I called, but he was high out of earshot.

The climb that took Grandpa most of the day, took me less than five minutes. I went up like a squirrel, grabbing a discarded generator here, a transmission housing there. I pocketed a trinket or two on the way and used a discarded fanbelt to rappel down to a foothold on a rusted drive-shaft, and scrabble up from an easier angle.

'Cool, Grandpa,' I said when I reached him and saw the prize in his grip. It was a bowling trophy done in the pedestrian style of the early 1950s. A brass figure with a brass bowling ball in its hand, stepping up to the lane. Imagining the figure on the hood of a car made me smile. Only Grandpa could choose something like that for a hood ornament.

'You okay, Gramps?' I said. But he didn't hear me. 'Can you get down?' I said.

Again, he remained silent, stretched over the peak of the scrap pile, the bowling trophy in his right hand, his left gripping the door handle of an old tailgate. I crawled to his other side to get his ear, and now I could hear my father doing his two-pinkied whistle somewhere down below. Grandpa was gazing out over the salvage yard and I expected him to say, in his soft broken English, 'No kill yourself, Nunzio. Go nice and easy. Rest a little.' But he said no such thing. I touched his back and it felt soft, his flannel shirt warm from the sun. Letting myself drop to an elbow, I looked closer at his face.

'Hey, Grandpa, come on.'

I looked into his eyes and found them flat. Something in my body lurched, a flood of adrenaline. I knew my grandfather was dead. I had to get to my feet and yell, but I couldn't. I touched his warm shirt again, hoping for a pulse. I felt a strange anger inside. Why couldn't he have just sat home in his easy chair and watched TV like other old men who have done all they could in life? Who would bury his fig tree when winter came? Who would unearth it in spring?

'Dad,' I tried to yell it out, but there was no sound to carry it. Nor did there need to be. When I looked down, my father and Danny Boy were standing near The Crusher, shielding their eyes from the late-day August glare and looking up. They saw Grandpa's still torso frozen at the peak like Ira Hayes and the flag. They saw the tears streaking grease on my face, running down my cheek like wet ashes.

My father and brother grabbed at the scrap pile and went up side by side. When they reached the top, they looked at Grandpa. My hand was still on his back, and I was rubbing it, like I used to do on Sundays after dinner to help him digest.

'Balls,' my father cursed, as if only his truck broke down, or he had dropped a wrench into an engine compartment. 'Balls.' But I knew what this was covering; I saw it in his eyes as he climbed to his father's side. The three of us sat on that scrap tower just looking at Grandpa's rigid legs. Danny Boy moved the hard scrap from under Grandpa's ear and removed the sombrero. He lay our grandfather's head in his lap as if to protect it.

'Danny,' my father said. He didn't say Pop, or Nunzio. He didn't even say Jesus or *Dio*.

'Danny,' he said again, and my brother looked at him, unsure of what to do. My brother reached for him. Big Dan seemed to be numb with shock, and Danny Boy gently took him in his arms and held him, nearly causing the two to slide down the pile. I grabbed my father, too – more to keep him and Danny from falling than anything else – and the three of us sat on that pile of junk near Grandpa's still body, not even aware that the sun had dropped behind the fence and a light rain was beginning to fall, making oil-slick rainbows.

Grandpa would have nodded in approval at the manner in which his body was taken down from the crest of the scrap mountain. It was just his kind of resourceful planning. Danny Boy gently rolled the old man onto the detached hood of a sedan, and Dad used the Caterpillar forks to gingerly lift his father's body, inch by careful inch, off the pile and safely to the ground. I could almost hear Grandpa giving the instructions as my father sat high on the machine, fixed on doing the job right.

We would wait for Mr Egger from the funeral parlor before we made the dreadful journey home to face Nonni. I did not want to see Mr Egger and his son, Junior Egger, put my grandfather into a green plastic bag and zipper it. When they came through the gate in their red El Camino, I ran toward the back of the yard, holding the bowling trophy in both hands. It was the last thing Grandpa touched and I didn't want to let it go. I took it to Area 51, went into the shed and sat in the old man's lawn chair. The trophy, a small brass plate said, was awarded to the Portuguese Scovillites, an ethnic bowling team from Scovill Brass in nearby Waterbury, presented by the Brassworkers Local 569.

It seemed absurd.

But perfect just the same. I could have sat there and cried like my insides wanted to, but it seemed useless, sitting there, surrounded by Grandpa's inventions. And so I did what seemed like the only appropriate thing to do: I donned Grandpa's welding helmet, opened the acetylene valve and began to weld the Portuguese Scovillites' bowling trophy to the hood of the *Proletario*. Sparks danced and smoke choked the shed, and I lost myself in the task, knowing full well that Grandpa was already in that green plastic bag being laid in the back of the Eggers' El Camino.

I finished the job.

Grandpa was waked, in the Italian tradition, for forty-eight hours, most of which rained so hard, The Little Boot gardens resembled beds of wet coffee grounds, and small frogs came out in droves.

Mayor Longo had let it be known he was coming to our house after the funeral to offer condolences. This disturbed Danny Boy. The house would grow quiet with respect, he predicted, and Nonni would smile through her tears, clutching the mayor's hand, savoring the sympathy from the dignitary. Grandpa's eighty years, my brother said, would be plowed beneath Mayor Frankie's ten minutes in the kitchen. Me, I was ambivalent about the mayor's promise. How many mayors of a city came to console the relatives of a former millhand and salvage broker? It was hard to find fault with this act of respect no matter what other suspicions we had about our city leader.

'Then,' Danny Boy complained, 'they'll be fighting over who gets Grandpa's sausage grinder in the morning. And his Buick.'

So when Danny left the cemetery, I went with him, deciding it best to avoid a *bocci* ball war or a tense moment with Mayor Longo sitting on our sofa, sipping Sanka. We drove across Genoa Street and down the steep decline leading toward the corner where the Lithuanian section began to mix with Italian. Danny Boy pulled over, staring into the lit window of Yolanda's little house where she ran her Hair Salon and Consignment Shop. An electric bug zapper flickered blue on her porch. 'I'll be right back,' he said.

Yolanda came to the screendoor. She was in a blue sweatsuit and towering white turban and she appeared a touch embarrassed because she was washing her hair, she said. She stepped out onto her porch and looked past my brother, squinting at me in the car.

'Danny . . .' she said, and then I heard her say something about Grandpa and how sorry she was.

'Yolanda, I need to see you. I know it's late . . .'

Yolanda looked at him and I saw her weakness for his eyes. She told Cousin Lena once while she was rummaging through the consignment shop that when she looked at Danny's eyes she felt a need to have his babies. This was related, and highly enjoyed, at dinner one Sunday, to which my father had said, 'She's a desperate woman, that Perugini woman.'

Dad may have had a point; Yolanda let my brother into her house with a kind of urgency, locking the door behind her. All I could figure was that Danny Boy, in his despondent state, needed a woman like Yolanda. A motherly type who would hold him, let him cry, maybe have sex with him, do his laundry, and send him home with a tray of lasagna.

But he came back out so quickly, I had little time to speculate. And when he stepped out on the porch, his mission became clear. Indeed, he held a foil tray covered with more foil on top and bearing all the signs of a homemade lasagna, but Danny Boy had gone in for a haircut. His normal styling would have taken an hour with a blow dry; this was a simple cut, shaved on each side with a long dark tuft remaining in the center. A shocking haircut, that's what it was.

A mohawk.

CHAPTER TWENTY-ONE
Three-card Monte

The exit that took us along the Sound was nearly flooded, but Danny punched gas, set his jaw and took us through. I sat quiet as we went up the streets into the residential neigborhoods, toward Guy Valle's dark little lane.

'Why we going to the Padrone's?' I said.

My brother ignored me, his mind far off as he drove slowly past the house once. He backed up in a neighbor's drive then coursed by again, and now we saw someone cross the lit window, looking out. On the third, slow pass, we heard the piano. And then light washed the driveway, spreading wider as the garage door went up. The little Bolivian housekeeper was leaving for the night, carrying her bulky purse and a small grocery bag overloaded with corn. Her face was set stern like before.

Danny Boy sped up, but the woman lifted a hand to us – and I ducked – but she never looked again, kept walking toward the sidewalk and away. She was just giving a cursory wave to a neighbor she didn't know. We pulled over at the curb, just beyond the brick ranch. Danny shut the car down. He seemed afraid to remove his hands from the wheel, but after a breath, he did, leaving the key in the ignition.

'Ray isn't gonna own her no more,' he said.

'What do you mean?'

'He's getting a notice from the electric company. His power's about to be shut off.'

'Danny,' I said, but he was out and at the trunk, lifting it and removing a dirty blue towel.

'Hey,' a voice said from the shrubs, and I saw my brother step back, nervous.

There was a man standing at the curb, holding a large green trashbag in one hand and a Budweiser beer in the other. He was shamelessly shirtless for a fat man, and he wore Bermuda shorts and sandals. His presence – safe, suburban and dough-bellied – put me at ease even as he grumbled about Danny parking in front of the trash.

'When's the garbage man come?' Danny asked.

'Four-thirty. In the morning. This car better be out of here, Chief.'

'It will be.'

'Where you going?' the man asked. He was now looking in at me as if searching for some sign of young mischief.

'Where am I going?' Danny stammered.

'Yeah. Where you going that you got to park here. In front of my trash cans.'

'I'm going to see Mr Valle.'

The man looked at Danny Boy. He took a swallow of cold beer. That's when I noticed that Danny was holding the tray of lasagna that Yolanda gave him, and he pointed his chin at it as if this explained his visit.

'Oh, right. Valle,' the man finally said. He secured a lid on a plastic drum and watched Danny Boy walk down the curb, the short towel-wrapped object under an arm like a loaf of bread.

'Hey, Chief,' the guy said, smiling now. 'He's a nice old guy, sends over more tomatoes and squash than we can eat. But do me a favor. Ask him if he can play anything other than Verdi or Bellini.'

'Sure,' Danny Boy said.

'And tell him that his dog's been crapping in my yard again.'

Danny Boy walked off.

'Hey, Chief,' the man called out again; he was becoming a thorn. 'No, don't tell him that.'

'About the dog shit or the piano?'

'Neither. Don't tell him what I said about the dog shit, or the piano. Just tell him Chicky the Polack said thanks again for the squash.'

The man winked at me, pleased with himself, and he carried his large belly down his driveway and into his garage which was indeed brimming with produce. When he racked the overhead closed, I whirled in the frontseat, trying to catch sight of my brother.

Inside, the piano was going with passion, left hand running up the bass keys, right hand tinkling down. Oh, *God*. I wondered if Danny knocked or rang the bell. I couldn't see the house through the shrubs. Over the piano now, I could hear a dog barking. My brother was in the house, I knew he was. With a gun wrapped in a towel, he was in the house. The dog stopped barking. But some others were barking now from across the street.

I studied the bushes, listening. The old man was still playing. There was still time to reach Danny Boy. I went out the driver's door and through the shrubs, running across Guy Valle's manicured front lawn. The piano was building to the final refrain and it was so loud I almost sympathized with Chicky the Polack next door. A side porch entrance was open, the aluminum screendoor still slightly ajar. I went up the steps, hesitated on the porch – changed my mind and ran back down – then decided I was committed, and I went back up, saying the name St Anthony four times.

Then I was in.

My heart drubbed when I saw the doberman standing in the kitchen. It was the size of a small horse, its tail bobbed, body long and whippet-like. It stared at me, curled back its lip, then plunged its head back down into the tray that Danny Boy had obviously set on the floor. It was not lasagna, it was *manicotti* and the doberman didn't mind at all. When I took another step in, the dog growled, but it was only in defense of its heaping gift of ricotta and red sauce.

I gave him a berth, moved past him. The house smelled like wax fruit and cleaning compounds. The kitchen was lit, but the living room was dim, drawing its light from a hallway. The baby grand was being played with an almost religious passion, and Danny Boy stood over it, in the corner, his legs rigid as he aimed the sawed-off shotgun. The towel was wrapped around both the stock and his hand as a sound muffler. Guy Valle must have been so engrossed in his music, he didn't notice the improbable assassin standing over him. Or he played with his eyes closed; or he didn't care and chose to keep playing in the face of death. For a second, I wondered if it was this simple for De Niro to kill Fanucci in his own home.

The old Padrone kept playing, banging the keys until the low sustaining rumble of the bass notes brought the song to a dramatic close; one last key, the very last deep and dissonant ivory. But it hung in the air, stayed there.

'Son of a bitch,' Danny said.

'No,' I called out. 'Don't do it, Danny.'

I entered the living room. Danny Boy looked over his shoulder at me. He lowered the gun and turned slightly.

There was no one at the piano.

And no sound now but for the sloppy chomping of *manicotti* from the kitchen. Slowly, I edged forward, as if on broken glass and I looked at the floor under the big walnut grand to see if the Padrone was laying there in a dark pool.

He was not. And there was something ghostly about the living room. The sofa and chairs, and even an ottoman, were draped in clean white bedsheets. The carpet had been vacuumed so frequently and so hard, it was grooved with Hoover tracks and smelled like pet-stain remover. The plants – and there were close to a dozen – were all lush and well-watered.

'Son of a *bitch*,' Danny Boy said again as if overcome by a revelation.

I stepped up beside him and looked at the piano. It was a restored antique with a burl walnut case and embossed gold letters across the face reading: *Pianola – Savin Rock Amusement Park, 1928*. The music roll that had been scrolling read *La Traviata*. Beside the rolls was a coin mechanism and a small carved lion face. Danny Boy and I stood in the slipstream of our breath. I reached in my pocket and removed the small brass token I had been carrying all summer. Moving slowly, so my hands didn't quake and lose the coin, I fit the rim of the slug into the slot, looked up at Danny, and let it go.

It made a primitive mechanical sound as it dropped down and in, triggering a thousand intricate little parts. Nothing happened for a moment. Then the piano keys began to move like devil's magic and Danny Boy and I started our progress backward, toward the kitchen as that familiar haunting aria filled the little house; the scroll turned, the words appeared on the music roll: *La Forza del Destino*. It was a dark, sad music, growing sadder still, as we backed across a large section of heavy plastic that was stapled over bare oak where a section of carpet had been neatly trimmed away.

'He hasn't been here in months,' Danny said.

'Where is he?'

Danny moved slowly toward the kitchen, his eyes still on the player piano. 'He's on a cruise,' he said.

Minutes later we were driving for Port Jefferson, the two of us silent. Danny fishtailed up near the watch gate where the same security guard sat in his little nest. We looked for the big barge sitting in the turbid saltwater but couldn't spot it behind others. Danny Boy got out and looked across the roof of his car, searching.

'Too late, pal,' the guard said, self-pleased.

Danny Boy searched the quiet waters of Long Island Sound. I watched him standing there, eyes off across the water where a summer haze lay after the heavy rain. 'How's destiny look to you now, Mr Valle?' he said. And then, taking one last look before pulling away from the docks, he held his face in the open window, inhaled the scent of motor oil and saltwater and said, 'Sayonara, Motherfucker.'

'Angelo,' Danny said into the pay phone, 'stop yelling.'

We were at the Meritt gas station, halfway home, me at the self-serve tanks, pumping regular into the Cutlass, Danny Boy a few feet away at the phone.

'Ange,' he hissed, 'stop, Ange – listen. I've got a nucleur fucking shit bomb to drop.'

He had to yell at Goomba Angelo a few times to get a word in. 'Angelo, shut the hell up and listen to me. Guy Valle. Yeah, Ange – I know who he is. Ange, would you shut the—' Danny Boy raised the phone like it was a hammer and said, with disgust, 'He's cocked.'

He struck the receiver against the metal booth and let it fall, dangling on its cord, then hurried off to pay for the gas. I lingered by the car for a moment then grabbed the phone.

'*Goomba?*'

'The fuck's *this*?' he yelled too loud into the phone.

'Me, Nunzio.'

'Tell your brother to go back to High School.'

'We're coming to see you. We need to talk to you.'

'You better, Numb Nuts. I've got the funnel. I saw my pigeons.'

'What's this?'

'I know how they're getting the money into City Hall. They're going to feast on the day of the Feast, *capisce*?'

It sounded as if the phone fell to the floor; I could hear Ruby Lee scraping about and Angelo cursing her in language not even a monkey deserved.

Then the line went dead.

The peace cross at Holy Hill USA was glowing azure over the city when we returned on the interstate at a broken speed limit. The feral dogs were making a rumpus up in the Gaza Strip and South End dogs were howling back. At Dunn's Convalarium and Assisted Living Complex, the windows – some lit, some unlit – made a vertical checkerboard that suggested disorder. Some people slept, some were up watching TV, some paced and banged their heads on sheet rock, but there was no certain rhythm to the place.

Me and Danny Boy moved quickly over the soiled carpet of the fourth-floor corridor, hurrying our steps when we heard Johnny yelling. At least there was a tempo to Goomba Angelo's apartment: Johnny came, the two yelled at each other, and Johnny went again. But now it sounded like she had the upperhand, screaming, 'You motherfucker, you dumb-ass motherfucker.'

Somebody next door yelled back in Spanish.

'Cuckoos' nest,' Danny mumbled to himself.

The door was ajar and Danny pushed his way in, me in tow. Inside, Johnny was making a falsetto sound like she was treating the fourth floor to a little Minnie Ripperton. Chaos was laying in wait for us, I knew it.

The black chanteuse was standing over Angelo near the window, and he was giving her his shining eye stare to taunt her as she wailed at him. She must've heard us come in because she wheeled, her voice still climbing high. But she wasn't singing. She wasn't complaining. She was crying. In a kind of stunned terror, she was crying, her eyes welling, a little mascara on her strong bones. 'The dumb ass mother*fucker*,' she said, so high-pitched she could have shattered crystal if Angelo had any.

Angelo sat in his chair, eyes fixed on the wall opposite, his tongue showing just a little at his bottom lip like he had lost his grip on a

Judge's Cave. One of his straight front teeth looked broken, and behind him, on the window, there was a wet spritz the color of clay. On his wheelchair tray was a tableau of Bicycle playing cards, sticky with spilled alcohol.

'Oh, Jesus,' Danny Boy said.

Ruby was huddled in a corner, trembling like a chided dog. On the floor, between Ruby and the wheelchair, Angelo's .38 Chief Special lay in loose cat litter. 'He done it,' Johnny said. 'My Angel, he gone and done it.'

The floor came up fast, struck my knees. I wanted to vomit but my belly was empty.

'*Jesus*,' Danny said again. And again. I could not look at Angelo, keeping my eyes on the monkey who was in near seizure in the corner, unkempt and panting like a cat with heat stroke. She peered up at me, blinking nervously, and I took her gently in my arms to compose her. But she would not be consoled. Her torso was knotted, small velvety hands curled in at her belly as if the back-kick from the handgun bruised her, or simply frightened her into a spasm. Turning her gently in my arms, I saw that she was clutching something crimped against her belly.

When she climbed to my shoulder, two Bicycle playing cards fell from her tiny hands. I gathered them and realized there was a third stuck to the spade: a three of spades, an eight of diamonds and the King of hearts. *What was Ruby doing with the cards if she had been squeezing the trigger on a handgun?* Was she dealing out Napoleon or three-card Monte when someone entered the apartment and stood over the drunken Angelo, knowing that he had talked to his pigeons?

Johnny was making pained falsetto sounds from her throat, her big shoulders heaving as a procession of people came in and out: several paramedics, a police officer, and a woman wearing a plastic rain hat who announced herself as Mrs Moynihan. She had a small cat carrier with her and Ruby Lee did not hesitate to climb into it.

It may have been minutes or an hour, I was too stunned to follow time, but me and Danny eventually found ourselves alone in the apartment. Paramedics had covered Angelo with an old army blanket and wheeled him out with Johnny wailing behind.

'Jesus, why?' my brother whispered. He was staring from a hard angle at the wet blood on the glass. 'Why'd he do it? What did he have, what did he find out, made him want to do this?'

'He saw his pigeons,' I said. 'He found the funnel. Said that they were going to feast on the day of the feast.'

'The feast? What else did he say to you?'

'He said that . . . he said to tell you that you should go back to fucking High School.'

'He had to get one in, didn't he?' Danny Boy looked at me, saw the cards in my hand.

'He was playing three-card Monte.' I disarranged the cards, fanned them. 'Ruby had these in her hands – so how could she have been holding a gun?

Danny Boy reached for the cards, looked them over. 'A three, an eight and the King of hearts.'

'What was he trying to tell us?'

'A three and an eight. .38? And the Hara-Kiri king.' He handed the high card back to me, the King putting his own sword through his head, the suicide king.

'He was telling us goodbye,' Danny said.

CHAPTER TWENTY-TWO

The Feast of Saint Donato

'Ain't that just like my Cousin Angelo,' Dad said, dunking a Stella D'oro in his warm milk and sugar. 'He shoots himself in the nut on the night of my father's funeral.'

Dawn was on us and Big Dan had the obituary page spread under his breakfast. He was livid. 'That's just like him. He knew the whole family would be looking in the obituaries, and so he puts himself in there, his picture – look at him. In his cop uniform. That's his way of giving my mother high blood pressure.'

'Dan,' Mom said, setting out the orange juice. 'That'd be taking spite a wee bit up the brae, don't you think?'

On the obituary page, there was the picture of Angelo Volpe after graduating from the academy; I had only seen the shot in Nonni's album from the shoulders down. He had been a young man then, with that hair-tonic look men in their early twenties have, like they haven't grown all the way into their big ears yet. But there he was. Angie, the cop.

'Look what it says here, Nancy. "No surviving relatives." Thank God.'

Dad pondered this then noticed that I was sullen over my cereal. Danny Boy was not yet at the table.

'He drink last night? Danny, he get loaded?'

'No.'

'I've got some good news for him,' Big Dan said, turning to the Sports page.

'Dad,' I said. 'Angelo was a good cop.'

'Sure,' Dad said. 'Let's make a saint out of him now that he's gone.'

'Let Nunzi believe in the good,' Mom said.

'Like my father, they'll make a saint out of him. That's how people are.'

'That's right,' Mom said. 'Guid willie, that's how people are.'

'I'm not trying to be sacrilegious, Nancy. I'm just saying, people die and all of a sudden they want to put a shrine up at Holy Hill.'

'God, I hope not,' I said. 'They'll end up under the new Mall.'

'They should call a spade a spade – that's all I'm saying.'

'So on Goomba Angelo's headstone they should put what, Dad? "Here lays a crooked cop who dragged a dead girl out in the parking lot"?'

'Why not? Why put a goddamned poem by Robert Frost on there?'

Mom and I stared at Dad as he dunked another anisette cookie in warm milk.

'Where's Danny Boy? We've got a surprise for him,' Mom said, hoping to lift the clouds from the kitchen table.

'We're working half a day today, 'Dad said. 'It's the feast. You don't have to go.'

'I want to go,' I said.

'Why?'

'I'm Italian.'

Dad stared at me, and when he saw that I meant it, his eyes warmed a little. He looked back down at the paper. 'I never heard you say that before, Nunzio. Why now?'

I didn't know how to explain it myself, but I no longer wished my name was Douglas Spalding or James West. Danny Boy came out of the bathroom wearing a red head-rag and his black sleeveless T-shirt. There was a quiet air about him, like a man playing poker and parceling his energies. He traded my mother a kiss good morning for a tall Tang.

'You should've been here last night,' Dad said. 'The mayor showed up.'

'So I hear.'

'He stayed two hours, ate the *maccherone* with us. Guess what he says? He says that the towing service under the city contract, Johnny's Garage, is getting terminated. He wants to give us the contract. City contract to impound cars and what not.'

'He's all compassion, isn't he?' Danny said, tinder-dry.

'I'll put you on the buffalo hunts. You'll run the towing for the city. For Saukiwog, Danny.'

'The mayor can take his patronage job and cram it.'

Big Dan looked up from the paper, not sure he heard right. 'What's this?'

'Longo's a crook, Dad. He and Campobosso and his aldermen are taking pay-offs from the S and L to okay building projects for Carmella. And Carmella's giving the contracts to construction and demolition companies that are tied to the Bridgeport Mob.'

I had a mouthful of toast, but it wasn't going anywhere. Mom was rapt, too, standing in the kitchen with a pitcher of Tang.

'What the *hell* are you talking about, kid?' Dad said.

'And what are *we*, Dad? The Beachcombers? The guys who salvage shipwrecks?'

'I'm asking you a question, Danny.'

'We the clean-up crew?'

'Who was that at the wake with you? Was that the Puerto Rican? I'm asking you.'

'I'm asking *you*: are we the clean-up crew?'

'You're talking about aldermen and what not. What'd you do, meet a topless politician down the Thirsty Turtle? Get that *mopine* off your head.'

Danny Boy unveiled his mohawk. It appeared lewd under the ceiling lamp. I was running, but I heard my mother say, '*Och, dear Columba*,' and I heard Big Dan's spoon hit a plate hard. And I heard Danny Boy get up and say, 'Let's go to the feast. I'll lead the parade.'

'That's it,' Dad said. He pushed his chair out, stood tall and said, 'Hook her up.'

Saukiwog hosted several Italian festivals during the summer; each of them, the Festa di San Donato being no exception, became official with the opening ceremony. In years past, it was morning Mass and then the blessing of the statue, and then Lou Napolitano-Massi singing 'Return to Me'. But this year, the day would begin with a ritual of another kind: the offering of an Oldsmobile Cutlass to the rusted, albeit insatiable, Crusher.

Danny Boy, wearing his head-rag, sat on a short stack of tires, arms folded watching as Dad air-gunned the tires off, and I rummaged inside salvaging what I could: the jar with my brother's bottled affliction, the Bell & Howell Super 8, and the towel-wrapped gun from under the seat. I stowed them in Grandpa's shed then returned to watch Danny's car go through. When it came out the back end, another flattened car to commemorate Danny's trespasses, I stood near my brother and set a sympathetic hand on his arm. Dad shut down the machine and his giant Caterpillar, and sat there for a moment, looking down at Danny Boy.

'I hope you like walking to Hollywood, Pacino,' he said, but I was certain he meant De Niro. 'Because you can't even hitch-hike with a haircut like that. You look like an escapee from Southbury.'

Danny Boy walked off toward the tire bunker and I watched Dad collect the crushed Cutlass on the big Caterpillar forks and drive it around back. I followed and saw him set the flattened vehicle beside Danny's others. He shut down the payloader and sat, high on the seat, elbows resting on the wheel. He didn't see me watching him; he sat in silence, back there along the south fence.

'Dad,' I said. 'I'm sorry.'

My father didn't look my way. 'What are you sorry for?'

'I'm sorry for ever opening that trunk.'

I couldn't tell if he was looking down at me now, or looking away; he was a shadow in sunspots, sitting high on his two-pronged Caterpillar. But the silence told me he was ruminating on what I had just said. 'Nunzio,' he finally spoke, sounding tired. 'We did what we set out to do, didn't we? We made a man out of you. I only wanted what was best for you, Nunzio.'

'Dad,' I said, not sure if I'd ever be able to get the words out. 'Cousin Tina talks all the time about first generation and third generation and all that, and I never understood what she was saying.'

'College girl,' Dad said.

'But I understand it now. Grandpa got to dream. He got to dream about going to the New Country. Danny gets to dream. So do I. But you . . .'

My father was looking at me now, his brow knitted.

'You got stuck holding the bag.'

'Maybe,' Dad said, quietly.

'Grandpa loved you, Dad.'

'What's this?'

'He couldn't say it. Not to you. I think he told me because he knew he was going to die soon, and he wanted me to know. He said it, Dad. I promise you he said it. He said it in Italian, but I understood it.'

My father looked horrified for a moment. Not by what I said, but by what he felt his face doing. He took in a breath but it didn't come back out. 'I think I'm gonna have to miss the feast this year,' Dad said. 'Got a lot of work to do.'

'Three-card Monte,' Danny Boy said. He had sought me out in a deep alley between used tires. 'Let me see them cards again.'

I pulled them from the back pocket of my jeans, King up. Danny Boy took them, planted a boot on a fat radial and fanned them across his knee. 'Three, Eight, King,' he said.

'Suicide King.'

'Go back to High School,' Danny said, remembering Angelo's last words, and then he dealt out the Bicycle cards in a new order. Eight, three, King.

'So you think he was playing Pyramid?'

'No, you dumb shit. Eight, three, King. Eighty-three King.'

'Eighty-three King?'

'Go back to High School. 83 King Street – that's my old school. That's the old Kirby High building. That's where Carmella leases three floors of office space from the city.'

'Holy shit.'

'Yeah, holy shit.'

'They're going to feast, Angelo said. On the day of the feast.'

Danny Boy looked out toward the Big Clock tower. It was twenty minutes after eleven. He broke into a jog but stopped halfway down the rubber alley, regarding his crushed Cutlass.

I looked at the square block that was once a cream puff; we had no way out.

Then I saw something flint up in my brother's lampblack eyes. He had me by the sleeve and he was running again, and I was running with him.

*   *   *

It came alive with the over-tuned idle of a lawnmower and filled the shed with a harsh black smoke. Danny was behind the wheel, me beside him, and I showed him how to use the old 1950's push buttons to power the booster.

The *Proletario* rolled out of the shed, and Danny Boy seemed startled by the sheer power of the hotchpotch machine. Each time he kicked the accelerator, the car bulleted forward with such velocity, he seemed compelled to slam on the brake which emitted a train-like *whish-shuh* from somewhere in the undercarriage.

Dad was crossing the yard on foot, carrying a rim in each hand. He stopped when he heard the roaring, and then he jogged out of the way when his father's backyard invention surged past, its wheels pulverizing the earth. Instinctively, I dropped to the floor to hide. Danny had no such luxury; he had to hold fast to the wheel just to contain the finned machine that took to the paved road out and went from 0 to 60 in four seconds. I heard Dad's shrill, two-pinkied whistle way behind us, but there was nothing that could stop the car. It was making its maiden voyage at the hands of Donato Paradiso's grandsons.

Four hundred horses thundered out the gate.

On Route 8, we overtook some thirty vehicles before I even climbed back up in my seat. Danny Boy, no longer terrified, broke a nervous smile as he pushed the overdrive button. 'Man Oh-Manicotti,' he said as he cut the wheel to make the exit toward the center of Saukiwog. 'This thing's got *balls*.'

I wondered what the woman in the red Chevette at the light thought when she looked in her rearview and saw a finned tank with a bowling trophy on the hood, coming up fast, and with the sound of three Firebirds. She ran the light, and we jumped it with her, past her – she was screaming, and Danny tried to yell, 'Sorry!' as he pumped the Russian tractor clutch and tried to downshift.

Inside ten minutes, we were pulling up with a loud throb at 83 King Street.

The old building, a four-story, Art Moderne monolith of brick, sat high and remote behind fieldstone walls and dead vines. It would always be Kirby High to my brother.

To me, it appeared another ghost site in the same pantheon with the defunct drive-in, the holy shrine, and the old rolling mills. The football field was overgrown and in disrepair, too, but I found my brother staring at it as he rolled slowly past. I had to look at it, too; I hadn't since the day Danny lay unconscious at the thirty-yard line. Maybe Danny Boy's lost spirit jogged after us a block and hopped in the backseat, but Danny Boy's eyes appeared sharp and focused. He looked like the Junkyard Dog again as he parked in the school's breezeway and bailed.

He knew the front doors would be locked so he led me over a cement wall and to a first-floor window. Watching him shove the double hung down an inch, I realized he had done this in years past, maybe trying to sneak back in for sixth period. He slipped a hand in, turned the lock then opened the lower window high. We moved through the halls and upstairs, my brother going with a kind of quick-footed second nature. Only now, he was carrying an object wrapped in a blue towel and there was much more at stake than detention. The stairwells smelled like old chalkboards and damp asbestos, the scent getting stronger the higher we ascended.

When we reached the fourth-floor landing, Danny peered through the small pane on the door that kept us from Mr Carmella's rented office space. I envisioned his secretaries and accountants sitting at undersized school desks, doing their work while Mr Butterscotch Sunday stood at the blackboard with a wedge of chalk, drawing foundation plans for the Indian Bingo Palace.

'It's locked,' Danny whispered.

'Can we pick it or something?'

'No. This place was like Alcatraz.' He rested against the massive door for a moment, calculating, then he broke into a hurried descent back down to the third floor, me in tow. We ran the length of the hall until Dannny was skidding on his army boots to make the turn into a small janitor's room and up a narrow flight of stairs. We came out in another custodial room in the center of a long dark corridor, and when we crept out, Danny's steel-shanks went right through the fourth floor.

Water was dripping at a steady measure from the ceiling overhead and the corridor flooring was so water damaged that the linoleum had been torn away leaving planks of rotten spruce. The smell was fetid and corky with a hint of sanitation stink. Carefully, and without a whisper, we moved down the hall, sloshing through water traps and looking into vacant classrooms where walls had fallen away with water rot, exposing old lead pipe and chalky asbestos.

We sloshed out into the condemned corridor, then Danny stopped suddenly. Noises were coming from a classroom. Shuffling noises, like someone sorting through papers. Danny Boy approached the door, and he lifted the gun slightly. I considered the ghost of a wizened old math teacher, correcting homework in purgatory, but ghosts were the least of our ordeal.

Again, we heard the noise.

Danny Boy shoved the door open and squared himself. Something erupted from the salvage with a sound like two rattlesnakes fighting. We both fell back, and I went down on wet spruce. Pigeons thundered out. A dozen of them, wings buffeting, stray feathers falling about and a dozen more funneled out the door and then out a fourth floor window like bats leaving a cavern in force. More came out in mad flutter and that's when I became aware of the strong pigeon stink. My brother sat on the floor, registering the discovery. In his left hand was a great clump of pink, wet insulation that had come away with his grip when he stumbled. 'We found the hole in the insulation,' he said, no longer whispering and fairly exultant.

I stared at his handful of what looked like cotton candy until I realized it wasn't the insulation he was talking about. 'Carmella pays twenty-five grand a month to the city for this? This is his three floors of office space?'

'It's a dump,' I said.

'Pigeons,' Danny Boy said, shaking the wet material off his fingers, and climbing to his feet. 'Angie must have sat in his wheelchair on the corner, watching the top floors to see who might be coming and going. He must have seen pigeons coming out the windows, going back in. Some office rental, right? This is how Carmella kicks money back to the mayor. It's a shill, a fake rental.'

I wanted to whoop, or slap Danny five, or sing some Roy Orbison, but I didn't get the chance. There were more sounds coming from the stairwell and we both looked that way, tense. It was more scuffing noise and then, a concussive bang and echo. 'Maybe rats,' I said.

Danny Boy held a finger upside his nose and listened. It was silent again. Or maybe just the ghosts of knickered kids from the 1920's going up and down stairs. 'Let's go,' my brother finally whispered.

We made a move for the janitor closet, but another loud sound made Danny balk. A door shut in the hall beneath us and a light went on down there, sending it up through the damaged planks and gaping slats. Then a voice echoed as if in a deep tank. A second voice laughed with a more casual assonance. We stood motionless, trying not to cast shadows down onto the third floor. Men were talking. Directly beneath us, they were talking; two men that I hoped might be security guards checking on the two figures who had pulled up in an illegal roadster and had entered the abandoned school. But then one of the men walked directly beneath us, stopped and said, 'Hey, *guaglione*.'

It was Sally Testa.

My heart stalled, and I squeezed my brother's arm. Danny turned his eyes on me. Then a third man coming from the opposite end of the hall made some little joke and laughed, then said, 'What are you all dressed up for? The feast?'

'Yeah,' Sally said, and I could see him strike a pose below, a mock gentleman's stance. He was wearing a Dacron shirt the color of a Miami sunset. His slacks were pink and too high and tight on his lower belly. 'I want to get over there before they cut that layer cake,' he said.

'Shit,' the third man said, and I saw it was Mr Campobosso, the mayor's aging mentor. 'It's got thirty-three layers. You got time.'

'Yeah, about thirty-three minutes, the way they put away that *torta*.'

'What the hell was that?' the second man said. He stepped up alongside Sally, and I recognized Mr Sforza, one of the aldermen.

Me and Danny weren't breathing, afraid to move on the sagging floorboards. The men went silent also, holding still, just listening. There was indeed a banging from the landing – we heard it now, too. The big oak door unlocked and a little man came down the hall, jangling keys. 'I can't wait for the wrecking ball to take out this sonuvabitch,' he said, and I thought I knew the voice. 'You can get salmonella from the pigeons, you know.'

'No, that's turtles,' Sally Testa said. 'You get salmonella from them little turtles, not pigeons.'

'How are you, Sal?' the little man said, chewing something. He, like the other three, was just under Danny and me; I could see the top of his head, a cruel bald spot catching the light off the wall. It was Mr Carmella – Mr Butterscotch Sunday himself – sucking on his signature candy. He was wearing a light blue suit and carrying a portfolio the reddish color of a new catcher's mitt.

I moved my eyes to Danny, searching for his appraisal. But my brother remained motionless, eyes passive. He turned his wrist to glimpse his watch. I saw it, too. It was five minutes past noon.

'Where's the kid?' Sally said. 'He at the festival already?'

'Hey, Sal, come on,' Mr Campobosso groaned.

'Hey, I'm sorry,' Sally said. 'The mayor, I mean. I call him the kid because . . . he *is* a kid, right? Hell, at my age, everybody's a kid. I'm getting so fucking old I have to carry an empty Chlorox bottle in my car so I can take a leak every ten minutes.'

'Frankie was six years old when I joined the Party,' Mr Carmella said. 'He'll always be the kid. Even when *his* prostate finally goes, he'll still be the kid.'

The men laughed, deceptive echoes coming from the far end of the hall.

'Okay,' Mr Carmella said. 'Let's close this. My kids are waiting to get to the feast.'

Something fell lightly near my feet. Danny Boy's shadow was changing ever so slightly as he moved his right arm slowly from his side. The dirty blue towel was wrapped around his hand, the gray metal extruding. Without breathing, he took careful aim. I wanted to protest what he was about to do, but the words knew their place, somewhere down in my throat, and my hands were going numb.

Danny, don't, I wanted to say.

Don't throw your life away for these crooks. We've got them. We've got the funnel. Let's just sit tight and let them leave. We can go to the newspaper or the state police. This is real, it's not a drive-in movie. Don't shoot!

But Danny Boy trained the weapon in a double grip, setting his sight through the gap in the floorboards. His target seemed to be

Sally, my third *goomba* and the acting capo of the Bridgeport Mob. There was nothing I could do to stop it.

Danny Boy planted his heels and squeezed the trigger.

I closed my eyes. There was no bang or muffled blast. Just a muted and rapid clicking. Opening an eye, I saw the Super 8, catching light and shadow. I let a breath out in careful increments.

'This is for the aldermen,' Mr Sunday said, rolling the candy around in his molars. He rapped a hand off the portfolio. 'There's fifteen, for building and engineering. Ten for zoning. There'll be another twenty-five when the project's done.'

Mr Sunday handed the portfolio to Mr Sforza. 'Frankie will have his hundred grand out of the lease by next month. So I think we're square, boys.'

Now, they were looking patiently toward Sally Testa who was peering down at his white shoes as if troubled by a scuff mark.

'Sal?' Mr Campobosso said, softly. 'What's the old man say? He still on the fence about the Bingo Hall?'

The Super 8 was clicking faster, tiny motor spinning, as Danny Boy aimed it at the light beneath us. A pigeon suddenly fluttered out from the wall behind me and did some aggressive cooing over my head. I waved a hand at it and it landed on a piece of broken desk, just looking at me with a stubborn gaze.

Sally glanced up as if stirred from deep thought. 'What's that?'

'Valle. Where's he at on this? He want in?'

'I told you. Uncle Guy's got the hardening-of-the-arteries. He sits at the piano, playing Verdi all day long, thinks he's back in Naples. I run Bridgeport now.'

I heard a sound catch in my brother's mouth. He knew where Guy Valle was and he wasn't playing the piano.

Sally reached into his back pocket and pulled out a folded envelope, stuffed and sealed. He handed it to Campobosso, and the former GOP chairman slipped it inside his jacket.

'We're set to take down the old mill,' Sally said. 'Soon as you guys say the word.'

Whether to conceal himself, or to ensure a steady shot, Danny Boy had not drawn a breath for as long as he could, but now he broke. He lowered the camera and let out a rush of air that sounded like a truck just let some diesel. The men didn't notice.

But then the sentinel pigeon came back at me, flapping at my head. I ducked and prayed that it would go off somewhere, but it had its sights on me.

'What the fuck was that?' Mr Sforza said.

Mr Sunday broke his hard candy in his teeth, looked behind him. 'Pigeons,' he said.

The men shook hands, laughed off some remark about the game on TV the night before, then split into the two directions they had come from and started away.

And it came back.

My feathered aggressor struck my head blind side. Feathers flew as I batted a hand at the pigeon, knocking my cap up over my eyes. It fell forward and I clutched at, but lost it. It was falling toward the gap in the floorboards. Danny made a deft one-handed grab for it, but wasn't fast enough. The bright red Renaissance City ball cap fell through the cranny, nose-weighted by its bill. It floated like a sinking kite and landed in the center of the corridor where the men had been standing. I didn't hear it make a sound, and I was hopeful the men hadn't either.

Danny Boy and I stared down at the cap, listening to the footsteps of the men. It was hard to tell with all the echoes, how far down they'd gone or even if they were on the same floor. And then Mr Sunday appeared directly under us again. He was staring down at the cap. Sally appeared from the other side and bent with a groan to fetch it. 'This thing yours?'

'No. I thought maybe Dom dropped it.'

Mr Campobosso shook his head as he approached. The men huddled around the cap, baffled. Sally sniffed it for some reason, and this made me tense. Then he looked at the plastic strap at the back of the hat and studied how many holes it was adjusted to. 'Someone with a little fucking head,' he said.

'Yeah, but where'd it come from?' Mr Campobosso said.

Just as he said this, all four men looked straight up. Danny Boy and I were too frozen to move. Any scuffle would make untold noise so we just hoped we couldn't be spotted in shadow.

'There's somebody up there,' Mr Sforza said. 'Is it kids?'

'I see somebody,' Sally said. Then he yelled, 'Who's that? Who's up there?'

Danny Boy stayed on a knee, as motionless as a cathedral carving.

Not me.

I broke for the janitor closet and a rotten piece of linoleum cracked under me and followed the same course as the hat. Half a plank of punky spruce went down behind Danny Boy as he rushed the closet behind me, then ahead of me, holding my sleeve and leading me down the stairwell.

'We're screwed, Danny,' I chuffed, stumbling behind him. He led me out into the third-floor corridor where the men had been, and we could hear doors slamming above us, below us; footsteps scuffing, dress shoes clicking at a run – all of it echoing deceptively. The city officials were yelling to each other across distances as they tried to find us.

Bursting out onto the third floor, we saw Mr Sforza. He stopped running when he saw us, and he stood with an almost relieved look, as if he was satisfied that the intruders were mere kids, stray punks. But then Sally Testa emerged from the landing, breathing like a bull mastiff. When he saw us, he shoved his glasses up on the bridge of his nose and said something awful under his breath to Mr Sforza. The two remained still for a moment. Then they made a sudden run for us, Sally yelling for us to stop.

Danny led me through the door of the old vice-principal's office, then swung open a door to an inner room and hoofed it down a back stairway. 'Homefield advantage.' He knew that the girls' locker room had a fire door at the far end.

In the alley, the *Proletario* sat where we had parked it. I got in the passenger seat, leaned across to turn the ignition. But my eye caught something silver in the mouth of the cobblestone breezeway. A fresh-waxed, silver Camaro, idling high. It sat there, in the mouth, like a mako shark just waiting. Ray Beans, wearing a Chicago Bulls ballcap, was getting out, one arm in a cast, the other probing at his waistband. The Camaro's trunk was open and Uncas Fontenot stepped out from behind the lid, wielding what looked like a heavy machinist's hammer.

'Come on, Danny,' I begged, looking at the open fire door. Ray Beans and Uncas Fontenot came storming at the car and I could see by their eyes they had never seen such a machine. This put a slight hesitance in their step. Still they came at me, Ray with a small black gun in his left hand, the same one he had held at my brother's head weeks back. Uncas Fontenot may not have been Indian, but he wielded the hammer like a tomahawk as he rushed me.

Danny was still in the old school, directing a home movie that was sure to blow the brass roof off the city – if we could get out alive. Looking for the sawed-off, I popped the glove box, but the only item inside was the Hellman's jar full of my brother's spiritual poison. Maybe it was my belief in Old Country superstition, or maybe it was just desperation – but I needed magic now.

So I grabbed the jar and held it like a football for a moment. It was warm and heavy and I had to strain to cock it back, but I did, and I hurled it out the window in the direction of Ray Beans and Uncas Fontenot. It struck the cobblestone alley with a muffled POP and exploded in a slick of black oil and stale water and all the dark power of the *mal'occhio*.

Magic or not, Ray Beans slid first, his torso lurching one way, his arm cast the other, and he went down on his muscled cheeks, sliding in the oil and yelling, '*Fauk* you.' Uncas was dancing on the black sheen. He did a pirouette, holding his hammer high across his body like a soldier in ice maneuvers. The two collided, grabbing at each other for balance. Then they both went down, hips first. Ray slid on his side with a strange look on his face, coming to rest against the brick wall.

The Super 8 was in my lap suddenly, and Danny Boy was at the wheel. He fired the engine, leaned into first gear and gunned down the alley, swinging out onto King Street. The 455 SuperDuty opened wide, but someone was behind us, leaning on a horn, and making shock waves themselves: a red Monte Carlo was coming up fast, Sally at the wheel, Mr Carmella in the passenger seat. I caught a glimpse of Mr Sforza and Mr Campobosso, walking north as if nothing eventful had transpired. But Mr Sforza was holding the leather portfolio under an arm like it was a ticking bomb. We roared past Ray Beans and Uncas Fontenot, and Ray went into a crouch, aiming the handgun in a double grip as he yelled something. But when Sally blew the horn again, the two thugs got into the backseat of the Monte Carlo and joined the pursuit.

'What we gonna do, Danny? Can we go to the police station?'

'No. We're going to New Haven, the Feds.'

'They're chasing us, Danny!'

I didn't know what kind of power plant Sally Testa had in his Monte, but he was riding our bumper with ease. In the side mirror, I saw him grinning like a school kid chasing a carload of sophomore girls. Mr Sunday however, was sitting erect, looking ashen. His eyes appeared closed behind his thick glasses. In the backseat, Ray Beans and Uncas Fontenot leaned over the front, watching every turn we made.

'We can hit Route 8 at the underpass,' Danny said, thinking homefield advantage again. He maneuvered toward Genoa Avenue and our own neighborhood.

'But Danny—' I said.

It was too late. We roared onto Genoa and into a strobe effect of police and fire engine lights. A roadblock awaited us, Sergeant Kelly standing there, waving some cars in, and directing others east. Danny Boy punched the horn and made an awful sound from his belly.

The *Proletario* was obviously not a common street car, and a loud cheer rose up from some kids sitting on the back of the fire engine. Sergeant Kelly blew his whistle and waved us forward, yelling, 'Slow her down, slow her down. Head toward the church.'

We were, to our shared consternation, in the middle of the Feast of San Donato. In front of us was a papier mâché float carrying a Punch and Judy puppet show, and a flatbed truck from Johnny's Garage creating a mobile stage for Lou Napolitano-Massi and his band. The air was jubilant, filled with the scent and sound of carnival games, frying *zeppole* and hot sausage. Above it all was Louie Nap's accordion and boisterous rendition of 'Hey, Goombare'.

'I could screw up a wet dream,' my brother said, looking in the side mirror.

Behind us marched a group of Italian-American war veterans from the VFW. Tailing them was Sally Testa's red Monte Carlo. It tried to pass the veterans to no avail while Danny made an effort to overtake the floats. But we were swarmed by the celebration, a part of it even as we fled. I looked out at the friendly, cheering faces, and felt hands coming in through the window. Mrs Orsini was there,

smiling and praising the strange machine, and when she saw me
in the passenger seat she kissed her fingers and piped, '*Bella, bella
macchina*,' in her squeaky voice.

Danny forced a smile, waved, and prayed for some benevolence
from our patron saint. Louie Nap had by now noticed the car and
he was directing the song to us, drawing even more attention
as he sang, '*A toot da toot, a zing a zing, a plink a plink, il
mandolino . . .*'

'Shit, we're trapped,' Danny said.

'What's this over here?' Louie barked husky into the microphone.
'A hot rod? Stock car? *Hey, Goombare, c'e fa sonare?*'

The streets applauded as we climbed the hilly section of Genoa. I
could see Mayor Longo out in front of our train. He was wearing a
casual blazer and leading six men who carried the ceramic statue of
San Donato on their shoulders. He waved to the crowded sidewalks.
Bastard, I thought to myself, but I knew Danny Boy was thinking
it, too: the mayor was out here waving to my grandmother and
the Italian population while the money they had invested in Casa
Bank was greasing the way for a Bingo Hall that promised to be
their salvation.

I knew Dad was out there somewhere, too – he never missed the
feast – and I dreaded each ten yards of the two miles we would
have to go to reach the church.

'Nunzio!' someone called into my window. It was Eddie Coco,
his lip hairs dusted with confectionery sugar. 'Is this it?' he said.
'This the car your Grandpa built? Can I ride with you's?'

'No,' I said, under the cheering crowd. I lifted the Super 8. 'Eddie,
take this. Take it and go hide it in your cellar. *Go!*'

Eddie looked confused, but reached for it just the same. I could
hear a voice on the sidewalk, drawing near. 'Excuse me, *Gooma*,'
somebody said, jostling toward my window, and Ray Beans came
into view, burrowing through fat women in floral print dresses,
reaching out for the camera as Eddie took it by the trigger. I
yanked it back just as Danny Boy punched fuel and we kept pace
with the parade. In the side mirror I saw Ray Beans swallowed in
the crowd.

Behind us, Sally was still at the wheel, talking to a fireman who
walked alongside the Monte Carlo. He was pointing to us, saying

something and the fireman was on his radio now, quickening his step and moving toward my brother's window. We roared past Punch and Judy and Louie Nap, and bore down on the statue carriers and His Honor.

People cheered and whistled as Grandpa's car thundered upstreet, passing the statue then cutting down Mary Street which was lined with pastry booths. The Italian festa song gave a deceptive opera-buffa air to the road race. My Cousin Giustina covered her ears when we gunned past her, and she rolled her eyes; nobody knew we were the objects of a mob hit.

The Monte Carlo, adorned in random confetti, followed us. I was turned in my seat, monitoring the chase, but I saw something else: up at Genoa and Mary, the parade had stopped momentarily. Mayor Longo had broken his cadence to look down the side street at where the Monte Carlo laid rubber behind the custom vehicle with a brass bowling trophy hood ornament. He tried to watch but the procession moved him out of eyeshot.

'Yeah,' Danny Boy said. 'You better hold tight to that saint, you son of a bitch.'

We descended at a dangerous pace, down the networks of side streets and steep drops and under the trestle, and then again down another falling network of streets until we dog-legged back onto River Avenue which, as Danny well knew, had no offshoots, no way out. It dropped off steep beneath stucco houses and cinderblock garages and tiered gardens, and it crossed a train track before dying back at the banks of the Mattatuck River. 'We'll ride the track,' he said, hopeful, gaining speed.

'We can't,' I said, watching the Monte Carlo bear down, Ray Beans hanging his bulky cast out the back window. 'The old caboose. It's on the track.'

And there it was, rusted and long idle, sitting abandoned on the rails. Danny Boy braked the car with a hydraulic hiss and fixed his eyes on the rearview. 'Where's reverse?'

'There *is* none.'

They had us. We were trapped. And in a convenient place: a remote cul-de-sac along the polluted river. The Monte braked to a stop behind us.

'Go in the water,' I said.

'What?'

'Drive into the river.'

'Nunz, man—'

'Danny, go!'

Sally grabbed for the driver's door handle just as Danny slammed the gas pedal and released the Russian clutch, and we went forward in a haphazard *baja*, down the bank and into the polluted river, nose first. The car floated and bobbed, but did not stall.

'Throw the two red toggles,' I said. Danny Boy flipped them down, the two together.

'Punch it,' I said, watching Sally stumble behind us and curse the greenish mud that got on his shoes. Danny Boy stomped the gas pedal and we began motoring across the river like a water craft with a small Evinrude. The two boat propellers beneath the bumper chopped murk and threw up a frothy wash. God bless Grandpa, I thought to myself as we left Sally and his two associates standing on the bank, awed. Mr Sunday remained in the car, no less stunned.

Danny Boy punched a fist off the wheel in a kind of triumph. I clung to the dash, watching the opposite bank draw closer. Cars moved north on the highway just above the waterline; some slowed when they spotted the amphibious car. A few horns blew.

'Toggles,' I said, when we reached the green shallows. Mud and detritus was roiling with the exhaust. Danny Boy flipped the red switches back up. With a muddy trundle in first gear, we crested the bank then stopped there for a moment. Danny Boy was breathing again. He turned his eyes on me. '*Proletario*,' he said, in a homage to a car commercial. 'There is no substitute.'

'Yes, there is,' I said. 'It's called common sense.'

Only fifty feet down along the river was the old Hayes Bridge, crossing to the highway. The Monte Carlo was more than halfway across, the men inside looking down at us as they sped along. 'Well,' Danny said in frustration, throwing the wheel hard left, 'you know we don't have any of *that*.'

We were four exits past the New Haven route, and we had little recourse. Driving the wrong way into traffic would be as certain a disaster as losing the race to Sally and his foot soldiers.

Danny Boy got into the fast lane and drove as hard as he could. Water and sludge sputtered from the pipes and the car threatened to stall a few times. The Monte Carlo was nearly across the bridge when we passed it, doing seventy. It hit the highway at a comparable speed, nearly lost control, then got with us again. Sally Testa was nothing if not relentless.

'Where we going?'

'There's no place else *to* go.'

Sally's Monte Carlo was out of view. We had left him in the dust of the rust bowl.

'We can't go to the yard,' I said. 'He'll expect that.'

'He'll expect us to expect that,' Danny Boy said.

We got off the junkyard exit and raced for the home gates. Maybe Danny was thinking homefield advantage, or maybe this was just what people did under duress; chased in circles, they went to family ground. Indeed, Paradise Salvage never looked more welcoming as we high-geared up the long road in. When I jumped out to open the gate I saw a sign mounted there, magic marker on cardboard: *Closed at Noon for Feast.*

I wanted to close the gate behind Danny and lock it, but the red Monte Carlo turned onto the junkyard road with a throaty gravel scratch and it was roaring toward us. I got back in and we bulled up to the main building, the Monte right behind us. Danny shut the *Proletario* down, and the car proceeded to make a sound like a single-engine plane, cooling after a transatlantic flight. Then it died with a wet sputter.

Big Dan was gone. The wind moved loose chrome down in the acres of dead cars. Other than that, the wrecking yard was tomb still as the Monte Carlo pulled alongside us and Sally shut it down.

'Run,' Danny said. 'Take the camera and run. Don't let it go.'

As I leapt out, I saw Danny running to the trunk, the car keys jangling in his nervous hands. His sawed-off was in there, I concluded; the portend of gunshots cracking the air in a junkyard on a Saturday, with me hiding under some junker Renault, brought my pulse into my face. But there would be no exchange of gunfire. Danny Boy's hands fumbled with the trunk key but never got a handle, and Ray Beans and Uncas Fontenot were on him.

'You kick a dog in the ass, he always runs home, don't he?' Ray said, coming at my brother in his short, muscle-bound strut, gun high. Uncas Fontenot held his machine hammer, but appeared to see no reason to lift it now. From their side of the conflict, we couldn't have led them to a better place. I was running. But someone had me by the shirt in a mean twist.

'This shit's done, fellas,' Sally Testa said. He pulled me toward him and reached for the camera, but I tossed it over the trunk of the *Proletario* to my brother. Danny Boy caught it cleanly, held it. But he was going nowhere either. And now Mr Carmella felt safe enough to climb out of the car. He pointed a finger at me and said, 'You're in a lot of trouble, you boys.'

Sally shifted his weight from one white shoe to the other. 'You taking movie pictures, Danny? We making a movie?'

Danny stood tense, eyes going from Sally, to me, to Ray.

'It was you, Charlie,' Sally said in his untutored Brando. Ray and Uncas Fontenot laughed at the humor. 'We're making a movie picture over here, fellas,' Sally announced, turning to Mr Carmella who was not finding any levity in it.

'You don't even know who you faukin' with, do you?' Ray said, thrusting the handgun toward my brother's chin. 'Faukin' grease monkey. This man over here, you don't even know who he is.'

'Shut the fuck up, Ray,' Sally said. Then he stood there for a moment, pulled a hanky and worked it in a nostril, as if deliberating.

Danny looked hard at Ray Beans. 'You're tough, Ray. Shot a ninety-year-old man and a quadriplegic in a wheelchair.'

Ray tightened his neck, his jaw. Everything about him tightened. But it was his grip on the gun that was making his knuckles pale, finger at the trigger.

'Danny,' Sally said, 'you're a screw-up. Your old man knows it. But doing what you just did, that's the top level of screwing up, *capisce*? If they gave medals for fucking up, you'd get the Bronze. Ray would get the Gold. Now give me the movie picture camera and get on a train to New York. Summer's over, *guaglione*.'

Danny Boy looked over his shoulder. 'It's *my* movie,' he said.

The silence was profound for a baited moment. Then Sally began laughing, jabbing at my arm. 'It's his movie,' he said. Uncas Fontenot laughed; Ray smirked, shook his head at such brashness. Sally chuckled himself pink in the cheeks, but when he stopped smiling, I saw that it was the ruddy color of wrath.

He released his grip on me and walked over to the *Proletario*, inspecting its fins. 'What's this fucking piece of shit?' he said.

'Our grandfather made it,' I said, defiance in my voice.

Sally saw the keys on the ground, bent for them, groaning. Danny Boy stood firm. 'You're a good actor, Sally,' he said. Then he raised the camera to his eye and began filming Salvatore Testa. 'You're in the movie, Sally. So are you, Ray. Mr Carmella. It's a movie about a man in the trunk of a '73 Pontiac. A man they called the Padrone – Guy Valle. And how his nephew had him taken out so he could make the big bucks in a ring that goes from the bank to City Hall. It was *you*, Sally. Say *bingo*!'

'Fuck you. How's that?'

'That's good, Sally. Try it again, but imagine yourself bending over for the soap in the shower at Somers. Dig down deep, Sally. Think hard about where you're going.'

Sally grinned into the Super 8, his face the color of raw pork. He made no attempt to mask his anger on camera, and so I knew we would not be leaving the junkyard alive. He singled out the trunk key and stuck it in the cargo lock of Grandpa's car. He gave it a nonchalant lift and it opened with the smooth yawn of hydraulics. 'And you,' he said to Danny Boy, 'you think hard about where your little brother's going.'

Sally had me by the elbow. 'Get in the trunk,' he said.

'Oh, Jesus,' Mr Sunday said, looking about the yard.

'This little fucker caused me big problems, Dom,' Sally said. 'Big fucking problems.'

'No,' Danny said. Then, as if in reflex, he tossed the camera to Sally, and the big man caught it against his chest. Sally smiled, but his eyes were cold as he kept his grip on my elbow.

He knew how to reach my brother. Then he released me.

'Let's get out of here,' he said. 'I've seen enough junk for today.' And with the Bell & Howell in hand, he got in behind the wheel of his Monte. The others got in, too, Ray the last one, still glaring at Danny.

'You ain't on the 6:10 tomorrow morning, sucker, I'm coming for you.'

That's when a sound rose up from the earth, a grinding sound, like a giant wasp nest had busted open and loosed a fury; a hundred million wasps making a violent chainsaw buzz down in The Boneyard where the city ghosts sat dormant in their wrecked cars. All of us looked up, startled. Dust was rising and sunspots burned through it. Something powerful was rising up out of The Boneyard. It was a yellow giant, two pronged and crushing dirt beneath massive tires. The Caterpillar was coming up the lane between the death cars and hills of cast iron. It was straining full-throttle in high third. Up in the seat, Big Dan gripped the wheel like Ahab at his harpoon. He was wearing his green *I've Been to Carlsbad Caverns* visor, his eyes shaded, his jaw set businesslike. He was barreling up fast, and Danny and I moved out of the way. Sally was smiling, bent at the dash and watching my father through the passenger window. He put the car in park, and started to get out with a confident air. That's when Dad dropped the massive forks onto the hood of the red Monte and folded sheet metal over the engine. Sally let out a sudden yell of protest. Mr Sunday sat stunned, momentarily, then he began pushing back against his seat, shouting but making no sound. Dad reversed a few yards, lowered the forks, and came again like a man riding a triceratops. He pierced the car through the windows but high enough to just miss heads, and he proceeded to lift the car up off the ground.

'Ho!' Sally yelled, four feet up. 'You gone fucking nuts, Paradiso?'

'Holy shit,' Danny Boy said, standing beside me, watching Big Dan raise the car another four feet. We could hear Ray Beans yelling, and Uncas Fontenot wailing in what may or may not have been an Indian tongue as he tried to open his door. Dad swung the big forklift around, stuck his fingers in his mouth and let fly a sharp whistle.

Danny Boy knew what this meant, but he was frozen in place for a spell. Then he broke into a run, leading Dad and his cargo to The Crusher. He grabbed the ether can, gave it a spray into the plugs and pipes and fired the machine up. The Crusher came alive with a retching noise that now overtook all sound. In the Monte, Sally and Mr Carmella's hands were slapping at the outer door handles, but it was a futile effort. I breasted a tire pile and watched from a safe distance as Big Dan slammed the Monte down on the gangway. When Ray Beans tried to open the back door and bail, Dad moved one fork with the finesse of a carving tool, and folded the door in, locking it permanently. When Ray squared himself in the window and lifted his little .22, I yelled, 'Dad, look out!' and the forks came back down and smashed the gun into the door, melding metal to metal and breaking the hit man's arm in a new place.

The Crusher was drawing the Monte Carlo in; the hood was already eaten, and now Sally went over the front seat, landing in back and obviously on Ray's broken arm, because Ray's head was thrashing and Sally was across his lap. Mr Carmella was afraid to move, but when the jaws came down and compressed the front seat, he rolled himself over the headrest and just got himself clear, leaving one of his dress loafers under flat metal. The four men were jammed together in the backseat like High School joyriders, only there was no joy in the half-crushed Monte Carlo – just terror like I had never seen on grown men's faces in my life. Jonah was alive when he went into the belly of the whale and so was Sally Testa going through the wrecking machine, but I couldn't imagine Jonah screaming any louder than Sally Testa. Sally Sheet Metal was about to become his own nickname.

I had to look away.

But with the car half-eaten, Dad drew a finger across his throat, and Danny Boy shut The Crusher down. Big Dan turned off the Caterpillar, and it took both machines thirty seconds of belching and knocking as they warmed down to a hard silence.

Some glass shards tinkled from the Monte, and metal creaked where Sally's back was pressed, and somebody – I think it was Uncas Fontenot – was hyperventilating.

Dad remained high up on his captain's chair, studying the situation. He removed his visor, and wiped some sweat from his brow. He looked like he needed a cold soda, but it seemed inappropriate to suggest such a thing. Danny Boy climbed up on the gangway and peered in at the trapped men. Sally was breathing like he had asthma and Ray Beans was making pained sounds. Other than that, the car was quiet as the men eyed my father in dreaded anticipation of his next move. Danny Boy looked into the flattened front seat, dug a hand in, and carefully extracted the Super 8 which had a broken lens.

'Your uncle paid my father's way to this country,' Big Dan said, his arms resting over the wheel of the machine. The silence itself seemed to listen to my father. 'The old man did what he had to do to make a living, Sally. I've done what I had to do. Everybody's got a piper to pay.'

Sally was twisted in the backseat, looking up over his bent tinted glasses at the man on the big forklift. Me and Danny traded looks and drew closer to the Caterpillar. 'Fare's been paid, Sally. The buck stops here,' he said. 'With these boys. My sons.'

'Can we talk, Dan?' Sally said from somewhere in the crushed metal.

'Remember this day,' my father said.

Sally wouldn't forget. Neither would I.

Nor would I ever forget the look on the face of Danny Boy as he stood with his secondhand Super 8 under an arm, his eyes on our father. We all lingered for a time – the men in the crushed car had no choice – and the world seemed to have stopped spinning to let us off for a breather. Dad had no idea what Danny Boy was holding in his hand; everything we had tried to tell him all summer was inside that small box with the hotshoe and trigger. Our summer was in that Bell & Howell, in Super 8 sound; it wasn't *Apocalypse Now*, but it held more demons than Pandora's proverbial box, or Nonni's Hellman's jar, or the '73 Pontiac Bonneville that was somewhere out on the high August seas.

Danny Boy had made his movie. And my father, for the first time in his life, was living outside the shadow of Vesuvio and the grip of *La Via Vecchia*, the old ways.

Me: my ceramic saints had not failed me, but I was in dire need of a visit to the Porcelain God.

Big Dan once said that he would rather pole a skiff up the Amazon than drive through downtown New Haven, so it was a testament to his resolve that he drove us into the heart of that big city, looking for Court Street and the Federal Office Building.

We must have cut a curious sight, the three of us, walking in our junkyard clothes and heavy boots down the blue carpet of the fifth floor which led to a massive glass wall with an official seal and the imposing name: Federal Bureau of Investigation. Danny Boy was wearing a ball cap at Dad's insistence, to hide the mohawk, and he had a duffel bag slung over his shoulder in which he carried the

Super 8. Dad had called Trooper Fisher who had once bartered the defective K-9 shepherd, Primo Canero, for a set of camshafts, and the trooper directed us to the New Haven Field Office of the FBI and a friend of his named S.A. Schinto.

Big Dan fingered two Tums into his mouth and set to work dissolving them as we sat on metal folding chairs in an office that was no more exotic than the Motor Vehicle Department. I didn't know what I expected, but not the cheap-looking honeycomb of cubicles we were ushered through, nor the special agent who didn't carry a gun and who looked about as adventurous as my industrial arts teacher. But Dad was impressed and he raised his brow at me when we were escorted into an empty office and asked to sit while they had the film footage developed at an outside service.

After nearly two hours, S.A. Schinto returned with a willowy black man named S.A. Riddick, who smelled like aftershave, and who, to my great delight, did indeed wear a gun in a shoulder holster over a pair of fancy suspenders, and he carried a cardboard tray of fast food coffee. He asked me if I liked to play video poker. 'Got a video poker game on my desk,' he said. 'You can go down the hall and play a little while we discuss a few things.'

'Nunzio is a part of this,' my brother said. S.A. Schinto studied me, nodded, then gestured toward the coffee tray.

'We had your film transferred to three quarter-inch tape,' S.A. Riddick said. 'Why is it in black and white?'

'Excuse me?' Danny Boy said.

'The film footage. Why is it in black and white? I found that odd.'

'It was a creative decision, sir.'

'A creative decision?' said S.A. Schinto.

'Yeah, for mood. I wanted the film to have a kind of *noir* feel.'

'A kind of what feel?' my father said.

'*Noir*. It's French.'

The room went silent. S.A. Schinto was looking over the rims of his reading glasses at my brother with a trace of a smirk. S.A. Riddick was studying him also, nodding tentatively.

'How'd it come out?' Danny Boy said, finally.

S.A. Schinto was staring at my brother in a terrible way. His silence was excruciating, and I feared that the footage in the condemned school building did not develop. Maybe the FBI agent had just spent his Saturday night watching a bad amateur movie in black and white. Then when S.A. Riddick began to chuckle quietly, I was certain we were about to be escorted to a cell for wasting federal time. 'Noir,' S.A. Riddick laughed.

'Well, Dan,' S.A. Schinto finally said. 'If you're telling me that the bank president is leasing that rat-trap from the city for twenty-five grand a month, and that the guy passing the portfolio *is* this financial officer and also a city developer, and the guy he's passing it to is one of the aldermen in your town . . . well, Dan, I'd say you did a hell of a piece of citizen vigilance and we have more than ample grounds to go into City Hall.'

Danny Boy nodded, relieved, and he moved his eyes onto Big Dan who was nodding also, but with a bewildered look on his face.

'And,' S.A. Riddick said, looking down at a report of some kind, 'if the heavyset white male who is seen handing an envelope to the former GOP chairman –' he looked at his report suddenly. 'Is that who—'

'Yes, sir,' Danny Boy said. 'That's Mr Campobosso who takes the envelope from Salvatore Testa.'

'Okay. If this Salvatore Testa is involved in a construction deal with the officer from the thrift, then I don't think I'm being overzealous in saying that by the time you wake up tomorrow morning, the atmosphere of Saukiwog Mills will be somewhat charged.'

'The fit's gonna hit the shan,' S.A. Schinto underscored.

Danny Boy nodded again, his face set stern. 'What about the first part of the film, sir?'

'The first part?'

'Yeah, the first forty feet.'

S.A. Riddick glanced back down at his report. 'You mean, the Italian family eating on the beach, and cleaning fish, and that part?'

'Yes, sir. And the shot from the knife and the fish that cuts to the Spanish girl, looking out the window.'

'I didn't get it,' S.A. Schinto said.

'Me neither,' I chimed, and Danny Boy only looked slightly disappointed.

'What's this?' Dad said, nonplussed.

'Look, guys,' S.A. Schinto said, quite comfortable with us, because his shoes were off and his feet were up on the table, 'you say the violators, the gentlemen in the footage, pursued you, trying to confiscate this evidence?'

'Yes, sir, that's right,' Danny Boy said. 'With a gun.'

'Where are they now, these fellows?'

Danny Boy hesitated, then looked at Big Dan. I was already looking at him and so were S.A. Schinto and S.A. Riddick. Dad crushed a Tum in his molars and ruminated for a time.

'They're waiting in the car,' he said.

CHAPTER TWENTY-THREE

6:10

'The Feds are in City Hall.'

Word traveled as word did in The Little Boot and Little Lithuania, in the Hispanic South End and the black neighborhoods of the North End. 'Twenty-four FBI and IRS agents are in Longo's office and house.' And if anyone hadn't heard, it was there to see on the front page of the Saukiwog *Republican*: FEDERAL AUTHORITIES SUBPOENA CITY RECORDS.

Residents gathered outside City Hall, watching federal agents cart away box after box of documents. When Mayor Longo exited after seven hours, some folks cheered him in support, and he waved a dismissive hand at the whole débâcle around him.

But Pandora's Box was open; so were the filing cabinets.

Within ten days, federal regulators removed Mr Carmella from Casa Savings and Loan and issued what the newspaper called a cease-and-desist order. The cardboard boxes revealed land transaction contracts involving the thrift, BCD and Saukiwog city officials.

'He was like a son to me,' Nonni cried from her front porch. She gathered with Gooma Rosa and Mrs Coco and together they wept for Mayor Frankie. But when she learned that the six thousand dollars in stock she had purchased was now worthless paper, she wept and made a pair of horns with her fingers, aiming them toward City Hall.

Nonni was one of the lucky ones.

Old Mr Paternostro, the retired millworker, had invested his life savings in stock at Casa Bank. He lost it all. Eddie Coco's father lost half of his life's cache and so had dozens more. The more filing cabinets that were carried out of City Hall, the more dirt came back. Job training funds that the mayor had fought for had been invested in BCD developments. The newspaper reported this and people spread the word in the check-out lines at IGA.

'And here I am standing in the unemployment line,' Dave Zuraitas moaned from where he sat on the Asa Bean fountain with a cigarette. Suddenly the blacks he was in line with felt more like kindred victims and less like an enemy Zuraitas was searching for.

Guy Valle meanwhile was heading into the melting pot. Literally. By the time the remains of the man who once brought the Italian millworkers to Saukiwog reached Japan, the evidence of the leased office space in the dilapidated Kirby building tied Mr Campobosso and the aldermen to the spokes of 'a wheel of municipal corruption, Casa Savings and Loan being the hub,' as the newspaper described it.

'He's young, they took advantage of him,' Mrs Crocco said when I went in for an Italian ice. 'He was set up.'

Maybe she was right. The FBI discovered that within a month of Frank Longo's appointment as mayor, the men who helped get him elected, Campobosso and the aldermen and Mr Carmella, were orchestrating real-estate investments between the city, the thrift and Guy Valle. They promised Frankie he could get rich, very rich, without anyone ever tracing it back to him. Now the city wanted to know how much he was rewarded for diverting over $3 million in state affordable housing funds into developments citywide.

We had reached the King of Diamonds.

Longo tried to keep his composure. He met a small cheering crowd at City Hall and told them he was a candidate for re-election and would remain so no matter the outcome of the investigation that he called bogus. But on the very same day, he made a statement in his office about Carmella talking too much, and an IRS agent interpreted it as a threat. Within hours, Mayor Longo was remanded into federal custody. There appeared in the *American* an unflattering photo of him being led away in leg irons with his hands cuffed and his Rolex forced halfway up his forearm. His Renaissance City was falling in around him.

'Poor Frankie,' Cousin Giustina said at Sunday dinner. 'He couldn't handle the power. He was a kid in a candy store.'

As for Sally Testa, while the Pianola continued to play on that quiet street in Bridgeport, and the Bolivian housekeeper watered the garden, Sally Sheet Metal was held without bail in federal prison in Danbury on bribery and assault charges. Ray Beans was reportedly in a prison hospital getting his arm recast and his fingers printed.

On opening night of *Ten Little Indians* at the Saukiwog Playhouse, there were more city residents than had turned out to support the accused mayor. Mr Pembroke was breathing quick with excitement when he peered out from behind the curtains and told us it was standing room only. My father and mother were there with Giustina, Lena and Pina Maria. There were dozens of kids I knew, sitting with their parents; and more than a hundred people I did not know, but they well represented the ethnic mix of our city.

Backstage, we were all smiling, but holding our breath when the house fell silent and dark, and Mr Pembroke gave Danny the cue. Wearing a white suit and formal driving cap, the overweight Danny Boy carried a basket of props up the steps and emerged Stage Right. For a time, it remained silent out there and I leaned into the curtain to see why.

Danny Boy was standing at his mark but the lines weren't coming; he was staring out at the faces of the city.

I saw my father watching him, intently.

And then Danny Boy delivered his line: 'First lot to arrive in Jim's boat. Lemons, tomatoes, cream, eggs and butter.'

There was a deep silence in the house, and it seemed that the audience was waiting for more. Then someone in the back applauded. The applause carried from a corner and across the seats and I saw my father clapping, smiling with a mix of pride and amusement. And then, as if overcome with something deeper than pride, he rose up on his dress shoes and clapped. It was as if he wanted Danny to see him at that moment. He didn't intend for Mrs Doyle to rise behind him, and it may have just been so she could see, but the audience began to follow suit. Two dozen people were now on their feet, applauding; someone whistled, and soon the house became a rush of sound, a standing ovation for Narracott who everyone recognized as Danny Paradiso. When the main actors entered Stage Left, they had to wait a full minute to begin their lines.

And Danny Boy exited. He had delivered the lines as himself, not De Niro, and he was pretty good.

All he had to do now was die off-stage, so he sat in the shadows, popped open a soda and let a deep sigh free. It was over. When he saw me looking at him, he winked.

In the parking lot after the show, Johnny called to us from the window of her big land barge. 'That was a good story,' she said. 'But I knew who the murderer be right off. I'm good at that shit.'

'No kidding,' my brother said.

'Where you going?' I was looking into the backseat where we had grown so accustomed to seeing the upright figure of the Pinkerton Man and Ruby Lee. Now, there were two suitcases and a large cardboard box. She was going to Myrtle Beach, she said. She had some business to take care of. In the front seat beside her was a small Judge's Cave cigar box held shut with Scotch tape. 'I'm taking my Angel to Myrtle Beach,' she said. 'Put him to rest. Let the man rest.'

My godfather was in a cigar box and he was leaving Saukiwog Mills.

Johnny squeezed my hand and gave me a look that made me want to hug her. But I didn't. She took my brother's hand, smiled, then drove off on four second-hand, steel-belted Firestones, toward the interstate on the last day of August which I knew was my last day on Earth as an unconfirmed Christian.

In the morning my Confirmation went off without so much as a sneeze in the balcony pew. Zi Bap wore a blue suit with brass buttons and Buster Browns that were out of fashion. But he was there half an hour early and ready to sponsor my ascent. The Archbishop from Hartford led the ceremony and services with a kind bearing while Father Vario flanked him, studying the manner of each one of us as we approached for Communion.

Zi Bap had his rugged hand on my shoulder as we went up for the Host and wine. When he failed to follow me back to the pew, I turned to find him still drinking from the chalice. He not only drank the blood of Christ, he finished off the cup and the ceremony had to pause a moment as the altar boys refilled it. I feared that Zi Bap was going to tell the Archbishop that the vino was a little on the dry side and he might try California grapes this fall.

But my last remaining godfather was polite and he seemed satiated as he followed me back to our seats to let the Host dissolve in his cheek. It was done. I had entered the church an unconfirmed pilgrim; I would be leaving a Christian. When Father Vario gave a closing sermon, he mentioned the recent trouble in our city and said, 'A new day has begun.' When I looked behind me, I saw my father staring straight at me. He knew I would be leaving the church a soldier, too.

Out in the cool air, church bells deafening, Nonni held my hand and walked me to Dad's Bel Aire, a peaceful smile on her face. She wanted to be near me, she said, because God had kissed my cheek and the Devil would give me a gracious berth.

Thanks'a God. *Grazia Dio.*

A small girl was looking at me from across the lot. It was Don Gustavo's granddaughter, Graziella, in her Confirmation dress and white shoes. She lowered her eyes and smiled, and life was full of wonder again.

A postcard arrived soon after at Paradise Salvage and Dad pinned it up with his collection of people he never knew. Beneath the words *Greetings from Myrtle Beach* was a picture of the sand and the ocean and an empty lawn chair. On the back:

Dear Numb Nuts,
  You will love to know that I put Angel to rest in the sand on M Beach. As he had wished, I faced the ocean and sang that Roy Orbison shit 'Dream Baby'. When the funeral was done, I turned and saw twenty patrons standing on the deck of the Surfside Café, crying their drunk ass. Man hired mine at the Surfside Piano Bar. I am a hit. I repeat: a hit.

Always Too Hot For You, Baby,

But I love you, (yes I do!)

Johnny

Epilogue

'Junk?' Big Dan said. '*Junk?* Never call it that. It's *salvage*, Nunzio. Redemption.'

'Like diving for shipwrecks,' I said.

'Like Jacques Cousteau,' he agreed.

'Only we're not French,' I said.

'One man's junk,' Danny Boy added. 'Another man's treasure.'

'There you go,' Dad said. 'That's it.'

We were in the tow truck, me, Nunzio, squeezed between my brother and Big Dan as we motored up Grand Street. Dad downshifted and I hasped my legs to protect the nuts. We passed City Hall but only Big Dan looked at the building where the fountain was running and a murder of crows rimmed the well. A block away, a banner hung over the street, flapping in a light autumn wind:

AMERICA'S RENAISSANCE CITY

We drove under the Big Clock tower. The east face read 6:00 and in the station, the 6:10 was getting some diesel and oil, and getting ready to head south to Grand Central. Passengers were boarding; some looked like commuters, others day-shoppers, a few like Danny Boy, young pilgrims with duffel bags and the *New York Post* under an arm. Danny Boy carried the *Village Voice* and one of Mom's old tweed suitcases. He wore the Saukiwog Mills tuxedo: a black T-shirt, blue jeans and his army boots unlaced. His Mohawk had been fashioned into a hip crewcut, compliments of Yolanda who also gave him a paper bag of *soprasatta*. Nonni had packed him a larger bag of angel cookies, some *peccorino* cheese and two small jars of eggplant.

The Pontelandolfo Club had raised five hundred dollars for him and Big Dan kicked in a hundred; he was ready to leave. On the platform, Dad and I stood with him and made small talk about diesel fuel, switchers and how far the world had come since steam. Then Dad said, 'I'm proud of you.'

'What?' Danny Boy said.

'I said be careful down there. They'll zook you. With ice picks. And muggers. Be careful. And watch your wallet. They're sharp down there.'

'I will,' Danny said.

I hugged my brother and he turned it into a half-Nelson and a choke-hold and he kissed the crown of my cap. 'Bye, Dante.'

A loud mufferless car pulled in and a half-dozen people looked over at the racket. The yellow Le Mans parked and Desiree got out looking disorganized and rushed, but excited just the same. She wore a man's tweed blazer over a Danskin, high-waisted jeans and a vintage pork pie jazz hat that my brother had salvaged, steamed and gifted her. With a clove smoke in her lips, she carried two small suitcases and ran as best she could in her ankle-strapped sandals; her bracelets and earrings tambourined as she mounted the platform. Danny Boy took one of her bags, kissed her, then looked up at the station clock. 'I'll call,' he said.

Desiree grabbed the brim of my cap and shoved it down over my eyes, teasing. 'Be good, Nunzio.' She hugged me. 'This is so exciting,' she whispered. 'I hope they have a girl's room on the train. I got to pee, *coqui*. Man, I got to pee.'

She handed Big Dan her car keys and smiled when he bent his brow. 'The engine's got like a million miles,' she said. 'But Nunzio says two of the tires still have tread.'

'You got class,' Dad said, suddenly. She drew back a step and looked at him over her sunglasses. 'We'll take care of the car,' he said.

The train let a whistle rip and I covered my ears.

'Well, Dad,' my brother said, moving into line.

'You got the ticket?'

My brother showed him the ticket, slapped it off my head and let Desiree go before him, onto the train.

'Goodbye, Danny,' Dad said. 'Don't get off the wrong stop, and hold onto the ticket.'

They were gone, Danny Boy and Desiree Vega, boarding in hurried steps, luggage catching in the narrow passages. Dad gave me a little science on why diesel fuel needs a certain mix in winter and why narrow-gauge track is faster, and his eyes welled up as he went on about how much grease it takes to keep bogie wheels and side rods running smoothly.

Danny Boy was on his way.

I thought of him sitting there at the train window with his bag of bread and cheese and a whole new *storia* ahead of him. Grandpa had spoken often about a place called Santa Lucia, the last piece of land the emigrants could see as they sailed away from Naples. My brother's last view was the Day-Glo peace cross high on Holy Hill and the rubble of the last mills.

'Hook her up,' Dad said.

We towed the yellow beater out onto Grand, short cut by the Green and *The Soldier's Horse*, and I saw Don Gustavo Martone in the window of his café, baking the first breads of the morning. A white cat slept in the window.

'Hey, what can you do?' Dad shrugged. Beyond him, out on the horizon I could see the north face of the clock-tower.

'Hey, Dad, look. It's working. The north face is on time. It's working again.'

'A fine city,' Dad said. 'A Big Clock city.'

He let me out at the corner of Queen and America with half an hour before the school bell. It was what I wanted. I had my skateboard in the back of the truck, and a brown bag with the name Nunzi on it.

'Nunzio,' Dad said. 'I'm sorry.'

'For what, Dad?'

'For taking away your summer.'

'I wouldn't trade it back for nothing.'

My father nodded, looked away. He was proud, I could see that.

'Dad?'

'Yeah?'

Words wouldn't break the surface. Dad sat in the tow truck with his signal light clicking slow and cars moving past.

'Hey,' Dad said, reaching around behind the seat and pulling up a small jacket, what looked like a faux-satin hockey jacket with someone else's name large across the back. 'This is for you.'

I didn't play hockey, and my name wasn't Douglas. But Big Dan was smiling as he helped me punch one arm into a sleeve and then the other. 'Nice one,' he said. 'Found it in a '65 Plymouth. They don't make them like that anymore. Kids would go nuts for that one.'

He worked a thumbnail in a molar and drove away, towing the old yellow car. I put my board to the walk, got it going.

I passed the corner of Genoa and did a careful slalom around a dozen grape boxes stacked between a truck and the Paternostros' cellar door; Mr Paternostro was getting ready to make his autumn wine. The smells of The Little Boot were wondrous as I passed Mary Street and heard Eddie Coco let a whistle fly. He was running across the yards and through the gardens, his lunch box under his arm; he gestured toward the next street over to let me know he'd catch me at the school doors. Mrs Orsini was coming out of Coangelo's with fresh bread. '*Buono figlio*,' she sang out to me as I passed her. 'Thanks'a God for the children.'

I got my board rolling downhill on America Street, moving toward a place where faith and magic came together like a wind at my back and Godspeed at four-hundred horse. *Il Destino* couldn't catch me now. Summer was gone and September looked like a wild pony on an open plain.

I caught a light tail wind and held my arms out like sails.

I was moving.